I0646598

A Terrible Temptation

Charles Reade

Contents

A TERRIBLE TEMPTATION

BY

Charles Reade

CHAPTER I.

THE morning-room of a large house in Portman Square, London.
A gentleman in the prime of life stood with his elbow on the broad mantel-piece, and made himself agreeable to a young lady, seated a little way off, playing at work.

To the ear he was only conversing, but his eyes dwelt on her with loving admiration all the time. Her posture was favorable to this furtive inspection, for she leaned her fair head over her work with a pretty, modest, demure air, that seemed to say, "I suspect I am being admired: I will not look to see: I might have to check it."

The gentleman's features were ordinary, except his brow--that had power in it--but he had the beauty of color; his sunburned features glowed with health, and his eye was bright. On the whole, rather good-looking when he smiled, but ugly when he frowned; for his frown was a scowl, and betrayed a remarkable power of hating.

Miss Arabella Bruce was a beauty. She had glorious masses of dark red hair, and a dazzling white neck to set it off; large, dove-like eyes, and a blooming oval face, which would have been classical if her lips had been thin and finely chiseled; but here came in her Anglo-Saxon breed, and spared society a Minerva by giving her two full and rosy lips. They made a smallish mouth at rest, but parted ever so wide when they smiled, and ravished the beholder with long, even rows of dazzling white teeth.

Her figure was tall and rather slim, but not at all commanding. There are people whose very bodies express character; and this tall, supple, graceful frame of Bella Bruce breathed womanly subservience; so did her gestures. She would take up or put down her own scissors half timidly, and look around before threading her needle, as if to see whether any soul objected. Her favorite word was "May I?" with a stress on the "May," and she used it where most girls would say "I will," or nothing, and do it.

Mr. Richard Bassett was in love with her, and also conscious that her fifteen thousand pounds would be a fine addition to his present income, which was small, though his distant expectations were great. As he had known her but one month, and she seemed rather amiable than inflammable, he had the prudence to proceed by degrees; and that is why, though his eyes gloated on her, he merely regaled her with the gossip of the day, not worth recording here. But when he had actually taken his hat to go, Bella Bruce put him a question that had been on her mind the whole time, for which reason she had reserved it to the very last moment.

"Is Sir Charles Bassett in town?" said she, mighty carelessly, but bending a little lower over her embroidery.

"Don't know," said Richard Bassett, with such a sudden brevity and asperity that Miss Bruce looked up and opened her lovely eyes. Mr. Richard Bassett replied to this mute inquiry, "We don't speak." Then, after a pause, "He has robbed me of my inheritance."

"Oh, Mr. Bassett!"

"Yes, Miss Bruce, the Bassett and Huntercombe estates were mine by right of birth. My father was the eldest son, and they were entailed on him. But Sir Charles's father persuaded my old, doting grandfather to cut off the entail, and settle the estates on him and his heirs; and so they robbed me of every acre they could. Luckily my little estate of Highmore was settled on my mother and her issue too tight for the villains to undo."

These harsh expressions, applied to his own kin, and the abruptness and heat they were uttered with, surprised and repelled his gentle listener. She shrank a little away from him. He observed it. She replied not to his words, but to her own thought:

"But, after all, it does seem hard." She added, with a little fervor, "But it wasn't poor Sir Charles's doing, after all."

"He is content to reap the benefit," said Richard Bassett, sternly.

Then, finding he was making a sorry impression, he tried to get away from the subject. I say tried, for till a man can double like a hare he will never get away from his hobby. "Excuse me," said he; "I ought never to speak about it. Let us talk of something else. You cannot enter into my feelings; it makes my blood boil. Oh, Miss Bruce! you can't conceive what a disinherited man feels--and I live at the very door: his old trees, that ought to be mine, fling their shadows over my little flower beds; the sixty chimneys of Huntercombe Hall look down on my cottage; his acres of lawn run up to my little garden, and nothing but a ha-ha between us."

"It *is* hard," said Miss Bruce, composedly; not that she entered into a hardship of this vulgar sort, but it was her nature to soothe and please people.

"Hard!" cried Richard Bassett, encouraged by even this faint sympathy; "it would be unendurable but for one thing--I shall have my own some day."

"I am glad of that," said the lady; "but how?"

"By outliving the wrongful heir."

Miss Bruce turned pale. She had little experience of men's passions. "Oh, Mr. Bassett!" said she--and there was something pure and holy in the look of sorrow and alarm she cast on the presumptuous speaker--"pray do not cherish such thoughts. They will do you harm. And remember life and death are not in our hands. Besides--"

"Well?"'

"Sir Charles might--"

"Well?"

"Might he not--marry--and have children?" This with more hesitation and a deeper blush than appeared absolutely necessary.

"Oh, there's no fear of that. Property ill-gotten never descends. Charles is a worn-out rake. He was fast at Eton--fast at Oxford--fast in London. Why, he looks ten years older than I, and he is three years younger. He had a fit two years ago. Besides, he is not a marrying man. Bassett and Huntercombe will be mine. And oh! Miss Bruce, if ever they are mine--"

"Sir Charles Bassett!" trumpeted a servant at the door; and then waited, prudently, to know whether his young lady, whom he had caught blushing so red with one gentleman, would be at home to another.

"Wait a moment," said Miss Bruce to him. Then, discreetly ignoring what Bassett had said last, and lowering her voice almost to a whisper, she said, hurriedly: "You should not blame him for the faults of others. There--I have not been long acquainted with either, and am little entitled to inter--But it is such a pity you are not friends. He is very good, I assure you, and very nice. Let me reconcile you two. *May* I?"

This well-meant petition was uttered very sweetly; and, indeed--if I may be permitted--in a way to dissolve a bear.

But this was not a bear, nor anything else that is placable; it was a man with a hobby grievance; so he replied in character:

"That is impossible so long as he keeps me out of my own." He had the grace, however, to add, half sullenly, "Excuse me; I feel I have been too vehement."

Miss Bruce, thus repelled, answered, rather coldly:

"Oh, never mind *that;* it was very natural.--I am at home, then," said she to the servant.

Mr. Bassett took the hint, but turned at the door, and said, with no little agitation, "I was not aware he visits you. One word--don't let his ill-gotten acres make you quite forget the disinherited one." And so he left her, with an imploring look.

She felt red with all this, so she slipped out at another door, to cool her cheeks and imprison a stray curl for Sir Charles.

He strolled into the empty room, with the easy, languid air of fashion. His features were well cut, and had some nobility; but his sickly complexion and the lines under his eyes told a tale of dissipation. He appeared ten years older than he was, and thoroughly *blase.*

Yet when Miss Bruce entered the room with a smile and a little blush, he brightened up and looked handsome, and greeted her with momentary warmth.

After the usual inquiries she asked him if he had met any body.

"Where?"

"Here; just now."

"No."

"What, nobody at all?"

"Only my sulky cousin; I don't call him anybody," drawled Sir Charles, who was now relapsing into his normal condition of semi-apathy.

"Oh," said Miss Bruce gayly, "you must expect him to be a little cross. It is not so very nice to be disinherited, let me tell you."

"And who has disinherited the fellow?"

"I forget; but you disinherited him among you. Never mind; it can't be helped now. When did you come back to town? I didn't see you at Lady d'Arcy's ball, did I?"

"You did not, unfortunately for me; but you would if I had known you were to be there. But about Richard: he may tell you what he likes, but he was not disinherited; he was bought out. The fact is, his father was uncommonly fast. My grandfather paid his debts again and again; but at last the old gentleman found he was dealing with the Jews for his reversion. Then there was an awful row. It ended in my grandfather outbidding the Jews. He bought the reversion of his estate from his own son for a large sum of money (he had to raise it by mortgages); then they cut off the entail between them, and he entailed the mortgaged estate on his other son, and his grandson (that was me), and on my heir-at-law. Richard's father squandered his thirty thousand pounds before he died; my father husbanded the estates, got into Parliament, and they put a tail to his name."

Sir Charles delivered this version of the facts with a languid composure that contrasted deliciously with Richard's heat in telling the story his way (to be sure, Sir Charles had got Huntercombe and Bassett, and it is easier to be philosophical on the right side of the boundary hedge), and wound up with a sort of corollary: "Dick Bassett suffers by his father's vices, and I profit by mine's virtues. Where's the injustice?"

"Nowhere, and the sooner you are reconciled the better."

Sir Charles demurred. "Oh, I don't want to quarrel with the fellow: but he is a regular thorn in my side, with his little trumpery estate, all in broken patches. He shoots my pheasants in the unfairest way." Here the landed proprietor showed real irritation, but only for a moment. He concluded calmly, "The fact is, he is not quite a gentleman. Fancy his coming and whining to you about our family affairs, and then telling you a falsehood!"

"No, no; he did not mean. It was his way of looking at things. You can afford to forgive him."

"Yes, but not if he sets you against me."

"But he cannot do that. The more any one was to speak against you, the more I--of course."

This admission fired Sir Charles; he drew nearer, and, thanks to his cousin's interference, spoke the language of love more warmly and directly than he had ever done before.

The lady blushed, and defended herself feebly. Sir Charles grew warmer, and at last elicited from her a timid but tender avowal, that made him supremely happy.

When he left her this brief ecstasy was succeeded by regrets on account of the years he had wasted in follies and intrigues.

He smoked five cigars, and pondered the difference between the pure creature who now honored him with her virgin affections and beauties of a different character who had played their parts in his luxurious life.

After profound deliberation he sent for his solicitor. They lighted the inevitable cigars, and the following observations struggled feebly out along with the smoke.

"Mr. Oldfield, I'm going to be married."

"Glad to hear it, Sir Charles." (Vision of settlements.) "It is a high time you were." (Puff-puff.)

"Want your advice and assistance first."

"Certainly."

"Must put down my pony-carriage now, you know."

"A very proper retrenchment; but you can do that without my assistance."

"There would be sure to be a row if I did. I dare say there will be as it is. At any rate, I want to do the thing like a gentleman."

"Send 'em to Tattersall's." (Puff.)

"And the girl that drives them in the park, and draws all the duchesses and countesses at her tail--am I to send her to Tattersall's?" (Puff.)

"Oh, it is *her* you want to put down, then?"

"Why, of course."

CHAPTER II.

SIR CHARLES and Mr. Oldfield settled that lady's retiring pension, and Mr. Oldfield took the memoranda home, with instructions to prepare a draft deed for Miss Somerset's approval.

Meantime Sir Charles visited Miss Bruce every day. Her affections for him grew visibly, for being engaged gave her the courage to love.

Mr. Bassett called pretty often; but one day he met Sir Charles on the stairs, and scowled.

That scowl cost him dear, for Sir Charles thereupon represented to Bella that a man with a grievance is a bore to the very eye, and asked her to receive no more visits from his scowling cousin. The lady smiled, and said, with soft complacency, "I obey."

Sir Charles's gallantry was shocked.

"No, don't say 'obey.' It is a little favor I ventured to ask."

"It is like you to ask what you have a right to command. I shall be out to him in future, and to every one who is disagreeable to you. What! does 'obey' frighten you from my lips? To me it is the sweetest in the language. Oh, please let me 'obey' you! *May* I?"

Upon this, as vanity is seldom out of call, Sir Charles swelled like a turkey-cock, and loftily consented to indulge Bella Bruce's strange propensity. From that hour she was never at home to Mr. Bassett.

He began to suspect; and one day, after he had been kept out with the loud, stolid "Not at home" of practiced mendacity, he watched, and saw Sir Charles admitted.

He divined it all in a moment, and turned to wormwood. What! was he to be robbed of the lady he loved--and her fifteen thousand pounds--by the very man who had robbed him of his ancestral fields? He dwelt on the double grievance till it nearly frenzied him. But he could do nothing: it was his fate. His only hope was that Sir Charles, the arrant flirt, would desert this beauty after a time, as he had the others.

But one afternoon, in the smoking-room of his club, a gentleman said to him, "So your cousin Charles is engaged to the Yorkshire beauty, Bell Bruce?"

"He is flirting with her, I believe," said Richard.

"No, no," said the other; "they are engaged. I know it for a fact. They are to be married next month."

Mr. Richard Bassett digested this fresh pill in moody silence, while the gentlemen of the club discussed the engagement with easy levity. They soon passed to a topic of wider interest, viz., who was to succeed Sir Charles with La Somerset. Bassett began to listen attentively, and learned for the first time Sir Charles Bassett's connection with that lady, and also that she was a woman of a daring nature and furious temper. At first he was merely surprised; but soon hatred and jealousy whispered in his ear that with these materials it must be possible to wound those who had wounded him.

Mr. Marsh, a young gentleman with a receding chin, and a mustache between hay and straw, had taken great care to let them all know he was acquainted with Miss Somerset. So Richard got Marsh alone, and sounded him. Could he call upon the lady without ceremony?

"You won't get in. Her street door is jolly well guarded, I can tell you."

"I am very curious to see her in her own house."

"So are a good many fellows."

"Could you not give me an introduction?"

Marsh shook his head sapiently for a considerable time, and with all this shaking, as it appeared, out fell words of wisdom. "Don't see it. I'm awfully spooney on her myself; and, you know, when a fellow introduces another fellow, that fellow always cuts the other out." Then, descending from the words of the wise and their dark sayings to a petty but pertinent fact, he added, *"Besides,* I'm only let in myself about once in five times."

"She gives herself wonderful airs, it seems," said Bassett, rather bitterly.

Marsh fired up. "So would any woman that was as beautiful, and as witty and as much run after as she is. Why she is a leader of fashion. Look at all the ladies following her round the park. They used to drive on the north side of the Serpentine. She just held up her finger, and now they have cut the Serpentine, and followed her to the south drive."

"Oh, indeed!" said Bassett. "Ah then this is a great lady; a poor country squire must not venture into her august presence." He turned savagely on his heel, and Marsh went and made sickly mirth at his expense.

By this means the matter soon came to the ears of old Mr. Woodgate, the father of that club, and a genial gossip. He got hold of Bassett in the dinner-room and examined him. "So you want an introduction to La Somerset, and Marsh refuses--Marsh, hitherto celebrated for his weak head rather than his hard heart?"

Richard Bassett nodded rather sullenly. He had not bargained for this rapid publicity.

The venerable chief resumed: "We all consider Marsh's conduct unclubable and a thing to be combined against. Wanted--an Anti-dog-in-the-manger League. I'll introduce you to the Somerset."

"What! do *you* visit her?" asked Bassett, in some astonishment.

The old gentleman held up his hands in droll disclaimer, and chuckled merrily "No, no; I enjoy from the shore the disasters of my youthful friends--that sacred pleasure is left me. Do you see that elegant creature with the little auburn beard and mustache, waiting sweetly for his dinner. He launched the Somerset."

"Launched her?"

"Yes; but for him she might have wasted her time breaking hearts and slapping faces in some country village. He it was set her devastating society; and with his aid she shall devastate you. Vandeleur, will you join Bassett and me?"

Mr. Vandeleur, with ready grace, said he should be delighted, and they dined together accordingly.

Mr. Vandeleur, six feet high, lank, but graceful as a panther, and the pink of politeness, was, beneath his varnish, one of the wildest young men in London--gambler, horse-racer, libertine, what not?--but in society charming, and his manners singularly elegant and winning. He never obtruded his vices in good company; in fact, you might dine with him all your life and not detect him. The young serpent was torpid in wine; but he came out, a bit at a time, in the sunshine of Cigar.

After a brisk conversation on current topics, the venerable chief told him plainly they were both curious to know the history of Miss Somerset, and he must tell it them.

"Oh, with pleasure," said the obliging youth. "Let us go into the smoking-room."

"Let--me--see. I picked her up by the sea-side. She promised well at first. We put her on my chestnut mare, and she showed lots of courage, so she soon learned to ride; but she kicked, even down there."

"Kicked!--whom?"

"Kicked all round; I mean showed temper. And when she got to London, and had ridden a few times in the park, and swallowed flattery, there was no holding her. I stood her cheek for a good while, but at last I told the servants they must not turn her out, but they could keep her out. They sided with me for once. She had ridden over them, as well. The first time she went out they bolted the doors, and handed her boxes up the area steps."

"How did she take that?"

"Easier than we expected. She said, 'Lucky for you beggars that I'm a lady, or I'd break every d--d window in the house.'"

This caused a laugh. It subsided. The historian resumed.

"Next day she cooled, and wrote a letter."

"To you?"

"No, to my groom. Would you like to see it? It is a curiosity."

He sent one of the club waiters for his servant, and his servant for his desk, and produced the letter.

"There!" said Vandeleur. "She looks like a queen, and steps like an empress, and this is how she writes:

"'DEAR JORGE--i have got the sak, an' praps your turn nex. dear jorge he alwaies promise me the grey oss, which now an oss is life an death to me. If you was to ast him to lend me the grey he wouldn't refuse you,

"'Yours respecfully,

"'RHODA SOMERSET.'"

When the letter and the handwriting, which, unfortunately, I cannot reproduce, had been duly studied and approved, Vandeleur continued--

"Now, you know, she had her good points, after all. If any creature was ill, she'd sit up all night and nurse them, and she used to go to church on Sundays, and come back with the sting out of her; only then she would preach to a fellow, and bore him. She is awfully fond of preaching. Her dream is to jump on a first-rate hunter, and ride across country, and preach to the villages. So, when George came grinning to me with the letter, I told him to buy a new side-saddle for the gray, and take her the lot, with my compliments. I had noticed a slight spavin in his near foreleg. She rode him that very day in the park, all alone, and made such a sensation that next day my gray was standing in Lord Hailey's stables. But she rode Hailey, like my gray, with a long spur, and he couldn't stand it. None of 'em could except Sir Charles Bassett, and he doesn't play fair--never goes near her."

"And that gives him an unfair advantage over his fascinating predecessors?" inquired the senior, slyly.

"Of course it does," said Vandeleur, stoutly. "You ask a girl to dine at Richmond once a month, and keep out of her way all the rest of the time, and give her lots of money--she will never quarrel with you."

"Profit by this information, young man," said old Woodgate, severely; "it comes too late for me. In my day there existed no sure method of pleasing the fair. But now that is invented, along with everything else. Richmond and--absence, equivalent to 'Richmond and victory!' Now, Bassett, we have heard the truth from the fountain-head, and it is rather serious. She swears, she kicks, she preaches. Do you still desire an introduction? As for me, my manly spirit is beginning to quake at Vandeleur's revelations, and some lines of Scott recur to my Gothic memory--

"'From the chafed tiger rend his prey, Bar the fell dragon's blighting way, But shun that lovely snare.'"

Bassett replied, gravely, that he had no such motive as Mr. Woodgate gave him credit for, but still desired the introduction.

"With pleasure," said Vandeleur; "but it will be no use to you. She hates me like poison; says I have no heart. That is what all ill-tempered women say."

Notwithstanding his misgivings the obliging youth called for writing materials, and produced the following epistle--

"DEAR MISS SOMERSET--Mr. Richard Bassett, a cousin of Sir Charles, wishes very much to be introduced to you, and has begged me to assist in an object so laudable. I should hardly venture to present myself, and, therefore, shall feel surprised as well as flattered if you will receive Mr. Bassett on my introduction, and my assurance that he is a respectable country gentleman, and bears no resemblance in character to

"Yours faithfully,

"ARTHUR VANDELEUR."

Next day Bassett called at Miss Somerset's house in May Fair, and delivered his introduction.

He was admitted after a short delay and entered the lady's boudoir. It was Luxury's nest. The walls were rose colored satin, padded and puckered; the voluminous curtains were pale satin, with floods and billows of real lace; the chairs embroidered, the tables all buhl and ormolu, and the sofas felt like little seas. The lady herself, in a delightful peignoir, sat nestled cozily in a sort of ottoman with arms. Her finely formed hand, clogged with brilliants, was just conveying brandy and soda-water to a very handsome mouth when Richard Bassett entered.

She raised herself superbly, but without leaving her seat, and just looked at a chair in a way that seemed to say, "I permit you to sit down;" and that done, she carried the glass to her lips with the same admirable firmness of hand she showed in driving. Her lofty manner, coupled with her beautiful but rather haughty features, smacked of imperial origin. Yet she was the writer to "jorge," and four years ago a shrimp-girl, running into the sea with legs as brown as a berry.

So swiftly does merit rise in this world which, nevertheless, some morose folk pretend is a wicked one.

I ought to explain, however, that this haughty reception was partly caused by a breach of propriety. Vandeleur ought first to have written to her and asked permission to present Richard Bassett. He had no business to send the man and the introduction together. This law a Parliament of Sirens had passed, and the slightest breach of it was a bitter offense Equilibrium governs the world. These ladies were bound to be overstrict in something or other, being just a little lax in certain things where other ladies are strict.

Now Bassett had pondered well what he should say, but he was disconcerted by her superb presence and demeanor and her large gray eyes, that rested steadily upon his face.

However, he began to murmur mellifluously. Said he had often seen her in public, and admired her, and desired to make her acquaintance, etc., etc.

"Then why did you not ask Sir Charles to bring you here?" said Miss Somerset, abruptly, and searching him with her eyes, that were not to say bold, but singularly brave, and examiners pointblank.

"I am not on good terms with Sir Charles. He holds the estates that ought to be mine; and now he has robbed me of my love. He is the last man in the world I would ask a favor of."

"You came here to abuse him behind his back, eh?" asked the lady with undisguised contempt.

Bassett winced, but kept his temper. "No, Miss Somerset; but you seem to think I ought to have come to you through Sir Charles. I would not enter your house if I did not feel sure I shall not meet him here."

Miss Somerset looked rather puzzled. "Sir Charles does not come here every day, but he comes now and then, and he is always welcome."

"You surprise me."

"Thank you. Now some of my gentlemen friends think it is a wonder he does not come every minute."

"You mistake me. What surprises me is that you are such good friends under the circumstances."

"Circumstances! what circumstances?"

"Oh, you know. You are in his confidence, I presume?"--this rather satirically. So the lady answered, defiantly:

"Yes, I am; he knows I can hold my tongue, so he tells me things he tells nobody else."

"Then, if you are in his confidence, you know he is about to be married."

"Married! Sir Charles married!"

"In three weeks."

"It's a lie! You get out of my house this moment!"

Mr. Bassett colored at this insult. He rose from his seat with some little dignity, made her a low bow, and retired. But her blood was up: she made a wonderful rush, sweeping down a chair with her dress as she went, and caught him at the door, clutched him by the shoulder and half dragged him back, and made him sit down again, while she stood opposite him, with the knuckles of one hand resting on the table.

"Now," said she, panting, "you look me in the face and say that again."

"Excuse me; you punish me too severely for telling the truth."

"Well, I beg your pardon--there. Now tell me--this instant. Can't you speak, man?" And her knuckles drummed the table.

"He is to be married in three weeks."

"Oh! Who to?"

"A young lady I love."

"Her name?"

"Miss Arabella Bruce."

"Where does she live?"

"Portman Square."

"I'll stop that marriage."

"How?" asked Richard, eagerly.

"I don't know; that I'll think over. But he shall not marry her--never!"

Bassett sat and looked up with almost as much awe as complacency at the fury he had evoked; for this woman was really at times a poetic impersonation of that fiery passion she was so apt to indulge. She stood before him, her cheek pale, her eyes glittering and roving savagely, and her nostrils literally expanding, while her tall body quivered with wrath, and her clinched knuckles pattered on the table.

"He shall not marry her. I'll kill him first!"

CHAPTER III.

RICHARD BASSETT eagerly offered his services to break off the obnoxious match. But Miss Somerset was beginning to be mortified at having shown so much passion before a stranger.

"What have you to do with it?" said she, sharply.

"Everything. I love Miss Bruce."

"Oh, yes; I forgot that. Anything else? There is, now. I see it in your eye. What is it?"

"Sir Charles's estates are mine by right, and they will return to my line if he does not marry and have issue."

"Oh, I see. That is so like a man. It's always love, and something more important, with you. Well, give me your address. I'll write if I want you."

"Highly flattered," said Bassett, ironically-wrote his address and left her.

Miss Somerset then sat down and wrote:

"DEAR SIR CHARLES--please call here, I want to speak to you.

yours respecfuly,

"RHODA SOMERSET."

Sir Charles obeyed this missive, and the lady received him with a gracious and smiling manner, all put on and catlike. She talked with him of indifferent things for more than an hour, still watching to see if he would tell her of his own accord.

When she was quite sure he would not, she said,

"Do you know there's a ridiculous report about that you are going to be married?"

"Indeed!"

"They even tell her name--Miss Bruce. Do you know the girl?"

"Yes."

"Is she pretty?"

"Very."

"Modest?"

"As an angel."

"And are you going to marry her?"

"Yes."

"Then you are a villain."

"The deuce I am!"

"You are, to abandon a woman who has sacrificed all for you."

Sir Charles looked puzzled, and then smiled; but was too polite to give his thoughts vent. Nor was it necessary; Miss Somerset, whose brave eyes never left the person she was speaking to, fired up at the smile alone, and she burst into a torrent of remonstrance, not to say vituperation. Sir Charles endeavored once or twice to stop it, but it was not to be stopped; so at last he quietly took up his hat, to go.

He was arrested at the door by a rustle and a fall. He turned round, and there was Miss Somerset lying on her back, grinding her white teeth and clutching the air.

He ran to the bell and rang it violently, then knelt down and did his best to keep her from hurting herself; but, as generally happens in these cases, his interference made her more violent. He had hard work to keep her from battering her head against the floor, and her arms worked like windmills.

Hearing the bell tugged so violently, a pretty page ran headlong into the room--saw--and; without an instant's diminution of speed, described a curve, and ran headlong out, screaming "Polly! Polly!"

The next moment the housekeeper, an elderly woman, trotted in at the door, saw her mistress's condition, and stood stock-still, calling, "Polly," but with the most perfect tranquillity the mind can conceive.

In ran a strapping house-maid, with black eyes and brown arms, went down on her knees, and said, firmly though respectfully, "Give her me, sir."

She got behind her struggling mistress, pulled her up into her own lap, and pinned her by the wrists with a vigorous grasp.

The lady struggled, and ground her teeth audibly, and flung her arms abroad. The maid applied all her rustic strength and harder muscle to hold her within bounds. The four arms went to and fro in a magnificent struggle, and neither could the maid hold the mistress still, nor the mistress shake off the maid's grasp, nor strike anything to hurt herself.

Sir Charles, thrust out of the play looked on with pity and anxiety, and the little page at the door--combining art and nature--stuck stock-still in a military attitude, and blubbered aloud.

As for the housekeeper, she remained in the middle of the room with folded arms, and looked down on the struggle with a singular expression of countenance. There was no agitation whatever, but a sort of thoughtful examination, half cynical, half admiring.

However, as soon as the boy's sobs reached her ear she wakened up, and said, tenderly, "What is the child crying for? Run and get a basin of water, and fling it all over her; that will bring her to in a minute."

The page departed swiftly on this benevolent errand.

Then the lady gave a deep sigh, and ceased to struggle.

Next she stared in all their faces, and seemed to return to consciousness.

Next she spoke, but very feebly. "Help me up," she sighed.

Sir Charles and Polly raised her, and now there was a marvelous change. The vigorous vixen was utterly weak, and limp as a wet towel--a woman of jelly. As such they handled her, and deposited her gingerly on the sofa.

Now the page ran in hastily with the water. Up jumps the poor lax sufferer, with flashing eyes: "You dare come near me with it!" Then to the female servants: "Call yourselves women, and water my lilac silk, not two hours old?" Then to the housekeeper: "You old monster, you wanted it for your Polly. Get out of my sight, *the lot!*"

Then, suddenly remembering how feeble she was, she sank instantly down, and turned piteously and languidly to Sir Charles. "They eat my bread, and rob me, and hate me," said she, faintly. "I have but one friend on earth." She leaned tenderly toward Sir Charles as that friend; but before she quite reached him she started back, her eyes filled with sudden horror. "And he forsakes me!" she cried; and so turned away from him despairingly, and began to cry bitterly, with head averted over the sofa, and one hand hanging by her side for Sir Charles to take and comfort her. He tried to take it. It resisted; and, under cover of that little disturbance, the other hand dexterously whipped two pins out of her hair. The long brown tresses--all her own--fell over her eyes and down to her waist, and the picture of distressed beauty was complete.

Even so did the women of antiquity conquer male pity--"solutis crinibus."

The females interchanged a meaning glance, and retired; then the boy followed them with his basin, sore perplexed, but learning life in this admirable school.

Sir Charles then, with the utmost kindness, endeavored to reconcile the weeping and disheveled fair to that separation which circumstances rendered necessary. But she was inconsolable, and he left the house, perplexed and grieved; not but what it gratified his vanity a little to find himself beloved all in a moment, and the Somerset unvixened. He could not help thinking how wide must be the circle of his charms, which had won the affections of two beautiful women so opposite in character as Bella Bruce and La Somerset.

The passion of this latter seemed to grow. She wrote to him every day, and begged him to call on her.

She called on him--she who had never called on a man before.

She raged with jealousy; she melted with grief. She played on him with all a woman's artillery; and at last actually wrung from him what she called a reprieve.

Richard Bassett called on her, but she would not receive him; so then he wrote to her, urging co-operation, and she replied, frankly, that she took no interest in his affairs; but that she was devoted to Sir Charles, and should keep him for herself. Vanity tempted her to add that he (Sir Charles) was with her every day, and the wedding postponed.

This last seemed too good to be true, so Richard Bassett set his servant to talk to the servants in Portman Square. He learned that the wedding was now to be on the 15th of June, instead of the 31st of May.

Convinced that this postponement was only a blind, and that the marriage would never be, he breathed more freely at the news.

But the fact is, although Sir Charles had yielded so far to dread of scandal, he was ashamed of himself, and his shame became remorse when he detected a furtive tear in the dove-like eyes of her he really loved and esteemed.

He went and told his trouble to Mr. Oldfield. "I am afraid she will do something desperate," he said.

Mr. Oldfield heard him out, and then asked him had he told Miss Somerset what he was going to settle on her.

"Not I. She is not in a condition to be influenced by that, at present."

"Let me try her. The draft is ready. I'll call on her to-morrow." He did call, and was told she did not know him.

"You tell her I am a lawyer, and it is very much to her interest to see me," said Mr. Oldfield to the page.

He was admitted, but not to a **tete-a-tete.** Polly was kept in the room. The Somerset had peeped, and Oldfield was an old fellow, with white hair; if he had been a young fellow, with black hair, she might have thought that precaution less necessary.

"First, madam," said Oldfield, "I must beg you to accept my apologies for not coming sooner. Press of business, etc."

"Why have you come at all? That is the question," inquired the lady, bluntly.

"I bring the draft of a deed for your approval. Shall I read it to you?"

"Yes; if it is not very long." He began to read it. The lady interrupted him characteristically.

"It's a beastly rigmarole. What does it mean--in three words?"

"Sir Charles Bassett secures to Rhoda Somerset four hundred pounds a year, while single; this is reduced to two hundred if you marry. The deed further assigns to you, without reserve, the beneficial lease of this house, and all the furniture and effects, plate, linen, wine, etc."

"I see--a bribe."

"Nothing of the kind, madam. When Sir Charles instructed me to prepare this deed he expected no opposition on your part to his marriage; but he thought it due to him and to yourself to mark his esteem for you, and his recollection of the pleasant hours he has spent in your company."

Miss Somerset's eyes searched the lawyer's face. He stood the battery unflinchingly. She altered her tone, and asked, politely and almost respectfully, whether she might see that paper.

Mr. Oldfield gave it her. She took it, and ran her eye over it; in doing which, she raised it so that she could think behind it unobserved. She handed it back at last, with the remark that Sir Charles was a gentleman and had done the right thing.

"He has; and you will do the right thing too, will you not?"

"I don't know. I am just beginning to fall in love with him myself."

"Jealousy, madam, not love," said the old lawyer. "Come, now! I see you are a young lady of rare good sense; look the thing in the face: Sir Charles is a landed gentleman; he must marry, and, have heirs. He is over thirty, and his time has come. He has shown himself your friend; why not be his? He has given you the means to marry a gentleman of moderate income, or to marry beneath you, if you prefer it--"

"And most of us do--"

"Then why not make his path smooth? Why distress him with your tears and remonstrances?"

He continued in this strain for some time, appealing to her good sense and her better feelings.

When he had done she said, very quietly, "How about the ponies and my brown mare? Are they down in the deed?"

"I think not; but if you will do your part handsomely I'll guarantee you shall have them."

"You are a good soul." Then, after a pause, "Now just you tell me exactly what you want me to do for all this."

Oldfield was pleased with this question. He said, "I wish you to abstain from writing to Sir Charles, and him to visit you only once more before his marriage, just to shake hands and part, with mutual friendship and good wishes."

"You are right," said she, softly; "best for us both, and only fair to the girl." Then, with sudden and eager curiosity, "Is she very pretty?"

"I don't know."

"What, hasn't he told you?"

"He says she is lovely, and every way adorable; but then he is in love. The chances are she is not half so handsome as yourself."

"And yet he is in love with her?"

"Over head and ears."

"I don't believe it. If he was really in love with one woman he couldn't be just to another. *I* couldn't. He'll be coming back to me in a few months."

"God forbid!"

"Thank you, old gentleman."

Mr. Oldfield began to stammer excuses. She interrupted him: "Oh, bother all that; I like you none the worse for speaking your mind." Then, after a pause, "Now excuse me; but suppose Sir Charles should change his mind, and never sign this paper?"

"I pledge my professional credit."

"That is enough, sir; I see I can trust you. Well, then, I consent to break off with Sir Charles, and only see him once more--as a friend. Poor Sir Charles! I hope he will be happy" (she squeezed out a tear for him)--"happier than I am. And when he does come he can sign the deed, you know."

Mr. Oldfield left her, and joined Sir Charles at Long's, as had been previously agreed.

"It is all right, Sir Charles; she is a sensible girl, and will give you no further trouble."

"How did you get over the hysterics?"

"We dispensed with them. She saw at once it was to be business, not sentiment. You are to pay her one more visit, to sign, and part friends. If you please, I'll make that appointment with both parties, as soon as the deed is engrossed. Oh, by-the-by, she did shed a tear or two, but she dried them to ask me for the ponies and the brown mare."

Sir Charles's vanity was mortified. But he laughed it off, and said she should have them, of course.

So now his mind was at ease, his conscience was at rest, and he could give his whole time where he had given his heart.

Richard Bassett learned, through his servant, that the wedding-dresses were ordered. He called on Miss Somerset. She was out.

Polly opened the door and gave him a look of admiration--due to his fresh color--that encouraged him to try and enlist her in his service.

He questioned her, and she told him in a general way how matters were going. "But," said she, "why not come and talk to her yourself? Ten to one but she tells you. She is pretty outspoken."

"My pretty dear," said Richard, "she never will receive me."

"Oh, but I'll make her!" said Polly.

And she did exert her influence as follows:

"Lookee here, the cousin's a-coming to-morrow and I've been and promised he should see you."

"What did you do that for?"

"Why, he's a well-looking chap, and a beautiful color, fresh from the country, like me. And he's a gentleman, and got an estate belike; and why not put yourn to hisn, and so marry him and be a lady? You might have me about ye all the same, till my turn comes."

"No, no," said Rhoda; "that's not the man for me. If ever I marry, it must be one of my own sort, or else a fool, like Marsh, that I can make a slave of."

"Well, any way, you must see him, not to make a fool of *me,* for I did promise him; which, now I think on't, 'twas very good of me, for I could find in my heart to ask him down into the kitchen, instead of bringing him upstairs to you."

All this ended, somehow, in Mr. Bassett's being admitted.

To his anxious inquiry how matters stood, she replied coolly that Sir Charles and herself were parted by mutual consent.

"What! after all your protestations?" said Bassett, bitterly.

But Miss Somerset was not in an irascible humor just then. She shrugged her shoulders, and said:

"Yes, I remember I put myself in a passion, and said some ridiculous things. But one can't be always a fool. I have come to my senses. This sort of thing always does end, you know. Most of them part enemies, but he and I part friends and well-wishers."

"And you throw *me* over as if I was nobody," said Richard, white with anger.

"Why, what are you to me?" said the Somerset. "Oh, I see. You thought to make a cat's-paw of me. Well, you won't, then."

"In other words, you have been bought off."

"No, I have not. I am not to be bought by anybody--and I am not to be insulted by you, you ruffian! How dare you come here and affront a lady in her own house--a lady whose shoestrings your betters are ready to tie, you brute? If you want to be a landed proprietor, go and marry some ugly old hag that's got it, and no eyesight left to see you're no gentleman. Sir Charles's land you'll never have; a better man has got it, and means to keep it for him and his. Here, Polly! Polly! Polly! take this man down to the kitchen, and teach him manners if you can: he is not fit for my drawing-room, by a long chalk."

Polly arrived in time to see the flashing eyes, the swelling veins, and to hear the fair orator's peroration.

"What, you are in your tantrums again!" said she. "Come along, sir. Needs must when the devil drives. You'll break a blood-vessel some day, my lady, like your father afore ye."

And with this homely suggestion, which always sobered Miss Somerset, and, indeed, frightened her out of her wits, she withdrew the offender. She did not take him into the kitchen, but into the dining-room, and there he had a long talk with her, and gave her a sovereign.

She promised to inform him if anything important should occur.

He went away, pondering and scowling deeply.

CHAPTER IV.

SIR CHARLES BASSETT was now living in Elysium. Never was rake more thoroughly transformed. Every day he sat for hours at the feet of Bella Bruce, admiring her soft, feminine ways and virgin modesty even more than her beauty. And her visible blush whenever he appeared suddenly, and the soft commotion and yielding in her lovely frame whenever he drew near, betrayed his magnetic influence, and told all but the blind she adored him.

She would decline all invitations to dine with him and her father--a strong-minded old admiral, whose authority was unbounded, only, to Bella's regret, very rarely exerted. Nothing would have pleased her more than to be forbidden this and commanded that; but no! the admiral was a lion with an enormous paw, only he could not be got to put it into every pie.

In this charming society the hours glided, and the wedding-day drew close. So deeply and sincerely was Sir Charles in love that when Mr. Oldfield's letter came, appointing the day and hour to sign Miss Somerset's deed, he was unwilling to go, and wrote back to ask if the deed could not be sent to his house.

Mr. Oldfield replied that the parties to the deed and the witnesses must meet, and it would be unadvisable, for several reasons, to irritate the lady's susceptibility previous to signature; the appointment having been made at her house, it had better remain so.

That day soon came.

Sir Charles, being due in Mayfair at 2 P.M., compensated himself for the less agreeable business to come by going earlier than usual to Portman Square. By this means he caught Miss Bruce and two other young ladies inspecting bridal dresses. Bella blushed and looked ashamed, and, to the surprise of her friends, sent the dresses away, and set herself to talk rationally with Sir Charles--as rationally as lovers can.

The ladies took the cue, and retired in disgust.

Sir Charles apologized.

"This is too bad of me. I come at an unheard-of hour, and frighten away your fair friends; but the fact is, I have an appointment at two, and I don't know how long they will keep me, so I thought I would make sure of two happy hours at the least."

And delightful hours they were. Bella Bruce, excited by this little surprise, leaned softly on his shoulder, and prattled her maiden love like some warbling fountain.

Sir Charles, transfigured by love, answered her in kind--three months ago he could not--and they compared pretty little plans of wedded life, and had small differences, and ended by agreeing.

Complete and prompt accord upon two points: first, they would not have a single quarrel, like other people; their love should never lose its delicate bloom; second, they would grow old together, and die the same day--the same minute if possible; if not, they must be content with the same day, but, on that, inexorable.

But soon after this came a skirmish. Each wanted to obey t'other.

Sir Charles argued that Bella was better than he, and therefore more fit to conduct the pair.

Bella, who thought him divinely good, pounced on this reason furiously. He defended it. He admitted, with exemplary candor, that he was good now--"awfully good." But he assured her that he had been anything but good until he knew her; now she had been always good; therefore, he argued, as his goodness came originally from her, for her to obey him would be a little too much like the moon commanding the sun.

"That is too ingenious for me, Charles," said Bella. "And, for shame! Nobody was ever so good as you are. I look up to you and--Now I could stop your mouth in a minute. I have only to remind you that I shall swear at the altar to obey you, and you will not swear to obey me. But I will not crush you under the Prayer-book--no, dearest; but, indeed, to obey is a want of my nature, and I marry you to supply that want: and that's a story, for I marry you because I love and honor and worship and adore you to distraction, my own--own--own!" With this she flung herself passionately, yet modestly on his shoulder, and, being there, murmured, coaxingly, "You will let me obey you, Charles?"

Thereupon Sir Charles felt highly gelatinous, and lost, for the moment, all power of resistance or argument.

"Ah, you will; and then you will remind me of my dear mother. She knew how to command; but as for poor dear papa, he is very disappointing. In selecting an admiral for my parent, I made sure of being ordered about. Instead of that--now I'll show you--there he is in the next room, inventing a new system of signals, poor dear--"

She threw the folding-doors open.

"Papa dear, shall I ask Charles to dinner to-day?"

"As you please, my dear."

"Do you think I had better walk or ride this afternoon?"

"Whichever you prefer."

"There," said Bella, "I told you so. That is always the way. Papa dear, you used always to be firing guns at sea. Do, please, fire one in this house--just one--before I leave it, and make the very windows rattle."

"I beg your pardon, Bella; I never wasted powder at sea. If the convoy sailed well and steered right I never barked at them. You are a modest, sensible girl, and have always steered a good course. Why should I hoist a petticoat and play the small tyrant? Wait till I see you going to do something wrong or silly."

"Ah! then you *would* fire a gun, papa?"

"Ay, a broadside."

"Well, that is something," said Bella, as she closed the door softly.

"No, no; it amounts to just nothing," said Sir Charles; "for you never will do anything wrong or silly. I'll accommodate you. I have thought of a way. I shall give you some blank cards; you shall write on them, 'I think I should like to do so and so.' You shall be careless, and leave them about; I'll find them, and bluster, and say, 'I command you to do so and so, Bella Bassett'--the very thing on the card, you know."

Bella colored to the brow with pleasure and modesty. After a pause she said: "How sweet! The worst of it is, I should get my own way. Now what I want is to submit my will to yours. A gentle tyrant--that is what you must be to Bella Bassett.

Oh, you sweet, sweet, for calling me that!"

These projects were interrupted by a servant announcing luncheon. This made Sir Charles look hastily at his watch, and he found it was past two o'clock.

"How time flies in this house!" said he. "I must go, dearest; I am behind my appointment already. What do you do this afternoon?"

"Whatever you please, my own."

"I could get away by four."

"Then I will stay at home for you."

He left her reluctantly, and she followed him to the head of the stairs, and hung over the balusters as if she would like to fly after him.

He turned at the street-door, saw that radiant and gentle face beaming after him, and they kissed hands to each other by one impulse, as if they were parting for ever so long.

He had gone scarcely half an hour when a letter, addressed to her, was left at the door by a private messenger.

"Any answer?" inquired the servant.

"No."

The letter was sent up, and delivered to her on a silver salver.

She opened it; it was a thing new to her in her young life--an anonymous letter.

"MISS BRUCE--I am almost a stranger to you, but I know your character from others, and cannot bear to see you abused. You are said to be about to marry Sir Charles Bassett. I think you can hardly be aware that he is connected with a lady of doubtful repute, called Somerset, and neither your beauty nor your virtue has prevailed to detach him from that connection.

"If, on engaging himself to you, he had abandoned her, I should not have said a word. But the truth is, he visits her constantly, and I blush to say that when he leaves you this day it will be to spend the afternoon at her house.

"I inclose you her address, and you can learn in ten minutes whether I am a slanderer or, what I wish to be,

"A FRIEND OF INJURED INNOCENCE."

CHAPTER V.

SIR CHARLES was behind his time in Mayfair; but the lawyer and his clerk had not arrived, and Miss Somerset was not visible.

She appeared, however, at last, in a superb silk dress, the broad luster of which would have been beautiful, only the effect was broken and frittered away by six rows of gimp and fringe. But why blame her? This is a blunder in art as universal as it is amazing, when one considers the amount of apparent thought her sex devotes to dress. They might just as well score a fair plot of velvet turf with rows of box, or tattoo a blooming and downy cheek.

She held out her hand, like a man, and talked to Sir Charles on indifferent topics, till Mr. Oldfield arrived. She then retired into the background, and left the gentlemen to discuss the deed. When appealed to, she evaded direct replies, and put on languid and imperial indifference. When she signed, it was with the air of some princess bestowing a favor upon solicitation.

But the business concluded, she thawed all in a moment, and invited the gentlemen to luncheon with charming cordiality. Indeed, her genuine **bonhomie** after her affected indifference was rather comic. Everybody was content. Champagne flowed. The lady, with her good mother-wit, kept conversation going till the lawyer was nearly missing his next appointment. He hurried away; and Sir Charles only lingered, out of good-breeding, to bid Miss Somerset good-by. In the course of leave-taking he said he was sorry he left her with people about her of whom he had a bad opinion. "Those women have no more feeling for you than stones. When you lay in convulsions, your housekeeper looked on as philosophically as if you had been two kittens at play--you and Polly."

"I saw her."

"Indeed! You appeared hardly in a condition to see anything."

"I did, though, and heard the old wretch tell the young monkey to water my lilac dress. That was to get it for her Polly. She knew I'd never wear it afterward."

"Then why don't you turn her off?"

"Who'd take such a useless old hag, if I turned her off?"

"You carry a charity a long way."

"I carry everything. What's the use doing things by halves, good or bad?"

"Well, but that Polly! She is young enough to get her living elsewhere; and she is extremely disrespectful to you."

"That she is. If I wasn't a lady, I'd have given her a good hiding this very day for her cheek!"

"Then why not turn her off this very day for her cheek?"

"Well, I'll tell you, since you and I are parted forever. No, I don't like."

"Oh, come! No secrets between friends."

"Well, then, the old hag is--my mother."

"What?"

"And the young jade--is my sister."

"Good Heavens!"

"And the page--is my little brother."

"Ha, ha, ha!"

"What, you are not angry?"

"Angry? no. Ha, ha, ha!"

"See what a hornets' nest you have escaped from. My dear friend, those two women rob me through thick and thin. They steal my handkerchiefs, and my gloves, and my very linen. They drink my wine like fishes. They'd take the hair off my head, if it wasn't fast by the roots--for a wonder."

"Why not give them a ten-pound note and send them home?"

"They'd pocket the note, and blacken me in our village. That was why I had them up here. First time I went home, after running about with that little scamp, Vandeleur--do you know him?"

"I have not the honor."

"Then your luck beats mine. One thing, he is going to the dogs as fast as he can. Some day he'll come begging to me for a fiver. You mark my words now."

"Well, but you were saying--"

"Yes, I went off about Van. Polly *says* I've a mind like running water. Well, then, when I went home the first time--after Van, mother and Polly raised a virtuous howl. 'All right,' said I--for, of course, I know how much virtue there is under *their* skins. Virtue of the lower orders! Tell that to gentlefolks that don't know them. I do. I've been one of 'em--'I know all about that,' says I. 'You want to share the plunder, that is the sense of your virtuous cry.' So I had 'em up here; and then there was no more virtuous howling, but a deal of virtuous thieving, and modest drinking, and pure-minded selling of my street-door to the highest male bidder. And they will corrupt the boy; and if they do, I'll cuts their black hearts out with my riding-whip. But I suppose I must keep them on; they are my own flesh and blood; and if I was to be ill and dying, they'd do all they knew to keep me alive--for their own sakes. I'm their milch cow, these country innocents."

Sir Charles groaned aloud, and said, "My poor girl, you deserve a better fate than this. Marry some honest fellow, and cut the whole thing."

"I'll see about it. You try it first, and let us see how you like it."

And so they parted gayly.

In the hall, Polly intercepted him, all smiles. He looked at her, smiled in his sleeve, and gave her a handsome present. "If you please, sir," said she, "an old gentleman called for you."

"When?"

"About an hour ago. Leastways, he asked if Sir Charles Bassett was there. I said yes, but you wouldn't see no one."

"Who could it be? Why, surely you never told anybody I was to be here to-day?"

"La, no, sir! how could I?" said Polly, with a face of brass.

Sir Charles thought this very odd, and felt a little uneasy about it. All to Portman Square he puzzled over it; and at last he was driven to the conclusion that Miss Somerset had been weak enough to tell some person, male or female, of the coming interview, and so somebody had called there--doubtless to ask him a favor.

At five o'clock he reached Portman Square, and was about to enter, as a matter of course; but the footman stopped him. "I beg pardon, Sir Charles," said the man, looking pale and agitated; "but I have strict orders. My young lady is very ill."

"Ill! Let me go to her this instant."

"I daren't, Sir Charles, I daren't. I know you are a gentleman; pray don't lose me my place. You would never get to see her. We none of us know the rights, but there's something up. Sorry to say it, Sir Charles, but we have strict orders not to admit you. Haven't you the admiral's letter, sir?"

"No; what letter?"

"He has been after you, sir; and when he came back he sent Roger off to your house with a letter."

A cold chill began to run down Sir Charles Bassett. He hailed a passing hansom, and drove to his own house to get the admiral's letter; and as he went he asked himself, with chill misgivings, what on earth had happened.

What had happened shall be told the reader precisely but briefly..

In the first place, Bella had opened the anonymous letter and read its contents, to which the reader is referred.

There are people who pretend to despise anonymous letters. Pure delusion! they know they ought to, and so fancy they do; but they don't. The absence of a signature gives weight, if the letter is ably written and seems true.

As for poor Bella Bruce, a dove's bosom is no more fit to rebuff a poisoned arrow than she was to combat that foulest and direst of all a miscreant's weapons, an anonymous letter. She, in her goodness and innocence, never dreamed that any person she did not know could possibly tell a lie to wound her. The letter fell on her like a cruel revelation from heaven.

The blow was so savage that, at first, it stunned her.

She sat pale and stupefied; but beneath the stupor were the rising throbs of coming agonies.

After that horrible stupor her anguish grew and grew, till it found vent in a miserable cry, rising, and rising, and rising, in agony.

"Mamma! mamma! mamma!"

Yes; her mother had been dead these three years, and her father sat in the next room; yet, in her anguish, she cried to her mother--a cry the which, if your mother had heard, she would have expected Bella's to come to her even from the grave.

Admiral Bruce heard this fearful cry--the living calling on the dead--and burst through the folding-doors in a moment, white as a ghost.

He found his daughter writhing on the sofa, ghastly, and grinding in her hand the cursed paper that had poisoned her young life.

"My child! my child!"

"Oh, papa! see! see!" And she tried to open the letter for him, but her hands trembled so she could not.

He kneeled down by her side, the stout old warrior, and read the letter, while she clung to him, moaning now, and quivering all over from head to foot.

"Why, there's no signature! The writer is a coward and, perhaps, a liar. Stop! he offers a test. I'll put him to it this minute."

He laid the moaning girl on the sofa, ordered his servants to admit nobody into the house, and drove at once to Mayfair.

He called at Miss Somerset's house, saw Polly, and questioned her.

He drove home again, and came into the drawing-room looking as he had been seen to look when fighting his ship; but his daughter had never seen him so. "My girl," said he, solemnly, "there's nothing for you to do but to be brave, and hide your grief as well as you can, for the man is unworthy of your love. That coward spoke the truth. He is there at this moment."

"Oh, papa! papa! let me die! The world is too wicked for me. Let me die!"

"Die for an unworthy object? For shame! Go to your own room, my girl, and pray to your God to help you, since your mother has left us. Oh, how I miss her now! Go and pray, and let no one else know what we suffer. Be your father's daughter. Fight and pray."

Poor Bella had no longer to complain that she was not commanded. She kissed him, and burst into a great passion of weeping; but he led her to the door, and she tottered to her own room, a blighted girl.

The sight of her was harrowing. Under its influence the admiral dashed off a letter to Sir Charles, calling him a villain, and inviting him to go to France and let an indignant father write scoundrel on his carcass.

But when he had written this his good sense and dignity prevailed over his fury; he burned the letter, and wrote another. This he sent by hand to Sir Charles's house, and ordered his servants--but that the reader knows.

Sir Charles found the admiral's letter in his letter-rack. It ran thus:

"SIR--We have learned your connection with a lady named Somerset, and I have ascertained that you went from my daughter to her house this very day.

"Miss Bruce and myself withdraw from all connection with you, and I must request you to attempt no communication with her of any kind. Such an attempt would be an additional insult.

"I am, sir, your obedient servant,

"JOHN URQUHART BRUCE."

At first Sir Charles Bassett was stunned by this blow. Then his mind resisted the admiral's severity, and he was indignant at being dismissed for so common an offense. This gave way to deep grief and shame at the thought of Bella and her lost esteem. But soon all other feelings merged for a time in fury at the heartless traitor who had destroyed his happiness, and had dashed the cup of innocent love from his very lips. Boiling over with mortification and rage, he drove at once to that traitor's house. Polly opened the door. He rushed past her, and burst into the dining-room, breathless, and white with passion.

He found Miss Somerset studying the deed by which he had made her independent for life. She started at his strange appearance, and instinctively put both hands flat upon the deed.

"You vile wretch!" cried Sir Charles. "You heartless monster! Enjoy your work." And he flung her the admiral's letter. But he did not wait while she read it; he heaped reproaches on her; and, for the first time in her life, she did not reply in kind.

"Are you mad?" she faltered. "What have I done?"

"You have told Admiral Bruce."

"That's false."

"You told him I was to be here to-day."

"Charles, I never did. Believe me."

"You did. Nobody knew it but you. He was here to-day at the very hour."

"May I never get up alive off this chair if I told a soul. Yes, our Polly. I'll ring for her."

"No, you will not. She is your sister. Do you think I'll take the word of such reptiles against the plain fact? You have parted my love and me--parted us on the very day I had made you independent for life. An innocent love was waiting to bless me, and an honest love was in your power, thanks to me, your kind, forgiving friend and benefactor. I have heaped kindness on you from the first moment I had the misfortune to know you. I connived at your infidelities--"

"Charles! Don't say that. I never **was.**"

"I indulged your most expensive whims, and, instead of leaving you with a curse, as all the rest did that ever knew you, and as you deserve, I bought your consent to lead a respectable life, and be blessed with a virtuous love. You took the bribe, but robbed me of the blessing--viper! You have destroyed me, body and soul--monster! perhaps blighted her happiness as well; you she-devils hate an angel worse than Heaven hates you. But you shall suffer with us; not your heart, for you have none, but your pocket. You have broken faith with me, and sent all my happiness to hell; I'll send your deed to hell after it!" With this, he flung himself upon the deed, and was going to throw it into the fire. Now up to that moment she had been overpowered by this man's fury, whom she had never seen the least angry before; but when he laid hands on her property it acted like an electric shock. "No! no!" she screamed, and sprang at him like a wildcat.

Then ensued a violent and unseemly struggle all about the room; chairs were upset, and vases broken to pieces; and the man and woman dragged each other to and fro, one fighting for her property, as if it was her life, and the other for revenge.

Sir Charles, excited by fury, was stronger than himself, and at last shook off one of her hands for a moment, and threw the deed into the fire. She tried to break from him and save it, but he held her like iron.

Yet not for long. While he was holding her back, and she straining every nerve to get to the fire, he began to show sudden symptoms of distress. He gasped loudly, and cried, "Oh! oh! I'm choking!" and then his clutch relaxed. She tore herself from it, and, plunging forward, rescued the smoking parchment.

At that moment she heard a great stagger behind her, and a pitiful moan, and Sir Charles fell heavily, striking his head against the edge of the sofa. She looked round--as she knelt, and saw him, black in the face, rolling his eyeballs fearfully, while his teeth gnashed awfully, and a little jet of foam flew through his lips.

Then she shrieked with terror, and the blackened deed fell from her hands. At this moment Polly rushed into the room. She saw the fearful sight, and echoed her sister's scream. But they were neither of them women to lose their heads and beat the air with their hands. They got to him, and both of them fought hard with the unconscious sufferer, whose body, in a fresh convulsion, now bounded away from the sofa, and bade fair to batter itself against the ground.

They did all they could to hold him with one arm apiece, and to release his swelling throat with the other. Their nimble fingers whipped off his neck-tie in a moment; but the distended windpipe pressed so against the shirt-button they could not undo it. Then they seized the collar, and, pulling against each other, wrenched the shirt open so powerfully that the button flew into the air, and tinkled against a mirror a long way off.

A few more struggles, somewhat less violent, and then the face, from purple, began to whiten, the eyeballs fixed; the pulse went down; the man lay still.

"Oh, my God!" cried Rhoda Somerset. "He is dying! To the nearest doctor! There's one three doors off. No bonnet! It's life and death this moment. Fly!"

Polly obeyed, and Doctor Andrews was actually in the room within five minutes.

He looked grave, and kneeled down by the patient, and felt his pulse anxiously.

Miss Somerset sat down, and, being from the country, though she did not look it, began to weep bitterly, and rock herself in rustic fashion.

The doctor questioned her kindly, and she told him, between her sobs, how Sir Charles had been taken.

The doctor, however, instead of being alarmed by those frightful symptoms she related, took a more cheerful view directly. "Then do not alarm yourself unnecessarily," he said. "It was only an epileptic fit."

"Only!" sobbed Miss Somerset. "Oh, if you had seen him! And he lies like death."

"Yes," said Dr. Andrews; "a severe epileptic fit is really a terrible thing to look at; but it is not dangerous in proportion. Is he used to have them?"

"Oh, no, doctor--never had one before."

Here she was mistaken, I think.

"You must keep him quiet; and give him a moderate stimulant as soon as he can swallow comfortably; the quietest room in the house; and don't let him be hungry, night or day. Have food by his bedside, and watch him for a day or two. I'll come again this evening."

The doctor went to his dinner--tranquil.

Not so those he left. Miss Somerset resigned her own luxurious bedroom, and had the patient laid, just as he was, upon her bed. She sent the page out to her groom and ordered two loads of straw to be laid before the door; and she watched by the sufferer, with brandy and water by her side.

Sir Charles now might have seemed to be in a peaceful slumber, but for his eyes. They were open, and showed more white, and less pupil, than usual.

However, in time he began to sigh and move, and even mutter; and, gradually, some little color came back to his pale cheeks.

Then Miss Somerset had the good sense to draw back out of his sight, and order Polly to take her place by his side. Polly did so, and, some time afterward, at a fresh order, put a teaspoonful of brandy to his lips, which were still pale and even bluish.

The doctor returned, and brought his assistant. They put the patient to bed.

"His life is in no danger," said he. "I wish I was as sure about his reason."

At one o'clock in the morning, as Polly was snoring by the patient's bedside, a hand was laid on her shoulder. It was Rhoda.

"Go to bed, Polly: you are no use here."

"You'd be sleepy if you worked as hard as I do."

"Very likely," said Rhoda, with a gentleness that struck Polly as very singular. "Good-night."

Rhoda spent the night watching, and thinking harder than she had ever thought before.

Next morning, early, Polly came into the sick-room. There sat her sister watching the patient, out of sight.

"La, Rhoda! Have you sat there all night?"

"Yes. Don't speak so loud. Come here. You've set your heart on this lilac silk. I'll give it to you for your black merino."

"Not you, my lady; you are not so fond of mereeny, nor of me neither."

"I'm not a liar like you," said the other, becoming herself for a moment, "and what I say I'll do. You put out your merino for me in the dressing-room."

"All right," said Polly, joyfully.

"And bring me two buckets of water instead of one. I have never closed my eyes."

"Poor soul! and now you be going to sluice yourself all the same. Whatever you can see in cold water, to run after it so, I can't think. If I was to flood myself like you, it would soon float me to my long home."

"How do you know? ***You never gave it a trial.*** Come, no more chat. Give me my bath: and then you may wash yourself in a tea-cup if you like--only don't wash my spoons in the same water, for ***mercy's sake!"***

Thus affectionately stimulated in her duties, Polly brought cold water galore, and laid out her new merino dress. In this sober suit, with plain linen collar and cuffs, the Somerset dressed herself, and resumed her watching by the bedside. She kept more than ever out of sight, for the patient was now beginning to mutter incoherently, yet in a way that showed his clouded faculties were dwelling on the calamity which had befallen him.

About noon the bell was rung sharply, and, on Polly entering, Rhoda called her to the window and showed her two female figures plodding down the street. "Look," said she. "Those are the only women I envy. Sisters of Charity. Run you after them, and take a good look at those beastly ugly caps: then come and tell me how to make one."

"Here's a go!" said Polly; but executed the commission promptly.

It needed no fashionable milliner to turn a yard of linen into one of those ugly caps, which are beautiful banners of Christian charity and womanly tenderness to the sick and suffering. The monster cap was made in an hour, and Miss Somerset put it on, and a thick veil, and then she no longer thought it necessary to sit out of the patient's sight.

The consequence was that, in the middle of his ramblings, he broke off and looked at her. The sister puzzled him. At last he called to her in French.

She made no reply.

"Je suis a l'hopital, n'est ce pas bonne soeur?"

"I am English," said she, softly.

CHAPTER VI.

ENGLISH!" said Sir Charles. "Then tell me, how did I come here? Where am I?"

"You had a fit, and the doctor ordered you to be kept quiet; and I am here to nurse you."

"A fit! Ay, I remember. That vile woman!"

"Don't think of her: give your mind to getting well: remember, there is somebody who would break her heart if you--"

"Oh, my poor Bella! my sweet, timid, modest, loving Bella!" He was so weakened that he cried like a child.

Miss Somerset rose, and laid her forehead sadly upon the window-sill.

"Why do I cry for her, like a great baby?" muttered Sir Charles. "She wouldn't cry for me. She has cast me off in a moment."

"Not she. It is her father's doing. Have a little patience. The whole thing shall be explained to them; and then she will soon soften the old man. 'It is not as if you were really to blame."

"No more I was. It is all that vile woman."

"Oh, don't! She is so sorry; she has taken it all to heart. She had once shammed a fit, on the very place; and when you had a real fit there--on the very spot--oh, it was so fearful--and lay like one dead, she saw God's finger, and it touched her hard heart. Don't say anything more against her just now. She is trying so hard to be good. And, besides, it is all a mistake: she never told that old admiral; she never breathed a word out of her own house. Her own people have betrayed her and you. She has made me promise two things: to find out who told the admiral, and--"

"Well?"

"The second thing I have to do--Well, that is a secret between me and that unhappy woman. She is bad enough, but not so heartless as you think."

Sir Charles shook his head incredulously, but said no more; and soon after fell asleep.

In the evening he woke, and found the Sister watching.

She now turned her head away from him, and asked him quietly to describe Miss Bella Bruce to her.

He described her in minute and glowing terms. "But oh, Sister," said he, "it is not her beauty only, but the beauty of her mind. So gentle, so modest, so timid, so docile. She would never have had the heart to turn me off. But she will obey her father. She looked forward to obey me, sweet dove."

"Did she say so?"

"Yes, that is her dream of happiness, to obey."

The Sister still questioned him with averted head, and he told her what had passed between Bella and him the last time he saw her, and all their innocent plans of married happiness. He told her, with the tear in his eye, and she listened, with the tear in hers. "And then," said he, laying his hand on her shoulder, "is it not hard? I just went to Mayfair, not to please myself, but to do an act of justice--of more than justice; and then, for that, to have her door shut in my face. Only two hours between the height of happiness and the depth of misery."

The Sister said nothing, but she hid her face in her hands, and thought.

The next morning, by her order, Polly came into the room, and said, "You are to go home. The carriage is at the door." With this she retired, and Sir Charles's valet entered the room soon after to help him dress.

"Where am I, James?"

"Miss Somerset's house, Sir Charles."

"Then get me out of it directly."

"Yes, Sir Charles. The carriage is at the door."

"Who told you to come, James?"

"Miss Somerset, Sir Charles."

"That is odd."

"Yes, Sir Charles."

When he got home he found a sofa placed by a fire, with wraps and pillows; his cigar case laid out, and a bottle of salts, and also a small glass of old cognac, in case of faintness.

"Which of you had the gumption to do all this?"

"Miss Somerset, Sir Charles."

"What, has she been *here?*"

"Yes, Sir Charles."

"Curse her!"

"Yes, Sir Charles."

CHAPTER VII.
"LOVE LIES BLEEDING."

BELLA BRUCE was drinking the bitterest cup a young virgin soul can taste. Illusion gone--the wicked world revealed as it is, how unlike what she thought it was--love crushed in her, and not crushed out of her, as it might if she had been either proud or vain.

Frail men and women should see what a passionate but virtuous woman can suffer, when a revelation, of which they think but little, comes and blasts her young heart, and bids her dry up in a moment the deep well of her affection, since it flows for an unworthy object, and flows in vain. I tell you that the fair head severed from the chaste body is nothing to her compared with this. The fair body, pierced with heathen arrows, was nothing to her in the days of old compared with this.

In a word--for nowadays we can but amplify, and so enfeeble, what some old dead master of language, immortal though obscure, has said in words of granite-- here

"Love lay bleeding."

No fainting--no vehement weeping; but oh, such deep desolation; such weariness of life; such a pitiable restlessness. Appetite gone; the taste of food almost lost; sleep unwilling to come; and oh, the torture of waking--for at that horrible moment all rushed back at once, the joy that had been, the misery that was, the blank that was to come.

She never stirred out, except when ordered, and then went like an automaton. Pale, sorrow-stricken, and patient, she moved about, the ghost of herself; and lay down a little, and then tried to work a little, and then to read a little; and could settle to nothing but sorrow and deep despondency.

Not that she nursed her grief. She had been told to be brave, and she tried. But her grief was her master. It came welling through her eyes in a moment, of its own accord.

She was deeply mortified too. But, in her gentle nature, anger could play but a secondary part. Her indignation was weak beside her grief, and did little to bear her up.

Yet her sense of shame was vivid; and she tried hard not to let her father see how deeply she loved the man who had gone from her to Miss Somerset. Besides, he had ordered her to fight against a love that now could only degrade her; he had ordered, and it was for her to obey.

As soon as Sir Charles was better, he wrote her a long, humble letter, owning that, before he knew her, he had led a free life; but assuring her that, ever since that happy time, his heart and his time had been solely hers; as to his visit to Miss Somerset, it had been one of business merely, and this he could prove, if she would receive him. The admiral could be present at that interview, and Sir Charles hoped to convince him he had been somewhat hasty and harsh in his decision.

Now the admiral had foreseen Sir Charles would write to her; so he had ordered his man to bring all letters to him first.

He recognized Sir Charles's hand, and brought the latter in to Bella. "Now, my child," said he, "be brave. Here is a letter from that man."

"Oh, papa! I thought he would. I knew he would." And the pale face was flushed with joy and hope all in a moment.

"Do what?"

"Write and explain."

"Explain? A thing that is clear as sunshine. He has written to throw dust in your eyes again. You are evidently in no state to judge. *I* shall read this letter first."

"Yes, papa," said Bella, faintly.

He did read it, and she devoured his countenance all the time.

"There is nothing in it. He offers no real explanation, but only says he can explain, and asks for an interview--to play upon your weakness. If I give you this letter, it will only make you cry, and render your task more difficult. I must be strong for your good, and set you an example. I loved this young man too; but, now I know him"--then he actually thrust the letter into the fire.

But this was too much. Bella shrieked at the act, and put her hand to her heart, and shrieked again. "Ah! you'll kill us, you'll kill us both!" she cried. "Poor Charles! Poor Bella! You don't love your child--you have no pity." And, for the first time, her misery was violent. She writhed and wept, and at last went into violent hysterics, and frightened that stout old warrior more than cannon had ever frightened him; and presently she became quiet, and wept at his knees, and begged his forgiveness, and said he was wiser than she was, and she would obey him in everything, only he must not be angry with her if she could not live.

Then the stout admiral mingled his tears with hers, and began to realize what deep waters of affliction his girl was wading in.

Yet he saw no way out but firmness. He wrote to Sir Charles to say that his daughter was too ill to write; but that no explanation was possible, and no interview could be allowed.

Sir Charles, who, after writing, had conceived the most sanguine hopes, was now as wretched as Bella. Only, now that he was refused a hearing, he had wounded pride to support him a little under wounded love.

Admiral Bruce, fearing for his daughter's health, and even for her life--she pined so visibly--now ordered her to divide her day into several occupations, and exact divisions of time--an hour for this, an hour for that; an hour by the clock--and here he showed practical wisdom. Try it, ye that are very unhappy, and tell me the result.

As a part of this excellent system, she had to walk round the square from eleven to twelve A. M., but never alone; he was not going to have Sir Charles surprising her into an interview. He always went with her, and, as he was too stiff to walk briskly, he sat down, and she had to walk in sight. He took a stout stick with him--for Sir Charles. But Sir Charles was proud, and stayed at home with his deep wound.

One day, walking round the square with a step of Mercury and heart of lead, Bella Bruce met a Sister of Charity pacing slow and thoughtful; their eyes met and drank, in a moment, every feature of each other.

The Sister, apparently, had seen the settled grief on that fair face; for the next time they met, she eyed her with a certain sympathy, which did not escape Bella.

This subtle interchange took place several times and Bella could not help feeling a little grateful. "Ah!" she thought to herself, "how kind religious people are! I should like to speak to her." And the next time they met she looked wistfully in the Sister's face.

She did not meet her again, for she went and rested on a bench, in sight of her father, but at some distance from him. Unconsciously to herself, his refusal even to hear Sir Charles repelled her. That was so hard on him and her. It looked like throwing away the last chance, the last little chance of happiness.

By-and-by the Sister came and sat on the same bench.

Bella was hardly surprised, but blushed high, for she felt that her own eyes had invited the sympathy of a stranger; and now it seemed to be coming. The timid girl felt uneasy. The Sister saw that, and approached her with tact. "You look unwell," said she, gently, but with no appearance of extravagant interest or curiosity.

"I am--a little," said Bella, very reservedly.

"Excuse my remarking it. We are professional nurses, and apt to be a little officious, I fear."

No reply.

"I saw you were unwell. But I hope it is not serious. I can generally tell when the sick are in danger." A peculiar look. "I am glad not to see it in so young and-- good a face."

"You are young, too; very young, and--" she was going to say "beautiful," but she was too shy--"to be a Sister of Charity. But I am sure you never regret leaving such a world as this is."

"Never. I have lost the only thing I ever valued in it."

"I have no right to ask you what that was."

"You shall know without asking. One I loved proved unworthy."

The Sister sighed deeply, and then, hiding her face with her hands for a moment, rose abruptly, and left the square, ashamed, apparently, of having been betrayed into such a confession.

Bella, when she was twenty yards off, put out a timid hand, as if to detain her; but she had not the courage to say anything of the kind.

She never told her father a word. She had got somebody now who could sympathize with her better than he could.

Next day the Sister was there, and Bella bowed to her when she met her. This time it was the Sister who went and sat on the bench.

Bella continued her walk for some time, but at last could not resist the temptation. She came and sat down on the bench, and blushed; as much as to say, "I have the courage to come, but not to speak upon a certain subject, which shall be nameless."

The Sister, as may be imagined, was not so shy. She opened a conversation. "I committed a fault yesterday. I spoke to you of myself, and of the past: it is discouraged by our rules. We are bound to inquire the griefs of others; not to tell our own."

This was a fair opening, but Bella was too delicate to show her wounds to a fresh acquaintance.

The Sister, having failed at that, tried something very different.

"But I could tell you a pitiful case about another. Some time ago I nursed a gentleman whom love had laid on a sick-bed."

"A gentleman! What! can they love as we do?" said Bella, bitterly.

"Not many of them; but this was an exception. But I don't know whether I ought to tell these secrets to so young a lady."

"Oh, yes--please--what else is there in this world worth talking about? Tell me about the poor man who could love as we can."

The Sister seemed to hesitate, but at last decided to go on.

"Well, he was a man of the world, and he had not always been a good man; but he was trying to be. He had fallen in love with a young lady, and seen the beauty of virtue, and was going to marry her and lead a good life. But he was a man of honor, and there was a lady for whom he thought it was his duty to provide. He set his lawyer to draw a deed, and his lawyer appointed a day for signing it at her house. The poor man came because his lawyer told him. Do you think there was any great harm in that?"

"No; of course not."

"Well, then, he lost his love for that."

Miss Bruce's color began to come and go, and her supple figure to crouch a little. She said nothing.

The Sister continued: "Some malicious person went and told the young lady's father the gentleman was in the habit of visiting that lady, and would be with her at a certain hour. And so he was; but it was the lawyer's appointment, you know. You seem agitated."

"No, no; not agitated," said Bella, "but astonished; it is so like a story I know. A young lady, a friend of mine, had an anonymous letter, telling her that one she loved and esteemed was unworthy. But what you have told me shows me how deceitful appearances may be. What was your patient's name?"

"It is against our rules to tell that. But you said an 'anonymous letter.' Was your friend so weak as to believe an anonymous letter? The writer of such a letter is a coward, and a coward always is a liar. Show me your friend's anonymous letter. I may, perhaps, be able to throw a light on it."

The conversation was interrupted by Admiral Bruce, who had approached them unobserved. "Excuse me," said he, "but you ladies seem to have hit upon a very interesting theme."

"Yes, papa," said Bella. "I took the liberty to question this lady as to her experiences of sick-beds, and she was good enough to give me some of them."

Having uttered this with a sudden appearance of calmness that first amazed the Sister, then made her smile, she took her father's arm, bowed politely, and a little stiffly, to her new friend, and drew the admiral away.

"Oh!" thought the Sister. "I am not to speak to the old gentleman. He is not in her confidence. Yet she is very fond of him. How she hangs on his arm! Simplicity! Candor! We are all tarred with the same stick--we women."

That night Bella was a changed girl--exalted and depressed by turns, and with no visible reason.

Her father was pleased. Anything better than that deadly languor.

The next day Bella sat by her father's side in the square, longing to go to the Sister, yet patiently waiting to be ordered.

At last the admiral, finding her dull and listless, said, "Why don't you go and talk to the Sister? She amuses you. I'll join you when I have smoked this cigar."

The obedient Bella rose, and went toward the Sister as if compelled. But when she got to her her whole manner changed. She took her warmly by the hand, and said, trembling and blushing, and all on fire, "I have brought you the anonymous letter."

The elder actress took it and ran her eye over it--an eye that now sparkled like a diamond. "Humph!" said she, and flung off all the dulcet tones of her assumed character with mighty little ceremony. "This hand is disguised a little, but I think I know it. I am sure I do! The dirty little rascal!"

"Madam!" cried Bella, aghast with surprise at this language.

"I tell you I know the writer and his rascally motive. You must lend me this for a day or two."

"Must I?" said Bella. "Excuse me! Papa would be so angry."

"Very likely; but you will lend it to me for all that; for with this I can clear Miss Bruce's lover and defeat his enemies."

Bella uttered a faint cry, and trembled, and her bosom heaved violently. She looked this way and that, like a frightened deer. "But papa? His eye is on us."

"Never deceive your father!" said the Sister, almost sternly; "but," darting her gray eyes right into those dove-like orbs, "give me five minutes' start--IF YOU REALLY LOVE SIR CHARLES BASSETT."

With these words she carried off the letter; and Bella ran, blushing, panting, trembling, to her father, and clung to him.

He questioned her, but could get nothing from her very intelligible until the Sister was out of sight, and then she told him all without reserve.

"I was unworthy of him to doubt him. An anonymous slander. I'll never trust appearances again. Poor Charles! Oh, my darling! what he must have suffered if he loves like me." Then came a shower of happy tears; then a shower of happy kisses.

The admiral groaned, but for a long time he could not get a word in. When he did it was chilling. "My poor girl," said he, "this unhappy love blinds you. What, don't you see the woman is no nun, but some sly hussy that man has sent to throw dust in your eyes?"

Nothing she could say prevailed to turn him from this view, and he acted upon it with resolution: he confined her excursions to a little garden at the back of the house, and forbade her, on any pretense, to cross the threshold.

Miss Somerset came to the square in another disguise, armed with important information. But no Bella Bruce appeared to meet her.

All this time Richard Bassett was happy as a prince.

So besotted was he with egotism, and so blinded by imaginary wrongs, that he rejoiced in the lovers' separation, rejoiced in his cousin's attack.

Polly, who now regarded him almost as a lover, told him all about it; and already in anticipation he saw himself and his line once more lords of the two manors--Bassett and Huntercombe--on the demise of Sir Charles Bassett, Bart., deceased without issue.

And, in fact, Sir Charles was utterly defeated. He lay torpid.

But there was a tough opponent in the way--all the more dangerous that she was not feared.

One fine day Miss Somerset electrified her groom by ordering her pony carriage to the door at ten A. M.

She took the reins on the pavement, like a man, jumped in light as a feather, and away rattled the carriage into the City. The ponies were all alive, the driver's eye keen as a bird's; her courage and her judgment equal. She wound in and out among the huge vehicles with perfect composure; and on those occasions when, the traffic being interrupted, the oratorical powers were useful to fill up the time, she shone with singular brilliance. The West End is too often in debt to the City, but, in the matter of chaff, it was not so this day; for whenever she took a peck she returned a bushel; and so she rattled to the door of Solomon Oldfield, solicitor, Old Jewry.

She penetrated into the inner office of that worthy, and told him he must come with her that minute to Portman Square.

"Impossible, madam!" And, as they say in the law reports, gave his reasons.

"Certain, sir!" And gave no reasons.

He still resisted.

Thereupon she told him she should sit there all day and chaff his clients one after another, and that his connection with the Bassett and Huntercombe estates should end.

Then he saw he had to do with a termagant, and consented, with a sigh.

She drove him westward, wincing every now and then at her close driving, and told him all, and showed him what she was pleased to call her little game. He told her it was too romantic. Said he, "You ladies read nothing but novels; but the real world is quite different from the world of novels." Having delivered this remonstrance--which was tolerably just, for she never read anything but novels and sermons--he submitted like a lamb, and received her instructions.

She drove as fast as she talked, so that by this time they were at Admiral Bruce's door.

Now Mr. Oldfield took the lead, as per instructions. "Mr. Oldfield, solicitor, and a lady--on business."

The porter delivered this to the footman with the accuracy which all who send verbal messages deserve and may count on. "Mr. Oldfield and lady."

The footman, who represented the next step in oral tradition, without which form of history the Heathen world would never have known that Hannibal softened the rocks with vinegar, nor the Christian world that eleven thousand virgins dwelt in a German town the size of Putney, announced the pair as "Mr. and Mrs. Hautville."

"I don't know them, I think. Well, I will see them."

They entered, and the admiral stared a little, and wondered how this couple came together--the keen but plain old man, with clothes hanging on him, and the dashing beauty, with her dress in the height of the fashion, and her gauntleted hands. However, he bowed ceremoniously, and begged his visitors to be seated.

Now the folding-doors were ajar, and the *soi-disant* Mrs. Oldfield peeped. She saw Bella Bruce at some distance, seated by the fire, in a reverie.

Judge that young lady's astonishment when she looked up and observed a large white, well-shaped hand, sparkling with diamonds and rubies, beckoning her furtively.

The owner of that sparkling hand soon heard a soft rustle of silk come toward the door; the very rustle, somehow, was eloquent, and betrayed love and timidity, and something innocent yet subtle. The jeweled hand went in again directly.

CHAPTER VIII.

MEANTIME Mr. Oldfield began to tell the admiral who he was, and that he was come to remove a false impression about a client of his, Sir Charles Bassett.

"That, sir," said the admiral, sternly, "is a name we never mention here."

He rose and went to the folding-doors, and deliberately closed them.

The Somerset, thus defeated, bit her lip, and sat all of a heap, like a cat about to spring, looking sulky and vicious.

Mr. Oldfield persisted, and, as he took the admiral's hint and lowered his voice, he was interrupted no more, but made a simple statement of those facts which are known to the reader.

Admiral Bruce heard them, and admitted that the case was not quite so bad as he had thought.

Then Mr. Oldfield proposed that Sir Charles should be re-admitted.

"No," said the old admiral, firmly; "turn it how you will, it is too ugly; the bloom of the thing is gone. Why should my daughter take that woman's leavings? Why should I give her pure heart to a man about town?"

"Because you will break it else," said Miss Somerset, with affected politeness.

"Give her credit for more dignity, madam, if you please," replied Admiral Bruce, with equal politeness.

"Oh, bother dignity!" cried the Somerset.

At this free phrase from so well-dressed a lady Admiral Bruce opened his eyes, and inquired of Oldfield, rather satirically, who was this lady that did him the honor to interfere in his family affairs.

Oldfield looked confused; but Somerset, full of mother-wit, was not to be caught napping. "I'm a by-stander; and they always see clearer than the folk them-selves. You are a man of honor, sir, and you are very clever at sea, no doubt, and a fighter, and all that; but you are no match for land-sharks. You are being made a dupe and a tool of. Who do you think wrote that anonymous letter to your daughter? A friend of truth? a friend of injured innocence? Nothing of the sort. One Richard Bassett--Sir Charles's cousin. Here, Mr. Oldfield, please compare these two handwritings closely, and you will see I am right." She put down the anonymous letter and Richard Bassett's letter to herself; but she could not wait for Mr. Oldfield to compare the documents, now her tongue was set going. "Yes, gentlemen, this is new to you; but you'll find that little scheming rascal wrote them both, and with as base a motive and as black a heart as any other anonymous coward's. His game is to make Sir Charles Bassett die childless, and so then this dirty fellow would inherit the estate; and owing to you being so green, and swallowing an anonymous letter like pure water from the spring, he very nearly got his way. Sir Charles has been at death's door along of all this."

"Hush, madam! not so loud, please," whispered Admiral Bruce, looking uneas-ily toward the folding, doors.

"Why not?" bawled the Somerset. "THE TRUTH MAY BE BLAMED, BUT IT CAN'T BE SHAMED. I tell you that your precious letter brought Sir Charles Bassett to the brink of the grave. Soon as ever he got it he came tearing in his cab to Miss Somerset's house, and accused her of telling the lie to keep him--and he might have known better, for the jade never did a sneaking thing in her life. But, any way, he thought it must be her doing, miscalled her like a dog, and raged at her dreadful, and at last--what with love and fury and despair--he had the terriblest fit you ever saw. He fell down as black as your hat, and his eyes rolled, and his teeth gnashed, and he foamed at the mouth, and took four to hold him; and presently as white as a ghost, and given up for dead. No pulse for hours; and when his life came back his reason was gone."

"Good Heavens, madam!"

"For a time it was. How he did rave! and 'Bella' the only name on his lips. And now he lies in his own house as weak as water. Come, old gentleman, don't you be too hard; you are not a child, like your daughter; take the world as it is. Do you think you will ever find a man of fortune who has not had a lady friend? Why, every single gentleman in London that can afford to keep a saddle-horse has an article of that sort in some corner or other; and if he parts with her as soon as his banns are cried, that is all you can expect. Do you think any mother in Belgravia would make a row about that? They are downier than you are; they would shrug their aristocratic shoulders, and decline to listen to the *past* lives of their sons-in-law--unless it was all in the newspapers, mind you."

"If Belgravian mothers have mercenary minds, that is no reason why I should, whose cheeks have bronzed in the service of a virtuous queen, and whose hairs have whitened in honor."

On receiving this broadside the Somerset altered her tone directly, and said, obsequiously: "That is true, sir, and I beg your pardon for comparing you to the trash. But brave men are pitiful, you know. Then show your pity here. Pity a gentleman that repented his faults as soon as your daughter showed him there was a better love within reach, and now lies stung by an anonymous viper, and almost dying of love and mortification; and pity your own girl, that will soon lose her health, and perhaps her life, if you don't give in."

"She is not so weak, madam. She is in better spirits already."

"Ay, but then she didn't know what he had suffered for *her.* She does now, for I heard her moan; and she will die for him now, or else she will give you twice as many kisses as usual some day, and cry a bucketful over you, and then run away with her lover. I know women better than you do; I am one of the precious lot."

The admiral replied only with a look of superlative scorn. This incensed the Somerset; and that daring woman, whose ear was nearer to the door, and had caught sounds that escaped the men, actually turned the handle, and while her eye flashed defiance, her vigorous foot spurned the folding-doors wide open in half a moment.

Bella Bruce lay with her head sidewise on the table, and her hands extended, moaning and sobbing piteously for poor Sir Charles.

"For shame, madam, to expose my child," cried the admiral, bursting with indignation and grief. He rushed to her and took her in his arms.

She scarcely noticed him, for the moment he turned her she caught sight of Miss Somerset, and recognized her face in a moment. "Ah! the Sister of Charity!" she cried, and stretched out her hands to her, with a look and a gesture so innocent, confiding, and imploring, that the Somerset, already much excited by her own eloquence, took a turn not uncommon with termagants, and began to cry herself.

But she soon stopped that, for she saw her time was come to go, and avoid unpleasant explanations. She made a dart and secured the two letters. "Settle it among yourselves," said she, wheeling round and bestowing this advice on the whole party; then shot a sharp arrow at the admiral as she fled: "If you must be a tool of Richard Bassett, don't be a tool and a dupe by halves. *He* is in love with her too. Marry her to the blackguard, and then you will be sure to kill Sir Charles." Having delivered this with such volubility that the words pattered out like a roll of musketry, she flounced out, with red cheeks and wet eyes, rushed down the stairs, and sprang into her carriage, whipped the ponies, and away at a pace that made the spectators stare.

Mr. Oldfield muttered some excuses, and retired more sedately.

All this set Bella Bruce trembling and weeping, and her father was some time before he could bring her to anything like composure. Her first words, when she could find breath, were, "He is innocent; he is unhappy. Oh, that I could fly to him!"

"Innocent! What proof?"

"That brave lady said so."

"Brave lady! A bold hussy. Most likely a friend of the woman Somerset, and a bird of the same feather. Sir Charles has done himself no good with me by sending such an emissary."

"No, papa; it was the lawyer brought her, and then her own good heart *made her burst out.* Ah! she is not like me: she has courage. What a noble thing courage is, especially in a woman!"

"Pray did you hear the language of this noble lady?"

"Every word nearly; and I shall never forget them. They were diamonds and pearls."

"Of the sort you can pick up at Billingsgate."

"Ah, papa, she pleaded for *him* as I cannot plead, and yet I love him. It was true eloquence. Oh, how she made me shudder! Only think: he had a fit, and lost his reason, and all for me. What shall I do? What shall I do?"

This brought on a fit of weeping.

Her father pitied her, and gave her a crumb of sympathy: said he was sorry for

Sir Charles.

"But," said he, recovering his resolution, "it cannot be helped. He must expiate his vices, like other men. Do, pray, pluck up a little spirit and sense. Now try and keep to the point. This woman came from him; and you say you heard her language, and admire it. Quote me some of it."

"She said he fell down as black as his hat, and his eyes rolled, and his poor teeth gnashed, and--oh, my darling! my darling! oh! oh! oh!"

"There--there--I mean about other things."

Bella complied, but with a running accompaniment of the sweetest little sobs.

"She said I must be very green, to swallow an anonymous letter like spring water. Oh! oh!"

"Green? There was a word!"

"Oh! oh! But it is the right word. You can't mend it. Try, and you will see you can't. Of course I was green. Oh! And she said every gentleman who can afford to keep a saddle-horse has a female friend, till his banns are called in church. Oh! oh!"

"A pretty statement to come to your ears!"

"But if it is the truth! 'THE TRUTH MAY BE BLAMED, BUT IT CAN'T BE SHAMED.' Ah! I'll not forget that: I'll pray every night I may remember those words of the brave lady. Oh!"

"Yes, take her for your oracle."

"I mean to. I always try to profit by my superiors. She has courage: I have none. I beat about the bush, and talk skim-milk; she uses the very word. She said we have been the dupe and the tool of a little scheming rascal, an anonymous coward, with motives as base as his heart is black--oh! oh! Ay, that is the way to speak of such a man; I can't do it myself, but I reverence the brave lady who can. And she wasn't afraid even of you, dear papa. 'Come, old gentleman'--ha! ha! ha!--'take the world as it is; Belgravian mothers would not break *both* their hearts for what is past and gone.' What hard good sense! a thing I always *did* admire: because I've got none. But her *heart* is not hard; after all her words of fire, that went so straight instead of beating the bush, she ended by crying for me. Oh! oh! oh! Bless her! Bless her! If ever there was a good woman in the world, that is one. She was not born a lady, I am afraid; but that is nothing: she was born a woman, and I mean to make her acquaintance, and take her for my example in all things. No, dear papa, women are not so pitiful to women without cause. She is almost a stranger, yet she cried for me. Can you be harder to me than she is? No; pity your poor girl, who will lose her health, and perhaps her life. Pity poor Charles, stung by an anonymous viper, and laid on a bed of sickness for me. Oh! oh! oh!"

"I do pity you, Bella. When you cry like this, my heart bleeds."

"I'll try not to cry, papa. Oh! oh!"

"But most of all, I pity your infatuation, your blindness. Poor, innocent dove, that looks at others by the light of her own goodness, and so sees all manner of virtues in a brazen hussy. Now answer me one plain question. You called her 'the Sister!' Is she not the same woman that played the Sister of Charity?"

Bella blushed to the temples, and said, hesitatingly, she was not quite sure.

"Come, Bella. I thought you were going to imitate the jade, and not beat about the bush. Yes or no?"

"The features are very like."

"Bella, you know it is the same woman. You recognized her in a moment. That speaks volumes. But she shall find I am not to be made 'a dupe and a tool of' quite so easily as she thinks. I'll tell you what--this is some professional actress Sir Charles has hired to waylay you. Little simpleton!"

He said no more at that time; but after dinner he ruminated, and took a very serious, indeed almost a maritime, view of the crisis. "I'm overmatched now," thought he. "They will cut my sloop out under the very guns of the flagship if we stay much longer in this port--a lawyer against me, and a woman too; there's nothing to be done but heave anchor, hoist sail, and run for it."

He sent off a foreign telegram, and then went upstairs. "Bella, my dear," said he, "pack up your clothes for a journey. We start to-morrow."

"A journey, papa! A long one?"

"No. We shan't double the Horn this time."

"Brighton? Paris?"

"Oh, farther than that."

"The grave: that is the journey I should like to take."

"So you shall, some day; but just now it is a ***foreign*** port you are bound for. Go and pack."

"I obey." And she was creeping off, but he called her back and kissed her, and said, "Now I'll tell you where you are going; but you must promise me solemnly not to write one line to Sir Charles."

She promised, but cried as soon as she had promised; whereat the admiral inferred he had done wisely to exact the promise.

"Well, my dear," said he, "we are going to Baden. Your aunt Molineux is there. She is a woman of great delicacy and prudence, and has daughters of her own all well married, thanks to her motherly care. She will bring you to your senses better than I can."

Next evening they left England by the mail; and the day after Richard Bassett learned this through his servant, and went home triumphant, and, indeed, wondering at his success. He ascribed it, however, to the Nemesis which dogs the heels of those who inherit the estate of another.

Such was the only moral reflection he made, though the business in general, and particularly his share in it, admitted of several.

Miss Somerset also heard of it, and told Mr. Oldfield; he told Sir Charles Bassett.

That gentleman sighed deeply, and said nothing. He had lost all hope.

The whole matter appeared stagnant for about ten days; and then a delicate hand stirred the dead waters cautiously. Mr. Oldfield, of all people in the world, received a short letter from Bella Bruce.

"Konigsberg Hotel, BADEN.

"Miss Bruce presents her compliments to Mr. Oldfield, and will feel much obliged if he will send her the name and address of that brave lady who accompanied him to her father's house.

"Miss Bruce desires to thank that lady, personally, for her noble defense of one with whom it would be improper for her to communicate; but she can never be indifferent to his welfare, nor hear of his sufferings without deep sorrow."

"Confound it!" said Solomon Oldfield. "What am I to do? I mustn't tell her it is Miss Somerset." So the wary lawyer had a copy of the letter made, and sent to Miss Somerset for instructions.

Miss Somerset sent for Mr. Marsh, who was now more at her beck and call than ever, and told him she had a ticklish letter to write. "I can talk with the best," said she, "but the moment I sit down and take up a pen something cold runs up my shoulder, and then down my backbone, and I'm palsied; now you are always writing, and can't say 'Bo' to a goose in company. Let us mix ourselves; I'll walk about and speak my mind, and then you put down the cream, and send it."

From this ingenious process resulted the following composition:

"She whom Miss Bruce is good enough to call 'the brave lady' happened to know the truth, and that tempted her to try and baffle an anonymous slanderer, who was ruining the happiness of a lady and gentleman. Being a person of warm impulses, she went great lengths; but she now wishes to retire into the shade. She is flattered by Miss Bruce's desire to know her, and some day, perhaps, may remind her of it; but at present she must deny herself that honor. If her reasons were known, Miss Bruce would not be offended nor hurt; she would entirely approve them."

Soon after this, as Sir Charles Bassett sat by the fire, disconsolate, his servant told him a lady wanted to see him.

"Who is it?"

"Don't know, Sir Charles; but it is a kind of a sort of a nun, Sir Charles."

"Oh, a Sister of Charity! Perhaps the one that nursed me. Admit her, by all means."

The Sister came in. She had a large veil on. Sir Charles received her with profound respect, and thanked her, with some little hesitation, for her kind attention to him. She stopped him by saying that was merely her duty. "But," said she, softly, "words fell from you, on the bed of sickness, that touched my heart; and besides I happen to know the lady."

"You know my Bella!" cried Sir Charles. "Ah, then no wonder you speak so kindly; you can feel what I have lost. She has left England to avoid me."

"All the better. Where she is the door cannot be closed in your face. She is at Baden. Follow her there. She has heard the truth from Mr. Oldfield, and she knows who wrote the anonymous letter."

"And who did?"

"Mr. Richard Bassett."

This amazed Sir Charles.

"The scoundrel!" said he, after a long silence.

"Well, then, why let that fellow defeat you, for his own ends? I would go at once to Baden. Your leaving England would be one more proof to her that she has no rival. Stick to her like a man, sir, and you will win her, I tell you."

These words from a nun amazed and fired him. He rose from his chair, flushed with sudden hope and ardor. "I'll leave for Baden to-morrow morning."

The Sister rose to retire.

"No, no," cried Sir Charles. "I have not thanked you. I ought to go down on my knees and bless you for all this. To whom am I so indebted?"

"No matter, sir."

"But it does matter. You nursed me, and perhaps saved my life, and now you give me back the hopes that make life sweet. You will not trust me with your name?"

"We have no name."

"Your voice at times sounds very like--no, I will not affront you by such a comparison."

"I'm her sister," said she, like lightning.

This announcement quite staggered Sir Charles, and he was silent and uncomfortable. It gave him a chill.

The Sister watched him keenly, but said nothing.

Sir Charles did not know what to say, so he asked to see her face. "It must be as beautiful as your heart."

The Sister shook her head. "My face has been disfigured by a frightful disorder."

Sir Charles uttered an ejaculation of regret and pity.

"I could not bear to show it to one who esteems me as you seem to do. But perhaps it will not always be so."

"I hope not. You are young, and Heaven is good. Can I do nothing for you, who have done so much for me?"

"Nothing--unless--" said she, feigning vast timidity, "you could spare me that ring of yours, as a remembrance of the part I have played in this affair."

Sir Charles colored. It was a ruby of the purest water, and had been two centuries in his family. He colored, but was too fine a gentleman to hesitate. He said, "By all means. But it is a poor thing to offer *you.*"

"I shall value it very much."

"Say no more. I am fortunate in having anything you deign to accept."

And so the ring changed hands.

The Sister now put it on her middle finger, and held up her hand, and her bright eyes glanced at it, through her veil, with that delight which her sex in general feel at the possession of a new bauble. She recovered herself, however, and told him, soberly, the ring should return to his family at her death, if not before.

"I will give you a piece of advice for it," said she. "Miss Bruce has foxy hair; and she is very timid. Don't you take her advice about commanding her. She would like to be your slave! Don't let her. Coax her to speak her mind. Make a friend of her. Don't you put her to this--that she must displease you, or else deceive you. She might choose wrong, especially with that colored hair."

"It is not in her nature to deceive."

"It is not in her nature to displease. Excuse me; I am too fanciful, and look at women too close. But I know your happiness depends on her. All your eggs are in that one basket. Well, I have told you how to carry the basket. Good-by."

Sir Charles saw her out, and bowed respectfully to her in the hall, while his servant opened the street door. He did her this homage as his benefactress.

When admiral and Miss Bruce reached Baden Mrs. Molineux was away on a visit; and this disappointed Admiral Bruce, who had counted on her assistance to manage and comfort Bella. Bella needed the latter very much. A glance at her pale, pensive, lovely face was enough to show that sorrow was rooted at her heart. She was subjected to no restraint, but kept the house of her own accord, thinking, as persons of her age are apt to do, that her whole history must be written in her face. Still, of course, she did go out sometimes; and one cold but bright afternoon she was strolling languidly on the parade, when all in a moment she met Sir Charles Bassett face to face.

She gave an eloquent scream, and turned pale a moment, and then the hot blood came rushing, and then it retired, and she stood at bay, with heaving bosom--and great eyes.

Sir Charles held out both hands pathetically. "Don't you be afraid of me."

When she found he was so afraid of offending her she became more courageous. "How dare you come here?" said she, but with more curiosity than violence, for it had been her dream of hope he would come.

"How could I keep away, when I heard you were here?"

"You must not speak to me, sir; I am forbidden."

"Pray do not condemn me unheard."

"If I listen to you I shall believe you. I won't hear a word. Gentlemen can do things that ladies cannot even speak about. Talk to my aunt Molineux; our fate depends on her. This will teach you not to be so wicked. What business have gentlemen to be so wicked? Ladies are not. No, it is no use; I will not hear a syllable. I am ashamed to be seen speaking to you. You are a bad character. Oh, Charles, is it true you had a fit?"

"Yes."

"And have you been very ill? You look ill."

"I am better now, dearest."

"Dearest! Don't call me names. How dare you keep speaking to me when I request you not?"

"But I can't excuse myself, and obtain my pardon, and recover your love, unless I am allowed to speak."

"Oh, you can speak to my aunt Molineux, and she will read you a fine lesson."

"Where is she?"

"Nobody knows. But there is her house, the one with the iron gate. Get her ear first, if you really love me; and don't you ever waylay me again. If you do, I shall say something rude to you, sir. Oh, I'm so happy!"

Having let this out, she hid her face with her hands, and fled like the very wind.

At dinner-time she was in high spirits.

The admiral congratulated her.

"Brava, Bell! Youth and health and a foreign air will soon cure you of that folly."

Bella blushed deeply, and said nothing. The truth struggled within her, too, but she shrank from giving pain, and receiving expostulation.

She kept the house, though, for two days, partly out of modesty, partly out of an honest and pious desire to obey her father as much as she could.

The third day Mrs. Molineux arrived, and sent over to the admiral.

He invited Bella to come with him. She consented eagerly, but was so long in dressing that he threatened to go without her. She implored him not to do that; and after a monstrous delay, the motive of which the reader may perhaps divine, father and daughter called on Mrs. Molineux. She received them very affectionately. But when the admiral, with some hesitation, began to enter on the great subject, she said, quietly, "Bella, my dear, go for a walk, and come back to me in half an hour."

"Aunt Molineux!" said Bella, extending both her hands imploringly to that lady.

Mrs. Molineux was proof against this blandishment, and Bella had to go.

When she was gone, this lady, who both as wife and mother was literally a model, rather astonished her brother the admiral. She said: "I am sorry to tell you that you have conducted this matter with perfect impropriety, both you and Bella. She had no business to show you that anonymous letter; and when she did show it you, you should have taken it from her, and told her not to believe a word of it."

"And married my daughter to a libertine! Why, Charlotte, I am ashamed of you."

Mrs. Molineux colored high; but she kept her temper, and ignored the interruption. "Then, if you decided to go into so indelicate a question at all (and really you were not bound to do so on anonymous information), why, then, you should have sent for Sir Charles, and given him the letter, and put him on his honor to tell you the truth. He would have told you the fact, instead of a garbled version; and the fact is that before he knew Bella he had a connection, which he prepared to dissolve, on terms very honorable to himself, as soon as he engaged himself to your daughter. What is there in that? Why, it is common, universal, among men of fashion. I am so vexed it ever came to Bella's knowledge: really it is dreadful to me, as a mother, that such a thing should have been discussed before that child. Complete innocence means complete ignorance; and that is how all my girls went to their husbands. However, what we must do now is to tell her Sir Charles has satisfied me he was not to blame; and after that the subject must never be recurred to. Sir Charles has promised me never to mention it, and no more shall Bella. And now, my dear John, let me congratulate you. Your daughter has a high-minded lover, who adores her, with a fine estate: he has been crying to me, poor fellow, as men will to a woman of my age; and if you have any respect for my judgment--ask him to dinner."

She added that it might be as well if, after dinner, he were to take a little nap.

Admiral Bruce did not fall into these views without discussion. I spare the reader the dialogue, since he yielded at last; only he stipulated that his sister should do the dinner, and the subsequent siesta.

Bella returned looking very wistful and anxious.

"Come here, niece," said Mrs. Molineux. "Kneel you at my knee. Now look--me in the face. Sir Charles has loved you, and you only, from the day he first saw you. He loves you now as much as ever. Do you love him?"

"Oh, aunt! aunt!" A shower of kisses, and a tear or two.

"That is enough. Then dry your eyes, and dress your beautiful hair a little better than *that;* for he dines with me to-day!"

Who so bright and happy now as Bella Bruce?

The dreaded aunt did not stop there. She held that after the peep into real life Bella Bruce had obtained, for want of a mother's vigilance, she ought to be a wife as soon as possible. So she gave Sir Charles a hint that Baden was a very good place to be married in; and from that moment Sir Charles gave Bella and her father no rest till they consented.

Little did Richard Bassett, in England, dream what was going on at Baden. He now surveyed the chimneys of Huntercombe Hall with resignation, and even with growing complacency, as chimneys that would one day be his, since their owner would not be in a hurry to love again. He shot Sir Charles's pheasants whenever they strayed into his hedgerows, and he lived moderately and studied health. In a word, content with the result of his anonymous letter, he confined himself now to cannily out-living the wrongful heir--his cousin.

One fine frosty day the chimneys of Huntercombe began to show signs of life; vertical columns of blue smoke rose in the air, one after another, till at last there were about forty going.

Old servants flowed down from London. New ones trickled in, with their boxes, from the country. Carriages were drawn out into the stable-yard, horses exercised, and a whisper ran that Sir Charles was coming to live on his estates, and not alone.

Richard Bassett went about inquiring cautiously.

The rumor spread and was confirmed by some little facts.

At last, one fine day, when the chimneys were all smoking, the church-bells began to peal.

Richard Bassett heard, and went out, scowling deeply. He found the village all agog with expectation.

Presently there was a loud cheer from the steeple, and a flag floated from the top of Huntercombe House. Murmurs. Distant cheers. Approaching cheers. The clatter of horses' feet. The roll of wheels. Huntercombe gates flung wide open by a cluster of grooms and keepers.

Then on came two outriders, ushered by loud hurrahs, and followed by a carriage and four that dashed through the village amid peals of delight from the villagers. The carriage was open, and in it sat Sir Charles and Bella Bassett. She was lovelier than ever; she dazzled the very air with her beauty and her glorious hair. The hurrahs of the villagers made her heart beat; she pressed Sir Charles's hand tenderly, and literally shone with joy and pride; and so she swept past Richard Bassett; she saw him directly, shuddered a moment, and half clung to her husband; then on again, and passed through the open gates amid loud cheers. She alighted in her own hall, and walked, nodding and smiling sunnily, through two files of domestics and retainers; and thought no more of Richard Bassett than some bright bird that has flown over a rattlesnake and glanced down at him.

But a gorgeous bird cannot always be flying. A snake can sometimes creep under her perch, and glare, and keep hissing, till she shudders and droops and lays her plumage in the dust.

CHAPTER IX.

GENERALLY deliberate crimes are followed by some great punishment; but they are also often attended in their course by briefer chastisements--single strokes from the whip that holds the round dozen in reserve. These precursors of the grand expiation are sharp but kindly lashes, for they tend to whip the man out of the wrong road.

Such a stroke fell on Richard Bassett: he saw Bella Bruce sweep past him, clinging to her husband, and shuddering at himself. For this, then, he had plotted and intrigued and written an anonymous letter. The only woman he had ever loved at all went past him with a look of aversion, and was his enemy's wife, and would soon be the mother of that enemy's children, and blot him forever out of the coveted inheritance.

The man crept home, and sat by his little fireside, crushed. Indeed, from that hour he disappeared, and drank his bitter cup alone.

After a while it transpired in the village that he was very ill. The clergyman went to visit him, but was not admitted. The only person who got to see him was his friend Wheeler, a small but sharp attorney, by whose advice he acted in country matters. This Wheeler was very fond of shooting, and could not get a crack at a pheasant except on Highmore; and that was a bond between him and its proprietor. It was Wheeler who had first told Bassett not to despair of possessing the estates, since they had inserted Sir Charles's heir at law in the entail.

This Wheeler found him now so shrunk in body, so pale and haggard in face, and dejected in mind, that he was really shocked, and asked leave to send a doctor from a neighboring town.

"What to do?" said Richard, moodily. "It's my mind; it's not my body. Ah, Wheeler, it is all over. I and mine shall never have Huntercombe now."

"I'll tell you what it is," said Wheeler, almost angrily, "you will have six feet by two of it before long if you go on this way. Was ever such folly! to fret yourself out of this jolly world because you can't get one particular slice of its upper crust. Why, one bit of land is as good as another; and I'll show you how to get land--in this neighborhood, too. Ay, right under Sir Charles's nose."

"Show me that," said Bassett, gloomily and incredulously.

"Leave off moping, then, and I will. I advise the bank, you know, and 'Splatchett's' farm is mortgaged up to the eyes. It is not the only one. I go to the village inns, and pick up all the gossip I hear there."

"How am I to find money to buy land?"

"I'll put you up to that, too; but you must leave off moping. Hang it, man, never say die. There are plenty of chances on the cards. Get your color back, and marry a girl with money, and turn that into land. The first thing is to leave off grizzling. Why, you are playing the enemy's game. That can't be right, can it?"

This remark was the first that really roused the sick man.

Wheeler had too few clients to lose one. He now visited Bassett almost daily, and, being himself full of schemes and inventions, he got Bassett, by degrees, out of his lethargy, and he emerged into daylight again; but he looked thin, and yellow as a guinea, and he had turned miser. He kept but one servant, and fed her and himself at Sir Charles Bassett's expense. He wired that gentleman's hares and rabbits in his own hedges. He went out with his gun every sunny afternoon, and shot a brace or two of pheasants, without disturbing the rest; for he took no dog with him to run and yelp, but a little boy, who quietly tapped the hedgerows and walked the sunny banks and shaws. They never came home empty-handed.

But on those rarer occasions when Sir Charles and his friends beat the Bassett woods Richard was sure to make a large bag; for he was a cool, unerring shot, and flushed the birds in hedgerows, slips of underwood, etc., to which the fairer sportsmen had driven them.

These birds and the surplus hares he always sold in the market-town, and put the money into a box. The rabbits he ate, and also squirrels, and, above all, young hedgehogs: a gypsy taught him how to cook them, viz., by inclosing them in clay, and baking them in wood embers; then the bristles adhere to the burned clay, and the meat is juicy. He was his own gardener, and vegetables cost him next to nothing.

So he went on through all the winter months, and by the spring his health and strength were restored. Then he turned woodman, cut down every stick of timber in a little wood near his house, and sold it; and then set to work to grub up the roots for fires, and cleared it for tillage. The sum he received for the wood was much more than he expected, and this he made a note of.

He had a strong body, that could work hard all day, a big hate, and a mania for the possession of land. And so he led a truly Spartan life, and everybody in the village said he was mad.

While he led this hard life Sir Charles and Lady Bassett were the gayest of the gay. She was the beauty and the bride. Visits and invitations poured in from every part of the country. Sir Charles, flattered by the homage paid to his beloved, made himself younger and less fastidious to indulge her; and the happy pair often drove twelve miles to dinner, and twenty to dine and sleep--an excellent custom in that country, one of whose favorite toasts is worth recording: "MAY YOU DINE WHERE YOU PLEASE, AND SLEEP WHERE YOU DINE."

They were at every ball, and gave one or two themselves.

Above all, they enjoyed society in that delightful form which is confined to large houses. They would have numerous and well-assorted visitors staying at the house for a week or so, and all dining at a huge round table. But two o'clock P.M. was the time to see how hosts and guests enjoyed themselves. The hall door of Huntercombe was approached by a flight of stone steps, easy of ascent, and about twenty-four feet wide. At the riding hour the county ladies used to come, one after another, holding up their riding-habits with one hand, and perch about this gigantic flight of steps like peacocks, and chatter like jays, while the servants walked their horses about the gravel esplanade, and the four-in-hand waited a little in the rear. A fine champing of bits and fidgeting of thoroughbreds there was, till all were ready; then the ladies would each put out her little foot, with charming nonchalance, to the nearest gentleman or groom, with a slight preference for the grooms, who were more practiced. The man lifted, the lady sprang at the same time, and into her saddle like a bird--Lady Bassett on a very quiet pony, or in the carriage to please some dowager--and away they clattered in high spirits, a regular cavalcade. It was a hunting county, and the ladies rode well; square seat, light hand on the snaffle, the curb reserved for cases of necessity; and, when they had patted the horse on the neck at starting, as all these coaxing creatures must, they rode him with that well-bred ease and unconsciousness of being on a horse which distinguishes ladies who have ridden all their lives from the gawky snobbesses in Hyde Park, who ride, if riding it can be called, with their elbows uncouthly fastened to their sides as if by a rope, their hands at the pit of their stomachs, and both those hands, as heavy as a housemaid's, sawing the poor horse with curb and snaffle at once, while the whole body breathes pretension and affectation, and seems to say, "Look at me; I am on horseback! Be startled at that--as I am! and I have had lessons from a riding-master. He has taught me how a lady should ride"--in his opinion, poor devil.

The champing, the pawing, the mounting, and the clattering of these bright cavalcades, with the music of the women excited by motion, furnished a picture of wealth and gayety and happy country life that cheered the whole neighborhood, and contrasted strangely with the stern Spartan life of him who had persuaded himself he was the rightful owner of Huntercombe Hall.

Sir Charles Bassett was a magistrate, and soon found himself a bad one. One day he made a little mistake, which, owing to his popularity, was very gently handled by the Bench at their weekly meeting; but still Sir Charles was ashamed and mortified. He wrote directly to Oldfield for law books, and that gentleman sent him an excellent selection bound in smooth calf.

Sir Charles now studied three hours every day, except hunting days, when no squire can work; and as his study was his justice room, he took care to find an authority before he acted. He was naturally humane, and rustic offenders, especially poachers and runaway farm servants, used to think themselves fortunate if they were taken before him and not before Squire Powys, who was sure to give them the sharp edge of the law. So now Sir Charles was useful as well as ornamental.

Thus passed fourteen months of happiness, with only one little cloud--there was no sign yet of a son and heir. But let a man be ever so powerful, it is an awkward thing to have a bitter, inveterate enemy at his door watching for a chance. Sir Charles began to realize this in the sixteenth month of his wedded bliss. A small estate called "Splatchett's" lay on his north side, and a marginal strip of this property ran right into a wood of his. This strip was wretched land, and the owner, unable to raise any wheat crop on it, had planted it with larches.

Sir Charles had made him a liberal offer for "Splatchett's" about six years ago; but he had refused point-blank, being then in good circumstances.

Sir Charles now received a hint from one of his own gamekeepers that the old farmer was in a bad way, and talked of selling. So Sir Charles called on him, and asked him if he would sell "Splatchett's" now. "Why, I can't sell it twice," said the old man, testily. "You ha' got it, han't ye?" It turned out that Richard Bassett had been beforehand. The bank had pressed for their money, and threatened foreclosure; then Bassett had stepped in with a good price; and although the conveyance was not signed, a stamped agreement was, and neither vender nor purchaser could go back. What made it more galling, the proprietor was not aware of the feud between the Bassetts, and had thought to please Sir Charles by selling to one of his name.

Sir Charles Bassett went home seriously vexed. He did not mean to tell his wife; but love's eye read his face, love's arm went round his neck, and love's soft voice and wistful eyes soon coaxed it out of him. "Dear Charles," said she, "never mind. It is mortifying; but think how much you have, and how little that wicked man has. Let him have that farm; he has lost his self-respect, and that is worth a great many farms. For my part, I pity the poor wretch. Let him try to annoy you; your wife will try, against him, to make you happy, my own beloved; and I think I may prove as strong as Mr. Bassett," said she, with a look of inspiration.

Her sweet and tender sympathy soon healed so slight a scratch.

But they had not done with "Splatchett's" yet. Just after Christmas Sir Charles invited three gentlemen to beat his more distant preserves. Their guns bellowed in quick succession through the woods, and at last they reached North Wood. Here they expected splendid shooting, as a great many cock pheasants had already been seen running ahead.

But when they got to the end of the wood they found Lawyer Wheeler standing against a tree just within "Splatchett's" boundary, and one of their own beaters reported that two boys were stationed in the road, each tapping two sticks together to confine the pheasants to that strip of land, on which the low larches and high grass afforded a strong covert.

Sir Charles halted on his side of the boundary.

Then Wheeler told his man to beat, and up got the cock pheasants, one after another. Whenever a pheasant whirred up the man left off beating.

The lawyer knocked down four brace in no time, and those that escaped him and turned back for the wood were brought down by Bassett, firing from the hard road. Only those were spared that flew northward into "Splatchett's." It was a veritable slaughter, planned with judgment, and carried out in a most ungentlemanlike and unsportsmanlike manner.

It goaded Sir Charles beyond his patience. After several vain efforts to restrain himself, he shouldered his gun, and, followed by his friends, went bursting through the larches to Richard Bassett.

"Mr. Bassett," said he, "this is most ungentlernanly conduct."

"What is the matter, sir? Am I on your ground?"

"No, but you are taking a mean advantage of our being out. Who ever heard of a gentleman beating his boundaries the very day a neighbor was out shooting, and filling them with his game?"

"Oh, that is it, is it? When justice is against you you can talk of law, and when law is against you you appeal to justice. Let us be in one story or the other, please. The Huntercombe estates belong to me by birth. You have got them by legal trickery. Keep them while you live. ***They will come to me one day, you know.*** Meantime, leave me my little estate of 'Splatchett's.' For shame, sir; you have robbed me of my inheritance and my sweetheart; do you grudge me a few cock pheasants? Why, you have made me so poor they are an object to me now."

"Oh!" said Sir Charles, "if you are stealing my game to keep body and soul together, I pity you. In that case, perhaps you will let my friends help you fill your larder."

Richard Bassett hesitated a moment; but Wheeler, who had drawn near at the sound of the raised voices, made him a signal to assent.

"By all means," said he, adroitly. "Mr. Markham, your father often shot with mine over the Bassett estates. You are welcome to poor little 'Splatchett's.' Keep your men off, Sir Charles; they are noisy bunglers, and do more harm than good. Here, Tom! Bill! beat for the gentlemen. They shall have the sport. I only want the birds."

Sir Charles drew back, and saw pheasant after pheasant thunder and whiz into the air, then collapse at a report, and fall like lead, followed by a shower of feathers.

His friends seemed to be deserting him for Richard Bassett. He left them in charge of his keepers, and went slowly home.

He said nothing to Lady Bassett till night, and then she got it all from him. She was very indignant at many of the things; but as for Sir Charles, all his cousin's arrows glided off that high-minded gentleman, except one, and that quivered in his heart. "Yes, Bella," said he, "he told me he should inherit these estates. That is because we are not blessed with children."

Lady Bassett sighed. "But we shall be some day. Shall we not?"

"God knows," said Sir Charles, gloomily. "I wonder whether there was really anything unfair done on our side when the entail was cut off?"

"Is that likely, dearest? Why?"

"Heaven seems to be on his side."

"On the side of a wicked man?"

"But he may be the father of innocent children."

"Why, he is not even married."

"He will marry. He will not throw a chance away. It makes my head dizzy, and my heart sick. Bella, now I can understand two enemies meeting alone in some solitary place, and one killing the other in a moment of rage; for when this scoundrel insulted me I remembered his anonymous letter, and all his relentless malice. Bella, I could have raised my gun and shot him like a weasel."

Lady Bassett screamed faintly, and flung her arms round his neck. "Oh, Charles, pray to God against such thoughts. You shall never go near that man again. Don't think of our one disappointment: think of all the blessings we enjoy. Never mind that wretched man's hate. Think of your wife's love. Have I not more power to make you happy than he has to afflict you, my adored?" These sweet words were accompanied by a wife's divine caresses; with the honey of her voice, and the liquid sunshine of her loving eyes. Sir Charles slept peacefully that night, and forgot his one grief and his one enemy for a time.

Not so Lady Bassett. She lay awake all night and thought deeply of Richard Bassett and "his unrelenting, impenitent malice." Women of her fine fiber, when they think long and earnestly on one thing, have often divinations. The dark future seems to be lit a moment at a time by flashes of lightning, and they discern the indistinct form of events to come, And so it was with Lady Bassett: in the stilly night a terror of the future and of Richard Bassett crept over her--a terror disproportioned to his past acts and apparent power. Perhaps she was oppressed by having an enemy--she, who was born to be loved. At all events, she was full of feminine divinations and forebodings, and saw, by flashes, many a poisoned arrow fly from that quiver and strike the beloved breast. It had already discharged one that had parted them for a time, and nearly killed Sir Charles.

Daylight cleared away much of this dark terror, but left a sober dread and a strange resolution. This timid creature, stimulated by love, determined to watch the foe, and defend her husband with all her little power. All manner of devices passed through her head, but were rejected, because, if Love said "Do wonders," Timidity said "Do nothing that you have not seen other wives do." So she remained, scheming, and longing, and fearing, and passive, all day. But the next day she conceived a vague idea, and, all in a heat, rang for her maid. While the maid was coming she fell to blushing at her own boldness, and, just as the maid opened the door, her thermometer fell so low that--she sent her upstairs for a piece of work. Oh, lame and impotent conclusion!

Just before luncheon she chanced to look through a window, and to see the head gamekeeper crossing the park, and coming to the house. Now this was the very man she wanted to speak to. The sudden temptation surprised her out of her timidity. She rang the bell again, and sent for the man.

That Colossus wondered in his mind, and felt uneasy at an invitation so novel. However, he clattered into the morning-room, in his velveteen coat, and leathern gaiters up to his thigh, pulled his front hair, bobbed his head, and then stood firm in body as was he of Rhodes, but in mind much abashed at finding himself in her ladyship's presence.

The lady, however, did not prove so very terrible. "May I inquire your name, sir?" said she, very respectfully.

"Moses Moss, my lady."

"Mr. Moss, I wish to ask you a question or two. *May* I?"

"That you may, my lady."

"I want you to explain, if you will be so good, how the proprietor of 'Splatchett's' can shoot all Sir Charles's pheasants."

"Lord! my lady, we ain't come down to that. But he do shoot more than his share, that's sure an' sartin. Well, my lady, if you please, game is just like Christians: it will make for sunny spots. Highmore has got a many of them there, with good cover; so we breeds for him. As for 'Splatchett's,' that don't hurt we, my lady; it is all arable land and dead hedges, with no bottom; only there's one little tongue of it runs into North Wood, and planted with larch; and, if you please, my lady, there is always a kind of coarse grass grows under young larches, and makes a strong cover for game. So, beat North Wood which way you will, them artful old cocks will run ahead of ye, or double back into them larches. And you see Mr. Bassett is not a gentleman, like Sir Charles; he is always a-mouching about, and the biggest poacher in the parish; and so he drops on to 'em out of bounds."

"Is there no way of stopping all this, sir?"

"We might station a dozen beaters ahead. They would most likely get shot; but I don't think as they'd mind that much if you had set your heart on it, my lady. Dall'd if I would, for one."

"Oh, Mr. Moss! Heaven forbid that any man should be shot for me. No, not for all the pheasants in the world. I'll try and think of some other way. I should like to see the place. *May* I?"

"Yes, my lady, and welcome."

"How shall I get to it, sir?"

"You can ride to the 'Woodman's Rest,' my lady, and it is scarce a stone's-throw from there; but 'tis baddish traveling for the likes of you."

She appointed an hour, rode with her groom to the public-house, and thence was conducted through bush, through brier, to the place where her husband had been so annoyed.

Moss's comments became very intelligible to her the moment she saw the place. She said very little, however, and rode home.

Next day she blushed high, and asked Sir Charles for a hundred pounds to spend upon herself.

Sir Charles smiled, well pleased, and gave it her, and a kiss into the bargain.

"Ah! but," said she, "that is not all."

"I am glad of it. You spend too little money on yourself--a great deal too little."

"That is a complaint you won't have long to make. I want to cut down a few trees. *May* I?"

"Going to build?"

"Don't ask me. It is for myself."

"That is enough. Cut down every stick on the estate if you like. The barer it leaves us the better."

"Ah, Charles, you promised me not. I shall cut with great discretion, I assure you."

"As you please," said Sir Charles. "If you want to make me happy, deny yourself nothing. Mind, I shall be angry if you do."

Soon after this a gaping quidnunc came to Sir Charles and told him Lady Bassett was felling trees in North Wood.

"And pray who has a better right to fell trees in any wood of mine?"

"But she is building a wall."

"And who has a better right to build a wall?"

With the delicacy of a gentleman he would not go near the place after this till she asked him; and that was not long, She came into his study, all beaming, and invited him to a ride. She took him into North Wood, and showed him her work. Richard Bassett's plantation, hitherto divided from North Wood only by a boundary scarcely visible, was now shut off by a brick wall: on Sir Charles's side of that wall every stick of timber was felled and removed for a distance of fifty yards, and about twenty yards from the wall a belt of larches was planted, a little higher than cabbages.

Sir Charles looked amazed at first, but soon observed how thoroughly his enemy was defeated. "My poor Bella," said he, "to think of your taking all this trouble about such a thing!" He stopped to kiss her very tenderly, and she shone with joy and innocent pride. "And I never thought of this! You astonish me, Bella."

"Ay," said she, in high spirits now; "and, what is more, I have astonished Mr. Moss. He said, 'I wish I had your head-piece, my lady.' I could have told him Love sharpens a woman's wits; but I reserved that little adage for you."

"It's all mighty fine, fair lady, but you have told me a fib. You said it was to be all for yourself, and got a hundred pounds out of me."

"And so it was for myself, you silly thing. Are you not myself? and the part of myself I love the best?" And her supple wrist was round his neck in a moment.

They rode home together, like lovers, and comforted each other.

Richard Bassett, with Wheeler's assistance, had borrowed money on Highmore to buy "Splatchett's"; he now borrowed money on "Splatchett's," and bought Dean's Wood--a wood, with patches of grass, that lay on the east of Sir Charles's boundary. He gave seventeen hundred pounds for it, and sold two thousand pounds' worth of timber off it the first year. This sounds incredible; but, owing to the custom of felling only ripe trees, landed proprietors had no sure clew to the value of all the timber on an acre. Richard Bassett had found this out, and bought Dean's Wood upon the above terms--i.e., the vender gave him the soil and three hundred pounds gratis. He grubbed the roots and sold them for fuel, and planted larches to catch the overflow of Sir Charles's game. The grass grew beautifully, now the trees were down, and he let it for pasture.

He then, still under Wheeler's advice, came out into the world again, improved his dress, and called on several county families, with a view to marrying money.

Now in the country they do not despise a poor gentleman of good lineage, and Bassett was one of the oldest names in the county; so every door was open to him; and, indeed, his late hermit life had stimulated some curiosity. This he soon turned to sympathy, by telling them that he was proud but poor. Robbed of the vast estates that belonged to him by birth, he had been unwilling to take a lower position. However, Heaven had prospered him; the wrongful heir was childless; he was the heir at law, and felt he owed it to the estate, which must return to his line, to assume a little more public importance than he had done.

Wherever he was received he was sure to enlarge upon his wrongs; and he was believed; for he was notoriously the direct heir to Bassett and Huntercombe, but the family arrangement by which his father had been bought out was known only to a few. He readily obtained sympathy, and many persons were disgusted at Sir Charles's illiberality in not making him some compensation. To use the homely expression of Govett, a small proprietor, the baronet might as well have given him back one pig out of his own farrow--i.e., one of the many farms comprised in that large estate.

Sir Charles learned that Richard was undermining him in the county, but was too proud to interfere; he told Lady Bassett he should say nothing until some *gen-*

tleman should indorse Mr. Bassett's falsehoods.

One day Sir Charles and Lady Bassett were invited to dine and sleep at Mr. Hardwicke's, distance fifteen miles; they went, and found Richard Bassett dining there, by Mrs. Hardwicke's invitation, who was one of those ninnies that fling guests together with no discrimination.

Richard had expected this to happen sooner or later, so he was comparatively prepared, and bowed stiffly to Sir Charles. Sir Charles stared at him in return. This was observed. People were uncomfortable, especially Mrs. Hardwicke, whose thoughtlessness was to blame for it all.

At a very early hour Sir Charles ordered his carriage, and drove home, instead of staying all night.

Mrs. Hardwicke, being a fool, must make a little more mischief. She blubbered to her husband, and he wrote Sir Charles a remonstrance.

Sir Charles replied that he was the only person aggrieved; Mr. Hardwicke ought not to have invited a blackguard to meet *him.*

Mr. Hardwicke replied that he had never heard a Bassett called a blackguard before, and had seen nothing in Mr. Bassett to justify an epithet so unusual among gentlemen. "And, to be frank with you, Sir Charles," said he, "I think this bitterness against a poor gentleman, whose estates you are so fortunate as to possess, is not consistent with your general character, and is, indeed, unworthy of you."

To this Sir Charles Bassett replied:

"DEAR MR. HARDWICK--You have applied some remarks to me which I will endeavor to forget, as they were written in entire ignorance of the truth. But if we are to remain friends, I expect you to believe me when I tell you that Mr. Richard Bassett has never been wronged by me or mine, but has wronged me and Lady Bassett deeply. He is a dishonorable scoundrel, not entitled to be received in society; and if, after this assurance, you receive him, I shall never darken your doors again. So please let me know your decision.

"I remain

"Yours truly,

"CHARLES DYKE BASSETT."

Mr. Hardwicke chafed under this; but Prudence stepped in. He was one of the county members, and Sir Charles could command three hundred votes.

He wrote back to say he had received Sir Charles's letter with pain, but, of course, he could not disbelieve him, and therefore he should invite Mr. Bassett no more till the matter was cleared.

But Mr. Hardwicke, thus brought to book, was nettled at his own meanness; so he sent Sir Charles's letter to Mr. Richard Bassett.

Bassett foamed with rage, and wrote a long letter, raving with insults, to Sir Charles.

He was in the act of directing it when Wheeler called on him. Bassett showed him Sir Charles's letter. Wheeler read it.

"Now read what I say to him in reply."

Wheeler read Bassett's letter, threw it into the fire, and kept it there with the poker.

"Lucky I called," said he, dryly. "Saved you a thousand pounds or so. You must not write a letter without me."

"What, am I to sit still and be insulted? You're a pretty friend."

"I am a wise friend. This is a more serious matter than you seem to think."

"Libel?"

"Of course. Why, if Sir Charles had consulted *me,* I could not have dictated a better letter. It closes every chink a defendant in libel can creep out by. Now take your pen and write to Mr. Hardwicke."

"DEAR SIR--I have received your letter, containing a libel written by Sir Charles Bassett. My reply will be public.

"Yours very truly,

"RICHARD BASSETT."

"Is that all?"

"Every syllable. Now mind; you never go to Hardwicke House again; Sir Charles has got you banished from that house; special damage! There never was a prettier case for a jury--the rightful heir foully slandered by the possessor of his hereditary estates."

This picture excited Bassett, and he walked about raving with malice, and longing for the time when he should stand in the witness-box and denounce his enemy.

"No, no," said Wheeler, "leave that to counsel; you must play the mild victim in the witness-box. Who is the defendant solicitor? We ought to serve the writ on him at once."

"No, no; serve it on himself."

"What for? Much better proceed like gentlemen."

Bassett got in a passion at being contradicted in everything. "I tell you," said he, "the more I can irritate and exasperate this villain the better. Besides, he slandered me behind my back; and I'll have the writ served upon himself. I'll do everything I can to take him down. If a man wants to be my lawyer he must enter into my feelings a little."

Wheeler, to whom he was more valuable than ever now, consented somewhat reluctantly, and called at Huntercombe Hall next day with the writ, and sent in his card.

Lady Bassett heard of this, and asked if it was Mr. Bassett's friend.

The butler said he thought it was.

Lady Bassett went to Sir Charles in his study. "Oh, my dear," said she, "here is Mr. Bassett's lawyer."

"Well?"

"Why does he come here?"

"I don't know."

"Don't see him."

"Why not?"

"I am so afraid of Mr. Bassett. He is our evil genius. Let me see this person instead of you. *May* I?"

"Certainly not."

"Might I see him *first*, love?"

"You will not see him at all."

"Charles!"

"No, Bella; I cannot have these animals talking to my wife."

"But, dear love, I am so full of forebodings. You know, Charles, I don't often presume to meddle; but I am in torture about this man. If you receive him, may I be with you? Then we shall be two to one."

"No, no," said Sir Charles, testily. Then, seeing her beautiful eyes fill at the refusal and the unusual tone, he relented. "You may be in hearing if you like. Open that door, and sit in the little room."

"Oh, thank you!"

She stepped into the room--a very small sitting-room. She had never been in it before, and while she was examining it, and thinking how she could improve its appearance, Mr. Wheeler was shown into the study. Sir Charles received him standing, to intimate that the interview must be brief. This, and the time he had been kept waiting in the hall, roused Wheeler's bile, and he entered on his subject more bruskly than he had intended.

"Sir Charles Bassett, you wrote a letter to Mr. Hardwicke, reflecting on my client, Mr. Bassett--a most unjustifiable letter."

"Keep your opinion to yourself, sir. I wrote a letter, calling him what he is."

"No, sir; that letter is a libel."

"It is the truth."

"It is a malicious libel, sir; and we shall punish you for it. I hereby serve you with this copy of a writ. Damages, five thousand pounds."

A sigh from the next room passed unnoticed by the men, for their voices were now raised in anger.

"And so that is what you came here for. Why did you not go to my solicitor? You must be as great a blackguard as your client, to serve your paltry writs on me in my own house."

"Not blackguard enough to insult a gentleman in my own house. If you had been civil I might have accommodated matters; but now I'll make you smart--ugh!"

Nothing provokes a high-spirited man more than a menace. Sir Charles, threatened in his wife's hearing, shot out his right arm with surprising force and rapidity, and knocked Wheeler down in a moment.

In came Lady Bassett, with a scream, and saw the attorney lying doubled up, and Sir Charles standing over him, blowing like a grampus with rage and excitement.

But the next moment be staggered and gasped, and she had to support him to a seat. She rang the bell for aid, then kneeled, and took his throbbing temples to her wifely bosom.

Wheeler picked himself up, and, seated on his hams, eyed the pair with concentrated fury.

"Aha! You have hurt yourself more than me. Two suits against you now instead of one."

"Conduct this person from the house," said Lady Bassett to a servant who entered at that moment.

"All right, my lady," said Wheeler; "I'll remind you of that word when this house belongs to us."

CHAPTER X.

WITH this bitter reply Wheeler retired precipitately; the shaft pierced but one bosom; for the devoted wife, with the swift ingenuity of woman's love, had put both her hands right over her husband's ears that he might hear no more insults.

Sir Charles very nearly had a fit; but his wife loosened his neckcloth, caressed his throbbing head, and applied eau-de-Cologne to his nostrils. He got better, but felt dizzy for about an hour. She made him come into her room and lie down; she hung over him, curling as a vine and light as a bird, and her kisses lit softly as down upon his eyes, and her words of love and pity murmured music in his ears till he slept, and that danger passed.

For a day or two after this both Sir Charles and Lady Bassett avoided the unpleasant subject. But it had to be faced; so Mr. Oldfield was summoned to Huntercombe, and all engagements given up for the day, that he might dine alone with them and talk the matter over.

Sir Charles thought he could justify; but when it came to the point he could only prove that Richard had done several ungentleman-like things of a nature a stout jury would consider trifles.

Mr. Oldfield said of course they must enter an appearance; and, this done, the wisest course would be to let him see Wheeler, and try to compromise the suit. "It will cost you a thousand pounds, Sir Charles, I dare say; but if it teaches you never to write of an enemy or to an enemy without showing your lawyer the letter first, the lesson will be cheap. Somebody in the Bible says, 'Oh, that mine enemy would write a book!' I say, 'Oh, that he would write a letter--without consulting his solicitor.'"

It was Lady Bassett's cue now to make light of troubles. "What does it matter,

Mr. Oldfield? All they want is money. Yes, offer them a thousand pounds to leave him in peace."

So next day Mr. Oldfield called on Wheeler, all smiles and civility, and asked him if he did not think it a pity cousins should quarrel before the whole county.

"A great pity," said Wheeler. "But my client has no alternative. No gentleman in the county would speak to him if he sat quiet under such contumely."

After beating about the bush the usual time, Oldfield said that Sir Charles was hungry for litigation, but that Lady Bassett was averse to it. "In short, Mr. Wheeler, I will try and get Mr. Bassett a thousand pounds to forego this scandal."

"I will consult him, and let you know," said Wheeler. "He happens to be in the town."

Oldfield called again in an hour. Wheeler told him a thousand pounds would be accepted, with a written apology.

Oldfield shook his head. "Sir Charles will never write an apology: right or wrong, he is too sincere in his conviction."

"He will never get a jury to share it."

"You must not be too sure of that. You don't know the defense."

Oldfield said this with a gravity which did him credit.

"Do you know it yourself?" said the other keen hand.

Mr. Oldfield smiled haughtily, but said nothing. Wheeler had hit the mark.

"By the by," said the latter, "there is another little matter. Sir Charles assaulted me for doing my duty to my client. I mean to sue him. Here is the writ; will you accept service?"

"Oh, certainly, Mr. Wheeler and I am glad to find you do not make a habit of serving writs on gentlemen in person."

"Of course not. I did it on a single occasion, contrary to my own wish, and went in person--to soften the blow--instead of sending my clerk."

After this little spar, the two artists in law bade each other farewell with every demonstration of civility.

Sir Charles would not apologize.

The plaintiff filed his declaration.

The defendant pleaded not guilty, but did not disclose a defense. The law allows a defendant in libel this advantage.

Plaintiff joined issue, and the trial was set down for the next assizes.

Sir Charles was irritated, but nothing more. Lady Bassett, with a woman's natural shrinking from publicity, felt it more deeply. She would have given thousands of her own money to keep the matter out of court. But her very terror of Richard Bassett restrained her. She was always thinking about him, and had convinced herself he was the ablest villain in the wide world; and she thought to herself, "If, with his small means, he annoys Charles so, what would he do if I were to enrich him? He would crush us."

As the trial drew near she began to hover about Sir Charles in his study, like an anxious hen. The maternal yearnings were awakened in her by marriage, and she had no child; so her Charles in trouble was husband and child.

Sometimes she would come in and just kiss his forehead, and run out again, casting back a celestial look of love at the door, and, though it was her husband she had kissed, she blushed divinely. At last one day she crept in and said, very timidly, "Charles dear, the anonymous letter--is not that an excuse for libeling him--as they call telling the truth?"

"Why, of course it is. Have you got it?"

"Dearest, the brave lady took it away."

"The brave lady! Who is that?"

"Why, the lady that came with Mr. Oldfield and pleaded your cause with papa--oh, so eloquently! Sometimes when I think of it now I feel almost jealous. Who is she?"

"From what you have always told me, I think it was the Sister of Charity who nursed me."

"You silly thing, she was no Sister of Charity; that was only put on. Charles, tell me the truth. What does it matter *now?* It was some lady who loved you."

"Loved me, and set her wits to work to marry me to you?"

"Women's love is so disinterested--sometimes."

"No, no; she told me she was a sister of--, and no doubt that is the truth."

"A sister of whom?"

"No matter: don't remind me of the past; it is odious to me; and, on second thoughts, rather than stir up all that mud, it would be better not to use the anonymous letter, even if you could get it again."

Lady Bassett begged him to take advice on that; meantime she would try to get the letter, and also the evidence that Richard Bassett wrote it.

"I see no harm in that," said Sir Charles; "only confine your communication to Mr. Oldfield. I will not have you speaking or writing to a woman I don't know: and the more I think of her conduct the less I understand it."

"There are people who do good by stealth," suggested Bella timidly.

"Fiddledeedee!" replied Sir Charles; "you are a goose--I mean an angel."

Lady Bassett complied with the letter, but, goose or not, evaded the spirit of Sir Charles's command with considerable dexterity.

"DEAR MR. OLDFIELD--You may guess what trouble I am in. Sir Charles will soon have to appear in open court, and be talked against by some great orator. That anonymous letter Mr. Bassett wrote me was very base, and is surely some justification of the violent epithets my dear husband, in an unhappy moment of irritation, has applied to him. The brave lady has it. I am sure she will not refuse to send it me. I wish I dare ask her to give it me with her own hand; but I must not, I suppose. Pray tell her how unhappy I am, and perhaps she will favor us with a word of advice as well as the letter.

"I remain, yours faithfully,

"BELLA BASSETT."

This letter was written at the brave lady; and Mr. Oldfield did what was expected, he sent Miss Somerset a copy of Lady Bassett's letter, and some lines in his own hand, describing Sir Charles's difficulty in a more businesslike way.

In due course Miss Somerset wrote him back that she was in the country, hunting, at no very great distance from Huntercombe Hall; she would sent up to town for her desk; the letter would be there, if she had kept it at all.

Oldfield groaned at this cool conjecture, and wrote back directly, urging expedition.

This produced an effect that he had not anticipated.

One morning Lord Harrowdale's foxhounds met at a large covert, about five miles from Huntercombe, and Sir Charles told Lady Bassett she must ride to cover.

"Yes, dear. Charles, love, I have no spirit to appear in public. We shall soon have publicity enough."

"That is my reason. I have not done nor said anything I am ashamed of, and you will meet the county on this and on every public occasion."

"I obey," said Bella.

"And look your best."

"I will, dearest."

"And be in good spirits."

"Must I?"

"Yes."

"I will try. Oh!--oh!--oh!"

"Why, you poor-spirited little goose! Dry your eyes this moment."

"There. Oh!"

"And kiss me."

"There. Ah! kissing you is a great comfort."

"It is one you are particularly welcome to. Now run away and put on your habit. I'll have two grooms out; one with a fresh horse for me, and one to look after you."

"Oh, Charles! Pray don't make me hunt."

"No, no. Not so tyrannical as that; hang it all!"

"Do you know what I do while you are hunting? I pray all the time that you may not get a fall and be hurt; and I pray God to forgive you and all the gentlemen for your cruelty in galloping with all those dogs after one poor little inoffensive thing, to hunt it and kill it--kill it twice, indeed; once with terror, and then over again with mangling its poor little body."

"This is cheerful," said Sir Charles, rather ruefully. "We cannot all be angels, like you. It is a glorious excitement. There! you are too good for this world; I'll let you off going."

"Oh no, dear. I won't be let off, now I know your wish. Only I beg to ride home as soon as the poor thing runs away. You wouldn't get me out of the thick covers if I were a fox. I'd run round and round, and call on all my acquaintances to set them running."

As she said this her eyes turned toward each other in a peculiar way, and she looked extremely foxy; but the look melted away directly.

The hounds met, and Lady Bassett, who was still the beauty of the county, was surrounded by riders at first; but as the hounds began to work, and every now and then a young hound uttered a note, they cantered about, and took up different posts, as experience suggested.

At last a fox was found at the other end of the cover, and away galloped the hunters in that direction, all but four persons, Lady Bassett, and her groom, who kept respectfully aloof, and a lady and gentleman who had reined their horses up on a rising ground about a furlong distant.

Lady Bassett, thus left alone, happened to look round, and saw the lady level an opera-glass toward her and look through it.

As a result of this inspection the lady cantered toward her. She was on a chestnut gelding of great height and bone, and rode him as if they were one, so smoothly did she move in concert with his easy, magnificent strides.

When she came near Lady Bassett she made a little sweep and drew up beside her on the grass.

There was no mistaking that tall figure and commanding face. It was the brave lady. Her eyes sparkled; her cheek was slightly colored with excitement; she looked healthier and handsomer than ever, and also more feminine, for a reason the sagacious reader may perhaps discern if he attends to the dialogue.

"So," said she, without bowing or any other ceremony, "that little rascal is troubling you again."

Lady Bassett colored and panted, and looked lovingly at her, before she could speak. At last she said, "Yes; and you have come to help us again."

"Well, the lawyer said there was no time to lose; so I have brought you the anonymous letter."

"Oh, thank you, madam, thank you."

"But I'm afraid it will be of no use unless you can prove Mr. Bassett wrote it. It is in a disguised hand."

"But you found him out by means of another letter."

"Yes; but I can't give you that other letter to have it read in a court of law, because--Do you see that gentleman there?"

"Yes."

"That is Marsh."

"Oh, is it?"

"He is a fool; but I am going to marry him. I have been very ill since I saw you, and poor Marsh nursed me. Talk of women nurses! If ever you are ill in earnest, as I was, write to me, and I'll send you Marsh. Oh, I have no words to tell you his patience, his forbearance, his watchfulness, his tenderness to a sick woman. It is no use--I must marry him; and I could have no letter published that would give him pain."

"Of course not. Oh, madam, do you think I am capable of doing anything that would give you pain, or dear Mr. Marsh either?"

"No, no; you are a good woman."

"Not half so good as you are."

"You don't know what you are saying."

"Oh yes, I do."

"Then I say no more; it is rude to contradict. Good-by, Lady Bassett."

"Must you leave me so soon? Will you not visit us? May I not know the name of so good a friend?"

"Next week I shall be **Mrs. Marsh."**

"And you will give me the great pleasure of having you at my house--you and your husband?"

The lady showed some agitation at this--an unusual thing for her. She faltered: "Some day, perhaps, if I make him as good a wife as I hope to. What a lady you are! Vulgar people are ashamed to be grateful; but you are a born lady. Good-by, before I make a fool of myself; and they are all coming this way, by the dogs' music."

"Won't you kiss me, after bringing me this?"

"Kiss you?" and she opened her eyes.

"If you please," said Lady Bassett, bending toward her, with eyes full of gratitude and tenderness.

Then the other woman took her by the shoulders, and plunged her great gray orbs into Bella's.

They kissed each other.

At that contact the stranger seemed to change her character all in a moment. She strained Bella to her bosom and kissed her passionately, and sobbed out, wildly, "O God! you are good to sinners. This is the happiest hour of my life--it is a forerunner. Bless you, sweet dove of innocence! You will be none the worse, and I am all the better--Ah! Sir Charles. Not one word about me to him."

And with these words, uttered with sudden energy, she spurred her great horse, leaped the ditch, and burst through the dead hedge into the wood, and winded out of sight among the trees.

Sir Charles came up astonished. "Why, who was that?"

Bella's eyes began to rove, as I have before described; but she replied pretty promptly, "The brave lady herself; she brought me the anonymous letter for your defense."

"Why, how came she to know about it?"

"She did not tell me that. She was in a great hurry. Her fiance was waiting for her."

"Was it necessary to kiss her in the hunting-field?" said Sir Charles, with something very like a frown.

"I'd kiss the whole field, grooms and all, if they did you a great service, as that dear lady has," said Bella. The words were brave, but the accent piteous.

"You are excited, Bella. You had better ride home," said Sir Charles, gently enough, but moodily.

"Thank you, Charles," said Bella, glad to escape further examination about this mysterious lady. She rode home accordingly. There she found Mr. Oldfield, and showed him the anonymous letter.

He read it, and said it was a defense, but a disagreeable one. "Suppose he says he wrote it, and the facts were true?"

"But I don't think he will confess it. He is not a gentleman. He is very untruthful. Can we not make this a trap to catch him, sir? *He* has no scruples."

Oldfield looked at her in some surprise at her depth.

"We must get hold of his handwriting," said he. "We must ransack the local banks; find his correspondents."

"Leave all that to me," said Lady Bassett, in a low voice.

Mr. Oldfield thought he might as well please a beautiful and loving woman, if he could; so he gave her something to do for her husband. "Very well; collect all the materials of comparison you can--letters, receipts, etc. Meantime I will retain the two principal experts in London, and we will submit your materials to them the night before the trial."

Lady Bassett, thus instructed, drove to all the banks, but found no clerk acquainted with Mr. Bassett's handwriting. He did not bank with anybody in the county.

She called on several persons she thought likely to possess letters or other writings of Richard Bassett. Not a scrap.

Then she began to fear. The case looked desperate.

Then she began to think. And she thought very hard indeed, especially at night.

In the dead of night she had an idea. She got up, and stole from her husband's side, and studied the anonymous letter.

Next day she sat down with the anonymous letter on her desk, and blushed, and trembled, and looked about like some wild animal scared. She selected from the anonymous letter several words--"character, abused, Sir, Charles, Bassett, lady, abandoned, friend, whether, ten, slanderer" etc.--and wrote them on a slip of paper. Then she locked up the anonymous letter. Then she locked the door. Then she sat down to a sheet of paper, and, after some more wild and furtive glances all around, she gave her whole mind to writing a letter.

And to whom did she write, think you?

To Richard Bassett.

CHAPTER XI.

MR. BASSETT--I am sure both yourself and my husband will suffer in public estimation, unless some friend comes between you, and this unhappy lawsuit is given up.

"Do not think me blind nor presumptuous; Sir Charles, when he wrote that letter, had reason to believe you had done him a deep injury by unfair means. Many will share that opinion if this cause is tried. You are his cousin, and his heir at law. I dread to see an unhappy feud inflamed by a public trial. Is there no personal sacrifice by which I can compensate the affront you have received, without compromising Sir Charles Bassett's veracity, who is the soul of honor?

"I am, yours obediently,

"BELLA BASSETT."

She posted this letter, and Richard Bassett had no sooner received it than he mounted his horse and rode to Wheeler's with it.

That worthy's eyes sparkled. "Capital!" said he. "We must draw her on, and write an answer that will read well in court."

He concocted an epistle just the opposite of what Richard Bassett, left to himself, would have written. Bassett copied, and sent it as his own.

"LADY BASSETT--I thank you for writing to me at this moment, when I am weighed down by slander. Your own character stands so high that you would not deign to write to me if you believed the abuse that has been lavished on me. With you I deplore this family feud. It is not of my seeking; and as for this lawsuit, it is one in which the plaintiff is really the defendant. Sir Charles has written a defamatory letter, which has closed every house in this county to his victim. If, as I now feel sure, you disapprove the libel, pray persuade him to retract it. The rest our lawyers can settle,

"Yours very respectfully,

"RICHARD BASSETT."

When Lady Bassett read this, she saw she had an adroit opponent. Yet she wrote again:

"MR. BASSETT--There are limits to my influence with Sir Charles. I have no power to make him say one word against his convictions.

"But my lawyer tells me you seek pecuniary compensation for an affront. I offer you, out of my own means, which are ample, that which you seek--offer it freely and heartily; and I honestly think you had better receive it from me than expose yourself to the risks and mortifications of a public trial.

"I am, yours obediently,

"BELLA BASSETT."

"LADY BASSETT--You have fallen into a very natural error. It is true I sue Sir Charles Bassett for money; but that is only because the law allows me my remedy in no other form. What really brings me into court is the defense of my injured honor. How do you meet me? You say, virtually, 'Never mind your character: here is money.' Permit me to decline it on such terms.

"A public insult cannot be cured in private.

"Strong in my innocence, and my wrongs, I court what you call the risks of a public trial.

"Whatever the result, *you* have played the honorable and womanly part of peacemaker; and it is unfortunate for your husband that your gentle influence is limited by his vanity, which perseveres in a cruel slander, instead of retracting it while there is yet time.

"I am, madam, yours obediently,

"RICHARD BASSETT."

"MR. BASSETT--I retire from a correspondence which appears to be useless, and might, if prolonged, draw some bitter remark from me, as it has from you.

"After the trial, which you court and I deprecate, you will perhaps review my letters with a more friendly eye.

"I am, yours obediently,

"BELLA BASSETT."

In this fencing-match between a lawyer and a lady each gained an advantage.

The lawyer's letters, as might have been expected, were the best adapted to be read to a jury; but the lady, subtler in her way, obtained, at a small sacrifice, what she wanted, and that without raising the slightest suspicion of her true motive in the correspondence.

She announced her success to Mr. Oldfield; but, in the midst of it, she quaked with terror at the thought of what Sir Charles would say to her for writing to Mr. Bassett at all.

She now, with the changeableness of her sex, hoped and prayed Mr. Bassett would admit the anonymous letter, and so all her subtlety and pains prove superfluous.

Quaking secretly, but with a lovely face and serene front, she took her place at the assizes, before the judge, and got as near him as she could.

The court was crowded, and many ladies present.

Bassett v. Bassett was called in a loud voice; there was a hum of excitement, then a silence of expectation, and the plaintiff's counsel rose to address the jury.

CHAPTER XII.

MAY it please your Lordship: Gentlemen of the Jury--The plaintiff in this case is Richard Bassett, Esquire, the direct and lineal representative of that old and honorable family, whose monuments are to be seen in several churches in this county, and whose estates are the largest, I believe, in the county. He would have succeeded, as a matter of course, to those estates, but for an arrangement made only a year before he was born, by which, contrary to nature and justice, he was denuded of those estates, and they passed to the defendant. The defendant is nowise to blame for that piece of injustice; but he profits by it, and it might be expected that his good fortune would soften his heart toward his unfortunate relative. I say that if uncommon tenderness might be expected to be shown by anybody to this deserving and unfortunate gentleman, it would be by Sir Charles Bassett, who enjoys his cousin's ancestral estates, and can so well appreciate what that cousin has lost by no fault of his own."

"Hear! hear!"

"Silence in the court!"

The Judge.--I must request that there may be no manifestation of feeling.

Counsel.--I will endeavor to provoke none, my lord. It is a very simple case, and I shall not occupy you long. Well, gentlemen, Mr. Bassett is a poor man, by no fault of his; but if he is poor, he is proud and honorable. He has met the frowns of fortune like a gentleman--like a man. He has not solicited government for a place. He has not whined nor lamented. He has dignified unmerited poverty by prudence and self-denial; and, unable to forget that he is a Bassett, he has put by a little money every year, and bought a small estate or two, and had even applied to the Lord-Lieutenant to make him a justice of the peace, when a most severe and unexpected blow fell upon him. Among those large proprietors who respected him in spite of his humbler circumstances was Mr. Hardwicke, one of the county members. Well, gentlemen, on the 21st of last May Mr. Bassett received a letter from Mr. Hardwicke inclosing one purporting to be from Sir Charles Bassett--

The Judge.--Does Sir Charles Bassett admit the letter?

Defendant's Counsel (after a word with Oldfield).--Yes, my lord.

Plaintiff's Counsel.--A letter admitted to be written by Sir Charles Bassett. That letter shall be read to you.

The letter was then read.

The counsel resumed: "Conceive, if you can, the effect of this blow, just as my unhappy and most deserving client was rising a little in the world. I shall prove that it excluded him from Mr. Hardwicke's house, and other houses too. He is a man of too much importance to risk affronts. He has never entered the door of any gentleman in this county since his powerful relative published this cruel libel. He has drawn his Spartan cloak around him, and he awaits your verdict to resume that place among you which is due to him in every way--due to him as the heir in direct line to the wealth, and, above all, to the honor of the Bassetts; due to him as Sir Charles Bassett's heir at law; and due to him on account of the decency and fortitude with which he has borne adversity, and with which he now repels foul-mouthed slander."

"Hear! hear!"

"Silence in the court!"

"I have done, gentlemen, for the present. Indeed, eloquence, even if I possessed it, would be superfluous; the facts speak for themselves.--Call James Hardwicke, Esq."

Mr. Hardwicke proved the receipt of the letter from Sir Charles, and that he had sent it to Mr. Bassett; and that Mr. Bassett had not entered his house since then, nor had he invited him.

Mr. Bassett was then called, and, being duly trained by Wheeler, abstained from all heat, and wore an air of dignified dejection. His counsel examined him, and his replies bore out the opening statement. Everybody thought him sure of a verdict.

He was then cross-examined. Defendant's counsel pressed him about his unfair way of shooting. The judge interfered, and said that was trifling. If there was no substantial defense, why not settle the matter?

"There is a defense, my lord."

"Then it is time you disclosed it."

"Very well, my lord. Mr. Bassett, did you ever write an anonymous letter?"

"Not that I remember."

"Oh, that appears to you a trifle. It is not so considered."

The Judge.--Be more particular in your question.

"I will, my lord.--Did you ever write an anonymous letter, to make mischief between Sir Charles and Lady Bassett?"

"Never," said the witness; but he turned pale.

"Do you mean to say you did not write this letter to Miss Bruce? Look at the letter, Mr. Bassett, before you reply."

Bassett cast one swift glance of agony at Wheeler; then braced himself like iron. He examined the letter attentively, turned it over, lived an age, and said it was not his writing.

"Do you swear that?"

"Certainly."

Defendant's Counsel.--I shall ask your lordship to take down that reply. If persisted in, my client will indict the witness for perjury.

Plaintiff's Counsel.--Don't threaten the witness as well as insult him, please.

The Judge.--He is an educated man, and knows the duty he owes to God and the defendant.--Take time, Mr. Bassett, and recollect. Did you write that letter?"

"No, my lord."

Counsel waited for the judge to note the reply, then proceeded.

"You have lately corresponded with Lady Bassett, I think?"

"Yes. Her ladyship opened a correspondence with me."

"It is a lie!" roared Sir Charles Bassett from the door of the grand jury room.

"Silence in the court!"

The Judge.--Who made that unseemly remark?

Sir Charles.--I did, my lord. My wife never corresponded with the cur.

The Plaintiff.--It is only one insult more, gentlemen, and as false as the rest. Permit me, my lord. My own counsel would never have put the question. I would not, for the world, give Lady Bassett pain; but Sir Charles and his counsel have extorted the truth from me. Her ladyship did open a correspondence with me, and a friendly one.

The Plaintiff's Counsel.--Will your lordship ask whether that was after the defendant had written the libel?

The question was put, and answered in the affirmative.

Lady Bassett hid her face in her hands. Sir Charles saw the movement, and groaned aloud.

The Judge.--I beg the case may not be encumbered with irrelevant matter.

Counsel replied that the correspondence would be made evidence in the case. (To the witness.)--"You wrote this letter to Lady Bassett?"

"Yes."

"And every word in it?"

"And every word in it," faltered Bassett, now ashy pale, for he began to see the trap.

"Then you wrote this word 'character,' and this word 'injured,' and this word--"

The Judge (peevishly).--He tells you he wrote every word in those letters to Lady Bassett.--What more would you have?

Counsel.--If your lordship will be good enough to examine the correspondence, and compare those words in it I have underlined with the same words in the anonymous letter, you will perhaps find I know my business better than you seem to think. (The counsel who ventured on this remonstrance was a sergeant.)

"Brother Eitherside," said the judge, with a charming manner, "you satisfied me of that, to my cost, long ago, whenever I had you against me in a case. Please hand me the letters."

While the judge was making a keen comparison, counsel continued the cross-examination.

"You are aware that this letter caused a separation between Sir Charles Bassett and the lady he was engaged to?"

"I know nothing about it."

"Indeed! Well, were you acquainted with the Miss Somerset mentioned in this letter?"

"Slightly."

"You have been at her house?"

"Once or twice."

"Which? Twice is double as often as once, you know."

"Twice."

"No more?"

"Not that I recollect."

"You wrote to her?"

"I may have."

"Did you, or did you not?"

"I did."

"What was the purport of that letter?"

"I can't recollect at this distance of time."

"On your oath, sir, did you not write urging her to co-operate with you to keep Sir Charles Bassett from marrying his affianced, Miss Bella Bruce, to whom that anonymous letter was written with the same object?"

The perspiration now rolled in visible drops down the tortured liar's face. Yet still, by a gigantic effort, he stood firm, and even planted a blow.

"I did not write the anonymous letter. But I believe I told Miss Somerset I loved Miss Bruce, and that *her* lover was robbing me of mine, as he had robbed me of everything else."

"And that was all you said--on your oath?"

"All I can recollect." With this the strong man, cowed, terrified, expecting his letter to Somerset to be produced, and so the iron chain of evidence completed, gasped out, "Man, you tear open all my wounds at once!" and with this burst out sobbing, and lamenting aloud that he had ever been born.

Counsel waited calmly till he should be in a condition to receive another dose.

"Oh, will nobody stop this cruel trial?" said Lady Bassett, with the tears trickling down her face.

The judge heard this remark without seeming to do so.

He said to defendant's counsel, "Whatever the truth may be, you have proved enough to show Sir Charles Bassett might well have an honest conviction that Mr. Bassett had done a dastardly act. Whether a jury would ever agree on a question of handwriting must always be doubtful. Looking at the relationship of the parties, is it advisable to carry this matter further? If I might advise the gentlemen, they would each consent to withdraw a juror."

Upon this suggestion the counsel for both parties put their heads together in animated whispers; and during this the judge made a remark to the jury, intended for the public: "Since Lady Bassett's name has been drawn into this, I must say that I have read her letters to Mr. Bassett, and they are such as she could write without in the least compromising her husband. Indeed, now the defense is disclosed, they appear to me to be wise and kindly letters, such as only a good wife, a high-bred lady, and a true Christian could write in so delicate a matter."

Plaintiff's Counsel.--My lord, we are agreed to withdraw a juror.

Defendant's Counsel.--Out of respect for your lordship's advice, and not from any doubt of the result on *our* part.

The Crier.--WACE *v.* HALIBURTON!

And so the car of justice rolled on till it came to Wheeler v. Bassett.

This case was soon disposed of.

Sir Charles Bassett was dignified and calm in the witness-box, and treated the whole matter with high-bred nonchalance, as one unworthy of the attention the Court was good enough to bestow on it. The judge disapproved the assault, but said the plaintiff had drawn it on himself by unprofessional conduct, and by threatening a gentleman in his own house. Verdict for the plaintiff--40s. The judge refused to certify for costs.

Lady Bassett, her throat parched with excitement, drove home, and awaited her husband's return with no little anxiety. As soon as she heard him in his dressing-room she glided in and went down on her knees to him. "Pray, pray don't scold me; I couldn't bear you to be defeated, Charles."

Sir Charles raised her, but did not kiss her.

"You think only of me," said he, rather sadly. "It is a sorry victory, too dearly bought."

Then she began to cry.

Sir Charles begged her not to cry; but still he did not kiss her, nor conceal his mortification: he hardly spoke to her for several days.

She accepted her disgrace pensively and patiently. She thought it all over, and felt her husband was right, and loved her like a man. But she thought, also, that she was not very wrong to love him in her way. Wrong or not, she felt she could not sit idle and see his enemy defeat him.

The coolness died away by degrees, with so much humility on one side and so much love on both: but the subject was interdicted forever.

A week after the trial Lady Bassett wrote to Mrs. Marsh, under cover to Mr. Oldfield, and told her how the trial had gone, and, with many expressions of gratitude, invited her and her husband to Huntercombe Hall. She told Sir Charles what she had done, and he wore a very strange look. "Might I suggest that we have them alone?" said he dryly.

"By all means," said Lady Bassett. "I don't want to share my paragon with anybody."

In due course a reply came; Mr. and Mrs. Marsh would avail themselves some day of Lady Bassett's kindness: at present they were going abroad. The letter was written by a man's hand.

About this time Oldfield sent Sir Charles Miss Somerset's deed, canceled, and told him she had married a man of fortune, who was devoted to her, and preferred to take her without any dowry.

Bassett and Wheeler went home, crestfallen, and dined together. They discussed the two trials, and each blamed the other. They quarreled and parted: and Wheeler sent in an enormous bill, extending over five years. Eighty-five items began thus: "Attending you at your house for several hours, on which occasion you asked my advice as to whether--" etc.

Now as a great many of these attendances had been really to shoot game and dine on rabbits at Bassett's expense, he thought it hard the conversation should be charged and the rabbits not.

Disgusted with his defeat, and resolved to evade this bill, he discharged his servant, and put a retired soldier into his house, armed him with a blunderbuss, and ordered him to keep all doors closed, and present the weapon aforesaid at all rate collectors, tax collectors, debt collectors, and applicants for money to build churches or convert the heathen; but not to *fire* at anybody except his friend Wheeler, nor at him unless he should try to shove a writ in at some chink of the building.

This done, he went on his travels, third-class, with his eyes always open, and his heart full of bitterness.

Nothing happened to Richard Bassett on his travels that I need relate until one evening when he alighted at a small commercial inn in the city of York, and there met a person whose influence on the events I am about to relate seems at this moment incredible to me, though it is simple fact.

He found the commercial room empty, and rang the bell. In came the waiter, a strapping girl, with coal-black eyes and brows to match, and a brown skin, but glowing cheeks.

They both started at sight of each other. It was Polly Somerset.

"Why, Polly! How d'ye do? How do you come here?"

"It's along of you I'm here, young man," said Polly, and began to whimper. She told him her sister had found out from the page she had been colloguing with him, and had never treated her like a sister after that. "And when she married a gentleman she wouldn't have me aside her for all I could say, but she did pack me off into service, and here I be."

The girl was handsome, and had a liking for him. Bassett was idle, and time hung heavy on his hands: he stayed at the inn a fortnight, more for Polly's company than anything: and at last offered to put her into a vacant cottage on his own little estate of Highmore. But the girl was shrewd, and had seen a great deal of life this last three years; she liked Richard in her way, but she saw he was all self, and she would not trust him. "Nay," said she, "I'll not break with Rhoda for any young man in Britain. If I leave service she will never own me at all: she is as hard as iron."

"Well, but you might come and take service near me, and then we could often get a word together."

"Oh, I'm agreeable to that: you find me a good place. I like an inn best; one sees fresh faces."

Bassett promised to manage that for her. On reaching home he found a conciliatory letter from Wheeler, coupled with his permission to tax the bill according to his own notion of justice. This and other letters were in an outhouse; the old soldier had not permitted them to penetrate the fortress. He had entered into the spirit of his instructions, and to him a letter was a probable hand-grenade.

Bassett sent for Wheeler; the bill was reduced, and a small payment made; the rest postponed till better times. Wheeler was then consulted about Polly, and he told his client the landlady of the "Lamb" wanted a good active waitress; he thought he could arrange that little affair.

In due course, thanks to this artist, Mary Wells, hitherto known as Polly Somerset, landed with her boxes at the "Lamb "; and with her quick foot, her black eyes, and ready tongue soon added to the popularity of the inn. Richard Bassett, Esq., for one, used to sup there now and then with his friend Wheeler, and even sleep there after supper.

By-and-by the vicar of Huntercombe wanted a servant, and offered to engage Mary Wells.

She thought twice about that. She could neither write nor read, and therefore was dreadfully dull without company; the bustle of an inn, and people coming and going, amused her. However, it was a temptation to be near Richard Bassett; so she accepted at last. Unable to write, she could not consult him; and she made sure he would be delighted.

But when she got into the village the prudent Mr. Bassett drew in his horns, and avoided her. She was mortified and very angry. She revenged herself on her employer; broke double her wages. The vicar had never been able to convert a smasher; so he parted with her very readily to Lady Bassett, with a hint that she was rather unfortunate in glass and china.

In that large house her spirits rose, and, having a hearty manner and a clapper tongue, she became a general favorite.

One day she met Mr. Bassett in the village, and he seemed delighted at the sight of her, and begged her to meet him that night at a certain place where Sir Charles's garden was divided from his own by a ha-ha. It was a very secluded spot, shut out from view, even in daylight, by the trees and shrubs and the winding nature of the walk that led to it; yet it was scarcely a hundred yards from Huntercombe Hall.

Mary Wells came to the tryst, but in no amorous mood. She came merely to tell Mr. Bassett her mind, viz., that he was a shabby fellow, and she had had her cry, and didn't care a straw for him now. And she did tell him so, in a loud voice, and with a flushed cheek.

But he set to work, humbly and patiently, to pacify her; he represented that, in a small house like the vicarage, every thing is known; he should have ruined her character if he had not held aloof. "But it is different now," said he. "You can run out of Huntercombe House, and meet me here, and nobody be the wiser."

"Not I," said Mary Wells, with a toss. "The worse thing a girl can do is to keep company with a gentleman. She must meet him in holes and corners, and be flung off, like an old glove, when she has served his turn."

"That will never happen to you, Polly dear. We must be prudent for the present; but I shall be more my own master some day, and then you will see how I love you."

"Seeing is believing," said the girl, sullenly. "You be too fond of yourself to love the likes o' me."

Such was the warning her natural shrewdness gave her. But perseverance undermined it. Bassett so often threw out hints of what he would do some day, mixed with warm protestations of love, that she began almost to hope he would marry her. She really liked him; his fine figure and his color pleased her eye, and he had a plausible tongue to boot.

As for him, her rustic beauty and health pleased his senses; but, for his heart, she had little place in that. What he courted her for just now was to keep him informed of all that passed in Huntercombe Hall. His morbid soul hung about that place, and he listened greedily to Mary Wells's gossip. He had counted on her volubility; it did not disappoint him. She never met him without a budget, one-half of it lies or exaggerations. She was a born liar. One night she came in high spirits, and greeted him thus: "What d'ye think? I'm riz! Mrs. Eden, that dresses my lady's hair, she took ill yesterday, and I told the housekeeper I was used to dress hair, and she told my lady. If you didn't please our Rhoda at that, 'twas as much as your life was worth. You mustn't be thinking of your young man with her hair in your hand, or she'd rouse you with a good crack on the crown with a hair-brush. So I dressed my lady's hair, and handled it like old chaney; by the same token, she is so pleased with me you can't think. She is a real lady; not like our Rhoda. Speaks as civil to me as if I was one of her own sort; and, says she, 'I should like to have you about me, if I might.' I had it on my tongue to tell her she was mistress; but I was a little skeared at her at first, you know. But she will have me about her; I see it in her eye."

Bassett was delighted at this news, but he did not speak his mind all at once; the time was not come. He let the gypsy rattle on, and bided his time. He flattered her, and said he envied Lady Bassett to have such a beautiful girl about her. "I'll let my hair grow," said he.

"Ay, do," said she, "and then I'll pull it for you."

This challenge ended in a little struggle for a kiss, the sincerity of which was doubtful. Polly resisted vigorously, to be sure, but briefly, and, having given in, returned it.

One day she told him Sir Charles had met her plump, and had given a great start.

This made Bassett very uneasy. "Confound it, he will turn you away. He will say, 'This girl knows too much.'"

"How simple you be!" said the girl. "D'ye think I let him know? Says he, 'I think I have seen you before.' 'Yes, sir,' says I, 'I was housemaid here before my lady had me to dress her.' 'No,' says he, 'I mean in London--in Mayfair, you know.' I declare you might ha' knocked me down wi' a feather. So I looks in his face, as cool as marble, and I said, 'No, sir; I never had the luck to see London, sir,' says I. 'All the better for you,' says he; and he swallowed it like spring water, as sister Rhoda used to say when she told one and they believed it."

"You are a clever girl," said Bassett. "He would have turned you out of the house if he had known who you were."

She disappointed him in one thing; she was bad at answering questions. Morally she was not quite so great an egotist as himself, but intellectually a greater. Her volubility was all egotism. She could scarcely say ten words, except about herself. So, when Bassett questioned her about Sir Charles and Lady Bassett, she said "Yes," or "No," or "I don't know," and was off at a tangent to her own sayings and doings.

Bassett, however, by great patience and tact, extracted from her at last that Sir Charles and Lady Bassett were both sore at not having children, and that Lady Bassett bore the blame.

"That is a good joke," said he. "The smoke-dried rake! Polly, you might do me a good turn. You have got her ear; open her eyes for me. What might not happen?" His eyes shone fiendishly.

The young woman shook her head. "Me meddle between man and wife! I'm too fond of my place."

"Ah, you don't love me as I love you. You think only of yourself."

"And what do you think of? Do you love me well enough to find me a better place, if you get me turned out of Huntercombe Hall?"

"Yes, I will; a much better."

"That is a bargain."

Mary Wells was silly in some things, but she was very cunning, too; and she knew Richard Bassett's hobby. She told him to mind himself, as well as Sir Charles, or perhaps he would die a bachelor, and so his flesh and blood would never inherit Huntercombe. This remark entered his mind. The trial, though apparently a drawn battle, had been fatal to him--he was cut; he dared not pay his addresses to any lady in the county, and he often felt very lonely now. So everything combined to draw him toward Mary Wells--her swarthy beauty, which shone out at church like a black diamond among the other women; his own loneliness; and the pleasure these stolen meetings gave him. Custom itself is pleasant, and the company of this handsome chatterbox became a habit, and an agreeable one. The young woman herself employed a woman's arts; she was cold and loving by turns till at last he gave her what she was working for, a downright promise of marriage. She pretended not to believe him, and so led him further; he swore he would marry her.

He made one stipulation, however. She really must learn to read and write first.

When he had sworn this Mary became more uniformly affectionate; and as women who have been in service learn great self-government, and can generally please so long as it serves their turn, she made herself so agreeable to him that he began really to have a downright liking for her--a liking bounded, of course, by his incurable selfishness; but as for his hobby, that was on her side.

Now learning to read and write was wormwood to Mary Wells; but the prize was so great; she knew all about the Huntercombe estates, partly from her sister, partly from Bassett himself. (He must tell his wrongs even to this girl.) So she resolved to pursue matrimony, even on the severe condition of becoming a scholar. She set about it as follows: One day that she was doing Lady Bassett's hair she sighed several times. This was to attract the lady's attention, and it succeeded.

"Is there anything the matter, Mary?"

"No, my lady."

"I think there is."

"Well, my lady, I am in a little trouble; but it is my own people's fault for not sending of me to school. I might be married to-morrow if I could only read and write."

"And can you not?"

"No, my lady."

"Dear me! I thought everybody could read and write nowadays."

"La, no, my lady! not half of them in our village."

"Your parents are much to blame, my poor girl. Well, but it is not too late. Now I think of it, there is an adult school in the village. Shall I arrange for you to go to it?"

"Thank you, my lady. But then--"

"Well?"

"All my fellow-servants would have a laugh against me."

"The person you are engaged to, will he not instruct you?"

"Oh, he have no time to teach me. Besides, I don't want him to know, either. But I won't be his wife to shame him." (Another sigh.)

"Mary," said Lady Bassett, in the innocence of her heart, "you shall not be mortified, and you shall not lose a good marriage. I will try and teach you myself."

Mary was profuse in thanks. Lady Bassett received them rather coldly. She gave her a few minutes' instruction in her dressing-room every day; and Mary, who could not have done anything intellectual for half an hour at a stretch, gave her whole mind for those few minutes. She was quick, and learned very fast. In two months she could read a great deal more than she could understand, and could write slowly but very clearly.

Now by this time Lady Bassett had become so interested in her pupil that she made her read letters and newspapers to her at those parts of the toilet when her services were not required.

Mary Wells, though a great chatterbox, was the closest girl in England. Limpet never stuck to a rock as she could stick to a lie. She never said one word to Bassett about Lady Bassett's lessons. She kept strict silence till she could write a letter, and then she sent him a line to say she had learned to write for love of him, and she hoped he would keep his promise.

Bassett's vanity was flattered by this. But, on reflection, he suspected it was a falsehood. He asked her suddenly, at their next meeting, who had written that note for her.

"You shall see me write the fellow to it when you like," was the reply.

Bassett resolved to submit the matter to that test some day. At present, however, he took her word for it, and asked her who had taught her.

"I had to teach myself. Nobody cares enough for me to teach me. Well, I'll forgive you if you will write me a nice letter for mine."

"What! when we can meet here and say everything?"

"No matter; I have written to you, and you might write to me. They all get letters, except me; and the jades hold 'em up to me: they see I never get one. When you are out, post me a letter now and then. It will only cost you a penny. I'm sure I don't ask you for much."

Bassett humored her in this, and in one of his letters called her his wife that was to be.

This pleased her so much that the next time they met she hung round his neck with a good deal of feminine grace.

Richard Bassett was a man who now lived in the future. Everybody in the county believed he had written that anonymous letter, and he had no hope of shining by his own light. It was bitter to resign his personal hopes; but he did, and sullenly resolved to be obscure himself, but the father of the future heirs of Huntercombe. He would marry Mary Wells, and lay the blame of the match upon Sir Charles, who had blackened him in the county, and put it out of his power to win a lady's hand.

He told Wheeler he was determined to marry; but he had not the courage to tell him all at once what a wife he had selected.

The consequence of this half confession was that Wheeler went to work to find him a girl with money, and not under county influence.

One of Wheeler's clients was a retired citizen, living in a pretty villa near the market town. Mr. Wright employed him in little matters, and found him active and attentive. There was a Miss Wright, a meek little girl, palish, on whom her father doted. Wheeler talked to this girl of his friend Bassett, his virtues and his wrongs, and interested the young lady in him. This done, he brought him to the house, and the girl, being slight and delicate, gazed with gentle but undisguised admiration on Bassett's *torso.* Wheeler had told Richard Miss Wright was to have seven thousand pounds on her wedding-day, and that excited a corresponding admiration in the athletic gentleman.

After that Bassett often called by himself, and the father encouraged the intimacy. He was old, and wished to see his daughter married before he left her and this seemed an eligible match, though not a brilliant one; a bit of land and a good name on one side, a smart bit of money on the other. The thing went on wheels. Richard Bassett was engaged to Jane Wright almost before he was aware.

Now he felt uneasy about Mary Wells, very uneasy; but it was only the uneasiness of selfishness.

He began to try and prepare; he affected business visits to distant places, etc., in order to break off by degrees. By this means their meetings were comparatively few. When they did meet (which was now generally by written appointment), he tried to prepare by telling her he had encountered losses, and feared that to marry her would be a bad job for her as well as for him, especially if she should have children.

Mary replied she had been used to work, and would rather work for a husband than any other master.

On another occasion she asked him quietly whether a gentleman ever broke his oath.

"Never," said Richard.

In short, she gave him no opening. She would not quarrel. She adhered to him as she had never adhered to anything but a lie before.

Then he gave up all hope of smoothing the matter. He coolly cut her; never came to the trysting-place; did not answer her letters; and, being a reckless egotist, married Jane Wright all in a hurry, by special license.

He sent forward to the clerk of Huntercombe church, and engaged the ringers to ring the church-bells from six o'clock till sundown. This was for Sir Charles's ears.

It was a balmy evening in May. Lady Bassett was commencing her toilet in an indolent way, with Mary Wells in attendance, when the church-bells of Huntercombe struck up a merry peal.

"Ah!" said Lady Bassett; "what is that for? Do you know, Mary?"

"No, my lady. Shall I ask?"

"No; I dare say it is a village wedding."

"No, my lady, there's nobody been married here this six weeks. Our kitchen-maid and the baker was the last, you know. I'll send, and know what it is for." Mary went out and dispatched the first house-maid she caught for intelligence. The girl ran into the stable to her sweetheart, and he told her directly.

Meantime Lady Bassett moralized upon church-bells.

"They are always sad--saddest when they seem to be merriest. Poor things! they are trying hard to be merry now; but they sound very sad to me--sadder than usual, somehow."

The girl knocked at the door. Mary half opened it, and the news shot in--"'Tis for Squire Bassett; he is bringing of his bride home to Highmore to-day."

"Mr. Bassett--married--that is sudden. Who could he find to marry him?" There was no reply. The house-maid had flown off to circulate the news, and Mary Wells was supporting herself by clutching the door, sick with the sudden blow.

Close as she was, her distress could not have escaped another woman's eye, but Lady Bassett never looked at her. After the first surprise she had gone into a reverie, and was conjuring up the future to the sound of those church-bells. She requested Mary to go and tell Sir Charles; but she did not lift her head, even to give this order.

Mary crept away, and knocked at Sir Charles's dressing-room.

"Come in," said Sir Charles, thinking, of course, it was his valet.

Mary Wells just opened the door and held it ajar. "My lady bids me tell you, sir, the bells are ringing for Mr. Bassett; he's married, and brings her home tonight."

A dead silence marked the effect of this announcement on Sir Charles. Mary Wells waited.

"May Heaven's curse light on that marriage, and no child of theirs ever take my place in this house!"

"A-a-men!" said Mary Wells.

"Thank you, sir!" said Sir Charles. He took her voice for a man's, so deep and guttural was her "A--a--men" with concentrated passion.

She closed the door and crept back to her mistress.

Lady Bassett was seated at her glass, with her hair down and her shoulders bare. Mary clinched her teeth, and set about her usual work; but very soon Lady

Bassett gave a start, and stared into the glass. "Mary!" said she, "what *is* the matter? You look ghastly, and your hands are as cold as ice. Are you faint?"

"No."

"Then you are ill; very ill."

"I have taken a chill," said Mary, doggedly.

"Go instantly to the still-room maid, and get a large glass of spirits and hot water--quite hot."

Mary, who wanted to be out of the room, fastened her mistress's back hair with dogged patience, and then moved toward the door.

"Mary," said Lady Bassett, in a half-apologetic tone.

"My lady."

"I should like to hear what the bride is like."

"I'll know that to-night," said Mary, grinding her teeth.

"I shall not require you again till bedtime."

Mary left the room, and went, not to the still-room, but to her own garret, and there she gave way. She flung herself, with a wild cry, upon her little bed, and clutched her own hair and the bedclothes, and writhed all about the bed like a wild-cat wounded.

In this anguish she passed an hour she never forgot nor forgave. She got up at last, and started at her own image in the glass. Hair like a savage's, cheek pale, eyes blood-shot.

She smoothed her hair, washed her face, and prepared to go downstairs; but now she was seized with a faintness, and had to sit down and moan. She got the better of that, and went to the still-room, and got some spirits; but she drank them neat, gulped them down like water. They sent the devil into her black eye, but no color into her pale cheek. She had a little scarlet shawl; she put it over her head, and went into the village. She found it astir with expectation.

Mr. Bassett's house stood near the highway, but the entrance to the premises was private, and through a long white gate.

By this gate was a heap of stones, and Mary Wells got on that heap and waited.

When she had been there about half an hour, Richard Bassett drove up in a hired carriage, with his pale little wife beside him. At his own gate his eye encountered Mary Wells, and he started. She stood above him, with her arms folded grandly; her cheek, so swarthy and ruddy, was now pale, and her black eyes glittered like basilisks at him and his bride. The whole woman seemed lifted out of her low condition, and dignified by wrong.

He had to sustain her look for a few seconds, while the gate was being opened, and it seemed an age. He felt his first pang of remorse when he saw that swarthy, ruddy cheek so pale. Then came admiration of her beauty, and disgust at the woman for whom he had jilted her; and that gave way to fear: the hater looked into those glittering eyes, and saw he had roused a hate as unrelenting as his own.

CHAPTER XIII.

FOR the first few days Richard Bassett expected some annoyance from Mary Wells; but none came, and he began to flatter himself she was too fond of him to give him pain.

This impression was shaken about ten days after the little scene I have described. He received a short note from her, as follows:

"SIR--You must meet me to-night, at the same place, eight o'clock. If you do not come it will be the worse for you.

"M. W."

Richard Bassett's inclination was to treat this summons with contempt; but he thought it would be wiser to go and see whether the girl had any hostile intentions. Accordingly he went to the tryst. He waited for some time, and at last he heard a quick, firm foot, and Mary Wells appeared. She was hooded with her scarlet shawl, that contrasted admirably with her coal-black hair; and out of this scarlet frame her dark eyes glittered. She stood before him in silence.

He said nothing.

She was silent too for some time. But she spoke first.

"Well, sir, you promised one, and you have married another. Now what are you going to do for me?"

"What *can* I do, Mary? I'm not the first that wanted to marry for love, but money came in his way and tempted him."

"No, you are not the first. But that's neither here nor there, sir. That chalk-faced girl has bought you away from me with her money, and now I mean to have my share on't."

"Oh, if that is all," said Richard, "we can soon settle it. I was afraid you were going to talk about a broken heart, and all that stuff. You are a good, sensible girl;

and too beautiful to want a husband long. I'll give you fifty pounds to forgive me."

"Fifty pounds!" said Mary Wells, contemptuously. "What! when you promised me I should be your wife to-day, and lady of Huntercombe Hall by-and-by? Fifty pounds! No; not five fifties."

"Well, I'll give you seventy-five; and if that won't do, you must go to law, and see what you can get."

"What, han't you had your bellyful of law? Mind, it is an unked thing to for-swear yourself, and that is what you done at the 'sizes. I have seen what you did swear about your letter to my sister; Sir Charles have got it all wrote down in his study: and you swore a lie to the judge, as you swore a lie to me here under heaven, you villain!" She raised her voice very loud. "Don't you gainsay me, or I'll soon have you by the heels in jail for your lies. You'll do as I bid you, and very lucky to be let off so cheap. You was to be my master, but you chose her instead: well, then, you shall be my servant. You shall come here every Saturday at eight o'clock, and bring me a sovereign, which I never could keep a lump o' money, and I have had one or two from Rhoda; so I'll take it a sovereign a week till I get a husband of my own sort, and then you'll have to come down handsome once for all."

Bassett knitted his brows and thought hard. His natural impulse was to defy her; but it struck him that a great many things might happen in a few months; so at last he said, humbly, "I consent. I have been to blame. Only I'd rather pay you this money in some other way."

"My way, or none."

"Very well, then, I will bring it you as you say."

"Mind you do, then," said Mary Wells, and turned haughtily on her heel.

Bassett never ventured to absent himself at the hour, and, at first, the blackmail was delivered and received with scarcely a word; but by-and-by old habits so far revived that some little conversation took place.

Then, after a while, Bassett used to tell her he was unhappy, and she used to reply she was glad of it.

Then he began to speak slightingly of his wife, and say what a fool he had been to marry a poor, silly nonentity, when he might have wedded a beauty.

Mary Wells, being intensely vain, listened with complacency to this, although she replied coldly and harshly.

By-and-by her natural volubility overpowered her, and she talked to Bassett about herself and Huntercombe House, but always with a secret reserve.

Later--such is the force of habit--each used to look forward with satisfaction to the Saturday meeting, although each distrusted and feared the other at bottom.

Later still that came to pass which Mary Wells had planned from the first with deep malice, and that shrewd insight into human nature which many a low woman has--the cooler she was the warmer did Richard Bassett grow, till at last, contrasting his pale, meek little wife with this glowing Hebe, he conceived an unholy liking for the latter. She met it sometimes with coldness and reproaches, sometimes with affected alarm, sometimes with a half-yielding manner, and so tormented him to her heart's content, and undermined his affection for his wife. Thus she revenged herself on them both to her heart's content.

But malice so perverse is apt to recoil on itself; and women, in particular, should not undertake a long and subtle revenge of this sort; since the strongest have their hours of weakness, and are surprised into things they never intended. The subsequent history of Mary Wells will exemplify this. Meantime, however, meek little Mrs. Bassett was no match for the beauty and low cunning of her rival.

Yet a time came when she defended herself unconsciously. She did something that made her husband most solicitous for her welfare and happiness. He began to watch her health with maternal care, to shield her from draughts, to take care of her diet, to indulge her in all her whims instead of snubbing her, and to pet her, till she was the happiest wife in England for a time. She deserved this at his hands, for she assisted him there where his heart was fixed; she aided his hobby; did more for it than any other creature in England could.

To return to Huntercombe Hall: the loving couple that owned it were no longer happy. The hope of offspring was now deserting them, and the disappointment was cruel. They suffered deeply, with this difference--that Lady Bassett pined and Sir Charles Bassett fretted.

The woman's grief was more pure and profound than the man's. If there had been no Richard Bassett in the world, still her bosom would have yearned and pined, and the great cry of Nature, "Give me children or I die," would have been in her heart, though it would never have risen to her lips.

Sir Charles had, of course, less of this profound instinct than his wife, but he had it too; only in him the feeling was adulterated and at the same time imbittered by one less simple and noble. An enemy sat at his gate. That enemy, whose enduring malice had at last begotten equal hostility in the childless baronet, was now married, and would probably have heirs; and, if so, that hateful brood--the spawn of an anonymous letter-writer--would surely inherit Bassett and Huntercombe, succeeding to Sir Charles Bassett, deceased without issue. This chafed the childless man, and gradually undermined a temper habitually sweet, though subject, as we have seen, to violent ebullitions where the provocation was intolerable. Sir Charles, then, smarting under his wound, spoke now and then rather unkindly to the wife he loved so devotedly; that is to say, his manner sometimes implied that he blamed her for their joint calamity.

Lady Bassett submitted to these stings in silence. They were rare, and speedily followed by touching regrets; and even had it not been so she would have borne them with resignation; for this motherless wife loved her husband with all a wife's devotion and a mother's unselfish patience. Let this be remembered to her credit. It is the truth, and she may need it.

Her own yearning was too deep and sad for fretfulness; yet though, unlike her husband's, it never broke out in anger, the day was gone by when she could keep it always silent. It welled out of her at times in ways that were truly womanly and touching.

When she called on a wife the lady was sure to parade her children. The boasted tact of women--a quality the narrow compass of which has escaped their undiscriminating eulogists--was sure to be swept away by maternal egotism; and then poor Lady Bassett would admire the children loudly, and kiss them, to please the cruel egotist, and hide the tears that rose to her own eyes; but she would shorten her visit.

When a child died in the village Mary Wells was sure to be sent with words of comfort and substantial marks of sympathy.

Scarcely a day passed that something or other did not happen to make the wound bleed; but I will confine myself to two occasions, on each of which her heart's agony spoke out, and so revealed how much it must have endured in silence.

Since the day when Sir Charles allowed her to sit in a little room close to his study while he received Mr. Wheeler's visit she had fitted up that room, and often sat there to be near Sir Charles; and he would sometimes call her in and tell her his justice cases. One day she was there when the constable brought in a prisoner and several witnesses. The accused was a stout, florid girl, with plump cheeks and pale gray eyes. She seemed all health, stupidity, and simplicity. She carried a child on her left arm. No dweller in cities could suspect this face of crime. As well indict a calf.

Yet the witnesses proved beyond a doubt that she had been seen with her baby in the neighborhood of a certain old well on a certain day at noon; that soon after noon she had been seen on the road without her baby, and being asked what had become of it, had said she had left it with her aunt, ten miles off; and that about an hour after that a faint cry had been heard at the bottom of the old well--it was ninety feet deep; people had assembled, and a brave farmer's boy had been lowered in the bight of a cart-rope, and had brought up a dead hen, and a live child, bleeding at the cheek, having fallen on a heap of fagots at the bottom of the well; which child was the prisoner's.

Sir Charles had the evidence written down, and then told the accused she might make a counter-statement if she chose, but it would be wiser to say nothing at all.

Thereupon the accused dropped him a little short courtesy, looked him steadily in the face with her pale gray eyes, and delivered herself as follows:

"If you please, sir, I was a-sitting by th' old well, with baby in my arms; and I was mortal tired, I was, wi' carring of him; he be uncommon heavy for his age; and, if you please, sir, he is uncommon resolute; and while I was so he give a leap right out of my arms and fell down th' old well. I screams, and runs away to tell my brother's wife, as lives at top of the hill; but she was gone into North Wood for dry sticks to light her oven; and when I comes back they had got him out of the well, and I claims him directly; and the constable said we must come before you, sir; so here we be."

This she delivered very glibly, without tremulousness, hesitation, or the shadow of a blush, and dropped another little courtesy at the end to Sir Charles.

Thereupon he said not one word to her, but committed her for trial, and gave the farmer's boy a sovereign.

The people were no sooner gone than Lady Bassett came in, with the tears streaming, and threw herself at her husband's knees. "Oh, Charles! can such things be? Does God give a child to a woman that has the heart to kill it, and refuse one to me, who would give my heart's blood to save a hair of its little head? Oh, what have we done that he singles us out to be so cruel to us?"

Then Sir Charles tried to comfort her, but could not, and the childless ones wept together.

It began to be whispered that Mrs. Bassett was in the family way. Neither Sir Charles nor Lady Bassett mentioned this rumor. It would have been like rubbing vitriol into their own wounds. But this reserve was broken through one day. It was a sunny afternoon in June, just thirteen months after Mr. Bassett's wedding--Lady Bassett was with her husband in his study, settling invitations for a ball, and writing them--when the church-bells struck up a merry peal. They both left off, and looked at each other eloquently. Lady Bassett went out, but soon returned, looking pale and wild.

"Yes!" said she, with forced calmness. Then, suddenly losing her self-command, she broke out, pointing through the window at Highmore, *"He* has got a fine boy--to take our place here. Kill me, Charles! Send me to heaven to pray for you, and take another wife that will love you less but be like other wives. That villain has married a fruitful vine, and" (lifting both arms to heaven, with a gesture unspeakably piteous, poetic, and touching) "I am a barren stock."

CHAPTER XIV.

OF all the fools Nature produces with the help of Society, fathers of first-borns are about the most offensive.

The mothers of ditto are bores too, flinging their human dumplings at every head; but, considering the tortures they have suffered, and the anguish the little egotistical viper they have just hatched will most likely give them, and considering further that their love of their firstborn is greater than their pride, and their pride unstained by vanity, one must make allowances for them.

But the male parent is not so excusable. His fussy vanity is an inferior article to the mother's silly but amiable pride. His obtrusive affection is two-thirds of it egotism, and blindish egotism, too; for if, at the very commencement of the wife's pregnancy the husband is sent to India, or hanged, the little angel, as they call it--Lord forgive them!--is nurtured from a speck to a mature infant by the other parent, and finally brought into the world by her just as effectually as if her male confederate had been tied to her apron-string: all the time, instead of expatriated or hanged.

Therefore the Law--for want, I suppose, of studying Medicine--is a little inconsiderate in giving children to fathers, and taking them by force from such mothers *as can support them;* and therefore let Gallina go on clucking over her firstborn, but Gallus be quiet, or sing a little smaller.

With these preliminary remarks, let me introduce to you a character new in fiction, but terribly old in history--

THE CLUCKING COCK.

Upon the birth of a son and heir Mr. Richard Bassett was inflated almost to bursting. He became suddenly hospitable, collected all his few friends about him, and showed them all the Boy at great length, and talked Boy and little else. He went out into the world and made calls on people merely to remind them he had a son and heir.

His self-gratulation took a dozen forms; perhaps the most amusing, and the richest food for satire, was the mock-querulous style, of which he showed himself a master.

"Don't you ever marry," said he to Wheeler and others. "Look at me; do you think I am the master of my own house? Not I; I am a regular slave. First, there is a monthly nurse, who orders me out of my wife's presence, or graciously lets me in, just as she pleases; that is Queen 1. Then there's a wet-nurse, Queen 2, whom I must humor in everything, or she will quarrel with me, and avenge herself by souring her milk. But these are mild tyrants compared with the young King himself. If he does but squall we must all skip, and find out what he ails, or what he wants. As for me, I am looked upon as a necessary evil; the women seem to admit that a father is an incumbrance without which these little angels could not exist, but that is all."

He had a christening feast, and it was pretty well attended, for he reminded all he asked that the young Christian was the heir to the Bassett estates. They feasted, and the church-bells rang merrily.

He had his pew in the church new lined with cloth, and took his wife to be churched. The nurse was in the pew too, with his son and heir. It squalled and spoiled the Liturgy. Thereat Gallus chuckled.

He made a gravel-walk all along the ha-ha that separated his garden from Sir Charles's, and called it "The Heir's Walk." Here the nurse and child used to parade on sunny afternoons.

He got an army of workmen, and built a nursery fit for a duke's nine children. It occupied two entire stories, and rose in the form of a square tower high above the rest of his house, which, indeed, was as humble as "The Heir's Tower" was pretentious. "The Heir's Tower" had a flat lead roof easy of access, and from it you could inspect Huntercombe Hall, and see what was done on the lawn or at some of the windows.

Here, in the August afternoons, Mr. and Mrs. Bassett used to sit drinking their tea, with nurse and child; and Bassett would talk to his unconscious boy, and tell him that the great house and all that belonged to it should be his in spite of the arts that had been used to rob him of it.

Now, of course, the greater part of all this gratulation was merely amusing, and did no harm except stirring up the bile of a few old bachelors, and imbittering them worse than ever against clucking cocks, crowing hens, inflated parents, and matrimony in general.

But the overflow of it reached Huntercombe Hall, and gave cruel pain to the childless ones, over whom this inflated father was, in fact, exulting.

As for the christening, and the bells that pealed for it, and the subsequent churching, they bore these things with sore hearts, and bravely, being things of course. But when it came to their ears that Bassett and his family called his new gravel-walk "The Heir's Walk," and his ridiculous nursery "The Heir's Tower," this roused a bitter animosity, and, indeed, led to reprisals. Sir Charles built a long wall at the edge of his garden, shutting out "The Heir's Walk" and intercepting the view of his own premises from that walk.

Then Mr. Bassett made a little hill at the end of his walk, so that the heir might get one peep over the wall at his rich inheritance.

Then Sir Charles began to fell timber on a gigantic scale. He went to work with several gangs of woodmen, and all his woods, which were very extensive, rang with the ax, and the trees fell like corn. He made no secret that he was going to sell timber to the tune of several thousand pounds and settle it on his wife.

Then Richard Bassett, through Wheeler, his attorney, remonstrated in his own name, and that of his son, against this excessive fall of timber on an entailed estate.

Sir Charles chafed like a lion stung by a gad-fly, but vouchsafed no reply: the answer came from Mr. Oldfield; he said Sir Charles had a right under the entail to fell every stick of timber, and turn his woods into arable ground, if he chose; and even if he had not, looking at his age and his wife's, it was extremely improbable that Richard Bassett would inherit the estates: the said Richard Bassett was not personally named in the entail, and his rights were all in supposition: if Mr. Wheeler thought he could dispute both these positions, the Court of Chancery was open to his client.

Then Wheeler advised Bassett to avoid the Court of Chancery in a matter so debatable; and Sir Charles felled all the more for the protest. The dead bodies of the trees fell across each other, and daylight peeped through the thick woods. It was like the clearing of a primeval forest.

Richard Bassett went about with a witness and counted the fallen.

The poor were allowed the lopwood: they thronged in for miles round, and each built himself a great wood pile for the winter; the poor blessed Sir Charles: he gave the proceeds, thirteen thousand pounds, to his wife for her separate use. He did not tie it up. He restricted her no further than this: she undertook never to draw above 100 pounds at a time without consulting Mr. Oldfield as to the application. Sir Charles said he should add to this fund every year; his beloved wife should not be poor, even if the hated cousin should outlive him and turn her out of Huntercombe.

And so passed the summer of that year; then the autumn; and then came a singularly mild winter. There was more hunting than usual, and Richard Bassett, whom his wife's fortune enabled to cut a better figure than before, was often in the field, mounted on a great bony horse that was not so fast as some, being half-bred, but a wonderful jumper.

Even in this pastime the cousins were rivals. Sir Charles's favorite horse was a magnificent thoroughbred, who was seldom far off at the finish: over good ground Richard's cocktail had no chance with him; but sometimes, if toward the close of the run they came to stiff fallows and strong fences, the great strength of the inferior animal, and that prudent reserve of his powers which distinguishes the canny cocktail from the higher-blooded animal, would give him the advantage.

Of this there occurred, on a certain 18th of November, an example fraught with very serious consequences.

That day the hounds met on Sir Charles's estate. Sir Charles and Lady Bassett breakfasted in Pink; he had on his scarlet coat, white tie, irreproachable buckskins, and top-boots. (It seemed a pity a speck of dirt should fall on them.) Lady Bassett was in her riding-habit; and when she mounted her pony, and went to cover by his side, with her blue-velvet cap and her red-brown hair, she looked more like a brilliant flower than a mere woman.

A veteran fox was soon found, and went away with unusual courage and speed, and Lady Bassett paced homeward to wait her lord's return, with an anxiety men laugh at, but women can appreciate. It was a form of quiet suffering she had constantly endured, and never complained, nor even mentioned the subject to Sir Charles but once, and then he pooh-poohed her fancies.

The hunt had a burst of about forty minutes that left Richard Bassett's cocktail in the rear; and the fox got into a large beech wood with plenty of briars, and kept dodging about it for two hours, and puzzled the scent repeatedly.

Richard Bassett elected not to go winding in and out among trees, risk his horse's legs in rabbit-holes, and tire him for nothing. He had kept for years a little note book he called "Statistics of Foxes," and that told him an old dog-fox of uncommon strength, if dislodged from that particular wood, would slip into Bellman's Coppice, and if driven out of that would face the music again, would take the open country for Higham Gorse, and probably be killed before he got there; but once there a regiment of scythes might cut him out, but bleeding, sneezing fox-hounds would never work him out at the tail of a long run.

So Richard Bassett kept out of the wood, and went gently on to Bellman's Coppice and waited outside.

His book proved an oracle. After two hours' dodging and maneuvering the fox came out at the very end of Bellman's Coppice, with nothing near him but Richard Bassett. Pug gave him the white of his eye in an ugly leer, and headed straight as a crow for Higham Gorse.

Richard Bassett blew his horn, collected the hunt, and laid the dogs on. Away they went, close together, thunder-mouthed on the hot scent.

After a three miles' gallop they sighted the fox for a moment just going over the crest of a rising ground two furlongs off. Then the hullabbaloo and excitement grew furious, and one electric fury animated dogs, men, and horses. Another mile, and the fox ran in sight scarcely a furlong off; but many of the horses were distressed: the Bassetts, however, kept up, one by his horse being fresh, the other by his animal's native courage and speed.

Then came some meadows, bounded by a thick hedge, and succeeded by a plowed field of unusual size--eighty acres.

When the fox darted into this hedge the hounds were yelling at his heels; the hunt burst through the thin fence, expecting to see them kill close to it.

But the wily fox had other resources at his command than speed. Appreciating his peril, he doubled and ran sixty yards down the ditch, and the impetuous hounds rushed forward and overran the scent. They raved about to and fro, till at last one of the gentlemen descried the fox running down a double furrow in the middle of the field. He had got into this, and so made his way more smoothly than his four-footed pursuers could. The dogs were laid on, and away they went helter-skelter.

At the end of this stiff ground a stiffish leap awaited them; an old quickset had been cut down, and all the elm-trees that grew in it, and a new quickset hedge set on a high bank with double ditches.

The huntsman had an Irish horse that laughed at this fence; he jumped on to the bank, and then jumped off it into the next field.

Richard Bassett's cocktail came up slowly, rose high, and landed his forefeet in the field, and so scrambled on.

Sir Charles went at it rather rashly; his horse, tried hard by the fallow, caught his heels against the edge of the bank, and went headlong into the other ditch, throwing Sir Charles over his head into the field. Unluckily some of the trees were lying about, and Sir Charles's head struck one of these in falling; the horse blundered out again, and galloped after the hounds, but the rider lay there motionless.

Nobody stopped at first; the pace was too good to inquire; but presently Richard Bassett, who had greeted the accident with a laugh, turned round in his saddle, and saw his cousin motionless, and two or three gentlemen dismounting at the place. These were newcomers. Then he resigned the hunt, and rode back.

Sir Charles's cap was crushed in, and there was blood on his white waistcoat; he was very pale, and quite insensible.

The gentlemen raised him, with expressions of alarm and kindly concern, and inquired of each other what was best to be done.

Richard Bassett saw an opportunity to conciliate opinion, and seized it. "He must be taken home directly," said he. "We must carry him to that farmhouse, and get a cart for him."

He helped carry him accordingly. The farmer lent them a cart, with straw, and they laid the insensible baronet gently on it, Richard Bassett supporting his head. "Gentlemen," said he, rather pompously, "at such a moment everything but the tie of kindred is forgotten." Which resounding sentiment was warmly applauded by the honest squires.

They took him slowly and carefully toward Huntercombe, distant about two miles from the scene of the accident.

This 18th November Lady Bassett passed much as usual with her on hunting days. She was quietly patient till the afternoon, and then restless, and could not settle down in any part of the house till she got to a little room on the first floor, with a bay-window commanding the country over which Sir Charles was hunting. In this she sat, with her head against one of the mullions, and eyed the country-side as far as she could see.

Presently she heard a rustle, and there was Mary Wells standing and looking at her with evident emotion.

"What is the matter, Mary?" said Lady Bassett.

"Oh, my lady!" said Mary. And she trembled, and her hands worked.

Lady Bassett started up with alarm painted in her countenance.

"My lady, there's something wrong in the hunting field."

"Sir Charles!"

"An accident, they say."

Lady Bassett put her hand to her heart with a faint cry. Mary Wells ran to her.

"Come with me directly!" cried Lady Bassett. She snatched up her bonnet, and in another minute she and Mary Wells were on their road to the village, questioning every body they met.

But nobody they questioned could tell them anything. The stable-boy, who had told the report in the kitchen of Huntercombe, said he had it from a gentleman's groom, riding by as he stood at the gates.

The ill news thus flung in at the gate by one passing rapidly by was not confirmed by any further report, and Lady Bassett began to hope it was false.

But a terrible confirmation came at last.

In the outskirts of the village mistress and servant encountered a sorrowful procession: the cart itself, followed by five gentlemen on horseback, pacing slowly, and downcast as at a funeral.

In the cart Sir Charles Bassett, splashed all over with mud, and his white waistcoat bloody, lay with his head upon Richard Bassett's knee. His hair was wet with blood, some of which had trickled down his cheek and dried. Even Richard's buckskins were slightly stained with it.

At that sight Lady Bassett uttered a scream, which those who heard it never forgot, and flung herself, Heaven knows how, into the cart; but she got there, and soon had that bleeding head on her bosom. She took no notice of Richard Bassett, but she got Sir Charles away from him, and the cart took her, embracing him tenderly, and kissing his hurt head, and moaning over him, all through the village to Huntercombe Hall.

Four years ago they passed through the same village in a carriage-and-four--bells pealing, rustics shouting--to take possession of Huntercombe, and fill it with pledges of their great and happy love; and as they flashed past the heir at law shrank hopeless into his little cottage. Now, how changed the pageant!--a farmer's cart, a splashed and bleeding and senseless form in it, supported by a childless, despairing woman, one weeping attendant walking at the side, and, among the gentlemen pacing slowly behind, the heir at law, with his head lowered in that decent affectation of regret which all heirs can put on to hide the indecent complacency within.

CHAPTER XV.

A T the steps of Huntercombe Hall the servants streamed out, and relieved the strangers of the sorrowful load. Sir Charles was carried into the Hall, and Richard Bassett turned away, with one triumphant flash of his eye, quickly suppressed, and walked with impenetrable countenance and studied demeanor into Highmore House.

Even here he did not throw off the mask. It peeled off by degrees. He began by telling his wife, gravely enough, Sir Charles had met with a severe fall, and he had attended to him and taken him home.

"Ah, I am glad you did that, Richard," said Mrs. Bassett. "And is he very badly hurt?"

"I am afraid he will hardly get over it. He never spoke. He just groaned when they took him down from the cart at Huntercombe."

"Poor Lady Bassett!"

"Ay, it will be a bad job for her. Jane!"

"Yes, dear."

"There is a providence in it. The fall would never have killed him; but his head struck a tree upon the ground; and that tree was one of the very elms he had just cut down to rob our boy."

"Indeed?"

"Yes; he was felling the very hedgerow timber, and this was one of the old elms in a hedge. He must have done it out of spite, for elm-wood fetches no price; it is good for nothing I know of, except coffins. Well, he has cut down *his.*"

"Poor man! Richard, death reconciles enemies. Surely you can forgive him now."

"I mean to try."

Richard Bassett seemed now to have imbibed the spirit of quicksilver. His occupations were not actually enlarged, yet, somehow or other, he seemed full of business. He was all complacent bustle about nothing. He left off inveighing against Sir Charles. And, indeed, if you are one of those weak spirits to whom censure is intolerable, there is a cheap and easy way to moderate the rancor of detraction--you have only to die. Let me comfort genius in particular with this little recipe.

Why, on one occasion, Bassett actually snubbed Wheeler for a mere allusion. That worthy just happened to remark, "No more felling of timber on Bassett Manor for a while."

"For shame!" said Richard. "The man had his faults, but he had his good qualities too: a high-spirited gentleman, beloved by his friends and respected by all the county. His successor will find it hard to reconcile the county to his loss."

Wheeler stared, and then grinned satirically.

This eulogy was never repeated, for Sir Charles proved ungrateful--he omitted to die, after all.

Attended by first-rate physicians, tenderly nursed and watched by Lady Bassett and Mary Wells, he got better by degrees; and every stage of his slow but hopeful progress was communicated to the servants and the village, and to the ladies and gentlemen who rode up to the door every day and left their cards of inquiry.

The most attentive of all these was the new rector, a young clergyman, who had obtained the living by exchange. He was a man highly gifted both in body and mind--a swarthy Adonis, whose large dark eyes from the very first turned with glowing admiration on the blonde beauties of Lady Bassett.

He came every day to inquire after her husband; and she sometimes left the sufferer a minute or two to make her report to him in person. At other times Mary Wells was sent to him. That artful girl soon discovered what had escaped her mistress's observation.

The bulletins were favorable, and welcomed on all sides.

Richard Bassett alone was incredulous. "I want to see him about again," said he. "Sir Charles is not the man to lie in bed if he was really better. As for the doctors, they flatter a fellow till the last moment. Let me see him on his legs, and then I'll believe he is better."

Strange to say, obliging Fate granted Richard Bassett this moderate request.

One frosty but sunny afternoon, as he was inspecting his coming domain from "The Heir's Tower," he saw the Hall door open, and a muffled figure come slowly down the steps between two women: It was Sir Charles, feeble but convalescent. He crept about on the sunny gravel for about ten minutes, and then his nurses conveyed him tenderly in again.

This sight, which might have touched with pity a more generous nature, startled Richard Bassett, and then moved his bile. "I was a fool," said he; "nothing will ever kill that man. He will see me out; see us all out. And that Mary Wells nurses him, and I dare say in love with him by this time; the fools can't nurse a man without. Curse the whole pack of ye!" he yelled, and turned away in rage and disgust.

That same night he met Mary Wells, and, in a strange fit of jealousy, began to make hot protestations of love to her. He knew it was no use reproaching her, so he went on the other tack.

She received his vows with cool complacency, but would only stay a minute, and would only talk of her master and mistress, toward whom her heart was really warming in their trouble. She spoke hopefully, and said: "'Tisn't as if he was one of your faint-hearted ones as meet death half-way. Why, the second day, when he could scarce speak, he sees me crying by the bed, and says he, almost in a whisper, 'What are *you* crying for?' 'Sir,' says I, ''tis for you--to see you lie like a ghost.' 'Then you be wasting of salt-water,' says he. 'I wish I may, sir,' says I. So then he raised himself up a little bit. 'Look at me,' says he; 'I'm a Bassett. I am not the breed to die for a crack on the skull, and leave you all to the mercy of them that would have no mercy'--which he meant you, I suppose. So he ordered me to leave crying, which I behooved to obey; for he will be master, mind ye, while he have a finger to wag, poor dear gentleman, he will."

And, soon after this, she resisted all his attempts to detain her, and scudded back to the house, leaving Bassett to his reflections, which were exceedingly bitter.

Sir Charles got better, and at last used to walk daily with Lady Bassett. Their favorite stroll was up and down the lawn, close under the boundary wall he had built to shut out "The Heir's Walk."

The afternoon sun struck warm upon that wall and the walk by its side.

On the other side a nurse often carried little Dicky Bassett, the heir; but neither of the promenaders could see each other for the wall.

Richard Bassett, on the contrary, from "The Heir's Tower," could see both these little parties; and, as some men cannot keep away from what causes their pain, he used to watch these loving walks, and see Sir Charles get stronger and stronger, till at last, instead of leaning on his beloved wife, he could march by her side, or even give her his arm.

Yet the picture was, in a great degree, delusive; for, except during these blissful walks, when the sun shone on him, and Love and Beauty soothed him, Sir Charles was not the man he had been. The shake he had received appeared to have damaged his temper strangely. He became so irritable that several of his servants left him; and to his wife he repined; and his childless condition, which had been hitherto only a deep disappointment, became in his eyes a calamity that outweighed his many blessings. He had now narrowly escaped dying without an heir, and this seemed to sink into his mind, and, co-operating with the concussion his brain had received, brought him into a morbid state. He brooded on it, and spoke of it, and got back to it from every other topic, in a way that distressed Lady Bassett unspeakably. She consoled him bravely; but often, when she was alone, her gentle courage gave way, and she cried bitterly to herself.

Her distress had one effect she little expected; it completed what her invariable kindness had begun, and actually won the heart of a servant. Those who really know that tribe will agree with me that this was a marvelous conquest. Yet so it was; Mary Wells conceived for her a real affection, and showed it by unremitting attention, and a soft and tender voice, that soothed Lady Bassett, and drew many a silent but grateful glance from her dove-like eyes.

Mary listened, and heard enough to blame Sir Charles for his peevishness, and she began to throw out little expressions of dissatisfaction at him; but these were so promptly discouraged by the faithful wife that she drew in again and avoided that line. But one day, coming softly as a cat, she heard Sir Charles and Lady Bassett talking over their calamity. Sir Charles was saying that it was Heaven's curse; that all the poor people in the village had children; that Richard Bassett's weak, puny little wife had brought him an heir, and was about to make him a parent again; he alone was marked out and doomed to be the last of his race. "And yet," said he, "if I had married any other woman, and you had married any other man, we should have had children by the dozen, I suppose."

Upon the whole, though he said nothing palpably unjust, he had the tone of a man blaming his wife as the real cause of their joint calamity, under which she suffered a deeper, nobler, and more silent anguish than himself. This was hard to bear; and when Sir Charles went away, Mary Wells ran in, with an angry expression on the tip of her tongue.

She found Lady Bassett in a pitiable condition, lying rather than leaning on the table, with her hair loose about her, sobbing as if her heart would break.

All that was good in Mary Wells tugged at her heart-strings. She flung herself on her knees beside her, and seizing her mistress's hand, and drawing it to her bosom, fell to crying and sobbing along with her.

This canine devotion took Lady Bassett by surprise. She turned her tearful eyes upon her sympathizing servant, and said, "Oh, Mary!" and her soft hand pressed the girl's harder palm gratefully.

Mary spoke first. "Oh, my lady," she sobbed, "it breaks my heart to see you so. And what a shame to blame you for what is no fault of yourn. If I was your husband the cradles would soon be full in this house; but these fine gentlemen, they be old before their time with smoking of tobacco; and then to come and lay the blame on we!"

"Mary, I value you very much--more than I ever did a servant in my life; but if you speak against your master we shall part."

"La, my lady, I wouldn't for the world. Sir Charles is a perfect gentleman. Why, he gave me a sovereign only the other day for nursing of him; but he didn't ought to blame you for no fault of yourn, and to make you cry. It tears me inside out to see you cry; you that is so good to rich and poor. I wouldn't vex myself so for that: dear heart, 'twas always so; God sends meat to one house, and mouths to another."

"I could be patient if poor Sir Charles was not so unhappy," sighed Lady Bassett; "but if ever you are a wife, Mary, you will know how wretched it makes us to see a beloved husband unhappy."

"Then I'd make him happy," said Mary.

"Ah, if I only could!"

"Oh, I could tell you a way; for I have known it done; and now he is as happy as a prince. You see, my lady, some men are like children; to make them happy you must give them their own way; and so, if I was in your place, I wouldn't make two bites of a cherry, for sometimes I think he will fret himself out of the world for want on't."

"Heaven forbid!"

"It is my belief you would not be long behind him."

"No, Mary. Why should I?"

"Then--whisper, my lady!"

And, although Lady Bassett drew slightly back at this freedom, Mary Wells poured into her ear a proposal that made her stare and shiver.

As for the girl's own face, it was as unmoved as if it had been bronze.

Lady Bassett drew back, and eyed her askant with amazement and terror.

"What is this you have dared to say?"

"Why, it is done every day."

"By people of your class, perhaps. No; I don't believe it. Mary, I have been mistaken in you. I am afraid you are a vicious girl. Leave me, please. I can't bear the sight of you."

Mary went away, very red, and the tear in her eye.

In the evening Lady Bassett gave Mary Wells a month's warning, and Mary accepted it doggedly, and thought herself very cruelly used.

After this mistress and maid did not exchange an unnecessary word for many days.

This notice to leave was very bitter to Mary Wells, for she was in the very act of making a conquest. Young Drake, a very small farmer and tenant of Sir Charles, had fallen in love with her, and she liked him and had resolved he should marry her, with which view she was playing the tender but coy maiden very prettily. But Drake, though young and very much in love, was advised by his mother, and evidently resolved to go the old-fashioned way--keep company a year, and know the girl before offering the ring.

Just before her month was out a more serious trouble threatened Mary Wells.

Her low, artful amour with Richard Bassett had led to its natural results. By degrees she had gone further than she intended, and now the fatal consequences looked her in the face.

She found herself in an odious position; for her growing regard for young

Drake, though not a violent attachment, was enough to set her more and more against Richard Bassett, and she was preparing an entire separation from the latter when the fatal truth dawned on her.

Then there was a temporary revulsion of feeling; she told her condition to Bassett, and implored him, with many tears, to aid her to disappear for a time and hide her misfortune, especially from her sister.

Mr. Bassett heard her, and then gave her an answer that made her blood run cold. "Why do you come to me?" said he. "Why don't you go to the right man--young Drake?"

He then told her he had had her watched, and she must not think to make a fool of him. She was as intimate with the young farmer as with him, and was in his company every day.

Mary Wells admitted that Drake was courting her, but said he was a civil, respectful young man, who desired to make her his wife. "You have lost me that," said she, bursting into tears; "and so, for God's sake, show yourself a man for once, and see me through my trouble."

The egotist disbelieved, or affected not to believe her, and said, "When there are two it is always the gentleman you girls deceive. But you can't make a fool of me, Mrs. Drake. Marry the farmer, and I'll give you a wedding present; that is all I can do for any other man's sweetheart. I have got my own family to provide for, and it is all I can contrive to make both ends meet."

He was cold and inflexible to her prayers. Then she tried threats. He laughed at them. Said he, "The time is gone by for that: if you wanted to sue me for breach of promise, you should have done it at once; not waited eighteen months and taken another sweetheart first. Come, come; you played your little game. You made me come here week after week and bleed a sovereign. A woman that loved a man would never have been so hard on him as you were on me. I grinned and bore it; but when you ask me to own another man's child, a man of your own sort that you are in love with--you hate me--that is a little too much: no, Mrs. Drake; if that is your game we will fight it out--before the public if you like." And, having delivered this with a tone of harsh and loud defiance, he left her--left her forever. She sat down upon the cold ground and rocked herself. Despair was cold at her heart.

She sat in that forlorn state for more than an hour. Then she got up and went to her mistress's room and sat by the fire, for her limbs were cold as well as her heart.

She sat there, gazing at the fire and sighing heavily, till Lady Bassett came up to bed. She then went through her work like an automaton, and every now and then a deep sigh came from her breast.

Lady Bassett heard her sigh, and looked at her. Her face was altered; a sort of sullen misery was written on it. Lady Bassett was quick at reading faces, and this look alarmed her. "Mary," said she, kindly, "is there anything the matter?"

No reply.

"Are you unwell?"

"No."

"Are you in trouble?"

"Ay!" with a burst of tears.

Lady Bassett let her cry, thinking it would relieve her, and then spoke to her again with the languid pensiveness of a woman who has also her trouble. "You have been very attentive to Sir Charles, and a kind good servant to me, Mary."

"You are mocking me, my lady," said Mary, bitterly. "You wouldn't have turned me off for a word if I had been a good servant."

Lady Bassett colored high, and was silenced for a moment. At last she said, "I feel it must seem harsh to you. You don't know how wicked it was to tempt me. But it is not as if you had *done* anything wrong. I do not feel bound to mention mere words: I shall give you an excellent character, Mary--indeed I *have.* I think I have got a good place for you. I shall know to-morrow, and when it is settled we will look over my wardrobe together."

This proposal implied a boxful of presents, and would have made Mary's dark eyes flash with delight at another time; but she was past all that now. She interrupted Lady Bassett with this strange speech: "You are very kind, my lady; will you lend me the key of your medicine chest?"

Lady Bassett looked surprised, but said, "Certainly, Mary," and held out the keys.

But, before Mary could take them, she considered a moment, and asked her what medicine she required.

"Only a little laudanum."

"No, Mary; not while you look like that, and refuse to tell me your trouble. I am your mistress, and must exert my authority for your good. Tell me at once what is the matter."

"I'd bite my tongue off sooner."

"You are wrong, Mary. I am sure I should be your best friend. I feel much indebted to you for the attention and the affection you have shown me, and I am grieved to see you so despondent. Make a friend of me. There--think it over, and talk to me again to-morrow."

Mary Wells took the true servant's view of Lady Bassett's kindness. She looked at it as a trap; not, indeed, set with malice prepense, but still a trap. She saw that Lady Bassett meant kindly at present; but, for all that, she was sure that if she told the truth, her mistress would turn against her, and say, "Oh! I had no idea your trouble arose out of your own imprudence. I can do nothing for a vicious girl."

She resolved therefore to say nothing, or else to tell some lie or other quite wide of the mark.

Deplorable as this young woman's situation was, the duplicity and coarseness of mind which had brought her into it would have somewhat blunted the mental agony such a situation must inflict; but it was aggravated by a special terror; she knew that if she was found out she would lose the only sure friend she had in the world.

The fact is, Mary Wells had seen a great deal of life during the two years she was out of the reader's sight. Rhoda had been very good to her; had set her up in a lodging-house, at her earnest request. She misconducted it, and failed: threw it up in disgust, and begged Rhoda to put her in the public line. Rhoda complied. Mary made a mess of the public-house. Then Rhoda showed her she was not fit to govern anything, and drove her into service again; and in that condition, having no more cares than a child, and plenty of work to do, and many a present from Rhoda, she had been happy.

But Rhoda, though she forgave blunders, incapacity for business, and waste of money, had always told her plainly there was one thing she never would forgive.

Rhoda Marsh had become a good Christian in every respect but one. The male rake reformed is rather tolerant; but the female rake reformed is, as a rule, bitterly intolerant of female frailty; and Rhoda carried this female characteristic to an extreme both in word and in deed. They were only half-sisters, after all; and Mary knew that she would be cast off forever if she deviated from virtue so far as to be found out.

Besides the general warning, there had been a special one. When she read Mary's first letter from Huntercombe Hall Rhoda was rather taken aback at first; but, on reflection, she wrote to Mary, saying she could stay there on two conditions: she must be discreet, and never mention her sister Rhoda in the house, and she must not be tempted to renew her acquaintance with Richard Bassett. "Mind," said she, "if ever you speak to that villain I shall hear of it, and I shall never notice you again."

This was the galling present and the dark future which had made so young and unsentimental a woman as Mary Wells think of suicide for a moment or two; and it now deprived her of her rest, and next day kept her thinking and brooding all the time her now leaden limbs were carrying her through her menial duties.

The afternoon was sunny, and Sir Charles and Lady Bassett took their usual walk.

Mary Wells went a little way with them, looking very miserable. Lady Bassett observed, and said, kindly, "Mary, you can give me that shawl; I will not keep you; go where you like till five o'clock."

Mary never said so much as "Thank you." She put the shawl round her mistress, and then went slowly back. She sat down on the stone steps, and glared stupidly at the scene, and felt very miserable and leaden. She seemed to be stuck in a sort of slough of despond, and could not move in any direction to get out of it.

While she sat in this somber reverie a gentleman walked up to the door, and Mary Wells lifted her head and looked at him. Notwithstanding her misery, her eyes rested on him with some admiration, for he was a model of a man: six feet high, and built like an athlete. His face was oval, and his skin dark but glowing; his hair, eyebrows, and long eyelashes black as jet; his gray eyes large and tender. He was dressed in black, with a white tie, and his clothes were well cut, and seemed superlatively so, owing to the importance and symmetry of the figure they covered. It was the new vicar, Mr. Angelo.

He smiled on Mary graciously, and asked her how Sir Charles was.

She said he was better.

Then Mr. Angelo asked, more timidly, was Lady Bassett at home.

"She is just gone out, sir."

A look of deep disappointment crossed Mr. Angelo's face. It did not escape Mary Wells. She looked at him full, and, lowering her voice a little, said, "She is only in the grounds with Sir Charles. She will be at home about five o'clock."

Mr. Angelo hesitated, and then said he would call again at five. He evidently preferred a duet to a trio. He then thanked Mary Wells with more warmth than the occasion seemed to call for, and retired very slowly: he had come very quickly.

Mary Wells looked after him, and asked herself wildly if she could not make some use of him and his manifest infatuation.

But before her mind could fix on any idea, and, indeed, before the young clergyman had taken twenty steps homeward, loud voices were heard down the shrubbery.

These were followed by an agonized scream.

Mary Wells started up, and the young parson turned: they looked at each other in amazement.

Then came wild and piercing cries for help--in a woman's voice.

The young clergyman cried out, *"Her* voice! *her* voice!" and dashed into the shrubbery with a speed Mary Wells had never seen equaled. He had won the 200-yard race at Oxford in his day.

The agonized screams were repeated, and Mary Wells screamed in response as she ran toward the place.

CHAPTER XVI.

SIR CHARLES BASSETT was in high spirits this afternoon--indeed, a little too high.

"Bella, my love," said he, "now I'll tell you why I made you give me your signature this morning. The money has all come in for the wood, and this very day I sent Oldfield instructions to open an account for you with a London banker."

Lady Bassett looked at him with tears of tenderness in her eyes. "Dearest," said she, "I have plenty of money; but the love to which I owe this present, that is my treasure of treasures. Well, I accept it, Charles; but don't ask me to spend it on myself; I should feel I was robbing you."

"It is nothing to me how you spend it; I have saved it from the enemy."

Now that very enemy heard these words. He had looked from the "Heir's Tower," and seen Sir Charles and Lady Bassett walking on their side the wall, and the nurse carrying his heir on the other side.

He had come down to look at his child in the sun; but he walked softly, on the chance of overhearing Sir Charles and Lady Bassett say something or other about his health; his design went no further than that, but the fate of listeners is proverbial.

Lady Bassett endeavored to divert her husband from the topic he seemed to be approaching; it always excited him now, and did him harm.

"Do not waste your thoughts on that enemy. He is powerless."

"At this moment, perhaps; but his turn is sure to come again; and I shall provide for it. I mean to live on half my income, and settle the other half on you. I shall act on the clause in the entail, and sell all the timber on the estate, except about the home park and my best covers. It will take me some years to do this; I must not glut the market, and spoil your profits; but every year I'll have a fall, till I have denuded Mr. Bassett's inheritance, as he calls it, and swelled your banker's account to a Plum. Bella, I have had a shake. Even now that I am better such a pain goes through my head, like a bullet crushing through it, whenever I get excited. I don't think I shall be a long-lived man. But never mind, I'll live as long as I can; and, while I do live, I'll work for you, and against that villain."

"Charles," cried Lady Bassett, "I implore you to turn your thoughts away from that man, and to give up these idle schemes. Were you to die I should soon follow you; so pray do not shorten your life by these angry passions, or you will shorten mine."

This appeal acted powerfully on Sir Charles, and he left off suddenly with flushed cheeks and tried to compose himself.

But his words had now raised a corresponding fury on the other side of that boundary wall. Richard Bassett, stung with rage, and, unlike his high-bred cousin, accustomed to mix cunning even with his fury, gave him a terrible blow--a very *coup de Jarnac.* He spoke *at* him; he ran forward to the nurse, and said very loud: "Let me see the little darling. He does you credit. What fat cheeks!--what arms!--an infant hercules! There, take him up the mound. Now lift him in your arms, and let him see his inheritance. Higher, nurse, higher. Ay, crow away, youngster; all that is yours--house and land and all. They may steal the trees; they can't make away with the broad acres. Ha! I believe he understands every word, nurse. See how he smiles and crows."

At the sound of Bassett's voice Sir Charles started, and, at the first taunt, he uttered something between a moan and a roar, as of a wounded lion.

"Come away," cried Lady Bassett. "He is doing it on purpose."

But the stabs came too fast. Sir Charles shook her off, and looked wildly round for a weapon to strike his insulter with.

"Curse him and his brat!" he cried. "They shall neither of them--I'll kill them both."

He sprang fiercely at the wall, and, notwithstanding his weakly condition, raised himself above it, and glared over with a face so full of fury that Richard Bassett recoiled in dismay for a moment, and said, "Run! run! He'll hurt the child!"

But, the next moment, Sir Charles's hands lost their power; he uttered a miserable moan, and fell gasping under the wall in an epileptic fit, with all the terrible symptoms I have described in a previous portion of this story. These were new to his poor wife, and, as she strove in vain to control his fearful convulsions, her shrieks rent the air. Indeed, her screams were so appalling that Bassett himself sprang at the wall, and, by a great effort of strength, drew himself up, and peered down, with white face, at the glaring eyes, clinched teeth, purple face, and foaming lips of his enemy, and his body that bounded convulsively on the ground with incredible violence.

At that moment humanity prevailed over every thing, and he flung himself over the wall, and in his haste got rather a heavy fall himself. "It is a fit!" he cried, and running to the brook close by, filled his hat with water, and was about to dash it over Sir Charles's face.

But Lady Bassett repelled him with horror. "Don't touch him, you villain! You have killed him." And then she shrieked again.

At this moment Mr. Angelo dashed up, and saw at a glance what it was, for he had studied medicine a little. He said, "It is epilepsy. Leave him to me." He managed, by his great strength, to keep the patient's head down till the face got pale and the limbs still; then, telling Lady Bassett not to alarm herself too much, he lifted Sir Charles, and actually proceeded to carry him toward the house. Lady Bassett, weeping, proffered her assistance, and so did Mary Wells; but this athlete said, a little bruskly, "No, no; I have practiced this sort of thing;" and, partly by his rare strength, partly by his familiarity with all athletic feats, carried the insensible baronet to his own house, as I have seen my accomplished friend Mr. Henry Neville carry a tall actress on the mimic stage; only, the distance being much longer, the perspiration rolled down Mr. Angelo's face with so sustained an effort.

He laid him gently on the floor of his study, while Lady Bassett sent two grooms galloping for medical advice, and half a dozen servants running for this and that stimulant, as one thing after another occurred to her agitated mind. The very rustling of dresses and scurry of feet overhead told all the house a great calamity had stricken it.

Lady Bassett hung over the sufferer, sighing piteously, and was for supporting his beloved head with her tender arm; but Mr. Angelo told her it was better to keep the head low, that the blood might flow back to the vessels of the brain.

She cast a look of melting gratitude on her adviser, and composed herself to apply stimulants under his direction and advice.

Thus judiciously treated, Sir Charles began to recover consciousness in part. He stared and muttered incoherently. Lady Bassett thanked God on her knees, and then turned to Mr. Angelo with streaming eyes, and stretched out both hands to him, with an indescribable eloquence of gratitude. He gave her his hands timidly, and she pressed them both with all her soul. Unconsciously she sent a rapturous thrill through the young man's body: he blushed, and then turned pale, and felt for a moment almost faint with rapture at that sweet and unexpected pressure of her soft hands.

But at this moment Sir Charles broke out in a sort of dry, business-like voice, "I'll kill the viper and his brood!" Then he stared at Mr. Angelo, and could not make him out at first. "Ah!" said he, complacently, "this is my private tutor: a man of learning. I read Homer with him; but I have forgotten it, all but one line--

"[greek]"

"That's a beautiful verse. Homer, old boy, I'll take your advice. I'll kill the heir at law, and his brat as well, and when they are dead and well seasoned I'll sell them to that old timber-merchant, the devil, to make hell hotter. Order my horse, somebody, this minute!"

During this tirade Lady Bassett's hands kept clutching, as if to stop it, and her eyes filled with horror.

Mr. Angelo came again to her rescue. He affected to take it all as a matter of course, and told the servants they need not wait, Sir Charles was coming to himself by degrees, and the danger was all over.

But when the servants were gone he said to Lady Bassett, seriously, "I would not let any servant be about Sir Charles, except this one. She is evidently attached to you. Suppose we take him to his own room."

He then made Mary Wells a signal, and they carried him upstairs.

Sir Charles talked all the while with pitiable vehemence. Indeed, it was a continuous babble, like a brook.

Mary Wells was taking him into his own room, but Lady Bassett said, "No: into my room. Oh, I will never let him out of my sight again."

Then they carried him into Lady Bassett's bedroom, and laid him gently down on a couch there.

He looked round, observed the locality, and uttered a little sigh of complacency. He left off talking for the present, and seemed to doze.

The place which exerted this soothing influence on Sir Charles had a contrary and strange effect on Mr. Angelo.

It was of palatial size, and lighted by two side windows, and an oriel window at the end. The delicate stone shafts and mullions were such as are oftener seen in cathedrals than in mansions. The deep embrasure was filled with beautiful flowers and luscious exotic leaf-plants from the hot-houses. The floor was of polished oak, and some feet of this were left bare on all sides of the great Aubusson carpet made expressly for the room. By this means cleanliness penetrated into every corner: the oak was not only cleaned, but polished like a mirror. The curtains were French chintzes, of substance, and exquisite patterns, and very voluminous. On the walls was a delicate rose-tinted satin paper, to which French art, unrivaled in these matters, had given the appearance of being stuffed, padded, and divided into a thousand cozy pillows, by gold-headed nails.

The wardrobes were of satin-wood. The bedsteads, one small, one large, were plain white, and gold in moderation.

All this, however, was but the frame to the delightful picture of a wealthy young lady's nest.

The things that startled and thrilled Mr. Angelo were those his imagination could see the fair mistress using. The exquisite toilet table; the Dresden mirror, with its delicate china frame muslined and ribboned; the great ivory-handled brushes, the array of cut-glass gold-mounted bottles, and all the artillery of beauty; the baths of various shapes and sizes, in which she laved her fair body; the bath sheets, and the profusion of linen, fine and coarse; the bed, with its frilled sheets, its huge frilled pillows, and its eider-down quilt, covered with bright purple silk.

A delicate perfume came through the wardrobes, where strata of fine linen from Hamburg and Belfast lay on scented herbs; and this, permeating the room, seemed the very perfume of Beauty itself, and intoxicated the brain. Imagination conjured pictures proper to the scene: a goddess at her toilet; that glorious hair lying tumbled on the pillow, and burning in contrasted color with the snowy sheets and with the purple quilt.

From this reverie he was awakened by a soft voice that said, "How can I ever thank you enough, sir?"

Mr. Angelo controlled himself, and said, "By sending for me whenever I can be of the slightest use." Then, comprehending his danger, he added, hastily, "And I fear I am none whatever now." Then he rose to go.

Lady Bassett gave him both her hands again, and this time he kissed one of them, all in a flurry; he could not resist the temptation. Then he hurried away, with his whole soul in a tumult. Lady Bassett blushed, and returned to her husband's side.

Doctor Willis came, heard the case, looked rather grave and puzzled, and wrote the inevitable prescription; for the established theory is that man is cured by drugs alone.

Sir Charles wandered a little while the doctor was there, and continued to wander after he was gone.

Then Mary Wells begged leave to sleep in the dressing-room.

Lady Bassett thanked her, but said she thought it unnecessary; a good night's rest, she hoped, would make a great change in the sufferer.

Mary Wells thought otherwise, and quietly brought her little bed into the dressing-room and laid it on the floor.

Her judgment proved right; Sir Charles was no better the next day, nor the day after. He brooded for hours at a time, and, when he talked, there was an incoherence in his discourse; above all, he seemed incapable of talking long on any subject without coming back to the fatal one of his childlessness; and, when he did return to this, it was sure to make him either deeply dejected or else violent against Richard Bassett and his son; he swore at them, and said they were waiting for his shoes.

Lady Bassett's anxiety deepened; strange fears came over her. She put subtle questions to the doctor; he returned obscure answers, and went on prescribing medicines that had no effect.

She looked wistfully into Mary Wells's face, and there she saw her own thoughts reflected.

"Mary," said she, one day, in a low voice, "what do they say in the kitchen?"

"Some say one thing, some another. What can they say? They never see him, and never shall while I am here."

This reminded Lady Bassett that Mary's time was up. The idea of a stranger taking her place, and seeing Sir Charles in his present condition, was horrible to her. "Oh, Mary," said she, piteously, "surely you will not leave me just now?"

"Do you wish me to stay, my lady?"

"Can you ask it? How can I hope to find such devotion as yours, such fidelity, and, above all, such secrecy? Ah, Mary, I am the most unhappy lady in all England this day."

Then she began to cry bitterly, and Mary Wells cried with her, and said she would stay as long as she could; "but," said she, "I gave you good advice, my lady, and so you will find."

Lady Bassett made no answer whatever, and that disappointed Mary, for she wanted a discussion.

The days rolled on, and brought no change for the better. Sir Charles continued to brood on his one misfortune. He refused to go out-of-doors, even into the garden, giving as his reason that he was not fit to be seen. "I don't mind a couple of women," said he, gravely, "but no man shall see Charles Bassett in his present state. No. Patience! Patience! I'll wait till Heaven takes pity on me. After all, it would be a shame that such a race as mine should die out, and these fine estates go to blackguards, and poachers, and anonymous-letter writers."

Lady Bassett used to coax him to walk in the corridor; but, even then, he ordered Mary Wells to keep watch and let none of the servants come that way. From words he let fall it seems he thought "Childlessness" was written on his face, and that it had somehow degraded his features.

Now a wealthy and popular baronet could not thus immure himself for any length of time without exciting curiosity, and setting all manner of rumors afloat. Visitors poured into Huntercombe to inquire.

Lady Bassett excused herself to many, but some of her own sex she thought it best to encounter. This subjected her to the insidious attacks of curiosity admirably veiled with sympathy. The assailants were marvelously subtle; but so was the devoted wife. She gave kiss for kiss, and equivoque for equivoque. She seemed grateful for each visit; but they got nothing out of her except that Sir Charles's nerves were shaken by his fall, and that she was playing the tyrant for once, and insisting on absolute quiet for her patient.

One visitor she never refused--Mr. Angelo. He, from the first, had been her true friend; had carried Sir Charles away from the enemy, and then had dismissed the gaping servants. She saw that he had divined her calamity and she knew from things he said to her that he would never breathe a word out-of-doors. She confided in him. She told him Mr. Bassett was the real cause of all this misery: he had insulted Sir Charles. The nature of this insult she suppressed. "And oh, Mr. Angelo," said she, "that man is my terror night and day! I don't know what he can do, but I feel he will do something if he ever learns my poor husband's condition."

"I trust, Lady Bassett, you are convinced he will learn nothing from me. Indeed, I will tell the ruffian anything you like. He has been sounding me a little; called to inquire after his poor cousin--the hypocrite!"

"How good you are! Please tell him absolute repose is prescribed for a time, but there is no doubt of Sir Charles's ultimate recovery."

Mr. Angelo promised heartily.

Mary Wells was not enough; a woman must have a man to lean on in trouble, and Lady Bassett leaned on Mr. Angelo. She even obeyed him. One day he told her that her own health would fail if she sat always in the sick-room; she must walk an hour every day.

"Must I?" said she, sweetly.

"Yes, even if it is only in your own garden."

From that time she used to walk with him nearly every day.

Richard Bassett saw this from his tower of observation; saw it, and chuckled. "Aha!" said he. "Husband sick in bed. Wife walking in the garden with a young man--a parson, too. He is dark, she is fair. Something will come of this. Ha, ha!"

Lady Bassett now talked of sending to London for advice; but Mary Wells dissuaded her. "Physic can't cure him. There's only one can cure him, and that is yourself, my lady."

"Ah, would to Heaven I could!"

"Try *my* way, and you will see, my lady."

"What, *that* way! Oh, no, no!"

"Well, then, if you won't, nobody else can."

Such speeches as these, often repeated, on the one hand, and Sir Charles's melancholy on the other, drove Lady Bassett almost wild with distress and perplexity.

Meanwhile her vague fears of Richard Bassett were being gradually realized.

Bassett employed Wheeler to sound Dr. Willis as to his patient's condition.

Dr. Willis, true to the honorable traditions of his profession, would tell him nothing. But Dr. Willis had a wife. She pumped him: and Wheeler pumped her.

By this channel Wheeler got a somewhat exaggerated account of Sir Charles's state. He carried it to Bassett, and the pair put their heads together.

The consultation lasted all night, and finally a comprehensive plan of action was settled. Wheeler stipulated that the law should not be broken in the smallest particular, but only stretched.

Four days after this conference Mr. Bassett, Mr. Wheeler, and two spruce gentlemen dressed in black, sat upon the "Heir's Tower," watching Huntercombe Hall.

They watched, and watched, until they saw Mr. Angelo make his usual daily call.

Then they watched, and watched, until Lady Bassett and the young clergyman came out and strolled together into the shrubbery.

Then the two gentlemen went down the stairs, and were hastily conducted by Bassett to Huntercombe Hall.

They rang the bell, and the taller said, in a business-like voice, "Dr. Mosely, from Dr. Willis."

Mary Wells was sent for, and Dr. Mosely said, "Dr. Willis is unable to come to-day, and has sent me."

Mary Wells conducted him to the patient. The other gentleman followed.

"Who is this?" said Mary. "I can't let all the world in to see him."

"It is Mr. Donkyn, the surgeon. Dr. Willis wished the patient to be examined with the stethoscope. You can stay outside, Mr. Donkyn."

This new doctor announced himself to Sir Charles, felt his pulse, and entered at once into conversation with him.

Sir Charles was in a talking mood, and very soon said one or two inconsecutive things. Dr. Mosely looked at Mary Wells and said he would write a prescription.

As soon as he had written it he said, very loud, "Mr. Donkyn!"

The door instantly opened, and that worthy appeared on the threshold.

"Oblige me," said the doctor to his confrere, "by seeing this prescription made up; and you can examine the patient yourself; but do not fatigue him."

With this he retired swiftly, and strolled down the corridor, to wait for his companion.

He had not to wait long. Mr. Donkyn adopted a free and easy style with Sir Charles, and that gentleman marked his sense of the indignity by turning him out of the room, and kicking him industriously half-way down the passage.

Messrs. Mosely and Donkyn retired to Highmore.

Bassett was particularly pleased at the baronet having kicked Donkyn; so was Wheeler; so was Dr. Mosely. Donkyn alone did not share the general enthusiasm.

When Sir Charles had disposed of Mr. Donkyn he turned on Mary Wells, and rated her soundly for bringing strangers into his room to gratify their curiosity; and when Lady Bassett came in he made his formal complaint, concluding with a proposal that one of two persons should leave Huntercombe, forever, that afternoon-- Mary Wells or Sir Charles Bassett.

Mary replied, not to him, but to her mistress, "He came from Dr. Willis, my lady. It was Dr. Mosely; and the other gent was a surgeon."

"Two medical men, sent by Dr. Willis?" said Lady Bassett, knitting her brow with wonder and a shade of doubt.

"A couple of her own sweethearts, sent by herself," suggested Sir Charles.

Lady Bassett sat down and wrote a hasty letter to Dr. Willis. "Send a groom with it, as fast as he can ride," said she; and she was much discomposed and nervous and impatient till the answer came bade.

Dr. Willis came in person. "I sent no one to take my place," said he. "I esteem my patient too highly to let any stranger prescribe for him or even see him--for a few days to come."

Lady Bassett sank into a chair, and her eloquent face filled with an undefinable terror.

Mary Wells, being on her defense, put in her word. "I am sure he was a doctor; for he wrote a prescription, and here 'tis."

Dr. Willis examined the prescription, with no friendly eye.

"Acetate of morphia! The very worst thing that could be given him. This is the favorite of the specialists. This fatal drug has eaten away a thousand brains for one it has ever benefited."

"Ah!" said Lady Bassett. "'Specialists!' what are they?"

"Medical men, who confine their practice to one disease."

"Mad-doctors, he means," said the patient, very gravely.

Lady Bassett turned very pale. "Then those were mad-doctors."

"Never you mind, Bella," said Sir Charles. "I kicked the fellow handsomely."

"I am sorry to hear it, Sir Charles."

"Why?"

Dr. Willis looked at Lady Bassett, as much as to say, "I shall not give *him* my real reason;" and then said, "I think it very undesirable you should be excited and provoked, until your health is thoroughly restored."

Dr. Willis wrote a prescription, and retired.

Lady Bassett sank into a chair, and trembled all over. Her divining fit was on her; she saw the hand of the enemy, and filled with vague fears.

Mary Wells tried to, comfort her. "I'll take care no more strangers get in here," said she. "And, my lady, if you are afraid, why not have the keepers, and two or three more, to sleep in the house? for, as for them footmen, they be too soft to fight."

"I will," said Lady Bassett; "but I fear it will be no use. Our enemy has so many resources unknown to me. How can a poor woman fight with a shadow, that comes in a moment and strikes; and then is gone and leaves his victim trembling?"

Then she slipped into the dressing-room and became hysterical, out of her husband's sight and hearing.

Mary Wells nursed her, and, when she was better, whispered in her ear, "Lose no more time, then. Cure him. You know the way."

CHAPTER XVII.

IN the present condition of her mind these words produced a strange effect on Lady Bassett. She quivered, and her eyes began to rove in that peculiar way I have already noticed; and then she started up and walked wildly to and fro; and then she kneeled down and prayed; and then, alarmed, perplexed, exhausted, she went and leaned her head on her patient's shoulder, and wept softly a long time.

Some days passed, and no more strangers attempted to see Sir Charles.

Lady Bassett was beginning to breathe again, when she was afflicted by an unwelcome discovery.

Mary Wells fainted away so suddenly that, but for Lady Bassett's quick eye and ready hand, she would have fallen heavily.

Lady Bassett laid her head down and loosened her stays, and discovered her condition. She said nothing till the young woman was well, and then she taxed her with it.

Mary denied it plump; but, seeing her mistress's disgust at the falsehood, she owned it with many tears.

Being asked how she could so far forget herself, she told Lady Bassett she had long been courted by a respectable young man; he had come to the village, bound on a three years' voyage, to bid her good-by, and, what with love and grief at parting, they had been betrayed into folly; and now he was on the salt seas, little dreaming in what condition he had left her: "and," said she, "before ever he can write to me, and I to him, I shall be a ruined girl; that is why I wanted to put an end to myself; I *will,* too, unless I can find some way to hide it from the world."

Lady Bassett begged her to give up those desperate thoughts; she would think what could be done for her. Lady Bassett could say no more to her just then, for she was disgusted with her.

But when she came to reflect that, after all, this was not a lady, and that she appeared by her own account to be the victim of affection and frailty rather than of vice, she made some excuses; and then the girl had laid aside her trouble, her despair, and given her sorrowful mind to nursing and comforting Sir Charles. This would have outweighed a crime, and it made the wife's bowels yearn over the unfortunate girl. "Mary," said she, "others must judge you; I am a wife, and can only see your fidelity to my poor husband. I don't know what I shall do without you, but I think it is my duty to send you to him if possible. You are sure he really loves you?"

"Me cross the seas after a young man?" said Mary Wells. "I'd as lieve hang myself on the nighest tree and make an end. No, my lady, if you are really my friend, let me stay here as long as I can--I will never go downstairs to be seen--and then give me money enough to get my trouble over unbeknown to my sister; she is all my fear. She is married to a gentleman, and got plenty of money, and I shall never want while she lives, and behave myself; but she would never forgive me if she knew. She is a hard woman; she is not like you, my lady. I'd liever cut my hand off than I'd trust her as I would you."

Lady Bassett was not quite insensible to this compliment; but she felt uneasy.

"What, help you to deceive your sister?"

"For her good. Why, if any one was to go and tell her about me now, she'd hate them for telling her almost as much as she would hate me."

Lady Bassett was sore perplexed. Unable to see quite clear in the matter, she naturally reverted to her husband and his interest. That dictated her course. She said, "Well, stay with us, Mary, as long as you can; and then money shall not be wanting to hide your shame from all the world; but I hope when the time comes you will alter your mind and tell your sister. May I ask what her name is?"

Mary, after a moment's hesitation, said her name was Marsh.

"I know a Mrs. Marsh," said Lady Bassett; "but, of course, that is not your sister. My Mrs. Marsh is rather fair."

"So is my sister, for that matter."

"And tall?"

"Yes; but you never saw her. You'd never forget her it you had. She has got eyes like a lion."

"Ah! Does she ride?"

"Oh, she is famous for that; and driving, and all."

"Indeed! But no; I see no resemblance."

"Oh, she is only my half-sister."

"This is very strange."

Lady Bassett put her hand to her brow, and thought.

"Mary," said she, "all this is very mysterious. We are wading in deep waters."

Mary Wells had no idea what she meant.

The day was not over yet. Just before dinner-time a fly from the station drove to the door, and Mr. Oldfield got out.

He was detained in the hall by sentinel Moss.

Lady Bassett came down to him. At the very sight of him she trembled, and said, "Richard Bassett?"

"Yes," said Mr. Oldfield, "he is in the field again. He has been to the Court of Chancery ***ex parte,*** and obtained an injunction ***ad interim*** to stay waste. Not another tree must be cut down on the estate for the present."

"Thank Heaven it is no worse than that. Not another tree shall be felled on the grounds."

"Of course not. But they will not stop there. If we do not move to dissolve the injunction, I fear they will go on and ask the Court to administer the estate, with a view to all interests concerned, especially those of the heir at law and his son."

"What, while my husband lives?"

"If they can prove him dead in law."

"I don't understand you, Mr. Oldfield."

"They have got affidavits of two medical men that he is insane."

Lady Bassett uttered a faint scream, and put her hand to her heart.

"And, of course, they will use that extraordinary fall of timber as a further proof, and also as a reason why the Court should interfere to protect the heir at law. Their case is well got up and very strong," said Mr. Oldfield, regretfully.

"Well, but you are a lawyer, and you have always beaten them hitherto."

"I had law and fact on my side. It is not so now. To be frank, Lady Bassett, I don't see what I can do but watch the case, on the chance of some error or illegality.

It is very hard to fight a case when you cannot put your client forward--and I suppose that would not be safe. How unfortunate that you have no children!"

"Children! How could they help us?"

"What a question! How could Richard Bassett move the Court if he was not the heir at law?"

After a long conference Mr. Oldfield returned to town to see what he could do in the way of procrastination, and Lady Bassett promised to leave no stone unturned to cure Sir Charles in the meantime. Mr. Oldfield was to write immediately if any fresh step was taken.

When Mr. Oldfield was gone, Lady Bassett pondered every word he had said, and, mild as she was, her rage began to rise against her husband's relentless enemy. Her wits worked, her eyes roved in that peculiar half-savage way I have described. She became intolerably restless; and any one acquainted with her sex might see that some strange conflict was going on in her troubled mind.

Every now and then she would come and cling to her husband, and cry over him; and that seemed to still the tumult of her soul a little.

She never slept all that night, and next day, clinging in her helpless agony to the nearest branch, she told Mary Wells what Bassett was doing, and said, "What shall I do? He is not mad; but he is in so very precarious a state that, if they get at him to torment him, they will drive him mad indeed."

"My lady," said Mary Wells, "I can't go from my word. 'Tis no use in making two bites of a cherry. We must cure him: and if we don't, you'll never rue it but once, and that will be all your life."

"I should look on myself with horror afterward were I to deceive him now."

"No, my lady, you are too fond of him for that. Once you saw him happy you'd be happy too, no matter how it came about. That Richard Bassett will turn him out of this else. I am sure he will; he is a hard-hearted villain."

Lady Bassett's eyes flashed fire; then her eyes roved; then she sighed deeply.

Her powers of resistance were beginning to relax. As for Mary Wells, she gave her no peace; she kept instilling her mind into her mistress's with the pertinacity of a small but ever-dripping fount, and we know both by science and poetry that small, incessant drops of water will wear a hole in marble.

"Gutta cavat lapidem non vi sed saepe cadendo."

And in the midst of all a letter came from Mr. Oldfield, to tell her that Mr. Bassett threatened to take out a commission ***de lunatico,*** and she must prepare Sir Charles for an examination; for, if reported insane, the Court would administer the estates; but the heir at law, Mr. Bassett, would have the ear of the Court and the right of application, and become virtually master of Huntercombe and Bassett; and, perhaps, considering the spirit by which he was animated, would contrive to occupy the very Hall itself. Lady Bassett was in the dressing-room when she received this blow, and it drove her almost frantic. She bemoaned her husband; she prayed God to take them both, and let their enemy have his will. She wept and raved, and at the height of her distress came from the other room a feeble cry, "Childless! childless! childless!"

Lady Bassett heard that, and in one moment, from violent she became unnaturally and dangerously calm. She said firmly to Mary Wells, "This is more than I can bear. You pretend you can save him--do it."

Mary Wells now trembled in her turn; but she seized the opportunity. "My lady, whatever I say you'll stand to?"

"Whatever you say I'll stand to."

CHAPTER XVIII.

MARY WELLS, like other uneducated women, was not accustomed to think long and earnestly on any one subject; to use an expression she once applied with far less justice to her sister, her mind was like running water.

But gestation affects the brains of such women, and makes them think more steadily, and sometimes very acutely; added to which, the peculiar dangers and difficulties that beset this girl during that anxious period stimulated her wits to the very utmost. Often she sat quite still for hours at a time, brooding and brooding, and asking herself how she could turn each new and unexpected event to her own benefit. Now so much does mental force depend on that exercise of keen and long attention, in which her sex is generally deficient, that this young woman's powers were more than doubled since the day she first discovered her condition, and began to work her brains night and day for her defense.

Gradually, as events I have related unfolded themselves, she caught a glimpse of this idea, that if she could get her mistress to have a secret, her mistress would help her to keep her own. Hence her insidious whispers, and her constant praises of Mr. Angelo, who, she saw, was infatuated with Lady Bassett. Yet the designing creature was actually fond of her mistress: and so strangely compounded is a heart of this low kind that the extraordinary step she now took was half affectionate impulse, half egotistical design.

She made a motion with her hand inviting Lady Bassett to listen, and stepped into Sir Charles's room.

"Childless! childless! childless!"

"Hush, sir," said Mary Wells. "Don't say so. We shan't be many mouths without one, please Heaven."

Sir Charles shook his head sadly.

"Don't you believe me?"

"No."

"What, did ever I tell you a lie?"

"No: but you are mistaken. She would have told me."

"Well, sir, my lady is young and shy, and I think she is afraid of disappointing you after all; for you know, sir, there's many a slip 'twixt the cup and the lip. But 'tis as I tell you, sir."

Sir Charles was much agitated, and said he would give her a hundred guineas if that was true. "Where is my darling wife? Why do I hear this through a servant?"

Mary Wells cast a look at the door, and said, for Lady Bassett to hear, "She is receiving company. Now, sir, I have told you good news; will you do something to oblige me? You shouldn't speak of it direct to my lady just yet; and if you want all to go well, you mustn't vex my lady as you are doing now. What I mean, you mustn't be so downhearted-- there's no reason for't--and you mustn't coop yourself up on this floor: it sets the folks talking, and worries my lady. You should give her every chance, being the way she is."

Sir Charles said eagerly he would not vex her for the world. "I'll walk in the garden," said he; "but as for going abroad, you know I am not in a fit condition yet; my mind is clouded."

"Not as I see."

"Oh, not always. But sometimes a cloud seems to get into my head; and if I was in public I might do or say something discreditable. I would rather die."

"La, sir!" said Mary Wells, in a broad, hearty way--"a cloud in your head! You've had a bad fall, and a fit at top on't, and no wonder your poor head do ache at times. You'll outgrow that--if you take the air and give over fretting about the t'other thing. I tell you you'll hear the music of a child's voice and little feet a-pattering up and down this here corridor before so very long--if so be you take my advice, and leave off fretting my lady with fretting of yourself. You should consider: she is too fond of you to be well when you be ill."

"I'll get well for her sake," said Sir Charles, firmly.

At this moment there was a knock at the door. Mary Wells opened it so that the servant could see nothing.

"Mr. Angelo has called."

"My lady will be down directly."

Mary Wells then slipped into the dressing-room, and found Lady Bassett looking pale and wild. She had heard every word.

"There, he is better already," said Mary Wells. "He shall walk in the garden with you this afternoon."

"What have you done? I can't look him in the face now. Suppose he speaks to me?"

"He will not. I'll manage that. You won't have to say a word. Only listen to what I say, and don't make a liar of me. He is better already."

"How will this end?" cried Lady Bassett, helplessly. "What shall I do?"

"You must go downstairs, and not come here for an hour at least, or you'll spoil my work. Mr. Angelo is in the drawing-room."

"I will go to him."

Lady Bassett slipped out by the other door, and it was three hours, instead of one, before she returned.

For the first time in her life she was afraid to face her husband.

CHAPTER XIX.

MEANTIME Mary Wells had a long conversation with her master; and after that she retired into the adjoining room, and sat down to sew baby-linen clandestinely.

After a considerable tune Lady Bassett came in, and, sinking into a chair, covered her face with her hands. She had her bonnet on.

Mary Wells looked at her with black eyes that flashed triumph.

After so surveying her for some time she said: "I have been at him again, and there's a change for the better already. He is not the same man. You go and see else."

Lady Bassett now obeyed her servant: she rose and crept like a culprit into Sir Charles's room. She found him clean shaved, dressed to perfection, and looking more cheerful than she had seen him for many a long day. "Ah, Bella," said he, "you have your bonnet on; let us have a walk in the garden."

Lady Bassett opened her eyes and consented eagerly, though she was very tired.

They walked together; and Sir Charles, being a man that never broke his word, put no direct question to Lady Bassett, but spoke cheerfully of the future, and told her she was his hope and his all; she would baffle his enemy, and cheer his desolate hearth.

She blushed, and looked confused and distressed; then he smiled, and talked of indifferent matters, until a pain in his head stopped him; then he became confused, and, putting his hand piteously to his head, proposed to retire at once to his own room.

Lady Bassett brought him in, and he reposed in silence on the sofa.

The next day, and, indeed, many days afterward, presented similar features.

Mary Wells talked to her master of the bright days to come, of the joy that would fill the house if all went well, and of the defeat in store for Richard Bassett. She spoke of this man with strange virulence; said "she would think no more of sticking a knife into him than of eating her dinner;" and in saying this she showed the white of her eye in a manner truly savage and vindictive.

To hurt the same person is a surer bond than to love the same person; and this sentiment of Mary Wells, coupled with her uniform kindness to himself, gave her great influence with Sir Charles in his present weakened condition. Moreover, the young woman had an oily, persuasive tongue; and she who persuades us is stronger than he who convinces us.

Thus influenced, Sir Charles walked every day in the garden with his wife, and forbore all direct allusion to her condition, though his conversation was redolent of it.

He was still subject to sudden collapses of the intellect; but he became conscious when they were coming on; and at the first warning he would insist on burying himself in his room.

After some days he consented to take short drives with Lady Bassett in the open carriage. This made her very joyful. Sir Charles refused to enter a single house, so high was his pride and so great his terror lest he should expose himself; but it was a great point gained that she could take him about the county, and show him in the character of a mere invalid.

Every thing now looked like a cure, slow, perhaps, but progressive; and Lady Bassett had her joyful hours, yet not without a bitter alloy: her divining mind asked itself what she should say and do when Sir Charles should be quite recovered. This thought tormented her, and sometimes so goaded her that she hated Mary Wells for her well-meant interference, and, by a natural recoil from the familiarity circumstances had forced on her, treated that young woman with great coldness and hauteur.

The artful girl met this with extreme meekness and servility; the only reply she ever hazarded was an adroit one; she would take this opportunity to say, "How much better master do get ever since I took in hand to cure him!"

This oblique retort seldom failed. Lady Bassett would look at her husband, and her face would clear; and she would generally end by giving Mary a collar, or a scarf, or something.

Thus did circumstances enable the lower nature to play with the higher. Lady Bassett's struggles were like those of a bird in a silken net; they led to nothing. When it came to the point she could neither do nor say any thing to retard his cure. Any day the Court of Chancery, set in motion by Richard Bassett, might issue a commission *de lunatico,* and, if Sir Charles was not cured by that time, Richard Bassett would virtually administer the estate--so Mr. Oldfield had told her--and that, she felt sure, would drive Sir Charles mad for life.

So there was no help for it. She feared, she writhed, she hated herself; but Sir Charles got better daily, and so she let herself drift along.

Mary Wells made it fatally easy to her. She was the agent. Lady Bassett was silent and passive.

After all she had a hope of extrication. Sir Charles once cured, she would make him travel Europe with her. Money would relieve her of Mary Wells, and distance cut all the other cords.

And, indeed, a time came when she looked back on her present situation with wonder at the distress it had caused her. "I was in shallow water then," said she-- "but now!"

CHAPTER XX.

SIR CHARLES observed that he was never trusted alone. He remarked this, and inquired, with a peculiar eye, why that was.

Lady Bassett had the tact to put on an innocent look and smile, and say: "That is true, dearest. I *have* tied you to my apron-string without mercy. But it serves you right for having fits and frightening me. You get well, and my tyranny will cease at once."

However, after this she often left him alone in the garden, to remove from his mind the notion that he was under restraint from her.

Mr. Bassett observed this proceeding from his tower.

One day Mr. Angelo called, and Lady Bassett left Sir Charles in the garden, to go and speak to him.

She had not been gone many minutes when a boy ran to Sir Charles, and said, "Oh, sir, please come to the gate; the lady has had a fall, and hurt herself."

Sir Charles, much alarmed, followed the boy, who took him to a side gate opening on the high-road. Sir Charles rushed through this, and was passing between two stout fellows that stood one on each side the gate, when they seized him, and lifted him in a moment into a close carriage that was waiting on the spot. He struggled, and cried loudly for assistance; but they bundled him in and sprang in after him; a third man closed the door, and got up by the side of the coachman. He drove off, avoiding the village, soon got upon a broad road, and bowled along at a great rate, the carriage being light, and drawn by two powerful horses.

So cleverly and rapidly was it done that, but for a woman's quick ear, the deed might not have been discovered for hours; but Mary Wells heard the cry for help through an open window, recognized Sir Charles's voice, and ran screaming downstairs to Lady Bassett: she ran wildly out, with Mr. Angelo, to look for Sir Charles.

He was nowhere to be found. Then she ordered every horse in the stables to be saddled; and she ran with Mary to the place where the cry had been heard.

For some time no intelligence whatever could be gleaned; but at last an old man was found who said he had heard somebody cry out, and soon after that a carriage had come tearing by him, and gone round the corner: but this direction was of little value, on account of the many roads, any one of which it might have taken.

However, it left no doubt that Sir Charles had been taken away from the place by force.

Terror-stricken, and pale as death, Lady Bassett never lost her head for a moment. Indeed, she showed unexpected fire; she sent off coachman and grooms to scour the country and rouse the gentry to help her; she gave them money, and told them not to come back till they had found Sir Charles.

Mr. Angelo said, eagerly, "I'll go to the nearest magistrate, and we will arrest Richard Bassett on suspicion."

"God bless you, dear friend!" sobbed Lady Bassett. "Oh, yes, it is his doing--murderer!"

Off went Mr. Angelo on his errand.

He was hardly gone when a man was seen running and shouting across the fields. Lady Bassett went to meet him, surrounded by her humble sympathizers. It was young Drake: he came up panting, with a double-barreled gun in his hand (for he was allowed to shoot rabbits on his own little farm), and stammered out, "Oh, my lady--Sir Charles--they have carried him off against his will!"

"Who? Where? Did you see him?"

"Ay, and heerd him and all. I was ferreting rabbits by the side of the turnpike-road yonder, and a carriage came tearing along, and Sir Charles put out his head and cried to me,' Drake, they are kidnapping me. Shoot!' But they pulled him back out of sight."

"Oh, my poor husband! And did you let them? Oh!"

"Couldn't catch 'em, my lady: so I did as I was bid; got to my gun as quick as ever I could, and gave the coachman both barrels hot."

"What, kill him?"

"Lord, no; 'twas sixty yards off; but made him holler and squeak a good un. Put thirty or forty shots into his back, I know."

"Give me your hand, Mr. Drake. I'll never forget that shot." Then she began to cry.

"Doant ye, my lady, doant ye," said the honest fellow, and was within an ace of blubbering for sympathy. "We ain't a lot o' babies, to see our squire kidnaped. If you would lend Abel Moss there and me a couple o' nags, we'll catch them yet, my lady."

"That we will," cried Abel. "You take me where you fired that shot, and we'll follow the fresh wheel-tracks. They can't beat us while they keep to a road."

The two men were soon mounted, and in pursuit, amid the cheers of the now excited villagers. But still the perpetrators of the outrage had more than an hour's start; and an hour was twelve miles.

And now Lady Bassett, who had borne up so bravely, was seized with a deadly faintness, and supported into the house.

All this spread like wild-fire, and roused the villagers, and they must have a hand in it. Parson had said Mr. Bassett was to blame; and that passed from one to another, and so fermented that, in the evening, a crowd collected round Highmore House and demanded Mr. Bassett.

The servants were alarmed, and said he was not at home.

Then the men demanded boisterously what he had done with Sir Charles, and threatened to break the windows unless they were told; and, as nobody in the house could tell them, the women egged on the men, and they did break the windows; but they no sooner saw their own work than they were a little alarmed at it, and retired, talking very loud to support their waning courage and check their rising remorse at their deed.

They left a house full of holes and screams, and poor little Mrs. Bassett half dead with fright.

As for Lady Bassett, she spent a horrible night of terror, suspense, and agony. She could not lie down, nor even sit still; she walked incessantly, wringing her hands, and groaning for news.

Mary Wells did all she could to comfort her; but it was a situation beyond the power of words to alleviate.

Her intolerable suspense lasted till four o'clock in the morning; and then, in the still night, horses' feet came clattering up to the door.

Lady Bassett went into the hall. It was dimly lighted by a single lamp. The great door was opened, and in clattered Moss and Drake, splashed and weary and downcast.

"Well?" cried Lady Bassett, clasping her hands.

"My lady," said Moss, "we tracked the carriage into the next county, to a place thirty miles from here--to a lodge--and there they stopped us. The place is well guarded with men and great big dogs. We heerd 'em bark, didn't us, Will?"

"Ay," said Drake, dejectedly.

"The man as kept the lodge was short, but civil. Says he, 'This is a place nobody comes in but by law, and nobody goes out but by law. If the gentleman is here you may go home and sleep; he is safe enough.'"

"A prison? No!"

"A 'sylum, my lady."

CHAPTER XXI.

THE lady put her hand to her heart, and was silent a long time.

At last she said, doggedly but faintly, "You will go with me to that place to-morrow, one of you."

"I'll go, my lady," said Moss. "Will, here, had better not show his face. They might take the law on him for that there shot."

Drake hung his head, and his ardor was evidently cooled by discovering that Sir Charles had been taken to a mad-house.

Lady Bassett saw and sighed, and said she would take Moss to show her the way.

At eleven o'clock next morning a light carriage and pair came round to the Hall gate, and a large basket, a portmanteau, and a bag were placed on the roof under care of Moss; smaller packages were put inside; and Lady Bassett and her maid got in, both dressed in black.

They reached Bellevue House at half-past two. The lodge-gate was open, to Lady Bassett's surprise, and they drove through some pleasant grounds to a large white house.

The place at first sight had no distinctive character: great ingenuity had been used to secure the inmates without seeming to incarcerate them. There were no bars to the lower front windows, and the side windows, with their defenses, were shrouded by shrubs. The sentinels were out of sight, or employed on some occupation or other, but within call. Some patients were playing at cricket; some ladies looking on; others strolling on the gravel with a nurse, dressed very much like themselves, who did not obtrude her functions unnecessarily. All was apparent indifference, and Argus-eyed vigilance. So much for the surface.

Of course, even at this moment, some of the locked rooms had violent and miserable inmates.

The hall door opened as the carriage drew up; a respectable servant came forward.

Lady Bassett handed him her card, and said, "I am come to see my husband, sir."

The man never moved a muscle, but said, "You must wait, if you please, till I take your card in."

He soon returned, and said, "Dr. Suaby is not here, but the gentleman in charge will see you."

Lady Bassett got out, and, beckoning Mary Wells, followed the servant into a curious room, half library, half chemist's shop; they called it "the laboratory."

Here she found a tall man leaning on a dirty mantelpiece, who received her stiffly. He had a pale mustache, very thin lips, and altogether a severe manner. His head bald, rather prematurely, and whiskers abundant.

Lady Bassett looked him all over with one glance of her woman's eye, and saw she had a hard and vain man to deal with.

"Are you the gentleman to whom this house belongs?" she faltered.

"No, madam; I am in charge during Dr. Suaby's absence."

"That comes to the same thing. Sir, I am come to see my dear husband."

"Have you an order?"

"An order, sir? I am his wife."

Mr. Salter shrugged his shoulders a little, and said, "I have no authority to let any visitor see a patient without an order from the person by whose authority he is placed here, or else an order from the commissioners."

"But that cannot apply to his wife; to her who is one with him, for better for worse, in sickness or health."

"It seems hard; but I have no discretion in the matter. The patient only came yesterday--much excited. He is better to-day, and an interview with you would excite him again."

"Oh no! no! no! I can always soothe him. I will be so mild, so gentle. You can be present, and hear every word I say. I will only kiss him, and tell him who has done this, and to be brave, for his wife watches over him; and, sir, I will beg him to be patient, and not blame you nor any of the people here."

"Very proper, very proper; but really this interview must be postponed till you have an order, or Dr. Suaby returns. He can violate his own rules if he likes; but I cannot, and, indeed, I dare not."

"Dare not let a lady see her husband? Then you are not a man. Oh, can this be England? It is too inhuman."

Then she began to cry and wring her hands.

"This is very painful," said Mr. Salter, and left the room.

The respectable servant looked in soon after, and Lady Bassett told him, between her sobs, that she had brought some clothes and things for her husband. "Surely, sir," said she, "they will not refuse me that?"

"Lord, no, ma'am," said the man. "You can give them to the keeper and nurse in charge of him."

Lady Bassett slipped a guinea into the man's hand directly. "Let me see those people," said she.

The man winked, and vanished: he soon reappeared, and said, loudly, "Now, madam, if you will order the things into the hall."

Lady Bassett came out and gave the order.

A short, bull-necked man, and rather a pretty young woman with a flaunting cap, bestirred themselves getting down the things; and Mr. Salter came out and looked on.

Lady Bassett called Mary Wells, and gave her a five-pound note to slip into the man's hand. She telegraphed the girl, who instantly came near her with an India rubber bath, and, affecting ignorance, asked her what that was.

Lady Bassett dropped three sovereigns into the bath, and said, "Ten times, twenty times that, if you are kind to him. Tell him it is his cousin's doing, but his wife watches over him."

"All right," said the girl. "Come again when the doctor is here."

All this passed, in swift whispers, a few yards from Mr. Salter, and he now came forward and offered his arm to conduct Lady Bassett to the carriage.

But the wretched, heart-broken wife forgot her art of pleasing. She shrank from him with a faint cry of aversion, and got into her carriage unaided. Mary Wells followed her.

Mr. Salter was unwilling to receive this rebuff. He followed, and said, "The clothes shall be given, with any message you may think fit to intrust to me."

Lady Bassett turned away sharply from him, and said to Mary Wells, "Tell him to drive home. Home! I have none now. Its light is torn from me."

The carriage drove away as she uttered these piteous words.

She cried at intervals all the way home; and could hardly drag herself upstairs to bed.

Mr. Angelo called next day with bad news. Not a magistrate would move a finger against Mr. Bassett: he had the law on his side. Sir Charles was evidently insane; it was quite proper he should be put in security before he did some mischief to himself or Lady Bassett. "They say, why was he hidden for two months, if there was not something very wrong?"

Lady Bassett ordered the carriage and paid several calls, to counteract this fatal impression.

She found, to her horror, she might as well try to move a rock. There was plenty of kindness and pity; but the moment she began to assure them her husband was not insane she was met with the dead silence of polite incredulity. One or two old friends went further, and said, "My dear, we are told he could not be taken away without two doctors' certificates: now, consider, they must know better than you. Have patience, and let them cure him."

Lady Bassett withdrew her friendship on the spot from two ladies for contradicting her on such a subject; she returned home almost wild herself.

In the village her carriage was stopped by a woman with her hair all flying, who told her, in a lamentable voice, that Squire Bassett had sent nine men to prison for taking Sir Charles's part and ill-treating his captors.

"My lawyer shall defend them at my expense," said Lady Bassett, with a sigh.

At last she got home, and went up to her own room, and there was Mary Wells waiting to dress her.

She tottered in, and sank into a chair. But, after this temporary exhaustion, came a rising tempest of passion; her eyes roved, her fingers worked, and her heart seemed to come out of her in words of fire. "I have not a friend in all the county. That villain has only to say 'Mad,' and all turn from me, as if an angel of truth had said 'Criminal.' We have no friend but one, and she is my servant. Now go and envy wealth and titles. No wife in this parish is so poor as I; powerless in the folds of a serpent. I can't see my husband without an order from ***him.*** He is all power, I and mine all weakness." She raised her clinched fists, she clutched her beautiful hair as if she would tear it out by the roots. "I shall, go mad! I shall go mad! No!" said she, all of a sudden. "That will not do. That is what he wants--and then my darling ***would*** be defenseless. I will not go mad." Then suddenly grinding her white teeth: "I'll teach him to drive a lady to despair. I'll fight."

She descended, almost without a break, from the fury of a Pythoness to a strange calm. Oh! then it is her sex are dangerous.

"Don't look so pale," said she, and she actually smiled. "All is fair against so foul a villain. You and I will defeat him. Dress me, Mary."

Mary Wells, carried away by the unusual violence of a superior mind, was quite bewildered.

Lady Bassett smiled a strange smile, and said, "I'll show you how to dress me;" and she did give her a lesson that astonished her.

"And now," said Lady Bassett, "I shall dress you." And she took a loose full dress out of her wardrobe, and made Mary Wells put it on; but first she inserted some stuffing so adroitly that Mary seemed very buxom, but what she wished to hide was hidden. Not so Lady Bassett herself. Her figure looked much rounder than in the last dress she wore.

With all this she was late for dinner, and when she went down Mr. Angelo had just finished telling Mr. Oldfield of the mishap to the villagers.

Lady Bassett came in animated and beautiful.

Dinner was announced directly, and a commonplace conversation kept up till the servants were got rid of. She then told Mr. Oldfield how she had been refused admittance to Sir Charles at Bellevue House, a plain proof, to her mind, they knew her husband was not insane; and begged him to act with energy, and get Sir Charles out before his reason could be permanently injured by the outrage and the horror of his situation.

This led to a discussion, in which Mr. Angelo and Lady Bassett threw out various suggestions, and Mr. Oldfield cooled their ardor with sound objections. He was familiar with the Statutes de Lunatico, and said they had been strictly observed both in the capture of Sir Charles and in Mr. Salter's refusal to let the wife see the husband. In short, he appeared either unable or unwilling to see anything except the strong legal position of the adverse party.

Mr. Oldfield was one of those prudent lawyers who search for the adversary's strong points, that their clients may not be taken by surprise; and that is very wise of them. But wise things require to be done wisely: he sometimes carried this system so far as to discourage his client too much. It is a fine thing to make your client think his case the weaker of the two, and then win it for him easily; that gratifies your own foible, professional vanity. But suppose, with your discouraging him so, he flings up or compromises a winning case? Suppose he takes the huff and goes to some other lawyer, who will warm him with hopes instead of cooling him with a one-sided and hostile view of his case?

In the present discussion Mr. Oldfield's habit of beginning by admiring his adversaries, together with his knowledge of law and little else, and his secret conviction that Sir Charles was unsound of mind, combined to paralyze him; and, not being a man of invention, he could not see his way out of the wood at all; he could negative Mr. Angelo's suggestions and give good reasons, but he could not, or did not, suggest anything better to be done.

Lady Bassett listened to his negative wisdom with a bitter smile, and said, at last, with a sigh: "It seems, then, we are to sit quiet and do nothing, while Mr. Bassett and his solicitor strike blow upon blow. There! I'll fight my own battle; and do you try and find some way of defending the poor souls that are in trouble because they did not sit with their hands before them when their benefactor was outraged. Command my purse, if money will save them from prison."

Then she rose with dignity, and walked like a camelopard all down the room on the side opposite to Mr. Oldfield. Angelo flew to open the door, and in a whisper begged a word with her in private. She bowed ascent, and passed on from the room.

"What a fine creature!" said Mr. Oldfield. "How she walks!"

Mr. Angelo made no reply to this, but asked him what was to be done for the poor men: "they will be up before the Bench to-morrow."

Stung a little by Lady Bassett's remark, Mr. Oldfield answered, promptly, "We must get some tradesmen to bail them with our money. It will only be a few pounds apiece. If the bail is accepted, they shall offer pecuniary compensation, and get up a defense; find somebody to swear Sir Charles was sane--that sort of evidence is always to be got. Counsel must do the rest. Simple natives--benefactor outraged--honest impulse--regretted, the moment they understood the capture had been legally made. Then throw dirt on the plaintiff. He is malicious, and can be proved to have forsworn himself in Bassett *v.* Bassett."

A tap at the door, and Mary Wells put in her head. "If you please, sir, my lady is tired, and she wishes to say a word to you before she goes upstairs."

"Excuse me one minute," said Mr. Angelo, and followed Mary Wells. She ushered him into a boudoir, where he found Lady Bassett seated in an armchair, with her head on her hand, and her eyes fixed sadly on the carpet.

She smiled faintly, and said, "Well, what do you wish to say to me?"

"It is about Mr. Oldfield. He is clearly incompetent."

"I don't know. I snubbed him, poor man: but if the law is all against us!"

"How does he know that? He assumes it because he is prejudiced in favor of the enemy. How does he **know** they have done **everything** the Act of Parliament requires? And, if they have, Law is not invincible. When Law defies Morality, it gets baffled, and trampled on in all civilized communities."

"I never heard that before."

"But you would if you had been at Oxford," said he, smiling.

"Ah!"

"What we want is a man of genius, of invention; a man who will see every chance, take every chance, lawful or unlawful, and fight with all manner of weapons."

Lady Bassett's eye flashed a moment. "Ah!" said she; "but where can I find such a man, with knowledge to guide his zeal?"

"I think I know of a man who could at all events advise you, if you would ask him."

"Ah! Who?"

"He is a writer; and opinions vary as to his merit. Some say he has talent; others say it is all eccentricity and affectation. One thing is certain--his books bring about the changes he demands. And then he is in earnest; he has taken a good many alleged lunatics out of confinement."

"Is it possible? Then let us apply to him at once."

"He lives in London; but I have a friend who knows him. May I send an outline to him through that friend, and ask him whether he can advise you in the matter?"

"You may; and thank you a thousand times!"

"A mind like that, with knowledge, zeal, and invention, must surely throw some light."

"One would think so, dear friend."

"I'll write to-night and send a letter to Greatrex; we shall perhaps get an answer the day after to-morrow."

"Ah! you are not the one to go to sleep in the service of a friend. A writer, did you say? What does he write?"

"Fiction."

"What, novels?"

"And dramas and all."

Lady Bassett sighed incredulously. "I should never think of going to Fiction for wisdom."

"When the Family Calas were about to be executed unjustly, with the consent of all the lawyers and statesmen in France, one man in a nation saw the error, and fought for the innocent, and saved them; and that one wise man in a nation of fools was a writer of fiction."

"Oh! a learned Oxonian can always answer a poor ignorant thing like me. One swallow does not make summer, for all that."

"But this writer's fictions are not like the novels you read; they are works of laborious research. Besides, he is a lawyer, as well as a novelist."

"Oh, if he is a lawyer!"

"Then I may write?"

"Yes," said Lady Bassett, despondingly.

"What is to become of Oldfield?"

"Send him to the drawing-room. I will go down and endure him for another hour. You can write your letter here, and then please come and relieve me of Mr. Negative."

She rang, and ordered coffee and tea into the drawing-room; and Mr. Oldfield found her very cold company.

In half an hour Mr. Angelo came down, looking flushed and very handsome;

and Lady Bassett had some fresh tea made for him.

This done she bade the gentlemen goodnight, and went to her room. Here she found Mary Wells full of curiosity to know whether the lawyer would get Sir Charles out of the asylum.

Lady Bassett gave loose to her indignation, and said nothing was to be expected from such a Nullity. "Mary, he could not see. I gave him every opportunity. I walked slowly down the room before him after dinner; and I came into the drawing-room and moved about, and yet he could not see."

"Then you will have to tell him, that is all."

"Never; no more shall you. I'll not trust my fate, and Sir Charles's, to a man that has no eyes."

For this feminine reason she took a spite against poor Oldfield; but to Mr. Angelo she suppressed the real reason, and entered into that ardent gentleman's grounds of discontent, though these alone would not have entirely dissolved her respect for the family solicitor.

Next afternoon Angelo came to her in great distress and ire. "Beaten! beaten! and all through our adversaries having more talent. Mr. Bassett did not appear at first. Wheeler excused him on the ground that his wife was seriously ill through the fright. Bassett's servants were called, and swore to the damage and to the men, all but one. He got off. Then Oldfield made a dry speech; and a tradesman he had prepared offered bail. The magistrates were consulting, when in burst Mr. Bassett all in black, and made a speech fifty times stronger than Oldfield's, and sobbed, and told them the rioters had frightened his wife so she had been prematurely confined, and the child was dead. Could they take bail for a riot, a dastardly attack by a mob of cowards on a poor defenseless woman, the gentlest and most inoffensive creature in England? Then he went on: 'They were told I was not in the house; and then they found courage to fling stones, to terrify my wife and kill my child. Poor soul!' he said, 'she lies between life and death herself: and I come here in an agony of fear, but I come for justice; the man of straw, who offers bail, is furnished with the money by those who stimulated the outrage. Defeat that fraud, and teach these cowards who war on defenseless ladies that there is humanity and justice and law in the land.' Then Oldfield tried to answer him with his hems and his haws; but Bassett turned on him like a giant, and swept him away."

"Poor woman!"

"Ah! that is true: I am afraid I have thought too little of her. But you suffer, and so must she. It is the most terrible feud; one would think this was Corsica instead of England, only the fighting is not done with daggers. But, after this, pray lean no more on that Oldfield. We were all carried away at first; but, now I think of it, Bassett must have been in the court, and held back to make the climax. Oh, yes! it was another surprise and another success. They are all sent to jail. Superior generalship! If Wheeler had been our man, we should have had eight wives crying for pity, each with one child in her arms, and another holding on to her apron. Do, pray, Lady Bassett, dismiss that Nullity."

"Oh, I cannot do that; he is Sir Charles's lawyer; but I have promised you to seek advice elsewhere, and so I will."

The conversation was interrupted by the tolling of the church-bell.

The first note startled Lady Bassett, and she turned pale.

"I must leave you," said Angelo, regretfully. "I have to bury Mr. Bassett's little boy; he lived an hour."

Lady Bassett sat and heard the bell toll.

Strange, sad thoughts passed through her mind. "Is it saddest when it tolls, or when it rings--that bell? He has killed his own child by robbing me of my husband. We are in the hands of God, after all, let Wheeler be ever so cunning, and Oldfield ever so simple.--And I am not acting by that.--Where is my trust in God's justice?--Oh, thou of little faith!--What shall I do? Love is stronger in me than faith--stronger than anything in heaven or earth. God forgive me--God help me--I will go back.

"But oh, to stand still, and be good and simple, and to see my husband trampled on by a cunning villain!

"Why is there a future state, where everything is to be different? no hate; no injustice; all love. Why is it not all of a piece? Why begin wrong if it is to end all right? If I was omnipotent it should be right from the first.--Oh, thou of little faith!--Ah, me! it is hard to see fools and devils, and realize angels unseen. Oh, that I could shut my eyes in faith and go to sleep, and drift on the right path; for I shall never take it with my eyes open, and my heart bleeding for him."

Then her head fell languidly back, her eyes closed, and the tears welled through them: they knew the way by this time.

CHAPTER XXII.

NEXT morning in came Mr. Angelo, with glowing cheeks and sparkling eyes.

"I have got a letter, a most gratifying one. My friend called on Mr. Rolfe, and gave him my lines; and he replies direct to me. May I read you his letter?"

"Oh, yes."

"'DEAR SIR--The case you have sent me, of a gentleman confined on certificates by order of an interested relative--as you presume, for you have not seen the order--and on grounds you think insufficient, is interesting, and some of it looks true; but there are gaps in the statement, and I dare not advise in so nice a matter till these are filled; but that, I suspect, can only be done by the lady herself. She had better call on me in person; it may be worth her while. At home every day, 10--3, this week. As for yourself, you need not address me through Greatrex. I have seen you pull No. 6, and afterward stroke in the University boat, and you dived in Portsmouth Harbor, and saved a sailor. See "Ryde Journal," Aug. 10, p. 4, col. 3; cited in my Day-book Aug. 10, and also in my Index hominum, in voce "Angelo"--ha! ha! here's a fellow for detail!

"Yours very truly,

"'ROLFE.'"

"And did you?"

"Did I what?"

"Dive and save a sailor."

"No; I nailed him just as he was sinking."

"How good and brave you are!"

Angelo blushed like a girl. "It makes me too happy to hear such words from you. But I vote we don't talk about me. Will you call on Mr. Rolfe?"

"Is he married?"

Angelo opened his eyes at the question. "I think not," said he. "Indeed, I know he is not."

"Could you get him down here?"

Angelo shook his head. "If he knew you, perhaps; but can you expect him to come here upon your business? These popular writers are spoiled by the ladies. I doubt if he would walk across the street to advise a stranger. Candidly, why should he?"

"No; and it was ridiculous vanity to suppose he would. But I never called on a gentleman in my life."

"Take me with you. You can go up at nine, and be back to a late dinner."

"I shall never have the courage to go. Let me have his letter."

He gave her the letter, and she took it away.

At six o'clock she sent Mary Wells to Mr. Angelo, with a note to say she had studied Mr. Rolfe's letter, and there was more in it than she had thought; but his going off from her husband to boat-racing seemed trivial, and she could not make up her mind to go to London to consult a novelist on such a serious matter.

At nine she sent to say she should go, but could not think of dragging him there: she should take her maid.

Before eleven, she half repented this resolution, but her maid kept her to it; and at half past twelve next day they reached Mr. Rolfe's door; an old-fashioned, mean-looking house, in one of the briskest thoroughfares of the metropolis; a cab-stand opposite to the door, and a tide of omnibuses passing it.

Lady Bassett viewed the place discontentedly, and said to herself, "What a poky little place for a writer to live in; how noisy, how unpoetical!"

They knocked at the door. It was opened by a maid-servant.

"Is Mr. Rolfe at home?"

"Yes, ma'am. Please give me your card, and write the business."

Lady Bassett took out her card and wrote a line or two on the back of it. The maid glanced at it, and showed her into a room, while she took the card to her master.

The room was rather long, low, and nondescript; scarlet flock paper; curtains and sofas green Utrecht velvet; woodwork and pillars white and gold; two windows looking on the street; at the other end folding-doors with scarcely any wood-work, all plate-glass, but partly hidden by heavy curtains of the same color and material as the others. Accustomed to large, lofty rooms, Lady Bassett felt herself in a long box here; but the colors pleased her. She said to Mary Wells, "What a funny, cozy little place for a gentleman to live in!"

Mr. Rolfe was engaged with some one, and she was kept waiting; this was quite new to her, and discouraged her, already intimidated by the novelty of the situation.

She tried to encourage herself by saying it was for her husband she did this unusual thing; but she felt very miserable and inclined to cry.

At last a bell rang; the maid came in and invited Lady Bassett to follow her. She opened the glass folding-doors, and took them into a small conservatory, walled like a grotto, with ferns sprouting out of rocky fissures, and spars sparkling, water dripping. Then she opened two more glass folding-doors, and ushered them into an empty room, the like of which Lady Bassett had never seen; it was large in itself, and multiplied tenfold by great mirrors from floor to ceiling, with no frames but a narrow oak beading; opposite her, on entering, was a bay-window all plate-glass, the central panes of which opened, like doors, upon a pretty little garden that glowed with color, and was backed by fine trees belonging to the nation; for this garden ran up to the wall of Hyde Park.

The numerous and large mirrors all down to the ground laid hold of the garden and the flowers, and by double and treble reflection filled the room with delightful nooks of verdure and color.

To confuse the eye still more, a quantity of young India-rubber trees, with glossy leaves, were placed before the large central mirror. The carpet was a warm velvet-pile, the walls were distempered, a French gray, not cold, but with a tint of mauve that gave a warm and cheering bloom; this soothing color gave great effect to the one or two masterpieces of painting that hung on the walls and to the gilt frames; the furniture, oak and marqueterie highly polished; the curtains, scarlet merino, through which the sun shone, and, being a London sun, diffused a mild rosy tint favorable to female faces. Not a sound of London could be heard.

So far the room was romantic; but there was a prosaic corner to shock those who fancy that fiction is the spontaneous overflow of a poetic fountain fed by nature only; between the fireplace and the window, and within a foot or two of the wall, stood a gigantic writing-table, with the signs of hard labor on it, and of severe system. Three plated buckets, each containing three pints, full of letters to be answered, other letters to be pasted into a classified guard-book, loose notes to be pasted into various books and classified (for this writer used to sneer at the learned men who say, "I will look among my papers for it;" he held that every written scrap ought either to be burned, or pasted into a classified guard-book, where it could be found by consulting the index); five things like bankers' bill-books, into whose several compartments MS. notes and newspaper cuttings were thrown, as a preliminary toward classification in books.

Underneath the table was a formidable array of note-books, standing upright, and labeled on their backs. There were about twenty large folios of classified facts, ideas, and pictures--for the very wood-cuts were all indexed and classified on the plan of a tradesman's ledger; there was also the receipt-book of the year, treated on the same plan. Receipts on a file would not do for this romantic creature. If a tradesman brought a bill, he must be able to turn to that tradesman's name in a book, and prove in a moment whether it had been paid or not. Then there was a collection of solid quartos, and of smaller folio guard-books called Indexes. There was "Index rerum et journalium"-- "Index rerum et librorum,"--"Index rerum et hominum," and a lot more; indeed, so many that, by way of climax, there was a fat folio ledger entitled "Index ad Indices."

By the side of the table were six or seven thick pasteboard cards, each about the size of a large portfolio, and on these the author's notes and extracts were collected from all his repertories into something like a focus for a present purpose. He was writing a novel based on facts; facts, incidents, living dialogue, pictures, reflections, situations, were all on these cards to choose from, and arranged in headed columns; and some portions of the work he was writing on this basis of imagination and drudgery lay on the table in two forms, his own writing, and his secretary's copy thereof, the latter corrected for the press. This copy was half margin, and so provided for additions and improvements; but for one addition there were ten excisions, great and small. Lady Bassett had just time to take in the beauty and artistic character of the place, and to realize the appalling drudgery that stamped it a workshop, when the author, who had dashed into his garden for a moment's recreation, came to the window, and furnished contrast No. 3. For he looked neither like a poet nor a drudge, but a great fat country farmer. He was rather tall, very portly, small-ish head, commonplace features mild brown eye not very bright, short beard, and wore a suit of tweed all one color. Such looked the writer of romances founded on fact. He rolled up to the window--for, if he looked like a farmer, he walked like a sailor--and stepped into the room.

CHAPTER XXIII.

M R. ROLFE surveyed the two women with a mild, inoffensive, ox-like gaze, and invited them to be seated with homely civility.

He sat down at his desk, and turning to Lady Bassett, said, rather dreamily, "One moment, please: let me look at the case and my notes."

First his homely appearance, and now a certain languor about his manner, discouraged Lady Bassett more than it need; for all artists must pay for their excitements with occasional languor. Her hands trembled, and she began to gulp and try not to cry.

Mr. Rolfe observed directly, and said, rather kindly, "You are agitated; and no wonder."

He then opened a sort of china closet, poured a few drops of a colorless liquid from a tiny bottle into a wine-glass, and filled the glass with water from a filter. "Drink that, if you please."

She looked at him with her eyes brimming. *"Must* I?"

"Yes; it will do you good for once in a way. It is only Ignatia."

She drank it by degrees, and a tear along with it that fell into the glass.

Meantime Mr. Rolfe had returned to his notes and examined them. He then addressed her, half stiffly, half kindly:

"Lady Bassett, whatever may be your husband's condition--whether his illness is mental or bodily, or a mixture of the two--his clandestine examination by bought physicians, and his violent capture, the natural effect of which must have been to excite him and retard his cure, were wicked and barbarous acts, contrary to God's law and the common law of England, and, indeed, to all human law except our shallow, incautious Statutes de Lunatico: they were an insult to yourself, who ought at least to have been consulted, for your rights are higher and purer than Richard Bassett's; therefore, as a wife bereaved of your husband by fraud and violence and the bare letter of a paltry statute whose spirit has been violated, you are quite justified in coming to me or to any public man you think can help your husband and you." Then, with a certain ***bonhomie,*** "So lay aside your nervousness; let us go into this matter sensibly, like a big man and a little man, or like an old woman and a young woman, whichever you prefer."

Lady Bassett looked at him and smiled assent. She felt a great deal more at her ease after this opening.

"I dare not advise you yet. I must know more than Mr. Angelo has told me. Will you answer my questions frankly?"

"I will try, sir."

"Whose idea was it confining Sir Charles Bassett to the house so much?"

"His own. He felt himself unfit for society."

"Did he describe his ailment to you then?"

"Yes."

"All the better; what did he say?"

"He said that, at times, a cloud seemed to come into his head, and then he lost all power of mind; and he could not bear to be seen in that condition."

"This was after the epileptic seizure?"

"Yes, sir."

"Humph! Now will you tell me how Mr. Bassett, by mere words, could so enrage Sir Charles as to give him a fit?"

Lady Bassett hesitated.

"What did he say to Sir Charles?"

"He did not speak to him. His child and nurse were there, and he called out loud, for Sir Charles to hear, and told the nurse to hold up his child to look at his inheritance."

"Malicious fool! But did this enrage Sir Charles so much as to give him a fit?"

"Yes."

"He must be very sensitive."

"On that subject."

Mr. Rolfe was silent; and now, for the first time, appeared to think intently.

His study bore fruit, apparently; for he turned to Lady Bassett and said, suddenly, "What is the strangest thing Sir Charles has said of late--the very strangest?"

Lady Bassett turned red, and then pale, and made no reply.

Mr. Rolfe rose and walked up to Mary Wells.

"What is the maddest thing your master has ever said?"

Mary Wells, instead of replying, looked at her mistress.

The writer instantly put his great body between them. "Come, none of that," said he. "I don't want a falsehood--I want the truth."

"La, sir, I don't know. My master he is not mad, I'm sure. The queerest thing he ever said was--he did say at one time 'twas writ on his face as he had no children."

"Ah! And that is why he would not go abroad, perhaps."

"That was one reason, sir, I do suppose." Mr. Rolfe put his hands behind his back and walked thoughtfully and rather disconsolately back to his seat.

"Humph!" said he. Then, after a pause, "Well, well; I know the worst now; that is one comfort. Lady Bassett, you really must be candid with me. Consider: good advice is like a tight glove; it fits the circumstances, and it does not fit other circumstances. No man advises so badly on a false and partial statement as I do, for the very reason that my advice is a close fit. Even now I can't understand Sir Charles's despair of having children of his own."

The writer then turned his looks on the two women, with an entire absence of expression; the sense of his eyes was turned inward, though the orbs were directed toward his visitors.

With this lack-luster gaze, and in the tone of thoughtful soliloquy, he said, "Has Sir Charles Bassett no eyes? and are there women so furtive, so secret, or so bashful, they do not tell their husbands?"

Lady Bassett turned with a scared look to Mary Wells, and that young woman showed her usual readiness. She actually came to Mr. Rolfe and half whispered to him, "If you please, sir, gentlemen are blind, and my lady she is very bashful; but Sir Charles knows it now; he have known it a good while; and it was a great comfort to him; he was getting better, sir, when the villains took him--ever so much better."

This solution silenced Mr. Rolfe, though it did not quite satisfy him. He fastened on Mary Wells's last statement. "Now tell me: between the day when those two doctors got into his apartment and the day of his capture, how long?"

"About a fortnight."

"And in that particular fortnight was there a marked improvement?"

"La, yes, sir; was there not, my lady?"

"Indeed there was, sir. He was beginning to take walks with me in the garden, and rides in an open carriage. He was getting better every day; and oh, sir, that is what breaks my heart! I was curing my darling so fast, and now they will do all they can to destroy him. Their not letting his wife see him terrifies me."

"I think I can explain that. Now tell me--what time do you expect--a certain event?"

Lady Bassett blushed and cast a hasty glance at the speaker; but he had a piece of paper before him, and was preparing to take down her reply, with the innocent face of a man who had asked a simple and necessary question in the way of business.

Then Lady Bassett looked at Mary Wells, and this look Mr. Rolfe surprised, because he himself looked up to see why the lady hesitated.

After an expressive glance between the mistress and maid, the lady said, almost inaudibly, "More than three months;" and then she blushed all over.

Mr. Rolfe looked at the two women a moment, and seemed a little puzzled at their telegraphing each other on such a subject; but he coolly noted down Lady Bassett's reply on a card about the size of a foolscap sheet, and then set himself to write on the same card the other facts he had elicited.

While he was doing this very slowly, with great care and pains, the lady was eying him like a zoologist studying some new animal. The simplicity and straightforwardness of his last question won by degrees upon her judgment and reconciled her to her Inquisitor, the more so as he was quiet but intense, and his whole soul in her case. She began to respect his simple straightforwardness, his civility without a grain of gallantry, and his caution in eliciting all the facts before he would advise.

After he had written down his synopsis, looking all the time as if his life depended on its correctness, he leaned back, and his ordinary but mobile countenance was transfigured into geniality.

"Come," said he, "grandmamma has pestered you with questions enough; now you retort--ask me anything--speak your mind: these things should be attacked in every form, and sifted with every sieve."

Lady Bassett hesitated a moment, but at last responded to this invitation.

"Sir, one thing that discourages me cruelly--my solicitor seems so inferior to Mr. Bassett's. He can think of nothing but objections; and so he does nothing, and lets us be trampled on: it is his being unable to cope with Mr. Bassett's solicitor, Mr. Wheeler, that has led me in my deep distress to trouble you, whom I had not the honor of knowing."

"I understand your ladyship perfectly. Mr. Oldfield is a respectable solicitor, and Wheeler is a sharp country practitioner; and--to use my favorite Americanism--you feel like fighting with a blunt knife against a sharp one."

"That is my feeling, sir, and it drives me almost wild sometimes."

"For your comfort, then, in my earlier litigations--I have had sixteen lawsuits for myself and other oppressed people--I had often that very impression; but the result always corrected it. Legal battles are like other battles: first you have a skirmish or two, and then a great battle in court. Now sharp attorneys are very apt to win the skirmish and lose the battle. I see a general of this stamp in Mr. Wheeler, and you need not fear him much. Of course an antagonist is never to be despised; but I would rather have Wheeler against you than Oldfield. An honest man like Oldfield blunders into wisdom, the Lord knows how. Your Wheelers seldom get beyond cunning; and cunning does not see far enough to cope with men of real sagacity and forethought in matters so complicated as this. Oldfield, acting for Bassett, would have pushed rapidly on to an examination by the court. You would have evaded it, and put yourself in the wrong; and the inquiry, well urged, might have been adverse to Sir Charles. Wheeler has taken a more cunning and violent course--it strikes more terror, does more immediate harm; but what does it lead to? Very little; and it disarms them of their sharpest weapon, the immediate inquiry; for we could now delay and greatly prejudice an inquiry on the very ground of the outrage and unnecessary violence; and could demand time to get the patient as well as he was before the outrage. And, indeed, the court is very jealous of those who begin by going to a judge, and then alter their minds, and try to dispose of the case themselves. And to make matters worse, here they do it by straining an Act of Parliament opposed to equity."

"I wish it may prove so, sir; but, meantime, Mr. Wheeler is active, Mr. Oldfield is passive. He has not an idea. He is a mere negative."

"Ah, that is because he is out of his groove. A smattering of law is not enough here. It wants a smattering of human nature too."

"Then, sir, would you advise me to part with Mr. Oldfield?"

"No. Why make an enemy? Besides, he is the vehicle of communication with the other side. You must simply ignore him for a time."

"But is there nothing I can do, sir? for it is this cruel inactivity that kills me. Pray advise me--you know all now."

Mr. Rolfe, thus challenged, begged for a moment's delay.

"Let us be silent a minute," said he, "and think hard."

And, to judge by his face, he did think with great intensity.

"Lady Bassett," said he, very gravely, "I assume that every fact you and Mr. Angelo have laid before me is true, and no vital part is kept back. Well, then, your present course is--Delay. Not the weak delay of those who procrastinate what cannot be avoided; but the wise delay of a general who can bring up overpowering forces, only give him time. Understand me, there is more than one game on the cards; but I prefer the surest. We could begin fighting openly to-morrow; but that would be risking too much for too little. The law's delay, the insolence of office, the up-hill and thorny way, would hurt Sir Charles's mind at present. The apathy, the cruelty, the trickery, the routine, the hot and cold fits of hope and fear, would poison your blood, and perhaps lose Sir Charles the heir he pines for. Besides, if we give battle to-day we fight the heir at law; but in three or four months we may have him on our side, and trustees appointed by you. By that time, too, Sir Charles will have got over that abominable capture, and be better than he was a week ago, constantly soothed and consoled--as he will be--by the hope of offspring. When the right time comes, that moment we strike, and with a sledge-hammer. No letters to the commissioners then, no petitioning Chancery to send a jury into the asylum, stronghold of prejudice. I will cut your husband in two. Don't be alarmed. I will merely give him, with your help, an ***alter ego,*** who shall effect his liberation and ruin Richard Bassett--ruin him in damages and costs, and drive him out of the country, perhaps. Meantime you are not to be a lay figure, or a mere negative."

"Oh, sir, I am so glad of that!"

"Far from that: you will act defensively. Mr. Bassett has one chance; you must be the person to extinguish it. Injudicious treatment in the asylum might retard Sir

Charles's cure; their leeches and their sedatives, administered by sucking apoth-ecaries, who reason it *a priori,* instead of watching the effect of these things on the patient, might seriously injure your husband, for his disorder is connected with a weak circulation of blood in the vessels of the brain. We must therefore guard against that at once. To work, then. Who keeps this famous asylum?"

"Dr. Suaby."

"Suaby? I know that name. He has been here, I think. I must look in my Index rerum et hominum. Suaby? Not down. Try Asyla.--Asyla; 'Suaby: see letter-book for the year--, p. 368.' An old letter-book. I must go elsewhere for that."

He went out, and after some time returned with a folio letter-book.

"Here are two letters to me from Dr. Suaby, detailing his system and inviting me to spend a week at his asylum. Come, come; Sir Charles is with a man who does not fear inspection; for at this date I was bitter against private asylums--rather in-discriminately so, I fear. Stay! he visited me; I thought so. Here's a description of him: 'A pale, thoughtful man, with a remarkably mild eye: is against restraint of lu-natics, and against all punishment of them--Quixotically so. Being cross-examined, declares that if a patient gave him a black eye he would not let a keeper handle him roughly, being irresponsible.' No more would I, if I could give him a good licking myself. Please study these two letters closely; you may get a clew how to deal with the amiable writer in person."

"Oh, thank you, Mr. Rolfe," said Lady Bassett, flushing all over. She was so transported at having something to do. She quietly devoured the letters, and after she had read them said a load of fears was now taken off her mind.

Mr. Rolfe shook his head. "You must not rely on Dr. Suaby too much. In a pris-on or an asylum each functionary is important in exact proportion to his nominal insignificance; and why? Because the greater his nominal unimportance the more he comes in actual contact with the patient. The theoretical scale runs thus: 1st. The presiding physician. 2d. The medical subordinates. 3d. The keepers and nurses. The practical scale runs thus: 1st. The keepers and nurses. 2d. The medical attendants. 3d. The presiding physician."

"I am glad to hear you say so, sir; for when I went to the asylum, and the medi-cal attendant, Mr. Salter, would not let me see my husband. I gave his keeper and the nurse a little money to be kind to him in his confinement."

"You did! Yet you come here for advice? This is the way: a man discourses and argues, and by profound reasoning--that is, by what he thinks profound, and it isn't--arrives at the right thing; and lo! a woman, with her understanding heart and her hard, good sense, goes and does that wise thing humbly, without a word. SURSUM CORDA!--Cheer up, loving heart!" shouted he, like the roar of a lion in ecstasies; "you have done a masterstroke--without Oldfield, or Rolfe, or any other man."

Lady Bassett clasped her hands with joy, and some electric fire seemed to run through her veins; for she was all sensibilities, and this sudden triumphant roaring out of strong words was quite new to her, and carried her away.

"Well," said this eccentric personage, cooling quite as suddenly as he had fired, "the only improvement I can suggest is, be a little more precise at your next visit. Promise his keepers twenty guineas apiece the day Sir Charles is **cured;** and promise them ten guineas apiece not to administer one drop of medicine for the next two months; and, of course, no leech nor blister. The cursed sedatives they believe in are destruction to Sir Charles Bassett. His circulation must not be made too slow one day, and too fast the next, which is the effect of a sedative, but made regular by exercise and nourishing food. So, then, you will square the keepers by their cupidity; the doctor is on the right side **per se.** Shall we rely on these two, and ignore the medical attendants? No; why throw a chance away? What is the key to these medical attendants? Hum! Try flunkyism. I have great faith in British flunkyism. Pay your next visit with four horses, two outriders, and blazing liveries. Don't dress in perfect taste like **that;** go in finer clothes than you ever wore in the morning, or ought to wear, except at a wedding; go not as a petitioner, but as a queen; and dazzle snobs; the which being dazzled, then tickle their vanity: don't speak of Sir Charles as an injured man, nor as a man unsound in mind, but a gentleman who is rather ill; 'but **now,** gentlemen, I feel your remarkable skill will soon set him right.' Your husband runs that one risk; make him safe: a few smiles and a little flattery will do it; and if not, why, fight with all a woman's weapons. Don't be too nice: we must all hold a candle to the devil once in our lives. A wife's love sanctifies a woman's arts in fighting with a villain and disarming donkeys."

"Oh, I wish I was there now!"

"You are excited, madam," said he, severely. "That is out of place--in a deliberative assembly."

"No, no; only I want to be there, doing all this for my dear husband."

"You are very excited; and it is my fault. You must be hungry too: you have come a journey. There will be a reaction, and then you will be hysterical. Your temperament is of that kind."

He rang a bell and ordered his maid-servant to bring some beef-wafers and a pint of dry Champagne.

Lady Bassett remonstrated, but he told her to be quiet; "for," said he, "I have a smattering of medicine, as well as of law and of human nature. Sir Charles must correspond with you. Probably he has already written you six letters complaining of this monstrous act--a sane man incarcerated. Well, that class of letter goes into a letter-box in the hall of an asylum, but it never reaches its address. Please take a pen and write a formula." He dictated as follows:

"MY DEAR LOVE--The trifling illness I had when I came here is beginning to give way to the skill and attention of the medical gentlemen here. They are all most kind and attentive: the place, as it is conducted, is a credit to the country."

Lady Bassett's eyes sparkled. "Oh, Mr. Rolfe, is not this rather artful?"

"And is it not artful to put up a letter-box, encourage the writing of letters, and then open them, and suppress whatever is disagreeable? May every man who opens another man's letter find that letter a trap. Here comes your medicine. You never drink champagne in the middle of the day, of course?"

"Oh, no."

"Then it will be all the better medicine."

He made both mistress and maid eat the thin slices of beef and drink a glass of champagne.

While they were thus fortifying themselves he wrote his address on some stamped envelopes, and gave them to Lady Bassett, and told her she had better write to him at once if anything occurred. "You must also write to me if you really cannot get to see your husband. Then I will come down myself, with the public press at my back. But I am sure that will not be necessary in Dr. Suaby's asylum. He is a better Christian than I am, confound him for it! You went too soon; your husband had been agitated by the capture; Suaby was away; Salter had probably applied what he imagined to be soothing remedies, leeches--a blister--morphia. Result, the patient was so much worse than he was before they touched him that Salter was ashamed to let you see him. Having really excited him, instead of soothing him, Sawbones Salter had to pretend that *you* would excite him. As if creation contained any mineral, drug simple, leech, Spanish fly, gadfly, or showerbath, so soothing as a loving wife is to a man in affliction. New reading of an old song:

'If the heart of a man is oppressed with cares,   It makes him much worse when a woman appears.'

"Go to-morrow; you will see him. He will be worse than he was; but not much. Somebody will have told him that his wife put him in there--"

"Oh! oh!"

"And he won't have believed it. His father was a Bassett; his mother a Le Compton; his great-great-great-grandmother was a Rolfe: there is no cur's blood in him. After the first shock he will have found the spirit and dignity of a gentleman to sustain adversity: these men of fashion are like that; they are better steel than women--and writers."

When he had said this he indicated by his manner that he thought he had exhausted the subject, and himself.

Lady Bassett rose and said, "Then, sir, I will take my leave; and oh! I am sorry I have not your eloquent pen or your eloquent tongue to thank you. You have interested yourself in a stranger--you have brought the power of a great mind to bear on our distress. I came here a widow--now I feel a wife again. Your good words have warmed my very heart. I can only pray God to bless you, sir."

"Pray say no more, madam," said Mr. Rolfe, hastily. "A gentleman cannot be always writing lies; an hour or two given to truth and justice is a wholesome diversion. At all events, don't thank me till my advice has proved worth it."

He rang the bell; the servant came, and showed the way to the street door. Mr. Rolfe followed them to the passage only, whence he bowed ceremoniously once more to Lady Bassett as she went out.

As she passed into the street she heard a fearful clatter. It was her counselor tearing back to his interrupted novel like a distracted bullock.

"Well, I don't think much of *he,*" said Mary Wells.

Lady Bassett was mute to that, and all the journey home very absorbed and taciturn, impregnated with ideas she could not have invented, but was more able to execute than the inventor. She was absorbed in digesting Rolfe's every word, and fixing his map in her mind, and filling in details to his outline; so small-talk stung her: she gave her companion very short answers, especially when she disparaged Mr. Rolfe.

"You couldn't get in a word edgeways," said Mary Wells.

"I went to hear wisdom, and not to chatter."

"He doesn't think small beer of hisself, anyhow."

"How *can* he, and see other men?"

"Well. I don't think much of him, for my part."

"I dare say the Queen of Sheba's lady's-maid thought Solomon a silly thing."

"I don't know; that was afore my time" (rather pertly).

"Of course it was, or you couldn't imitate her."

On reaching home she ordered a light dinner upstairs, and sent directions to the coachman and grooms.

At nine next morning the four-in-hand came round, and they started for the asylum--coachman and two more in brave liveries; two outriders.

Twenty miles from Huntercombe they changed the wheelers, two fresh horses having been sent on at night.

They drove in at the lodge-gate of Bellevue House, which was left ostentatiously open, and soon drew up at the hall door, and set many a pale face peeping from the upper windows.

The door opened; the respectable servant came out with a respectful air.

"Is Mr. Salter at home, sir?"

"No, madam. Mr. Coyne is in charge to-day."

Lady Bassett was glad to hear that, and asked if she might be allowed to see Mr. Coyne.

"Certainly, madam. I'll tell him at once," was the reply.

Determined to enter the place, Lady Bassett requested her people to open the carriage door, and she was in the act of getting out when Mr. Coyne appeared, a little oily, bustling man, with a good-humored, vulgar face, liable to a subservient pucker; he wore it directly at sight of a fine woman, fine clothes, fine footmen, and fine horses.

"Mr. Coyne, I believe," said Lady Bassett, with a fascinating smile.

"At your service, madam."

"May I have a word in private with you, sir?"

"Certainly, madam."

"We have come a long way. May the horses be fed?"

"I am afraid," said the little man, apologetically, "I must ask you to send them to the inn. It is close by."

"By all means." (To one of the outriders:) "You will wait here for orders."

Mary Wells had been already instructed to wait in the hall and look out sharp for Sir Charles's keeper and nurse, and tell them her ladyship wanted to speak to them privately, and it would be money in their way.

Lady Bassett, closeted with Mr. Coyne, began first to congratulate herself. "Mr. Bassett," said she, "is no friend of mine, but he has done me a kindness in sending Sir Charles here, when he might have sent him to some place where he might have been made worse instead of better. Here, I conclude, gentlemen of your ability will soon cure his trifling disorder, will you not?"

"I have good hopes, your ladyship; he is better to-day."

"Now I dare say you could tell me to a month when he will be cured."

"Oh, your ladyship exaggerates my skill too much."

"Three months?"

"That is a short time to give us; but your ladyship may rely on it we will do our best."

"Will you? Then I have no fear of the result. Oh, by-the-by, Dr. Willis wanted me to take a message to you, Mr. Coyne. He knows you by reputation."

"Indeed! Really I was not aware that my humble--"

"Then you are better known than you in your modesty supposed. Let me see: what was the message? Oh, it was a peculiarity in Sir Charles he wished you to know. Dr. Willis has attended him from a boy, and he wished me to tell you that morphia and other sedatives have some very bad effects on him. I told Dr. Willis you would probably find that and every thing else out without a hint from him or any one else."

"Yes; but I will make a note of it, for all that."

"That is very kind of you. It will flatter the doctor, the more so as he has so high an opinion of you. But now, Mr. Coyne, I suppose if I am very good, and promise to soothe him, and not excite him, I may see my husband to-day?"

"Certainly, madam. You have an order from the person who--"

"I forgot to bring it with me. I relied on your humanity."

"That is unfortunate. I am afraid I must not--" He hesitated, looked very uncomfortable, and said he would consult Mr. Appleton; then, suddenly puckering his face into obsequiousness, "Would your ladyship like to inspect some of our arrangements for the comfort of our patients?"

Lady Bassett would have declined the proposal but for the singular play of countenance; she was herself all eye and mind, so she said, gravely, "I shall be very happy, sir."

Mr. Coyne then led the way, and showed her a large sitting-room, where some ladies were seated at different occupations and amusements: they kept more apart from each other than ladies do in general; but this was the only sign a far more experienced observer than Lady Bassett could have discovered, the nurses having sprung from authoritative into unobtrusive positions at the sound of Mr. Coyne's footstep outside.

"What!" said Lady Bassett; "are all these ladies--" She hesitated.

"Every one," said Mr. Coyne; "and some incurably."

"Oh, please let us retire; I have no right to gratify my curiosity. Poor things! they don't seem unhappy."

"Unhappy!" said Mr. Coyne. "We don't allow unhappiness here; our doctor is too fond of them; he is always contriving something to please them."

At this moment Lady Bassett looked up and saw a woman watching her over the rail of a corridor on the first floor. She recognized the face directly. The woman made her a rapid signal, and then disappeared into one of the rooms.

"Would there be any objection to our going upstairs, Mr. Coyne?" said Lady Bassett, with a calm voice and a heart thumping violently.

"Oh, none whatever. I'll conduct you; but then, I am afraid I must leave you for a time."

He showed her upstairs, blew a whistle, handed her over to an attendant, and bowed and smiled himself away grotesquely.

Jones was the very keeper she had feed last visit. She flushed with joy at sight of bull-necked, burly Jones. "Oh, Mr. Jones!" said she, putting her hands together with a look that might have melted a hangman.

Jones winked, and watched Mr. Coyne out of sight.

"I have seen your ladyship's maid," said Jones, confidentially. "It is all right. Mr. Coyne have got the blinkers on. Only pass me your word not to excite him."

"Oh no, sir, I will soothe him." And she trembled all over.

"Sally!" cried Jones.

The nurse came out of a room and held the door ajar; she whispered, "I have prepared him, madam; he is all right."

Lady Bassett, by a great effort, kept her feet from rushing, her heart from crying out with joy, and she entered the room. Sally closed the door like a shot, with a delicacy one would hardly have given her credit for, to judge from appearances.

Sir Charles stood in the middle of the room, beaming to receive her, but restraining himself. They met: he held her to his heart; she wept for joy and grief upon his neck. Neither spoke for a long time.

CHAPTER XXIV.

THEY were seated hand in hand, comparing notes and comforting each other. Then Lady Bassett met with a great surprise: forgetting, or rather not realizing, Sir Charles's sex and character, she began with a heavy heart to play the consoler; but after he had embraced her many times with tender rapture, and thanked God for the sight of her, lo and behold, this doughty baronet claimed his rights of manhood, and, in spite of his capture, his incarceration, and his malady, set to work to console her, instead of lying down to be consoled.

"My darling Bella," said he, "don't you make a mountain of a mole-hill. The moment you told me I should be a father I began to get better, and to laugh at Richard Bassett's malice. Of course I was terribly knocked over at first by being captured like a felon and clapped under lock and key; but I am getting over that. My head gets muddled once a day, that is all. They gave me some poison the first day that made me drunk twelve hours after; but they have not repeated it."

"Oh!" cried Lady Bassett, "then don't let me lose a moment. How could I forget?" She opened the door, and called in Mr. Jones and the nurse.

"Mr. Jones," said she, "the first day my husband came here Mr. Salter gave him a sedative, or something, and it made him much worse."

"It always do make 'em worse," said Jones, bluntly.

"Then why did he give it?"

"Out o' book, ma'am. His sort don't see how the medicines work; but we do, as are always about the patient."

"Mr. Jones," said Lady Bassett, "if Mr. Salter, or anybody, prescribes, it is you who *administer* the medicine."

Jones assented with a wink. Winking was his foible, as puckering of the face was Coyne's.

"Should you be offended if I were to offer you and the nurse ten guineas a month to pretend you had given him Mr. Salter's medicines, and not do it?"

"Oh, that is not much to do for a gentleman like Sir Charles," said Jones. "But I didn't ought to take so much money for that. To be sure, I suppose, the lady won't miss it."

"Don't be a donkey, Jones," said Sir Charles, cutting short his hypocrisy. "Take whatever you can get; only earn it."

"Oh, what I takes I earns."

"Of course," said Sir Charles. "So that is settled. You have got to physic those flower-pots instead of me, that is all."

This view of things tickled Jones so that he roared with laughter. However, he recollected himself all of a sudden, and stopped with ludicrous abruptness.

He said to Lady Bassett, with homely kindness, "You go home comfortable, my lady; you have taken the stick by the right end." He then had the good sense to retire from the room.

Then Lady Bassett told Sir Charles of her visit to London, and her calling on Mr. Rolfe.

He looked blank at his wife calling on a bachelor; but her description of the man, his age, and his simplicity, reconciled him to that; and when she told him the plan and order of campaign Mr. Rolfe had given her he approved it very earnestly.

He fastened in particular on something that Mr. Rolfe had dwelt lightly on. "Dear as the sight of you is to me, sweet as the sound of your loved voice is to my ears and my heart, I would rather not see you again until our hopes are realized than jeopardize *that.*"

Lady Bassett sighed, for this seemed rather morbid. Sir Charles went on: "So think of your own health first, and avoid agitations. I am tormented with fear lest that monster should take advantage of my absence to molest you. If he does, leave Huntercombe. Yes, leave it; go to London; go, even for my sake; my health and happiness depend on you; they cannot be much affected by anything that happens here. 'Stone walls do not a prison make, nor iron bars a cage.'"

Lady Bassett promised, but said she could not keep away from him, and he must often write to her. She gave him Rolfe's formula, and told him all letters would pass that praised the asylum.

Sir Charles made a wry face.

Lady Bassett's wrist went round his neck in a moment. "Oh, Charles, dear, for my sake--hold a little, little candle to the devil. Mr. Rolfe says we must. Oblige me in this--I am not so noble as you--and then I'll be very good and obedient in what your heart is set upon."

At last Sir Charles consented.

Then they made haste, and told each other everything that had happened, and it was late in the afternoon before they parted.

Lady Bassett controlled her tears at parting as well as she could.

Mr. Coyne had slyly hid himself, but emerged when she came down to the carriage, and she shook him warmly by the hand, and he bowed at the door incessantly, with his face all in a pucker, till the cavalcade dashed away.

CHAPTER XXV.

LADY BASSETT timed her next visit so that she found Dr. Suaby at home. He received her kindly, and showed himself a master; told her Sir Charles's was a mixed case, in which the fall, the fit, and a morbid desire for offspring had all played their parts.

He hoped a speedy cure, but said he counted on her assistance. There was no doubt what he meant.

Oh, for one thing, he said to her, rather slyly, "Coyne tells me you have been good enough to supply us with a hint as to his treatment; sedatives are opposed to his idiosyncrasy."

Lady Bassett blushed high, and said something about Dr. Willis.

"Oh, you are quite right, you and Dr. Willis; only you are not so very conversant with that idiosyncrasy. Why have you let him smoke twenty cigars every day of his life? the brain is accessible by other roads than the stomach. Well, we have got him down to four cigars, and in a month we will have him down to two. The effect of that, and exercise, and simple food, and the absence of powerful excitements--you will see. Do your part," said he, gayly, "we will do ours. He is the most interesting patient in the house, and born to adorn society, though by a concurrence of unhappy circumstances he is separated from it for a while."

She spent the whole afternoon with Sir Charles, and they dined together at the doctor's private table, with one or two patients who were touched, but showed no signs of it on that occasion; for the good doctor really acted like oil on the troubled waters.

Sir Charles and Lady Bassett corresponded, and so kept their hearts up; but after Rolfe's hint the correspondence was rather guarded. If these letters were read in the asylum the curious would learn that Sir Charles was far more anxious about his wife's condition than his own; but that these two patient persons were only waiting a certain near event to attack Richard Bassett with accumulated fury--that smoldering fire did not smoke by letter, but burned deep in both their sore and heavy, but enduring, Anglo-Saxon hearts.

Lady Bassett wrote to Mr. Rolfe, thanking him again for his advice, and telling him how it worked.

She had a very short reply from that gentleman.

But about six weeks after her visit he surprised her a little by writing of his own accord, and asking her for a formal introduction to Sir Charles Bassett, and begging her to back a request that Sir Charles would devote a leisure hour or two to correspondence with him. "Not," said he, "on his private affairs, but on a matter of general interest. I want a few of his experiences and observations in that place. I have the less scruple in asking it, that whatever takes him out of himself will be salutary."

Lady Bassett sent him the required introduction in such terms that Sir Charles at once consented to oblige his wife by obliging Mr. Rolfe.

"My DEAR SIR--In compliance with your wish, and Lady Bassett's, I send you a few desultory remarks on what I see here.

"1st. The lines,

'Great wits to madness nearly are allied,   And thin partitions do their bonds divide,'

are, in my opinion, exaggerated and untrue. Taking the people here as a guide, the insane in general appear to be people with very little brains, and enormous egotism.

"My next observation is, that the women have far less imagination than the men; they cannot even realize their own favorite delusions. For instance, here are two young ladies, the Virgin Mary and the Queen of England. How do they play their parts? They sit aloof from all the rest, with their noses in the air. But gauge their imaginations; go down on one knee, or both, and address them as a saint and a queen; they cannot say a word in accordance; yet they are cunning enough to see they cannot reply in character, so they will not utter a syllable to their adorers. They are like the shop-boys who go to a masquerade as Burleigh or Walsingham, and when you ask them who is Queen Bess's favorite just now, blush, and look offended, and pass sulkily on.

"The same class of male lunatics can speak in character; and this observation has made me doubt whether philosophers are not mistaken in saying that women generally have more imagination than men. I suspect they have infinitely less; and I believe their great love of novels, which has been set down to imagination, arises mainly from their want of it. You writers of novels supply that defect for them by a pictorial style, by an infinity of minute details, and petty aids to realizing, all which an imaginative reader can do for himself on reading a bare narrative of sterling facts and incidents.

"I find a monotony in madness. So many have inspirations, see phantoms, are the victims of vast conspiracies (principalities and powers combined against a fly); their food is poisoned, their wine is drugged, etc., etc.

"These, I think, are all forms of that morbid egotism which is at the bottom of insanity. So is their antipathy for each other. They keep apart, because a madman is all self, and his talk is all self; thus egotisms, clash, and an antipathy arises; yet it is not, I think, pure antipathy, though so regarded, but a mere form of their boundless egotism.

"If, in visiting an asylum, you see two or three different patients buttonhole a fourth and pour their grievances into a listening ear, you may safely suspect No. 4 of--sanity.

"On the whole, I think the doctor himself, and one of his attendants, and Jones, a keeper, have more solid eccentricity and variety about them than most of the patients."

Extract from Letter 2, written about a fortnight later:

"Some insane persons have a way of couching their nonsense in language that sounds rational, and has a false air of logical connection. Their periods seem stolen from sensible books, and forcibly fitted to incongruous bosh. By this means the ear is confused, and a slow hearer might fancy he was listening to sense.

"I have secured you one example of this. You must know that, in the evening, I sometimes collect a few together, and try to get them to tell their stories. Little comes of it in general but interruptions. But, one night, a melancholy Bagman responded in good set terms, and all in a moment; one would have thought I had put a torch to a barrel of powder, he went off so quickly, in this style:

"'You ask my story: it is briefly told. Initiated in commerce from my earliest years, and traveled in the cotton trade. As representative of a large house in Manchester, I visited the United States.

"'Unfortunately for me, that country was then the chosen abode of spirits; the very air was thick and humming with supernaturalia. Ere long spirit-voices whispered in my ear, and suggested pious aspirations at first. That was a blind, no doubt; for very soon they went on to insinuate things profane and indelicate, and urged me to deliver them in mixed companies; I forbore with difficulty, restrained by the early lessons of a pious mother, and a disinclination to be kicked downstairs, or flung out o' window.

"'I consulted a friend, a native of the country; he said, in its beautiful Doric, "Old oss, I reckon you'd better change the air." I grasped his hand, muttered a blessing, and sailed for England.

"'On ocean's peaceful bosom the annoyance ceased. But under this deceitful calm fresh dangers brooded. Two doctors had stolen into the ship, unseen by human eye, and bided their time. Unable to act at sea, owing to the combined effect of wind and current, they concealed themselves on deck under a black tarpaulin--that is to say, it had been black, but wind and weather had reduced it to a dirty brown--and there, adopting for the occasion the habits of the dormouse, the bear, the caterpillar, and other ephemeral productions, they lay torpid. But the moment the vessel touched the quay, profiting by the commotion, they emerged, and signed certificates with chalk on my portmanteau; then vanished in the crowd. The Custom-house read the certificates, and seized my luggage as contraband. I was too old a traveler to leave my luggage; so then they seized me, and sent us both down here. (With sudden and short-lived fury) that old hell-hound at the Lodge asked them where I was booked for. "For the whole journey," said a sepulchral voice unseen. That means the grave, my boys, the silent grave.'

"Notwithstanding this stern decree, Suaby expects to turn him out cured in a few months.

"Miss Wieland, a very pretty girl, put her arm in mine, and drew me mysteriously apart. 'So you are collecting the villainies,' said she, sotto voce. 'It will take you all your time. I'll tell you mine. There's a hideous old man wants me to marry him; and I won't. And he has put me in here, and keeps me prisoner till I will. They are all on his side, especially that sanctified old guy, Suaby. They drug my wine, they stupefy me, they give me things to make me naughty and tipsy; but it is no use; I never will marry that old goat--that for his money and him--I'll die first.'

"Of course my blood boiled; but I asked my nurse, Sally, and she assured me there was not one atom of truth in any part of the story. 'The young lady was put in here by her mother; none too soon, neither.' I asked her what she meant. 'Why, she came here with her throat cut, and strapping on it. She is a suicidal.'"

This correspondence led eventually to some unexpected results; but I am obliged to interrupt it for a time, while I deal with a distinct series of events which began about five weeks after Lady Bassett's visit to Mr. Rolfe, and will carry the reader forward beyond the date we have now arrived at.

It was the little dining-room at Highmore; a low room, of modest size, plainly furnished. An enormous fire-place, paved with plain tiles, on which were placed iron dogs; only wood and roots were burned in this room.

Mrs. Bassett had just been packed off to bed by marital authority; Bassett and Wheeler sat smoking pipes and sipping whisky-and-water. Bassett professed to like the smell of peat smoke in whisky; what he really liked was the price.

After a few silent whiffs, said Bassett, "I didn't think they would take it so quietly; did you?"

"Well, I really did not. But, after all, what can they do? They are evidently afraid to go to the Court of Chancery, and ask for a jury in the asylum; and what else can they do?"

"Humph! They might arrange an escape, and hide him for fourteen days; then we could not recapture him without fresh certificates; could we?"

"Certainly not."

"And the doors would be too well guarded; not a crack for two doctors to creep in at."

"You go too fast. *You* know the law from me, and you are a daring man that would try this sort of thing; but a timid woman, advised by a respectable muff like Oldfield! They will never dream of such a thing."

"Oldfield is not her head-man. She has got another adviser, and he is the very man to do something plucky."

"I don't know who you mean."

"Why, her lover, to be sure."

"Her lover? Lady Bassett's lover!"

"Ay, the young parson."

Wheeler smiled satirically. "You certainly are a good hater. Nothing is too bad for those you don't like. If that Lady Bassett is not a true wife, where will you find one?"

"She is the most deceitful jade in England."

"Oh! oh!"

"Ah! you may sneer. So you have forgotten how she outwitted us. Did the devil himself ever do a cunninger thing than that? tempting a fellow into a correspondence that seemed a piece of folly on her part, yet it was a deep diabolical trick to get at my handwriting. Did *you* see her game? No more than I did. You chuckled at her writing letters to the plaintiff ***pendente lite.*** We were both children, setting our wits against a woman's. I tell you I dread her, especially when I see her so unnaturally quiet, after what we have done. When you hook a large salmon, and he makes a great commotion, but all of a sudden lies like a stone, be on your guard; he means mischief."

"Well," said Wheeler, "this is all very true, but you have strayed from the point. What makes you think she has an improper attachment?"

"Is it so very unnatural? He is the handsomest fellow about, she is the loveliest woman; he is dark, she is fair; and they are thrown together by circumstances. Another thing: I have always understood that women admire the qualities they don't possess themselves--strength, for instance. Now this parson is a Hercules. He took Sir Charles up like a boy and carried him in his arms all the way from where he had the fit. Lady Bassett walked beside them. Rely on it, a woman does not see one man carry another so without making a comparison in favor of the strong, and against the weak. But what am I talking about? They walk like lovers, those two."

"What, hand in hand? he! he!"

"No, side by side; but yet like lovers for all that."

"You must have a good eye."

"I have a good opera-glass."

Mr. Wheeler smoked in silence.

"Well, but," said he, after a pause, "if this is so, all the better for you. Don't you see that the lover will never really help her to get the husband out of confinement? It is not in the nature of things. He may struggle with his own conscience a bit, being a clergyman, but he won't go too far; he won't break the law to get Sir Charles home, and so end these charming duets with his lady-love."

"By Jove, you are right!" cried Bassett, convinced in his turn. "I say, old fellow, two heads are better than one. I think we have got the clew, between us. Yes, by Heaven! it is so; for the carriage used to be out twice a week, but now she only goes about once in ten days. By-and-by it will be once a fortnight, then once a month, and the black-eyed rector will preach patience and resignation. Oh, it was a master-stroke, clapping him in that asylum! All we have got to do now is to let well alone. When she is over head and ears in love with Angelo she will come to easy terms with us, and so I'll move across the way. I shall never be happy till I live at Huntercombe, and administer the estate."

The maid-servant brought him a note, and said it was from her mistress. Bassett took it rather contemptuously, and said, "The little woman is always in a fidget now when you come here. She is all for peace." He read the letter. It ran thus:

"DEAREST RICHARD--I implore you to do nothing more to hurt Sir Charles. It is wicked, and it is useless. God has had pity on Lady Bassett, and have you pity on her too. Jane has just heard it from one of the Huntercombe servants."

"What does she mean with her 'its'? Why, surely--Read it, you."

They looked at each other in doubt and amazement for some time. Then Richard Bassett rushed upstairs, and had a few hasty words with his wife.

She told him her news in plainer English, and renewed her mild entreaties. He turned his back on her in the middle. He went out into the nursery, and looked at his child. The little fellow, a beautiful boy, slept the placid sleep of infancy. He leaned over him and kissed him, and went down to the dining-room.

His feet came tramp, tramp, very slowly, and when he opened the door Mr. Wheeler was startled at the change in his appearance. He was pale, and his countenance fallen.

"Why, what is the matter?" said Wheeler.

"She has done us. Ah, I was wiser than you; I feared her. It is the same thing over again; a woman against two children. This shows how strong she is; you can't realize what she has done--even when you see it. An heir was wanted to those estates. Love cried out for one. Hate cried out for one. Nature denied one. She has cut the Gordian knot; cut it as boldly as the lowest woman in Huntercombe would have cut it under such a terrible temptation."

"Oh, for shame!"

"Think, and use your eyes."

"My eyes have seen the lady; I think I see her now, kneeling like an angel over her husband, and pitying him for having knocked me down. I say her only lover is her husband."

"Oh, that was a long time ago. Time brings changes. You can't take the eyes out of my head."

"Suppose it should be only a false alarm?"

"Is that likely? However, I will learn. Whether it is or not, that child shall never rob mine of Bassett and Huntercombe. Anything is fair against such a woman."

CHAPTER XXVI.

THAT very night, after Wheeler had gone home, Richard Bassett wrote a cajoling letter to Mary Wells, asking her to meet him at the old place.

When the girl got this letter she felt a little faint for a moment; but she knew the man, his treachery, and his hard egotism and selfishness so well, that she tossed the letter aside, and resolved to take no notice. Her trust was all in her mistress, for whom, indeed, she had more real affection than for any living creature; as for Richard Bassett she absolutely detested him.

As the day wore on she took another view of matters: her deceiver was the enemy of her mistress; she might do her a service by going to this rendezvous, might learn something from him, and use it against him.

So she went to the rendezvous with a heart full of bitter hate.

Bassett, with all his assurance, could not begin his interrogatory all in a moment. He made a sort of apology, said he felt he had been unkind, and he had never been happy since he had deserted her.

She cut that short. "I have found a better than you," said she. "I am going to London very soon--to be married."

"I am glad to hear it."

"No doubt you are."

"I mean for your sake."

"For my sake? You think as little of me as I do of you. Come, now, what do you want of me--without a lie, if you *can?"*

"I wanted to see you, and talk to you, and hear your prospects."

"Well, I have told you." And she pretended to be going.

"Don't be in such a hurry. Tell us the news. Is it true that Lady Bassett is expected--"

"Oh, that is no news."

"It is to me."

"'Tain't no news in our house. Why, we have known it for months."

This took away the man's breath for a minute.

At last he said, with a great deal of intention:

"Will it be fair or dark?"

"As God pleases."

"I'll bet you five pounds to one that it is dark."

Mary shrugged her shoulders contemptuously, as if these speculations were too childish for her.

"It's my lady you want to talk about, is it? I thought it was to make me a wedding present."

He actually put his hand in his pocket and gave her two sovereigns. She took them with a grim smile.

He presumed on this to question her minutely.

She submitted to the interrogatory.

Only, as the questions were not always delicate, and the answer was invariably an untruth, it may be as well to pass over the rest of the dialogue. Suffice it to say that, whenever the girl saw the drift of a question she lied admirably; and when she did not, still she lied upon principle: it must be a good thing to deceive the enemy.

Richard Bassett was now perplexed, and saw himself in that very position which had so galled Lady Bassett six weeks or so before. He could not make any advantageous move, but was obliged to await events. All he could do was to spy a little on Lady Bassett, and note how often she went to the asylum.

After many days' watching he saw something new.

Mr. Angelo was speaking to her with a good deal of warmth, when suddenly she started from him, and then turned round upon him in a very commanding attitude, and with prodigious fire. Angelo seemed then to address her very humbly. But she remained rigid. At last Angelo retired and left her so; but he was no sooner out of sight than she dropped into a garden seat, and, taking out her handkerchief, cried a long time.

"Why doesn't the fool come back?" said Bassett, from his tower of observation.

He related this incident to Wheeler, and it impressed that worthy more than all he had ever said before on the same subject. But in a day or two Wheeler, who was a great gossip, and picked up every thing, came and told Bassett that the parson was looking out for a curate, and going to leave his living for a time, on the ground of health. "That is rather against your theory, Mr. Bassett," said he.

"Not a bit," said Bassett. "On the contrary, that is just what these artful women do who sacrifice virtue but cling all the more to reputation. I read French novels, my boy."

"Find 'em instructive?"

"Very. They cut deeper into human nature than our writers dare. Her turning away her lover *now* is just the act of what the French call a masterly woman--maitresse femme. She has got rid of him to close the mouth of scandal; that is her game."

"Well," said Wheeler, "you certainly are very ingenious, and so fortified in your opinions that with you facts are no longer stubborn things; you can twist them all your way. If he had stayed and buzzed about her, while her husband was incarcerated, you would have found her guilty: he goes to Rome and leaves her, and therefore you find her guilty. You would have made a fine hanging judge in the good old sanguinary times."

"I use my eyes, my memory, and my reason. She is a monster of vice and deceit. Anything is fair against such a woman."

"I am sorry to hear you say that," said Wheeler, becoming grave rather suddenly. "A woman is a woman, and I tell you plainly I have gone pretty well to the end of my tether with you."

"Abandon me, then," said Bassett, doggedly; "I can go alone."

Wheeler was touched by this, and said, "No, no; I am not the man to desert a friend; but pray do nothing rash--do nothing without consulting me."

Bassett made no reply.

About a week after this, as Lady Bassett was walking sadly in her own garden, a great Newfoundland dog ran up to her without any warning, and put his paws almost on her shoulder.

She screamed violently, and more than once.

One or two windows flew open, and among the women who put their heads out to see what was the matter, Mary Wells was the first.

The owner of the dog instantly whistled, and the sportive animal ran to him; but Lady Bassett was a good deal scared, and went in holding her hand to her side. Mary Wells hurried to her assistance, and she cried a little from nervousness when the young woman came earnestly to her.

"Oh, Mary! he frightened me so. I did not see him coming."

"Mr. Moss," said Mary Wells, "here's a villain come and frightened my lady. Go and shoot his dog, you and your son; and get the grooms, and fling him in the horse-pond directly."

"No!" said Lady Bassett, firmly. "You will see that he does not enter the house, that is all. Should he attempt that, then you will use force for my protection. Mary, come to my room."

When they were together alone Lady Bassett put both hands on the girl's shoulders, and made her turn toward her.

"I think you love me, Mary?" said she, drinking the girl's eyes with her own.

"Ah! that I do, my lady."

"Why did you look so pale, and your eyes flash, and why did you incite those poor men to--It might have led to bloodshed."

"It would; and that is what I wanted, my lady!"

"Oh, Mary!"

"What, don't you see?"

"No, no; I don't want to think so. It might have been an accident. The poor dog meant no harm; it was his way of fawning, that was all."

"The beast meant no harm, but the man did. He is worse than any beast that ever was born; he is a cruel, cunning, selfish devil; and if I had been a man he should never have got off alive."

"But are you sure?"

"Quite. I was upstairs, and saw it all."

This was not true; she had seen nothing till her mistress screamed.

"Then--anything is fair against such a villain."

"Of course it is."

"Let me think."

She leaned her head upon her hand, and that intelligent face of hers quite shone with hard thought.

At last, after long and intense thinking, she spoke.

"I'll teach you to be inhuman, Mr. Richard Bassett," said she, slowly, and with a strange depth of resolution.

Then Mary Wells and she put their heads together in close discussion; but now Lady Bassett took the lead, and revealed to her astonished adviser extraordinary and astounding qualities.

They had driven her to bay, and that is a perilous game to play with such a woman.

Mary Wells found herself a child compared with her mistress, now that that lady was driven to put out all her powers.

The conversation lasted about two hours: in that time the whole campaign was settled.

CHAPTER XXVII.

MARY WELLS by order went down, in a loose morning wrapper her mistress had given her, and dined in the servants' hall. She was welcomed with a sort of shout, half ironical; and the chief butler said, "Glad to see you come back to us, Miss Wells."

"The same to you, sir," said Mary, with more pertness than logic; "which I'm only come to take leave, for to-morrow I go to London, on business."

"La! what's the business, I wonder?" inquired a house-maid, irreverentially.

"Well, my business is not your business, Jane. However, if you want to know, I'm going to be married."

"And none too soon," whispered the kitchen-maid to a footman.

"Speak up, my dear," said Mary. "There's nothing more vulgarer than whispering in company."

"I said, 'What will Bill Drake say to that?'"

"Bill Drake will say he was a goose not to make up his mind quicker. This will learn him beauty won't wait for no man. If he cries when I am gone, you lend him your apron to wipe his eyes, and tell him women can't abide shilly-shallying men."

"That's a hexcellent sentiment," said John the footman, "and a solemn warning it is--"

"To all such as footmen be," said Mary.

"We writes it in the fly-leaf of our Bibles accordingly," said John.

"No, my man, write it somewhere where you'll have a chance to read it."

This caused a laugh; and when it was over, the butler, who did not feel strong enough to chaff a lady of this caliber, inquired obsequiously whether he might venture to ask who was the happy stranger to carry off such a prize.

"A civil question deserves a civil answer, Mr. Wright," said Mary. "It is a sea-faring man, the mate of a ship. He have known me a few years longer than any man in these parts. Whenever he comes home from a voyage he tells me what he has made, and asks me to marry him. I have said 'No' so many times I'm sick and tired; so I have said 'Yes' for once in a way. Changes are lightsome, you know."

Thus airily did Mary Wells communicate her prospects, and next morning early was driven to the station; a cart had gone before with her luggage, which tormented the female servants terribly; for, instead of the droll little servant's box, covered with paper, she had a large lady's box, filled with linen and clothes by the liberality of Lady Bassett, and a covered basket, and an old carpet-bag, with some minor packages of an unintelligible character. Nor did she make any secret that she had money in both pockets; indeed, she flaunted some notes before the groom, and told him none but her lady knew all she had done for Sir Charles. "But," said she, "he is grateful, you see, and so is she."

She went off in the train, as gay as a lark; but she was no sooner out of sight than her face changed its whole expression, and she went up to London very grave and thoughtful.

The traveling carriage was ordered at ten o'clock next day, and packed as for a journey.

Lady Bassett took her housekeeper with her to the asylum.

She had an interview with Sir Charles, and told him what Mr. Bassett had done, and the construction Mary Wells had put on it.

Sir Charles turned pale with rage, and said he could no longer play the patient game. He must bribe a keeper, make his escape, and kill that villain.

Lady Bassett was alarmed, and calmed it down.

"It was only a servant's construction, and she might be wrong; but it frightened me terribly; and I fear it is the beginning of a series of annoyances and encroachments; and I have lost Mr. Angelo; he has gone to Italy. Even Mary Wells left me this morning to be married. I think I know a way to turn all this against Mr. Bassett; but I will not say it, because I want to hear what you advise, dearest."

Sir Charles did not leave her long in doubt. He said, "There is but one way; you must leave Huntercombe, and put yourself out of that miscreant's way until our child is born."

"That would not grieve me," said Lady Bassett. "The place is odious to me, now you are not there. But what would censorious people say?"

"What could they say, except that you obeyed your husband?"

"Is it a command, then, dearest?"

"It is a command; and, although you are free, and I am a prisoner--although you are still an ornament to society, and I pass for an outcast, still I expect you to obey me when I assume a husband's authority. I have not taken the command of you quite so much as you used to say I must; but on this occasion I do. You will leave Huntercombe, and avoid that caitiff until our child is born."

"That ends all discussion," said Lady Bassett. "Oh, Charles, my only regret is that it costs me nothing to obey you. But when did it ever? My king!"

He had ordered her to do the very thing she wished to do.

She now gave her housekeeper minute instructions, settled the board wages of the whole establishment, and sent her home in the carriage, retaining her own boxes and packages at the inn.

Richard Bassett soon found out that Lady Bassett had left Huntercombe. He called on Wheeler and told him. Wheeler suggested she had gone to be near her husband.

"No," said Bassett, "she has joined her lover. I wonder at our simplicity in believing that fellow was gone to Italy."

"This is rich," said Wheeler. "A week ago she was guilty, and a Machiavel in petticoats; for why? she had quarreled with her Angelo, and packed him off to Italy. Now she is guilty; and why? because he is not gone to Italy--not that you know whether he is or not. You reason like a mule. As for me, I believe none of this nonsense--till you find them together."

"And that is just what I mean to do."

"We shall see."

"You will see."

Very soon after this a country gentleman met Wheeler on market-day, and drew him aside to ask him a question. "Do you advise Mr. Richard Bassett still?"

"Yes."

"Did you set him to trespass on Lady Bassett's lawn, and frighten her with a great dog in the present state of her health?"

"Heaven forbid! This is the first I've heard of such a thing."

"I am glad to hear you say that, Tom Wheeler. There, read that. Your client deserves to be flogged out of the county, sir." And he pulled a printed paper out of his pocket. It was dated from the Royal Hotel, Bath, and had been printed with blanks, as follows; but a lady's hand had filled in the dates.

"On the day ---- of ----, while I was walking alone in my garden, Mr. Richard Bassett, the person who has bereaved me by violence of my protector, came, without leave, into my private grounds, and brought a very large dog; it ran to me, and frightened me so that I nearly fainted with alarm. Mr. Bassett was aware of my condition. Next day I consulted my husband, and he ordered me to leave Huntercombe Hall, and put myself beyond the reach of trespassers and outrage.

"One motive has governed Mr. Bassett in all his acts, from his anonymous letter to me before my marriage--which I keep for your inspection, together with the proofs that he wrote it--to the barbarous seizure of my husband upon certificates purchased beforehand, and this last act of violence, which has driven me from the county for a time.

"Sir Charles and I have often been your hosts and your guests; we now ask you to watch our property and our legal rights, so long as through injustice and cruelty my husband is a prisoner, his wife a fugitive."

"There," said the gentleman, "these papers are going all round the county."

Wheeler was most indignant, and said he had never been consulted, and had never advised a trespass. He begged a loan of the paper, and took it to Bassett's that very same afternoon.

"So you have been acting without advice," said he, angrily; "and a fine mess you have made of it." And, though not much given to violent anger, he dashed the paper down on the table, and hurt his hand a little. Anger must be paid for, like other luxuries.

Bassett read it, and was staggered a moment; but he soon recovered himself, and said, "What is the foolish woman talking about?"

He then took a sheet of paper, and said he would soon give her a Roland for an Oliver.

"Ay," said Wheeler, grimly, "let us see how you will put down *the foolish woman.* I'll smoke a cigar in the garden, and recover my temper."

Richard Bassett's retort ran thus:

"I never wrote an anonymous letter in my life; and if I put restraint upon Sir Charles, it was done to protect the estate. Experienced physicians represented him homicidal and suicidal; and I protected both Lady Bassett and himself by the act she has interpreted so harshly.

"As for her last grievance, it is imaginary. My dog is gentle as a lamb. I did not foresee Lady Bassett would be there, nor that the poor dog would run and welcome her. She is playing a comedy: the real truth is, a gentleman had left Huntercombe whose company is necessary to her. She has gone to join him, and thrown the blame very adroitly upon

"RICHARD BASSETT."

When he had written this Bassett ordered his dog-cart.

Wheeler came in, read the letter, and said the last suggestion in it was a libel, and an indictable one into the bargain.

"What, if it is true--true to the letter?"

"Even then you would not be safe, unless you could prove it by disinterested witnesses."

"Well, if I cannot, I consent to cut this sentence out. Excuse me one minute, I must put a few things in my carpetbag."

"What! going away?"

"Of course I am."

"Better give me your address, then, in case anything turns up."

"If you were as sharp as you pass for you would know my address--Royal Hotel, Bath, to be sure."

He left Wheeler staring, and was back in five minutes with his carpet-bag and wraps.

"Wouldn't to-morrow morning do for this wild-goose chase?" asked Wheeler.

"No," said Richard. "I'm not such a fool. Catch me losing twelve hours. In that twelve hours they would shift their quarters. It is always so when a fool delays. I shall breakfast at the Royal Hotel, Bath."

The dog-cart came to the door as he spoke, and he rattled off to the railway.

He managed to get to the Royal Hotel, Bath, at 7 A.M., took a warm bath instead of bed, and then ordered breakfast; asked to see the visitors' book, and wrote a false name; turned the leaves, and, to his delight, saw Lady Bassett's name.

But he could not find Mr. Angelo's name in the book.

He got hold of Boots, and feed him liberally, then asked him if there was a handsome young parson there--very dark.

Boots could not say there was.

Then Bassett made up his mind that Angelo was at another hotel, or perhaps in lodgings, out of prudence.

"Lady Bassett here still?" said he.

Boots was not very sure; would inquire at the bar. Did inquire, and brought him word Lady Bassett had left for London yesterday morning.

Bassett ground his teeth with vexation.

No train to London for an hour and a half. He took a stroll through the town to fill up the time.

How often, when a man abandons or remits his search for a time, Fate sends in his way the very thing he is after, but has given up hunting just then! As he walked along the north side of a certain street, what should he see but the truly beautiful and remarkable eyes and eyebrows of Mr. Angelo, shining from afar.

That gentleman was standing, in a reverie, on the steps of a small hotel.

Bassett drew back at first, not to be seen. Looking round he saw he was at the door of a respectable house that let apartments. He hurried in, examined the drawing-room floor, took it for a week, paid in advance, and sent to the Royal for his bag.

He installed himself near the window, to await one of two things, and act accordingly. If Angelo left the place he should go by the same train, and so catch the parties together; if the lady doubled back to Bath, or had only pretended to leave it, he should soon know that, by diligent watch and careful following.

He wrote to Wheeler to announce this first step toward success.

CHAPTER XXVIII.

SOME days after this Mr. Rolfe received a line from Lady Bassett, to say she was at the Adelphi Hotel, in John Street. He put some letters into his pocket and called on her directly.

She received him warmly, and told him, more fully than she had by letter, how she had acted on his advice; then she told him of Richard Bassett's last act, and showed him her retort.

He knitted his brows at first over it; but said he thought her proclamation could do no harm.

"As a rule," said he, "I object to flicking with a lady's whip when I am going to crush, but--yes--it is able, and gives you a good excuse for keeping out of the way of annoyances till we strike the blow. And now I have something to consult you upon. May I read you some extracts from your husband's letters to me?"

"Oh, yes."

"Forgive a novelist; but this is a new situation, reading a husband's letters to his wife. However, I have a motive, and so I had in soliciting the correspondence with Sir Charles." He then read her the letters that are already before the reader, and also the following extracts:

"Mr. Johnson, a broken tradesman, has some imagination, though not of a poetic kind; he is imbued with trade, and, in the daytime, exercises several, especially a butcher's. When he sees any of us coming, he whips before the nearest door or gate, and sells meat. He sells it very cheap; the reason is, his friends allow him only a shilling or two in coppers, and as every madman is the center of the universe, he thinks that the prices of all commodities are regulated by the amount of specie in his pocket. This is his style, 'Come, buy, buy, choice mutton three farthings the carcass. Retail shop next door, ma'am. Jack, serve the lady. Bill, tell him he can send me home those twenty bullocks, at three half-pence each--' and so on. But at night he subsides into an auctioneer, and, with knocking down lots while others are conversing, gets removed occasionally to a padded room. Sometimes we humor him, and he sells us the furniture after a spirited competition, and debits the amounts, for cash is not abundant here. The other night, heated with business, he went on from the articles of furniture to the company, and put us all up in succession.

"Having a good many dislikes, he sometimes forgot the auctioneer in the man, and depreciated some lots so severely that they had to be passed; but he set Miss Wieland in a chair, and descanted on her beauty, good temper, and other gifts, in terms florid enough for Robins, or any other poet. Sold for eighteen pounds, and to a lady. This lady had formed a violent attachment to Miss W.; so next week they will be at daggers drawn. My turn came, and the auctioneer did me the honor to describe me as 'the lot of the evening.' He told the bidders to mind what they were about, they might never again be able to secure a live baronet at a moderate price, owing to the tightness of the money market. Well, sir, I was honored with bids from several ladies; but they were too timid and too honest to go beyond their means; my less scrupulous sex soared above these considerations, and I was knocked down for seventy-nine pounds fifteen shillings, amid loud applause at the spirited result. My purchaser is a shop-keeper mad after gardening. Dr. Suaby has given him a plot to cultivate, and he whispered in my ear, 'The reason I went to a fancy price was, I can kill two birds with one stone with you. You'll make a very good statee stuck up among my flowers; and you can hallo, and keep those plaguy sparrows off.'"

"Oh, what creatures for my darling to live among!" cried Lady Bassett piteously.

Mr. Rolfe stared, and said, "What, then, you are like all your sex--no sense of humor?"

"Humor! when my husband is in misery and degradation!"

"And don't you see that the brave writer of these letters is steeled against misery, and above degradation? Such men are not the mere sport of circumstances. Your husband carries a soul not to be quelled by three months in a well-ordered mad-house. But I will read no more, since what gives me satisfaction gives you pain."

"Oh, yes, yes! Don't let me lose a word my husband has ever uttered."

"Well, I'll go on; but I'm horribly discouraged."

"I'm so sorry for that sir. Please forgive me."

Mr. Rolfe read the letter next in date--

"We are honored with one relic of antiquity, a Pythagorean. He has obliged me with his biography. He was, to use his own words, engendered by the sun shining on a dunghill at his father's door,' and began his career as a flea; but his identity was, somehow, shifted to a boy of nine years old. He has had a long spell of humanity, and awaits the great change--which is to turn him to a bee. It will not find him unprepared; he has long practiced humming, in anticipation. A faithful friend, called Caffyn, used to visit him every week. Caffyn died last year, and the poor Pythagorean was very lonely and sad; but, two months ago, he detected his friend in the butcher's horse, and is more than consoled, for he says, Caffyn comes six times a week now, instead of once.'"

"Poor soul!" said Lady Bassett. "What a strange world for him to be living in. It seems like a dream."

"There is something stranger coming in this last letter."

"I have at last found one madman allied to Genius. It has taken me a fortnight to master his delusion, and to write down the vocabulary he has invented to describe the strange monster of his imagination. All the words I write in italics are his own.

"Mr. Williams says that a machine has been constructed for malignant purposes, which machine is an *air-loom.* It rivals the human machine in this, that it can operate either on mind or matter. It was invented, and is worked, by a gang of villains superlatively skillful in *pneumatic chemistry, physiology, nervous influence, sympathy,* and the *higher metaphysic,* men far beyond the immature science of the present era, which, indeed, is a favorite subject of their ridicule.

"The gang are seven in number, but Williams has only seen the four highest: *Bill, the King,* a master of the art of *magnetic impregnation; Jack, the schoolmaster,* the short-hand writer of the gang; *Sir Archy,* Chief Liar to the Association; and the *glove-woman,* so called from her always wearing cotton mittens. This personage has never been known to speak to any one.

"The materials used in the air-loom by these *pneumatic adepts* are infinite; but principally *effluvia of certain metals, poisons, soporific scents,* etc.

"The principal effects are:

"1st. EVENT-WORKING.--This is done by *magnetic manipulation* of kings, emperors, prime ministers, and others; so that, while the world is fearing and admiring them, they are, in reality, mere puppets played by the workers of the air-loom.

"2d. CUTTING SOUL FROM SENSE.--This is done *by diffusing the magnetic warp from the root of the nose under the base of the skull, till it forms a veil; so that the sentiments of the heart can have no communication with the operations of the intellect.*

"3d. KITING.--As boys raise a kite in the air, so the air-loom can lift an idea into the brain, where it floats and undulates for hours together. The victim cannot get rid of an idea so insinuated.

"4th. LOBSTER-CRACKING.--An external pressure of the magnetic atmosphere surrounding the person assailed. Williams has been so operated on, and says he felt as if he was grasped by an enormous pair of nut-crackers with teeth, and subjected to a piercing pressure, which he still remembers with horror. Death sometimes results from Lobster-cracking.

"5th. LENGTHENING THE BRAIN.--As the cylindrical mirror lengthens the countenance, so these assailants find means to *elon*gate the brain. This distorts the ideas, and subjects the most serious are made silly and ridiculous.

"6th. THOUGHT-MAKING.--While one of these villains sucks at the brain of the assailed, and extracts his existing sentiments, another will press into the vacuum ideas very different from his real thoughts. Thus his mind is physically enslaved."

Then Sir Charles goes on to say:

"Poor Mr. Williams seems to me an inventor wasted. I thought I would try and reason him out of his delusion. I asked if he had ever seen this gang and their machine.

"He said yes, they operated on him this morning. 'Then show them me,' said I. 'Young man,' said he, satirically, 'do you think these assassins, and their diabolical machine, would be allowed to go on, if they could be laid hands on so easily? The gang are fertile in disguise; the machine operates at considerable distances.'

"To drive him into a corner, I said, 'Will you give me a drawing of it?' He seemed to hesitate, so I said, 'If you can not draw it, you never saw it, and never will.' He assented to that, and I was vain enough to think I had staggered him; but yesterday he produced the inclosed sketch and explanation. After this I sadly fear he is incurable.

"There are three sane patients in this asylum, besides myself. I will tell you their stories when you come here, which I hope will be soon; for the time agreed on draws near, and my patience and self-control are sorely tried, as day after day rolls by, and sees me still in a madhouse."

"There, Lady Bassett," said Mr. Rolfe. "And now for my motive in reading these letters. Sir Charles may still have a crotchet, an inordinate desire for an heir; but, even if he has, the writer of these letters has nothing to fear from any jury; and, therefore, I am now ready to act. I propose to go down to the asylum to-morrow, and get him out as quickly as I can."

Lady Bassett uttered an ejaculation of joy. Then she turned suddenly pale, and her countenance fell. She said nothing.

Mr. Rolfe was surprised at this, since, at their last meeting, she was writhing at her inaction. He began to puzzle himself. She watched him keenly. He thought to himself, "Perhaps she dreads the excitement of meeting--for herself."

At last Lady Bassett asked him how long it would take to liberate Sir Charles.

"Not quite a week, if Richard Bassett is well advised. If he fights desperately it may take a fortnight. In any case I don't leave the work an hour till it is done. I can delay, and I can fight; but I never mix the two. Come, Lady Bassett, there is something on your mind you don't like to say. Well, what does it matter? I will pack my bag, and write to Dr. Suaby that he may expect me soon; but I will wait till I get a line from you to go ahead. Then I'll go down that instant and do the work."

This proposal was clearly agreeable to Lady Bassett, and she thanked him.

"You need not waste words over it," said he. "Write one word, 'ACT!' That will be the shortest letter you ever wrote."

The rest of the conversation is not worth recording.

Mr. Rolfe instructed a young solicitor minutely, packed his bag, and waited.

But day after day went by, and the order never came to act.

Mr. Rolfe was surprised at this, and began to ask himself whether he could have been deceived in this lady's affection for her husband. But he rejected that. Then he asked himself whether it might have cooled. He had known a very short incarceration produce that fatal effect. Both husband and wife interested him, and he began to get irritated at the delay.

Sir Charles's letters made him think they had already wasted time.

At last a letter came from Gloucester Place.

"Will my kind friend now ACT?

"Gratefully,

"BELLA BASSETT."

Mr. Rolfe, upon this, cast his discontent to the winds and started for Bellevue House.

On the evening of that day a surgeon called Boddington was drinking tea with his wife, and they were talking rather disconsolately; for he had left a fair business in the country, and, though a gentleman of undoubted skill, was making his way very slowly in London.

The conversation was agreeably interrupted by a loud knock at the door.

A woman had come to say that he was wanted that moment for a lady of title in Gloucester Place, hard by.

"I will come," said he, with admirably affected indifference; and, as soon as the woman was out of sight, husband and wife embraced each other.

"Pray God it may all go well, for your sake and hers, poor lady."

Mr. Boddington hurried to the number in Gloucester Place. The door was opened by the charwoman.

He asked her with some doubt if that was the house.

The woman said yes, and she believed it was a surprise. The lady was from the country, and was looking out for some servants.

This colloquy was interrupted by an intelligent maid, who asked, over the balusters, if that was the medical man; and, on the woman's saying it was, begged him to step upstairs at once.

He found his patient attended only by her maid, but she was all discretion, and intelligence. She said he had only to direct her, she would do anything for her dear mistress. Mr. Boddington said a single zealous and intelligent woman, who could obey orders, was as good as a number, or better.

He then went gently to the bedside, and his experience told him at once that the patient was in labor. He told the attendant so, and gave her his directions.

CHAPTER XXIX.

M E. ROLFE reached Bellevue House in time to make a hasty toilet, and dine with Dr. Suaby in his private apartments.

The other guests were Sir Charles Bassett, Mr. Hyam--a meek, sorrowful patient--an Exquisite, and Miss Wieland.

Dr. Suaby introduced him to everybody but the Exquisite.

Mr. Rolfe said Sir Charles Bassett and he were correspondents.

"So I hear. He tells you the secrets of the prison-house, eh?"

"The humors of the place, you mean."

"Yes, he has a good eye for character. I suppose he has dissected me along with the rest?"

"No, no; he has only dealt with the minor eccentricities. His pen failed at you. 'You must come and *see* the doctor,' he said. So here I am."

"Oh," said the doctor, "if your wit and his are both to be leveled at me, I had better stop your mouths. Dinner! dinner! Sir Charles, will you take Miss Wieland? Sorry we have not another lady to keep you company, madam."

"Are you? Then I'm not," said the lady smartly.

The dinner passed like any other, only Rolfe observed that Dr. Suaby took every fair opportunity of drawing the pluckless Mr. Hyam into conversation, and that he coldly ignored the Exquisite.

"I have seen that young man about town, I think," said Mr. Rolfe. "Where was it, I wonder?"

"The Argyll Rooms, or the Casino, probably."

"Thank you, doctor. Oh, I forgot; you owed me one. He is no favorite of yours."

"Certainly not. And I only invited him medicinally."

"Medicinally? That's too deep for a layman."

"To flirt with Miss Wieland. Flirting does her good."

"Medicine embraces a wider range than I thought."

"No doubt. You are always talking about medicine; but you know very little, begging your pardon."

"That is the theory of compensation. When you know very little about a thing you must talk a great deal about it. Well, I'm here for instruction; thirsting for it."

"All the better; we'll teach you to drink deep ere you depart."

"All right: but not of your favorite Acetate of Morphia; because that is the draught that takes the reason prisoner."

"It's no favorite of mine. Indeed, experience has taught me that all sedatives excite; if they soothe at first, they excite next day. My antidotes to mental excitement are packing in lukewarm water, and, best of all, hard bodily exercise and the perspiration that follows it. To put it shortly--prolonged bodily excitement antidotes mental excitement."

"I'll take a note of that. It is the wisest thing I ever heard from any learned physician."

"Yet many a learned physician knows it. But you are a little prejudiced against the faculty."

"Only in their business. They are delightful out of that. But, come now, nobody hears us--confess, the system which prescribes drugs, drugs, drugs at every visit and in every case, and does not give a severe selection of esculents the first place, but only the second or third, must be rotten at the core. Don't you despise a layman's eye. All the professions want it."

"Well, you are a writer; publish a book, call it *Medicina laici*, and send me a copy."

"To slash in the ***Lancet?*** Well, I will: when novels cease to pay and truth begins to."

In the course of the evening Mr. Rolfe drew Dr. Suaby apart, and said, "I must tell you frankly, I mean to relieve you of one of your inmates."

"Only one? I was in hopes you would relieve me of all the sane people. They say you are ingenious at it. All I know is, I can't get rid of an inmate if the person who signed the order resists. Now, for instance, here's a Mrs. Hallam came here unsound: religious delusion. Has been cured two months. I have reported her so to her son-in-law, who signed the order; but he will not discharge her. He is vicious, she scriptural; bores him about eternity. Then I wrote to the Commissioners in Lunacy; but they don't like to strain their powers, so they wrote to the affectionate son-in-law, and he politely declines to act. Sir Charles Bassett the same: three weeks ago I reported him cured, and the detaining relative has not even replied to me."

"Got a copy of your letter?"

"Of course. But what if I tell you there is a gentleman here who never had any business to come, yet he is as much a fixture as the grates. I took him blindfold along with the house. I signed a deed, and it is so stringent I can't evade one of my predecessor's engagements. This old rogue committed himself to my predecessor's care, under medical certificates; the order he signed himself."

"Illegal, you know."

"Of course; but where's the remedy? The person who signed the order must rescind it. But this sham lunatic won't rescind it. Altogether the tenacity of an asylum is prodigious. The statutes are written with bird-lime. Twenty years ago that old Skinflint found the rates and taxes intolerable; and doesn't everybody find them intolerable? To avoid these rates and taxes he shut up his house, captured himself, and took himself here; and here he will end his days, excluding some genuine patient, unless *you* sweep him into the street for me."

"Sindbad, I will try," said Rolfe, solemnly; "but I must begin with Sir Charles Bassett. By-the-by, about his crotchet?"

"Oh, he has still an extravagant desire for children. But the cerebral derangement is cured, and the other, standing by itself, is a foible, not a mania. It is only a natural desire in excess. If they brought me Rachel merely because she had said, 'Give me children, or I die,' and I found her a healthy woman in other respects, I should object to receive her on that score alone."

"You are deadly particular--compared with some of them," said Rolfe.

That evening he made an appointment with Sir Charles, and visited him in his room at 8 A. M. He told him he had seen Lady Bassett in London, and, of course, he had to answer many questions. He then told him he came expressly to effect his liberation.

"I am grateful to you, sir," said Sir Charles, with a suppressed and manly emotion.

"Here are my instructions from Lady Bassett; short, but to the point."

"May I keep that?"

"Why, of course."

Sir Charles kissed his wife's line, and put the note in his breast.

"The first step," said Rolfe, "is to cut you in two. That is soon done. You must copy in your own hand, and then sign, this writing." And he handed him a paper.

"I, Charles Dyke Bassett, being of sound mind, instruct James Sharpe, of Gray's Inn, my Solicitor, to sue the person who signed the order for my incarceration--in the Court of Common Pleas; and to take such other steps for my relief as may be advised by my counsel--Mr. Francis Rolfe."

"Excuse me," said Sir Charles, "if I make one objection. Mr. Oldfield has been my solicitor for many years. I fear it will hurt his feelings if I intrust the matter to a stranger. Would there be any objection to my inserting Mr. Oldfield's name, sir?"

"Only this: he would think he knew better than I do; and then I, who know better than he does, and am very vain and arrogant, should throw up the case in a passion, and go back to my MS.; and humdrum Oldfield would go to Equity instead of law; and all the costs would fall on your estate instead of on your enemy; and you would be here eighteen months instead of eight or ten days. No, Sir Charles, you can't mix champagne and ditch-water; you can't make Invention row in a boat with Antique Twaddle, and you mustn't ask me to fight your battle with a blunt knife, when I have got a sharp knife that fits my hand."

Mr. Rolfe said this with more irritation than was justified, and revealed one of the great defects in his character.

Sir Charles saw his foible, smiled, and said, "I withdraw a proposal which I see annoys you." He then signed the paper.

Mr. Rolfe broke out all smiles directly, and said, "Now you are cut in two. One you is here; but Sharpe is another you. Thus, one you works out of the asylum, and one in, and that makes all the difference. Compare notes with those who have tried the other way. Yet, simple and obvious as this is, would you believe it, I alone have discovered this method; I alone practice it."

He sent his secretary off to London at once, and returned to Sir Charles. "The authority will be with Sharpe at 2:30. He will be at Whitehall 3:15, and examine the order. He will take the writ out at once, and if Richard Bassett is the man, he will serve it on him to-morrow in good time, and send one of your grooms over here on horseback with the news. We serve the writ personally, because we have shufflers to deal with, and I will not give them a chance. Now I must go and write a lie or two for the public; and then inspect the asylum with Suaby. Before post-time I will write to a friend of mine who is a Commissioner of Lunacy, one of the strong-minded ones. We may as well have two strings to our bow."

Sir Charles thanked him gracefully, and said, "It is a rare thing, in this selfish world, to see one man interest himself in the wrongs of another, as you are good enough to do in mine."

"Oh," said Rolfe, "all work and no play makes Jack a dull boy. My business is Lying; and I drudge at it. So to escape now and then to the play-ground of Truth and Justice is a great amusement and recreation to poor me. Besides, it gives me fresh vigor to replunge into Mendacity; and that's the thing that pays."

With this simple and satisfactory explanation he rolled away.

Leaving, for the present, matters not essential to this vein of incident, I jump to what occurred toward evening.

Just after dinner the servant who waited told Dr. Suaby that a man had walked all the way from Huntercombe to see Sir Charles Bassett.

"Poor fellow!" said Dr. Suaby; "I should like to see him. Would you mind receiving him here?"

"Oh, no."

"On second thoughts, James, you had better light a candle in the next room--in case."

A heavy clatter was heard, and the burly figure of Moses Moss entered the room. Being bareheaded, he saluted the company by pulling his head, and it bobbed. He was a little dazzled by the lights at first, but soon distinguished Sir Charles, and his large countenance beamed with simple and affectionate satisfaction.

"How d'ye do, Moss?" said Sir Charles.

"Pretty well, thank ye, sir, in my body, but uneasy in my mind. There be a trifle too many rogues afoot to please me. However, I told my mistress this morning, says I, 'Before I puts up with this here any longer, I must go over there and see him; for here's so many lies a-cutting about,' says I, 'I'm fairly mazed.' So, if you please, Sir

Charles, will you be so good as to tell me out of your own mouth, and then I shall know: be you crazy or hain't you--ay or no?"

Suaby and Rolfe had much ado not to laugh right out; but Sir Charles said, gravely, he was not crazy. "Do I look crazy, Moss?"

"That ye doan't; you look twice the man you did. Why, your cheeks did use to be so pasty like; now you've got a color--but mayhap" (casting an eye on the decanters) "ye're flustered a bit wi' drink."

"No, no," said Rolfe, "we have not commenced our nightly debauch yet; only just done dinner."

"Then there goes another. This will be good news to home. Dall'd if I would not ha' come them there thirty miles on all-fours for't. But, sir, if so be you are not crazy, please think about coming home, for things ain't as they should be in our parts. My lady she is away for her groaning, and partly for fear of this very Richard Bassett; and him and his lawyer they have put it about as you are dead in law; that is the word: and so the servants they don't know what to think; and the village folk are skeared with his clapping four brace on 'em in jail: and Joe and I, we wants to fight un, but my dame she is timorous, and won't let us, because of the laayer. And th' upshot is, this here Richard Bassett is master after a manner, and comes on the very lawn, and brings men with a pole measure, and uses the place as his'n mostly; but our Joe bides in the Hall with his gun, and swears he'll shoot him if he sets foot in the house. Joe says he have my lady's leave and license so to do, but not outside."

Sir Charles turned very red, and was breathless with indignation.

Dr. Suaby looked uneasy, and said, "Control yourself, sir.'"

"I am not going to control *myself,*" cried Rolfe, in a rage. "Don't you take it to heart, Sir Charles. It shall not last long."

"Ah!"

"Dr. Suaby, can you lend me a gig or a dog-cart, with a good horse?"

"Yes. I have got a WONDERFUL roadster, half Irish, half Norman."

"Then, Mr. Moss, to-morrow you and I go to Huntercombe: you shall show me this Bassett, and we will give him a pill."

"Meantime," said Dr. Suaby, "I take a leaf out of your Medicina laici, and prescribe a hearty supper, a quart of ale, and a comfortable bed to Mr. Moss. James, see him well taken care of. Poor man!" said he, when Moss had retired. "What simplicity! what good sense! what ignorance of the world! what feudality, if I may be allowed the expression."

Sir Charles was manifestly discomposed, and retired to bed early.

Rolfe drove off with Moss at eight o'clock, and was not seen again all day. Indeed, Sir Charles was just leaving Dr. Suaby's room when he came in rather tired, and would not say a word till they gave him a cup of tea: then he brightened up and told his story.

"We went to the railway to meet Sharpe. The muff did not come nor send by the first train. His clerk arrived by the second. We went to Huntercombe village together, and on the road I gave him some special instructions. Richard Bassett not at home. We used a little bad language and threw out a skirmisher--Moss, to wit--to find him. Moss discovered him on your lawn, planning a new arrangement of the flower beds, with Wheeler looking over the boundary wall.

"We went up to Bassett, and the clerk served his copy of the writ. He took it quite coolly; but when he saw at whose suit it was he turned pale. He recovered himself directly, though, and burst out laughing. 'Suit of Sir Charles Bassett. Why, he can't sue: he is civiliter mortuus: mad as a March hare: in confinement.' Clerk told him he was mistaken; Sir Charles was perfectly sane. 'Good-day, sir.' So then Bassett asked him to wait a little. He took the writ away, and showed it Wheeler, no doubt. He came back, and blustered, and said, 'Some other person has instructed you: you will get yourself into trouble, I fear.' The little clerk told him not to alarm himself; Mr. Sharpe was instructed by Sir Charles Bassett, in his own handwriting and signature, and said, 'It is not my business to argue the case with you. You had better take the advice of counsel.' 'Thank you,' said Bassett; 'that would be wasting a guinea.' 'A good many thousand guineas have been lost by that sort of economy,' says the little clerk, solemnly. Oh, and he told him Mr. Sharpe was instructed to indict him for a trespass if he ever came there again; and handed him a written paper to that effect, which we two had drawn up at the station; and so left him to his reflections. We went into the house, and called the servants together, and told them to keep the rooms warm and the beds aired, since you might return any day."

Upon this news Sir Charles showed no premature or undignified triumph, but some natural complacency, and a good deal of gratitude.

The next day was blank of events, but the next after Mr. Rolfe received a letter containing a note addressed to Sir Charles Bassett. Mr. Rolfe sent it to him.

SIR--I am desired to inform you that I attended Lady Bassett last night, when she was safely delivered of a son. Have seen her again this morning. Mother and child are doing remarkably well.

"W. BODDINGTON, Surgeon, 17 Upper Gloucester Place."

Sir Charles cried, "Thank God! thank God!" He held out the paper to Mr. Rolfe, and sat down, overpowered by tender emotions.

Mr. Rolfe devoured the surgeon's letter at one glance, shook the baronet's hand eloquently, and went away softly, leaving him with his happiness.

Sir Charles, however, began now to pine for liberty; he longed so to join his wife and see his child, and Rolfe, observing this, chafed with impatience. He had calculated on Bassett, advised by Wheeler, taking the wisest course, and discharging him on the spot. He had also hoped to hear from the Commissioner of Lunacy. But neither event took place.

They could have cut the Gordian knot by organizing an escape: Giles and others were to be bought to that: but Dr. Suaby's whole conduct had been so kind, generous, and confiding, that this was out of the question. Indeed, Sir Charles had for the last month been there upon parole.

Yet the thing had been wisely planned, as will appear when I come to notice the advice counsel had given to Bassett in this emergency. But Bassett would not take advice: he went by his own head, and prepared a new and terrible blow, which Mr. Rolfe did not foresee.

But meantime an unlooked-for and accidental assistant came into the asylum, without the least idea Sir Charles was there.

Mrs. Marsh, early in her married life, converted her husband to religion, and took him about the county preaching. She was in earnest, and had a vein of natural eloquence that really went straight to people's bosoms. She was certainly a Christian, though an eccentric one. Temper being the last thing to yield to Gospel light, she still got into rages; but now she was very humble and penitent after them.

Well, then, after going about doing good, she decided to settle down and do good. As for Marsh, he had only to obey. Judge for yourself: the mild, gray-haired vicar of Calverly, who now leaned on la Marsh as on a staff, thought it right at the beginning to ascertain that she was not opposing her husband's views. He put a query of this kind as delicately as possible.

"My husband!" cried she. "If he refused to go to heaven with me, I'd take him there by the ear." And her eye flashed with the threat.

Well, somebody told this lady that Mr. Vandeleur was ruined, and in Dr. Suaby's asylum, not ten miles from her country-seat. This intelligence touched her. She contrasted her own happy condition, both worldly and spiritual, with that of this unfortunate reprobate, and she felt bound to see if nothing could be done for the poor wretch. A timid Christian would have sent some man to do the good work; but this was a lion-like one. So she mounted her horse, and taking only her groom with her, was at Bellevue in no time.

She dismounted, and said she must speak to Dr. Suaby, sent in her card, and was received at once.

"You have a gentleman here called Vandeleur?"

The doctor looked disappointed, but bowed.

"I wish to see him."

"Certainly, madam.--James, take Mrs. Marsh into a sitting-room, and send Mr. Vandeleur to her."

"He is not violent, is he?" said Mrs. Marsh, beginning to hesitate when she saw there was no opposition.

"Not at all, madam--the Pink of Politeness. If you have any money about you, it might be as well to confide it to me."

"What, will he rob me?"

"Oh, no: much too well conducted: but he will most likely wheedle you out of it."

"No fear of that, sir." And she followed James.

He took her to a room commanding the lawn. She looked out of the window, and saw several ladies and gentlemen walking at their ease, reading or working in the sun.

"Poor things!" she thought; "they are not so very miserable: perhaps God comforts them by ways unknown to us. I wonder whether preaching would do them any good? I should like to try. But they would not let me; they lean on the arm of flesh."

Her thoughts were interrupted at last by the door opening gently, and in came Vandeleur, with his graceful panther-like step, and a winning smile he had put on for conquest.

He stopped; he stared; he remained motionless and astounded.

At last he burst out, "Somer--Was it me you wished to see?"

"Yes," said she, very kindly. "I came to see you for old acquaintance. You must call me Mrs. Marsh now; I am married."

By this time he had quite recovered himself, and offered her a chair with ingratiating zeal.

"Sit down by me," said she, as if she was petting a child. "Are you sure you remember me?"

Says the Courtier, "Who could forget you that had ever had the honor--"

Mrs. Marsh drew back with sudden hauteur. "I did not come here for folly," said she. Then, rather naively, "I begin to doubt your being so very mad."

"Mad? No, of course I am not."

"Then what brings you here?"

"Stumped."

"What, have I mistaken the house? Is it a jail?"

"Oh, no! I'll tell you. You see I was dipped pretty deep, and duns after me, and the Derby my only chance; so I put the pot on. But a dark horse won: the Jews knew I was done: so now it was a race which should take me. Sloman had seven writs out: I was in a corner. I got a friend that knows every move to sign me into this asylum. They thought it was all up then, and he is bringing them to a shilling in the pound."

Before he could complete this autobiographical sketch Mrs. Marsh started up in a fury, and brought her whip down on the table with a smartish cut.

"You little heartless villain!" she screamed. "Is this, the way you play upon people: bringing me from my home to console a maniac, and, instead of that, you are only what you always were, a spendthrift and a scamp? Finely they will laugh at me."

She clutched the whip in her white but powerful hand till it quivered in the air, impatient for a victim.

"Oh!" she cried, panting, and struggling with her passion, "if I wasn't a child of

God, I'd--"

"You'd give me a devilish good hiding," said Vandeleur, demurely.

"That I *would,*" said she, very earnestly.

"You forget that I never told you I was mad. How could I imagine you would hear it? How could I dream you would come, even if you did?"

"I should be no Christian if I didn't come."

"But I mean we parted bad friends, you know."

"Yes, Van; but when I asked you for the gray horse you sent me a new side-saddle. A woman does not forget those little things. You were a gentleman, though a child of Belial."

Vandeleur bowed most deferentially, as much as to say, "In both those matters you are the highest authority earth contains."

"So come," said she, "here is plenty of writing-paper. Now tell me all your debts, and I will put them down."

"What is the use? At a shilling in the pound, six hundred will pay them all."

"Are you sure?"

"As sure as that I am not going to rob you of the money."

"Oh, I only mean to lend it you."

"That alters the case."

"Prodigiously." And she smiled satirically. "Now your friend's address, that is treating with your creditors."

"Must I?"

"Unless you want to put me in a great passion."

"Anything sooner than that." Then he wrote it for her.

"And now," said she, "grant me a little favor for old acquaintance. Just kneel you down there, and let me wrestle with Heaven for you, that you may be a brand plucked from the fire, even as I am."

The Pink of Politeness submitted, with a sigh of resignation.

Then she prayed for him so hard, so beseechingly, so eloquently, he was amazed and touched.

She rose from her knees, and laid her head on her hand, exhausted a little by her own earnestness.

He stood by her, and hung his head.

"You are very good," he said. "It is a shame to let you waste it on me. Look here--I want to do a little bit of good to another man, after you praying so beautifully."

"Ah! I am so glad. Tell me."

"Well, then, you mustn't waste a thought on me, Rhoda. I'm a gambler and a fool: let me go to the dogs at once; it is only a question of time: but there's a fellow here that is in trouble, and doesn't deserve it, and he was a faithful friend to you, I believe. I never was. And he has got a wife: and by what I hear, you could get him out, I think, and I am sure you would be angry with me afterward if I didn't tell you; you have such a good heart. It is Sir Charles Bassett."

"Sir Charles Bassett here! Oh, his poor wife! What drove him mad? Poor, poor Sir Charles!"

"Oh, he is all right. They have cured him entirely; but there is no getting him out, and he is beginning to lose heart, they say. There's a literary swell here can tell you all about it; he has come down expressly: but they are in a fix, and I think you could help them out. I wish you would let me introduce you to him."

"To whom?"

"To Mr. Rolfe. You used to read his novels."

"I adore him. Introduce me at once. But Sir Charles must not see me, nor know I am here. Say Mrs. Marsh, a friend of Lady Bassett's, begs to be introduced."

Sly Vandeleur delivered this to Rolfe; but whispered out of his own head, "A character for your next novel--a saint with the devil's own temper."

This insidious addition brought Mr. Rolfe to her directly.

As might be expected from their go-ahead characters, these two knew each other intimately in about twelve minutes; and Rolfe told her all the facts I have related, and Marsh went into several passions, and corrected herself, and said she had been a great sinner, but was plucked from the burning, and therefore thankful to anybody who would give her a little bit of good to do.

Rolfe took prompt advantage of this foible, and urged her to see the Commissioners in Lunacy, and use all her eloquence to get one of them down. "They don't act upon my letters," said he; "but it will be another thing if a beautiful, ardent woman puts it to them in person, with all that power of face and voice I see in you. You are all fire; and you can talk Saxon."

"Oh, I'll talk to them," said Mrs. Marsh, "and God will give me words; He always does when I am on His side. Poor Lady Bassett! my heart bleeds for her. I will go to London to-morrow; ay, to-night, if you like. To-night? I'll go this instant!"

"What!" said Rolfe: "is there a lady in the world who will go a journey without packing seven trunks--and merely to do a good action?"

"You forget. Penitent sinners must make up for lost time."

"At that rate impenitent ones like me had better lose none. So I'll arm you at once with certain documents, and you must not leave the commissioners till they promise to send one of their number down without delay to examine him, and discharge him if he is as we represent."

Mrs. Marsh consented warmly, and went with Rolfe to Dr. Suaby's study.

They armed her with letters and written facts, and she rode off at a fiery pace; but not before she and Rolfe had sworn eternal friendship.

The commissioners received Mrs. Marsh coldly. She was chilled, but not daunted. She produced Suaby's letter and Rolfe's, and when they were read she played the orator. She argued, she remonstrated, she convinced, she persuaded, she thundered. Fire seemed to come out of the woman.

Mr. Fawcett, on whom Mr. Rolfe had mainly relied, caught fire, and declared he would go down next day and look into the matter on the spot; and he kept his word. He came down; he saw Sir Charles and Suaby, and penetrated the case.

Mr. Fawcett was a man with a strong head and a good heart, but rather an arrogant manner. He was also slightly affected with official pomposity and reticence; so, unfortunately, he went away without declaring his good intentions, and discouraged them all with the fear of innumerable delays in the matter.

Now if Justice is slow, Injustice is swift. The very next day a thunder-clap fell on Sir Charles and his friends.

Arrived at the door a fly and pair, with three keepers from an asylum kept by Burdoch, a layman, the very opposite of the benevolent Suaby. His was a place where the old system of restraint prevailed, secretly but largely: strait-waistcoats, muffles, hand-locks, etc. Here fleas and bugs destroyed the patients' rest; and to counteract the insects morphia was administered freely. Given to the bugs and fleas, it would have been an effectual antidote; but they gave it to the patients, and so the insects won.

These three keepers came with an order correctly drawn, and signed by Richard Bassett, to deliver Sir Charles to the agents showing the order.

Suaby, who had a horror of Burdoch, turned pale at the sight of the order, and took it to Rolfe.

"Resist!" said that worthy.

"I have no right."

"On second thoughts, do nothing, but gain time, while I--Has Bassett paid you for Sir Charles's board?"

"No."

"Decline to give him up till that is done, and be some time making out the bill. Come what may, pray keep Sir Charles here till I send you a note that I am ready."

He then hastened to Sir Charles and unfolded his plans, to him.

Sir Charles assented eagerly. He was quite willing to run risks with the hope of immediate liberation, which Rolfe held out. His own part was to delay and put off till he got a line from Rolfe.

Rolfe then borrowed Vandeleur on parole and the doctor's dog-cart, and dashed into the town, distant two miles.

First he went to the little theater, and found them just concluding a rehearsal. Being a playwright, he was known to nearly all the people, more or less, and got five supers and one carpenter to join him--for a consideration.

He then made other arrangements in the town, the nature of which will appear in due course.

Meantime Suaby had presented his bill. One of the keepers got into the fly and took it back to the town. There, as Rolfe had anticipated, lurked Richard Bassett. He cursed the delay, gave the man the money, and urged expedition. The money was brought and paid, and Suaby informed Sir Charles.

But Sir Charles was not obliged to hurry. IIe took a long time to pack; and he was not ready till Vandeleur brought a note to him from Rolfe.

Then Sir Charles came down.

Suaby made Burdoch's keeper sign a paper to the effect that he had the baronet in charge, and relieved Suaby of all further responsibility.

Then Sir Charles took an affectionate leave of Dr. Suaby, and made him promise to visit him at Huntercombe Hall.

Then he got into the fly, and sat between two keepers, and the fly drove off.

Sir Charles at that moment needed all his fortitude. The least mistake or miscalculation on the part of his friends, and what might not be the result to him?

As the fly went slowly through the gate he saw on his right hand a light carriage and pair moving up; but was it coming after him, or only bringing visitors to the asylum?

The fly rolled on; even his stout heart began to quake. It rolled and rolled. Sir Charles could stand it no longer. He tried to look out of the window to see if the carriage was following.

One of the keepers pulled him in roughly. "Come, none of that, sir?"

"You insolent scoundrel!" said Sir Charles.

"Ay, ay," said the man; "we'll see about that when we get you home."

Then Sir Charles saw he had offended a vindictive blackguard.

He sank back in his seat, and a cold chill crept over him.

Just then they passed a little clump of fir-trees.

In a moment there rushed out of these trees a number of men in crape masks, stopped the horses, surrounded the carriage, and opened it with brandishing of bludgeons and life-preservers, and pointing of guns.

CHAPTER XXX.

A BIG man, who seemed the leader, fired a volley of ferocious oaths at the keepers, and threatened to send them to hell that moment if they did not instantly deliver up that gentleman.

The keepers were thoroughly terrified, and roared for mercy.

"Hand him out here, you scoundrels!"

"Yes! yes! Man alive, we are not resisting: what is the use?"

"Hand down his luggage."

It was done all in a flutter.

"Now get in again; turn your horses' heads the other way, and don't come back for an hour. You with your guns take stations in those trees, and shoot them dead if they are back before their time."

These threats were interlarded with horrible oaths, and Burdoch's party were glad to get off, and they drove away quickly in the direction indicated.

However, as soon as they got over their first surprise they began to smell a hoax; and, instead of an hour, it was scarcely twenty minutes when they came back.

But meantime the supers were paid liberally among the fir-trees by Vandeleur, pocketed their crape, flung their dummy guns into a cornfield, dispersed in different directions, and left no trace.

But Sir Charles was not detained for that: the moment he was recaptured he and his luggage were whisked off in the other carriage, and, with Rolfe and his secretary, dashed round the town, avoiding the main street, to a railway eight miles off, at a pace almost defying pursuit. Not that they dreaded it: they had numbers, arms, and a firm determination to fight if necessary, and also three tongues to tell the truth, instead of one.

At one in the morning they were in London. They slept at Mr. Rolfe's house;

and before breakfast Mr. Rolfe's secretary was sent to secure a couple of prize-fighters to attend upon Sir Charles till further notice. They were furnished with a written paper explaining the case briefly, and were instructed to hit first and talk afterward should a recapture be attempted. Should a crowd collect, they were to produce the letter. These measures were to provide against his recapture under the statute, which allows an alleged lunatic to be retaken upon the old certificates for fourteen days after his escape from confinement, but for no longer.

Money is a good friend in such contingencies as these.

Sir Charles started directly after breakfast to find his wife and child. The faithful pugilists followed at his heels in another cab.

Neither Sir Charles nor Mr. Rolfe knew Lady Bassett's address: it was the medical man who had written: but that did not much matter; Sir Charles was sure to learn his wife's address from Mr. Boddington. He called on that gentleman at 17 Upper Gloucester Place. Mr. Boddington had just taken his wife down to Margate for her health; had only been gone half an hour.

This was truly irritating and annoying. Apparently Sir Charles must wait that gentleman's return. He wrote a line, begging Mr. Boddington to send him Lady Bassett's address in a cab immediately on his return.

He told Mr. Rolfe this; and then for the first time let out that his wife's not writing to him at the asylum had surprised and alarmed him; he was on thorns.

Mr. Boddington returned in the middle of the night, and at breakfast time Sir Charles had a note to say Lady Bassett was at 119 Gloucester Place, Portman Square.

Sir Charles bolted a mouthful or two of breakfast, and then dashed off in a hansom to 119 Gloucester Place.

There was a bill in the window, "To be let, furnished. Apply to Parker & Ellis."

He knocked at the door. Nobody came. Knocked again. A lugubrious female opened the door.

"Lady Bassett?"

"Don't live here, sir. House to be let."

Sir Charles went to Mr. Boddington and told him.

Mr. Boddington said he thought he could not be mistaken; but he would look at his address-book. He did, and said it was certainly 119 Gloucester Place; "Perhaps she has left," said he. "She was very healthy--an excellent patient. But I should not have advised her to move for a day or two more."

Sir Charles was sore puzzled. He dashed off to the agents, Parker & Ellis.

They said, Yes; the house was Lady Bassett's for a few months. They were instructed to let it.

"When did she leave? I am her husband, and we have missed each other somehow."

The clerk interfered, and said Lady Bassett had brought the keys in her carriage yesterday.

Sir Charles groaned with vexation and annoyance.

"Did she give you no address?"

"Yes, sir. Huntercombe Hall."

"I mean no address in London?"

"No, sir; none."

Sir Charles was now truly perplexed and distressed, and all manner of strange ideas came into his head. He did not know what to do, but he could not bear to do nothing, so he drove to the *Times* office and advertised, requesting Lady Bassett to send her present address to Mr. Rolfe.

At night he talked this strange business over with Mr. Rolfe.

That gentleman thought she must have gone to Huntercombe; but by the last post a letter came from Suaby, inclosing one from Lady Bassett to her husband.

"119 Gloucester Place.

"DARLING--The air here is not good for baby, and I cannot sleep for the noise. We think of creeping toward home to-morrow, in an easy carriage. Pray God you may soon meet us at dear Huntercombe. Our first journey will be to that dear old comfortable inn at Winterfield, where you and I were so happy, but not happier, dearest darling, than we shall soon be again, I hope.

"Your devoted wife.

"BELLA BASSETT.

"My heartfelt thanks to Mr. Rolfe for all he is doing."

Sir Charles wanted to start that night for Winterfield, but Rolfe persuaded him not. "And mind," said he, "the faithful pugilists must go with you."

The morning's post rendered that needless. It brought another letter from Suaby, informing Mr. Rolfe that the Commissioners had positively discharged Sir Charles, and notified the discharge to Richard Bassett.

Sir Charles took leave of Mr. Rolfe as of a man who was to be his bosom friend for life, and proceeded to hunt his wife.

She had left Winterfield; but he followed her like a stanch hound, and when he stopped at a certain inn, some twenty miles from Huntercombe, a window opened, there was a strange loving scream; he looked up, and saw his wife's radiant face, and her figure ready to fly down to him. He rushed upstairs, into the right room by some mighty instinct, and held her, panting and crying for joy, in his arms.

That moment almost compensated what each had suffered.

CHAPTER XXXI.

So full was the joy of this loving pair that, for a long time, they sat rocking in each other's arms, and thought of nothing but their sorrows past, and the sea of bliss they were floating on.

But presently Sir Charles glanced round for a moment. Swift to interpret his every look, Lady Bassett rose, took two steps, came back and printed a kiss on his forehead, and then went to a door and opened it.

"Mrs. Millar!" said she, with one of those tones by which these ladies impregnate with meaning a word that has none at all; and then she came back to her husband.

Soon a buxom woman of forty appeared, carrying a biggish bank of linen and lace, with a little face in the middle. The good woman held it up to Sir Charles, and he felt something novel stir inside him. He looked at the little thing with a vast yearning of love, with pride, and a good deal of curiosity; and then turned smiling to his wife. She had watched him furtively but keenly, and her eyes were brimming over. He kissed the little thing, and blessed it, and then took his wife's hands, and kissed her wet eyes, and made her stand and look at baby with him, hand in hand. It was a pretty picture.

The buxom woman swelled her feathers, as simple women do when they exhibit a treasure of this sort; she lifted the little mite slowly up and down, and said, "Oh, you Beauty!" and then went off into various inarticulate sounds, which I recommend to the particular study of the new philosophers: they cannot have been invented after speech; that would be retrogression; they must be the vocal remains of that hairy, sharp-eared quadruped, our Progenitor, who by accident discovered language, and so turned Biped, and went ahead of all the other hairy quadrupeds, whose ears were too long or not sharp enough to stumble upon language.

Under cover of these primeval sounds Lady Bassett drew her husband a little apart, and looking in his face with piteous wistfulness, said, "You won't mind Richard Bassett and his baby now?"

"Not I."

"You will never have another fit while you live?"

"I promise."

"You will always be happy?"

"I must be an ungrateful scoundrel else, my dear."

"Then baby is our best friend. Oh, you little angel!" And she pounced on the mite, and kissed it far harder than Sir Charles had. Heaven knows what these gentle creatures are so rough with their mouths to children, but so it is.

And now how can a mere male relate all the pretty childish things that were done and said to baby, and of baby, before the inevitable squalling began, and baby was taken away to be consoled by another of his subjects.

Sir Charles and Lady Bassett had a thousand things to tell each other, to murmur in each other's ears, sitting lovingly close to each other.

But when all was quiet, and everybody else was in bed, Lady Bassett plucked up courage and said, "Charles, I am not quite happy. There is one thing wanting." And then she hid her face in her hands and blushed. "I cannot nurse him."

"Never mind," said Sir Charles kindly.

"You forgive me?"

"Forgive you, my poor girl! Why, is that a crime?"

"It leads to so many things. You don't know what a plague a nurse is, and makes one jealous."

"Well, but it is only for a time. Come, Bella, this is a little peevish. Don't let us be ungrateful to Heaven. As for me, while you and our child live, I am proof against much greater misfortunes than that."

Then Lady Bassett cleared up, and the subject dropped.

But it was renewed next morning in a more definite form.

Sir Charles rose early; and in the pride and joy of his heart, and not quite without an eye to triumphing over his mortal enemy and his cold friends, sent a mounted messenger with orders to his servants to prepare for his immediate reception, and to send out his landau and four horses to the "Rose," at Staveleigh, half-way between Huntercombe and the place where he now was. Lady Bassett had announced herself able for the journey.

After breakfast he asked her rather suddenly whether Mrs. Millar was not rather an elderly woman to select for a nurse. "I thought people got a young woman for that office."

"Oh," said Lady Bassett, "why, Mrs. Millar is not *the* nurse. Of course nurse is young and healthy, and from the country, and the best I could have in every way for baby. But yet--oh, Charles, I hope you will not be angry--who do you think nurse is? It is Mary Gosport--Mary Wells that was."

Sir Charles was a little staggered. He put this and that together, and said, "Why, she must have been playing the fool, then?"

"Hush! not so loud, dear. She is a married woman now, and her husband gone to sea, and her child dead. Most wet-nurses have a child of their own; and don't you think they must hate the stranger's child that parts them from their own? Now baby is a comfort to Mary. And the wet-nurse is always a tyrant; and I thought, as this one has got into a habit of obeying me, she might be more manageable; and then as to her having been imprudent, I know many ladies who have been obliged to shut their eyes a little. Why, consider, Charles, would good wives and good mothers leave their own children to nurse a stranger's? Would their husbands let them? And I thought," said she, piteously, "we were so fortunate to get a young, healthy girl, imprudent but not vicious, whose fault had been covered by marriage, and then so attached to us both as she is, poor thing!"

Sir Charles was in no humor to make mountains of mole-hills. "Why, my dear Bella," said he, "after all, this is your department, not mine."

"Yes, but unless I please you in every department there is no happiness for me."

"But you know you please me in everything; and the more I look into anything, the wiser I always think you. You have chosen the best wet-nurse possible. Send her to me."

Lady Bassett hesitated. "You will be kind to her. You know the consequence if anything happens to make her fret. Baby will suffer for it."

"Oh, I know. Catch me offending this she potentate till he is weaned. Dress for the journey, my dear, and send nurse to me."

Lady Bassett went into the next room, and after a long time Mary came to Sir Charles with baby in her arms.

Mary had lost for a time some of her ruddy color, but her skin was clearer, and somehow her face was softened. She looked really a beautiful and attractive young woman.

She courtesied to Sir Charles, and then took a good look at him.

"Well, nurse," said he, cheerfully, "here we are back again, both of us."

"That we be, sir." And she showed her white teeth in a broad smile. "La, sir, you be a sight for sore eyes. How well you do look, to be sure!"

"Thank you, Mary. I never was better in my life. You look pretty well too; only a little pale; paler than Lady Bassett does."

"I give my color to the child," said Mary, simply.

She did not know she had said anything poetic; but Sir Charles was so touched and pleased with her answer that he gave her a five-pound note on the spot; and he said, "We'll bring your color back if beef and beer and kindness can do it."

"I ain't afeard o' that, sir; and I'll arn it. 'Tis a lovely boy, sir, and your very image."

Inspection followed; and something or other offended young master; he began to cackle. But this nurse did not take him away, as Mrs. Millar had. She just sat down with him and nursed him openly, with rustic composure and simplicity.

Sir Charles leaned his arm on the mantel-piece, and eyed the pair; for all this was a new world of feeling to him. His paid servant seemed to him to be playing the mother to his child. Somehow it gave him a strange twinge, a sort of vicarious jealousy: he felt for his Bella. But I think his own paternal pride, in all its freshness, was hurt a little too.

At last he shrugged his shoulders, and was going out of the room, with a hint to Mary that she must wrap herself up, for it would be an open carriage--

"Your own carriage, sir, and horses?"

"Certainly."

"And do all the folk know as we are coming?"

Sir Charles laughed. "Most likely. Gossip is not dead at Huntercombe, I dare say."

Nurse's black eyes flashed. "All the village will be out. I hope *he* will see us ride in, the black-hearted villain!"

Sir Charles was too proud to let her draw him into that topic; he went about his business.

Lady Bassett's carriage, duly packed, came round, and Lady Bassett was ready soon afterward; so was Mrs. Millar; so was baby, imbedded now in a nest of lawn and lace and white fur. They had to wait for nurse. Lady Bassett explained **sotto voce** to her husband, "Just at the last moment she was seized with a desire to wear a silk gown I gave her. I argued with her, but she only pouted. I was afraid for baby. It is very hard upon **you,** dear."

Her face and voice were so piteous that Sir Charles burst out laughing.

"We must take the bitter along with the sweet. Don't you think the sweet rather predominates at present?"

Lady Bassett explored his face with all her eyes. "My darling is happy now; trifles cannot put him out."

"I doubt if anything could shake me while I have you and our child. As for that jade keeping us all waiting while she dons silk attire, it is simply delicious. I wish Rolfe was here, that is all. Ha! ha! ha!"

Mrs. Gosport appeared at last in a purple silk gown, and marched to the carriage without the slightest sign of the discomfort she really felt; but that was no wonder, belonging, as she did, to a sex which can walk not only smiling but jauntily, though dead lame on stilts, as you may see any day in Regent Street.

Sir Charles, with mock gravity, ushered King Baby and his attendants in first, then Lady Bassett, and got in last himself.

Before they had gone a mile Nurse No. 1 handed the child over to Nurse No. 2 with a lofty condescension, as who should say, "You suffice for porterage; I, the superior artist, reserve myself for emergencies." No. 2 received the invaluable bundle with meek complacency.

By-and-by Nurse 1 got fidgety, and kept changing her position.

"What is the matter, Mary?" said Lady Bassett, kindly. "Is the dress too tight?"

"No, no, my lady," said Mary, sharply; "the gownd's all right." And then she was quiet a little.

But she began again; and then Lady Bassett whispered Sir Charles, "I think she wants to sit forward: **may** I?"

"Certainly not. I'll change with her. Here, Mary, try this side. We shall have more room in the landau; it is double, with wide seats."

Mary was gratified, and amused herself looking out of the window. Indeed, she was quiet for nearly half an hour. At the expiration of that period the fit took her again. She beckoned haughtily for baby, "which did come at her command," as the song says. She got tired of baby, or something, and handed him back again.

Presently she was discovered to be crying.

General consternation! Universal but vague consolation!

Lady Bassett looked an inquiry at Mrs. Millar. Mrs. Millar looked back assent. Lady Bassett assumed the command, and took off Mary's shawl.

"Yes," said she to Mrs. Millar. "Now, Mary, be good; it *is* too tight."

Thus urged, the idiot contracted herself by a mighty effort, while Lady Bassett attacked the fastenings, and, with infinite difficulty, they unhooked three bottom hooks. The fierce burst open that followed, and the awful chasm, showed what gigantic strength vanity can command, and how savagely abuse it to maltreat nature.

Lady Bassett loosened the stays too, and a deep sigh of relief told the truth, which the lying tongue had denied, as it always does whenever the same question is put.

The shawl was replaced, and comfort gained till they entered the town of Staveleigh.

Nurse instantly exchanged places with Sir Charles, and took the child again. He was her banner in all public places.

When they came up to the inn they were greeted with loud hurrahs. It was market-day. The town was full of Sir Charles's tenants and other farmers. His return had got wind, and every farmer under fifty had resolved to ride with him into Huntercombe.

When five or six, all shouting together, intimated this to Sir Charles, he sent one of his people to order the butchers out to Huntercombe with joints a score, and then to gallop on with a note to his housekeeper and butler. "For those that ride so far with me must sup with me," said he; a sentiment that was much approved.

He took Lady Bassett and the women upstairs and rested them about an hour; and then they started for Huntercombe, followed by some thirty farmers and a dozen towns-people, who had a mind for a lark and to sup at Huntercombe Hall for once.

The ride was delightful; the carriage bowled swiftly along over a smooth road, with often turf at the side; and that enabled the young farmers to canter alongside without dusting the carriage party. Every man on horseback they overtook joined them; some they met turned back with them, and these were rewarded with loud cheers. Every eye in the carriage glittered, and every cheek was more or less flushed by this uproarious sympathy so gallantly shown, and the very thunder of so many horses' feet, each carrying a friend, was very exciting and glorious. Why, before they got to the village they had fourscore horsemen at their backs.

As they got close to the village Mary Gosport held out her arms for young master: this was not the time to forego her importance.

The church-bells rang out a clashing peal, the cavalcade clattered into the village. Everybody was out to cheer, and at sight of baby the women's voices were as loud as the men's. Old pensioners of the house were out bareheaded; one, with hair white as snow, was down on his knees praying a blessing on them.

Lady Bassett began to cry softly; Sir Charles, a little pale, but firm as a rock; both bowing right and left, like royal personages; and well they might; every house in the village belonged to them but one.

On approaching that one Mary Gosport turned her head round, and shot a glance round out of the tail of her eye. Ay, there was Richard Bassett, pale and gloomy, half-hid behind a tree at his gate: but Hate's quick eye discerned him: at the moment of passing she suddenly lifted the child high, and showed it him, pretending to show it to the crowd: but her eye told the tale; for, with that act of fierce hatred and cunning triumph, those black orbs shot a colored gleam like a furious leopardess's.

A roar of cheers burst from the crowd at that inspired gesture of a woman, whose face and eyes seemed on fire: Lady Bassett turned pale.

The next moment they passed their own gate, and dashed up to the hall steps of Huntercombe.

Sir Charles sent Lady Bassett to her room for the night. She walked through a row of ducking servants, bowing and smiling like a gentle goddess.

Mary Gosport, afraid to march in a long dress with the child, for fear of accidents, handed him superbly to Millar and strutted haughtily after her mistress, nodding patronage. Her follower, the meek Millar, stopped often to show the heir right and left, with simple geniality and kindness.

Sir Charles stood on the hall steps, and invited all to come in and take pot-luck.

Already spits were turning before great fires; a rump of beef, legs of pork, and pease-puddings boiling in one copper; turkeys and fowls in another; joints and pies baking in the great brick ovens; barrels of beer on tap, and magnums of champagne and port marching steadily up from the cellars, and forming in line and square upon sideboards and tables.

Supper was laid in the hall, the dining-room, the drawing-room, and the great kitchen.

Poor villagers trickled in: no man or woman was denied; it was open house that night, as it had been four hundred years ago.

CHAPTER XXXII.

WHEN Sharpe's clerk retired, after serving that writ on Bassett, Bassett went to Wheeler and treated it as a jest. But Wheeler looked puzzled, and Bassett himself, on second thoughts, said he should like advice of counsel. Accordingly they both went up to London to a solicitor, and obtained an interview with a counsel learned in the law. He heard their story, and said, "The question is, can you convince a jury he was insane at the time?"

"But he can't get into court," said Bassett. "I won't let him."

"Oh, the court will make you produce him."

"But I thought an insane person was civiliter mortuus, and couldn't sue."

"So he is; but this man is not insane in law. Shutting up a man on certificates is merely a preliminary step to a fair trial by his peers whether he is insane or not. Take the parallel case of a felon. A magistrate commits him for trial, and generally on better evidence than medical certificates; but that does not make the man a felon, or disentitle him to a trial by his peers; on the contrary, it entitles him to a trial, and he could get Parliament to interfere if he was not brought to trial. This plaintiff simply does what, he will say, you ought to have done; he tries himself; if he tries you at the same time, that is your fault. If he is insane now, fight. If he is not, I advise you to discharge him on the instant, and then compound."

Wheeler said he was afraid the plaintiff was too vindictive to come to terms.

"Well, then, you can show you discharged him the moment you had reason to think he was cured, and you must prove he was insane when you incarcerated him; but I warn you it will be uphill work if he is sane now; the jury will be apt to go by what they see."

Bassett and Wheeler retired; the latter did not presume to differ; but Bassett was dissatisfied and irritated.

"That fellow would only see the plaintiff's side," said he. "The fool forgets there is an Act of Parliament, and that we have complied with its provisions to a T."

"Then why did you not ask his construction of the Act?" suggested Wheeler.

"Because I don't want his construction. I've read it, and it is plain enough to anybody but a fool. Well, I have consulted counsel, to please you; and now I'll go my own way, to please myself."

He went to Burdoch, and struck a bargain, and Sir Charles was to be shifted to Burdoch's asylum, and nobody allowed to see him there, etc., etc.; the old system, in short, than which no better has as yet been devised for perpetuating, or even causing, mental aberration.

Rolfe baffled this, as described, and Bassett was literally stunned. He now saw that Sir Charles had an ally full of resources and resolution. Who could it be? He began to tremble. He complained to the police, and set them to discover who had thus openly and audaciously violated the Act of Parliament, and then he went and threatened Dr. Suaby.

But Rolfe and Sir Charles, who loved Suaby as he deserved, had provided against that; they had not let the doctor into their secret. He therefore said, with perfect truth, that he had no hand in the matter, and that Sir Charles, being bound upon his honor not to escape from Bellevue, would be in the asylum still if Mr. Bassett had not taken him out, and invoked brute force, in the shape of Burdoch. "Well, sir," said he, "it seems they have shown you two can play at that game." And so bade him good afternoon very civilly.

Bassett went home sickened. He remained sullen and torpid for a day or two; then he wrote to Burdoch to send to London and try and recapture Sir Charles.

But next day he revoked his instructions, for he got a letter from the Commissioners of Lunacy, announcing the authoritative discharge of Sir Charles, on the strong representation of Dr. Suaby and other competent persons.

That settled the matter, and the poor cousin had kept the rich cousin three months at his own expense, with no solid advantage, but the prospect of a lawsuit.

Sharpe, spurred by Rolfe, gave him no breathing time. With the utmost expedition the Declaration in Bassett *v.* Bassett followed the writ.

It was short, simple, and in three counts.

"For violently seizing and confining the plaintiff in a certain place, on a false pretense that he was insane.

"For detaining him in spite of evidence that he was not insane.

"For endeavoring to remove him to another place, with a certain sinister motive there specified.

"By which several acts the plaintiff had suffered in his health and his worldly affairs, and had endured great agony of mind."

And the plaintiff claimed damages, ten thousand pounds.

Bassett sent over for his friend Wheeler, and showed him the new document with no little consternation.

But their discussion of it was speedily interrupted by the clashing of triumphant bells and distant shouting.

They ran out to see what it was. Bassett, half suspecting, hung back; but Mary Gosport's keen eye detected him, and she held up the heir to him, with hate and triumph blazing in her face.

He crept into his own house and sank into a chair foudroye.

Wheeler, however, roused him to a necessary effort, and next day they took the Declaration to counsel, to settle their defense in due form.

"What is this?" said the learned gentleman. "Three counts! Why, I advised you to discharge him at once."

"Yes," said Wheeler, "and excellent advice it was. But my client--"

"Preferred to go his own road. And now I am to cure the error I did what I could to prevent."

"I dare say, sir, it is not the first time in your experience."

"Not by a great many. Clients, in general, have a great contempt for the notion that prevention is better than cure."

"He can't hurt me," said Bassett, impatiently. "He was separately examined by two doctors, and all the provisions of the statute exactly complied with."

"But that is no defense to this plaint. The statute forbids you to imprison an insane person without certain precautions; but it does not give you a right, under any circumstances, to imprison a sane man. That was decided in Butcher *v.* Butcher. The defense you rely on was pleaded as a second plea, and the plaintiff demurred to it directly. The question was argued before the full court, and the judges, led by the first lawyer of the age, decided unanimously that the provisions of the statute did not affect sane Englishmen and their rights under the common law. They ordered the plea to be struck off the record, and the case was reduced to a simple issue of sane or insane. Butcher *v.* Butcher governs all these cases. Can you prove him insane? If not, you had better compound on any terms. In Butcher's case the jury gave 3,000 pounds, and the plaintiff was a man of very inferior position to Sir Charles Bassett. Besides, the defendant, Butcher, had not persisted against evidence, as you have. They will award 5,000 pounds at least in this case."

He took down a volume of reports, and showed them the case he had cited; and, on reading the unanimous decision of the judges, and the learning by which they were supported, Wheeler said at once: "Mr. Bassett, we might as well try to knock down St. Paul's with our heads as to go against this decision."

They then settled to put in a single plea, that Sir Charles was insane at the time of his capture.

This done, to gain time, Wheeler called on Sharpe, and, after several conferences, got the case compounded by an apology, a solemn retractation in writing, and the payment of four thousand pounds; his counsel assured him his client was very lucky to get off so cheap.

Bassett paid the money, with the assistance of his wife's father: but it was a sickener; it broke his spirit, and even injured his health for some time.

Sir Charles improved the village with the money, and gave a copy-hold tenement to each of the men Bassett had got imprisoned. So they and their sons and their grandsons lived rent free--no, now I think of it, they had to pay four pence a year to the Lord of the Manor.

Defeated at every point, and at last punished severely, Richard Bassett fell into a deep dejection and solitary brooding of a sort very dangerous to the reason. He would not go out-of-doors to give his enemies a triumph. He used to sit by the fire and mutter, "Blow upon blow, blow upon blow. My poor boy will never be lord of Huntercombe now!" and so on.

Wheeler pitied him, but could not rouse him. At last a person for whose narrow attainments and simplicity he had a profound, though, to do him justice, a civil contempt, ventured to his rescue. Mrs. Bassett went crying to her father, and told him she feared the worst if Richard's mind could not be diverted from the Huntercombe estate and his hatred of Sir Charles and Lady Bassett, which had been the great misfortune of her life and of his own, but nothing would ever eradicate it. Richard had great abilities; was a linguist, a wonderful accountant; could her dear father find him some profitable employment to divert his thoughts?

"What! all in a moment?" said the old man. "Then I shall have to *buy* it; and if I go on like this I shall not have much to leave you."

Having delivered this objection, he went up to London, and, having many friends in the City, and laying himself open to proposals, he got scent at last of a new insurance company that proposed also to deal in reversions, especially to entailed estates. By prompt purchase of shares in Bassett's name, and introducing Bassett himself, who, by special study, had a vast acquaintance with entailed estates, and a genius for arithmetical calculation, he managed somehow to get him into the direction, with a stipend, and a commission on all business he might introduce to the office.

Bassett yielded sullenly, and now divided his time between London and the country.

Wheeler worked with him on a share of commission, and they made some money between them.

After the bitter lesson he had received Bassett vowed to himself he never would attack Sir Charles again unless he was sure of victory. For all this he hated him and Lady Bassett worse than ever, hated them to the death.

He never moved a finger down at Huntercombe, nor said a word; but in London he employed a private inquirer to find out where Lady Bassett had lived at the time of her confinement, and whether any clergyman had visited her.

The private inquirer could find out nothing, and Bassett, comparing his advertisements with his performance, dismissed him for a humbug.

But the office brought him into contact with a great many medical men, one after another. He used to say to each stranger, with an insidious smile, "I think you once attended my cousin--Lady Bassett."

CHAPTER XXXIII.

SIR CHARLES and Lady Bassett, relieved of their cousin's active enmity, led a quiet life, and one that no longer furnished striking incidents.

But dramatic incident is not everything: character and feeling show themselves in things that will not make pictures. Now it was precisely during this reposeful period that three personages of this story exhibited fresh traits of feeling, and also of character.

To begin with Sir Charles Bassett. He came back from the asylum much altered in body and mind. Stopping his cigars had improved his stomach; working in the garden had increased his muscular power, and his cheeks were healthy, and a little sunburned, instead of sallow. His mind was also improved: contemplation of insane persons had set him by a natural recoil to study self-control. He had returned a philosopher. No small thing could irritate him now. So far his character was elevated.

Lady Bassett was much the same as before, except a certain restlessness. She wanted to be told every day, or twice a day, that her husband was happy; and, although he was visibly so, yet, as he was quiet over it, she used to be always asking him if he was happy. This the reader must interpret as he pleases.

Mary Gosport gave herself airs. Respectful to her master and mistress, but not so tolerant of chaff in the kitchen as she used to be. Made an example of one girl, who threw a doubt on her marriage. Complained to Lady Bassett, affected to fret, and the girl was dismissed.

She turned singer. She had always sung psalms in church, but never a profane note in the house. Now she took to singing over her nursling; she had a voice of prodigious power and mellowness, and, provided she was not asked, would sing lullabies and nursery rhymes from another county that ravished the hearer. Horsemen have been known to stop in the road to hear her sing through an open window of

Huntercombe, two hundred yards off.

Old Mr. Meyrick, a farmer well-to-do, fascinated by Mary Gosport's singing, asked her to be his housekeeper when she should have done nursing her charge.

She laughed in his face.

A fanatic who was staying with Sir Charles Bassett offered her three years' education in Do, Ra, Mi, Fa, preparatory to singing at the opera.

Declined without thanks.

Mr. Drake, after hovering shyly, at last found courage to reproach her for deserting him and marrying a sailor.

"Teach you not to shilly-shally," said she. "Beauty won't go a-begging. Mind you look sharper next time."

This dialogue, being held in the kitchen, gave the women some amusement at the young farmer's expense.

One day Mr. Richard Bassett, from motives of pure affection no doubt, not curiosity, desired mightily to inspect Mr. Bassett, aged eight months and two days.

So, in his usual wily way, he wrote to Mrs. Gosport, asking her, for old acquaintance' sake, to meet him in the meadow at the end of the lawn. This meadow belonged to Sir Charles, but Richard Bassett had a right of way through it, and could step into it by a postern, as Mary could by an iron gate.

He asked her to come at eleven o'clock, because at that hour he observed she walked on the lawn with her charge.

Mary Gosport came to the tryst, but without Mr. Bassett.

Richard was very polite; she cold, taciturn, observant.

At last he said, "But where's the little heir?"

She flew at him directly. "It is him you wanted, not me. Did you think I'd bring him here--for you to kill him?"

"Come, I say."

"Ay, you'd kill him if you had a chance. But you never shall. Or if you didn't kill him, you'd cast the evil-eye on him, for you are well known to have the evil-eye. No; he shall outlive thee and thine, and be lord of these here manors when thou is gone to hell, thou villain."

Mr. Richard Bassett turned pale, but did the wisest thing he could--put his hands in his pockets, and walked into his own premises, followed, however, by

Mary Gosport, who stormed at him till he shut his postern in her face.

She stood there trembling for a little while, then walked away, crying.

But having a mind like running water, she was soon seated on a garden chair, singing over her nursling like a mavis: she had delivered him to Millar while she went to speak her mind to her old lover.

As for Richard Bassett, he was theory-bitten, and so turned every thing one way. To be sure, as long as the woman's glaring eyes and face distorted by passion were before him, he interpreted her words simply; but when he thought the matter over he said to himself, "The evil-eye! That is all bosh; the girl is in Lady Bassett's secrets; and I am not to see young master: some day I shall know the reason why."

Sir Charles Bassett now belonged to the tribe of clucking cocks quite as much as his cousin had ever done; only Sir Charles had the good taste to confine his clucks to his own first-floor. Here, to be sure, he richly indemnified himself for his self-denial abroad. He sat for hours at a time watching the boy on the ground at his knee, or in his nurse's arms.

And while he watched the infant with undisguised delight, Lady Bassett would watch *him* with a sort of furtive and timid complacency.

Yet at times she suffered from twinges of jealousy--a new complaint with her.

I think I have mentioned that Sir Charles, at first, was annoyed at seeing his son and heir nursed by a woman of low condition. Well, he got over that feeling by degrees, and, as soon as he did get over it, his sentiments took quite an opposite turn. A woman for whom he did very little, in his opinion--since what, in Heaven's name, were a servant's wages?--he saw that woman do something great for him; saw her nourish his son and heir from her own veins; the child had no other nurture; yet the father saw him bloom and thrive, and grow surprisingly.

A weak observer, or a less enthusiastic parent, might have overlooked all this; but Sir Charles had naturally an observant eye and an analytical mind, and this had been suddenly but effectually developed by the asylum and his correspondence with Rolfe.

He watched the nurse, then, and her maternal acts with a curious and grateful eye, and a certain reverence for her power.

He observed, too, that his child reacted on the woman: she had never sung in the house before; now she sang ravishingly--sang, in low, mellow, yet sonorous notes, some ditties that had lulled mediaeval barons in their cradles.

And what had made her vocal made her beautiful at times.

Before, she had appeared to him a handsome girl, with the hardish look of the lower classes; but now, when she sat in a sunny window, and lowered her black lashes on her nursling, with the mixed and delicious smile of an exuberant nurse relieving and relieved, she was soft, poetical, sculptorial, maternal, womanly.

This species of contemplation, though half philosophical, half paternal, and quite innocent, gave Lady Bassett some severe pangs.

She hid them, however; only she bided her time, and then suggested the propriety of weaning baby.

But Mrs. Gosport got Sir Charles's ear, and told him what magnificent children they reared in her village by not weaning infants till they were eighteen months old or so.

By this means, and by crying to Lady Bassett, and representing her desolate condition with a husband at sea, she obtained a reprieve, coupled, however, with a good-humored assurance from Sir Charles that she was the greatest baby of the two.

When the inevitable hour approached that was to dethrone her she took to reading the papers, and one day she read of a disastrous wreck, the **Carbrea Castle**--only seven saved out of a crew of twenty-three. She read the details carefully, and two days afterward she received a letter written by a shipmate of Mr. Gosport's, in a handwriting not very unlike her own, relating the sad wreck of the **Carbrea Castle,** and the loss of several good sailors, James Gosport for one.

Then the house was filled with the wailing and weeping of the bereaved widow; and at last came consolers and raised doubts; but then somebody remembered to have seen the loss of that very ship in the paper. The paper was found, and the fatal truth was at once established.

Upon this Mr. Bassett was weaned as quickly as possible, and the widow clothed in black at Lady Bassett's expense, and everything in reason done to pet her and console her.

But she cried bitterly, and said she would throw herself into the sea and follow her husband.

Huntercombe was nowhere near the coast.

At last, however, she relented, and concluded to remain on earth as dry-nurse to Mr. Bassett.

Sir Charles did not approve this: it seemed unreasonable to turn a wet-nurse into a dry-nurse when that office was already occupied by a person her senior and more experienced.

Lady Bassett agreed with him, but shrugged her shoulders and said, "Two nurses will not hurt, and I suspect it will not be for long. Mary does not feel her husband's loss one bit."

"Surely you are mistaken. She howls loud enough."

"Too loud--much," said Lady Bassett, dryly.

Her perspicuity was not deceived. In a very short time Mr. Meyrick, unable to get her for his housekeeper, offered her marriage.

"What!" said she, "and James Gosport not dead a month?"

"Say the word now, and take your own time," said he.

"Well, I might do worse," said she.

About six weeks after this Drake came about her, and in tender tones of consolation suggested that it is much better for a pretty girl to marry one who plows the land than one who plows the sea.

"That is true," said Mary, with a sigh; "I have found it to my sorrow."

After this Drake played a bit with her, and then relented, and one evening offered her marriage, expecting her to jump eagerly at his offer.

"You be too late, young man," said she, coolly; "I'm bespoke."

"Doan't ye say that! How can ye be bespoke? Why, t'other hain't been dead four months yet."

"What o' that? This one spoke for me within a week. Why, our banns are to be cried to-morrow; come to church and hear 'em; that will learn ye not to shilly-shally so next time."

"Next time!" cried Drake, half blubbering; then, with a sudden roar, "what, be you coming to market again, arter this?"

"Like enough: he is a deal older than I be. 'Tis Mr. Meyrick, if ye must know."

Now Mr. Meyrick was well-to-do, and so Drake was taken aback.

"Mr. Meyrick!" said he, and turned suddenly respectful.

But presently a view of a rich widow flitted before his eye.

"Well," said he, "you shan't throw it in my teeth again as I speak too late. I ask you now, and no time lost."

"What! am I to stop my banns, and jilt Farmer Meyrick for ***thee?***"

"Nay, nay. But I mean I'll marry you, if you'll marry me, as soon as ever the breath is out of that dall'd old hunks's body."

"Well, well, Will Drake," said Mary, gravely, "if I do outlive this one--and you bain't married long afore--and if you keeps in the same mind as you be now--and lets me know it in good time--I'll see about it."

She gave a flounce that made her petticoats whisk like a mare's tail, and off to the kitchen, where she related the dialogue with an appropriate reflection, the company containing several of either sex. "Dilly-Dally and Shilly-Shally, they belongs to us as women be. I hate and despise a man as can't make up his mind in half a minnut."

So the widow Gosport became Mrs. Meyrick, and lived in a farmhouse not quite a mile from the Hall.

She used often to come to the Hall, and take a peep at her lamb: this was the name she gave Mr. Bassett long after he had ceased to be a child.

About four years after the triumphant return to Huntercombe, Lady Bassett conceived a sudden coldness toward the little boy, though he was universally admired.

She concealed this sentiment from Sir Charles, but not from the female servants: and, from one to another, at last it came round to Sir Charles. He disbelieved it utterly at first; but, the hint having been given him, he paid attention, and discovered there was, at all events, some truth in it.

He awaited his opportunity and remonstrated: "My dear Bella, am I mistaken, or do I really observe a falling off in your tenderness for your child?"

Lady Bassett looked this way and that, as if she meditated flight, but at last she resigned herself, and said, "Yes, dear Charles; my heart is quite cold to him."

"Good Heavens, Bella! But why? Is not this the same little angel that came to our help in trouble, that comforted me even before his birth, when my mind was morbid, to say the least?"

"I suppose he is the same," said she, in a tone impossible to convey by description of mine.

"That is a strange answer."

"If he is, *I* am changed." And this she said doggedly and unlike herself.

"What!" said Sir Charles, very gravely, and with a sort of awe: "can a woman withdraw her affection from her child, her innocent child? If so, my turn may come next."

"Oh, Charles! Charles!" and the tears began to well.

"Why, who can be secure after this? What is so stable as a mother's love? If that is not rooted too deep for gusts of caprice to blow it away, in Heaven's name, what is?"

No answer to that but tears.

Sir Charles looked at her very long, attentively, and seriously, and said not another syllable.

But his dropping so suddenly a subject of this importance was rather suspicious, and Lady Bassett was too shrewd not to see that.

They watched each other.

But with this difference: Sir Charles could not conceal his anxiety, whereas the lady appeared quite tranquil.

One day Sir Charles said, cheerfully, "Who do you think dines here to-morrow, and stays all night? Dr. Suaby."

"By invitation, dear?" asked Lady Bassett, quietly.

Sir Charles colored a little, and said, quietly, "Yes."

Lady Bassett made no remark, and it was impossible to tell by her face whether the visit was agreeable or not.

Some time afterward, however, she said, "Whom shall I ask to meet Dr. Suaby?"

"Nobody, for Heaven's sake!"

"Will not that be dull for him?"

"I hope not."

"You will have plenty to say to him, eh, darling?"

"We never yet lacked topics. Whether or no, his is a mind I choose to drink neat."

"Drink him neat?"

"Undiluted with rural minds."

"Oh!"

She uttered that monosyllable very dryly, and said no more.

Dr. Suaby came next day, and dined with them, and Lady Bassett was charming; but rather earlier than usual she said, "Now I am sure you and Dr. Suaby must have many things to talk about," and retired, casting back an arch, and almost a cunning smile.

The door closed on her, the smile fled, and a somber look of care and suffering took its place.

Sir Charles entered at once on what was next his heart, told Dr. Suaby he was in some anxiety, and asked him if he had observed anything in Lady Bassett.

"Nothing new," said Dr. Suaby; "charming as ever."

Then Sir Charles confided to Dr. Suaby, in terms of deep feeling and anxiety, what I have coldly told the reader.

Dr. Suaby looked a little grave, and took time to think before he spoke.

At last he delivered an opinion, of which this is the substance, though not the exact words.

"It is sudden and unnatural, and I cannot say it does not partake of mental aberration. If the patient was a man I should fear the most serious results; but here we have to take into account the patient's sex, her nature, and her present condition. Lady Bassett has always appeared to me a very remarkable woman. She has no mediocrity in anything; understanding keen, perception wonderfully swift, heart large and sensitive, nerves high strung, sensibilities acute. A person of her sex, tuned so high as this, is always subject, more or less, to hysteria. It is controlled by her intelligence and spirit; but she is now, for the time being, in a physical condition that has often deranged less sensitive women than she is. I believe this about the boy to be a hysterical delusion, which will pass away when her next child is born. That is to say, she will probably ignore her first-born, and everything else, for a time; but these caprices, springing in reality from the body rather than the mind, cannot endure forever. When she has several grown-up children the first-born will be the favorite. It comes to that at last, my good friend."

"These are the words of wisdom," said Sir Charles; "God bless you for them!"

After a while he said, "Then what you advise is simply--patience?"

"No, I don't say that. With such a large house as this, and your resources, you might easily separate them before the delusion grows any farther. Why risk a calamity?"

"A calamity?" and Sir Charles began to tremble.

"She is only cold to the child as yet. She might go farther, and fancy she hated it. ***Obsta principiis:*** that is my motto. Not that I really think, for a moment, the child is in danger. Lady Bassett has mind to control her nerves with; but why run the shadow of a chance?"

"I will not run the shadow of a chance," said Sir Charles, resolutely; "let us come upstairs: my decision is taken."

The very next day Sir Charles called on Mrs. Meyrick, and asked if he could come to any arrangement with her to lodge Mr. Bassett and his nurse under her roof. "The boy wants change of air," said he.

Mrs. Meyrick jumped at the proposal, but declined all terms. "No," said she, "the child I have suckled shall never pay me for his lodging. Why should he, sir, when I'd pay *you* to let him come, if I wasn't afeard of offending you?"

Sir Charles was touched at this, and, being a gentleman of tact, said, "You are very good: well, then, I must remain your debtor for the present."

He then took his leave, but she walked with him a few yards, just as far as the wicket, gate that separated her little front garden from the high-road.

"I hope," said she, "my lady will come and see me when my lamb is with me; a sight of her would be good for sore eyes. She have never been here but once, and then she did not get out of her carriage."

"Humph!" said Sir Charles, apologetically; "she seldom goes out now; you understand."

"Oh, I've heard, sir; and I do put up my prayers for her; for my lady has been a good friend to me, sir, and if you will believe me, I often sets here and longs for a sight of her, and her sweet eyes, and her hair like sunshine, that I've had in my hand so often. Well, sir, I hope it will be a girl this time, a little girl with golden hair; that's what I wants this time. They'll be the prettiest pair in England."

"With all my heart," said Sir Charles; "girl or boy, I don't care which; but I'd give a few thousands if it was here, and the mother safe."

He hurried away, ashamed of having uttered the feelings of his heart to a farmer's wife. To avoid discussion, he sent Mrs. Millar and the boy off all in a hurry, and then told Lady Bassett what he had done.

She appeared much distressed at that, and asked what she had done.

He soothed her, and said she was not to blame at all; and she must not blame him either. He had done it for the best.

"After all, you are the master," said she, submissively.

"I am," said he, "and men will be tyrants, you know."

Then she flung her arm round her tyrant's neck, and there was an end of the discussion.

One day he inquired for her, and heard, to his no small satisfaction, she had driven to Mrs. Meyrick's, with a box of things for Mr. Bassett. She stayed at the farmhouse all day, and Sir Charles felt sure he had done the right thing.

Mrs. Meyrick found out to her cost the difference between a nursling and a rampageous little boy.

Her lamb, as she called him, was now a young monkey, vigorous, active, restless, and, unfortunately, as strong on his pins as most boys of six. It took two women to look after him, and smart ones too, so swiftly did he dash off into some mischief or other. At last Mrs. Meyrick simplified matters in some degree by locking the large gate, and even the small wicket, and ordering all the farm people and milkmaids to keep an eye on him, and bring him straight to her if he should stray, for he seemed to hate in-doors. Never was such a boy.

Nevertheless, such as had not the care of him admired the child for his beauty and his assurance. He seemed to regard the whole human race as one family, of which he was the rising head. The moment he caught sight of a human being he dashed at it and into conversation by one unbroken movement.

Now children in general are too apt to hide their intellectual treasures from strangers by shyness.

One day this ready converser was standing on the steps of the house, when a gentleman came to the wicket gate, and looked over into the garden.

Young master darted to the gate directly, and getting his foot on the lowest bar and his hands on the spikes, gave tongue.

"Who are you? *I'm* Mr. Bassett. I don't live here; I'm only staying. My home is Huncom Hall. I'm to have it for myself when papa dies. I didn't know dat till I come here. How old are you? I'm half past four--"

A loud scream, a swift rustle, and Mr. Bassett was clutched up by Mrs. Meyrick, who snatched him away with a wild glance of terror and defiance, and bore him swiftly into the house, with words ringing in her ears that cost Mr. Bassett dear, he being the only person she could punish. She sat down on a bench, flung young master across her knee in a minute, and bestowed such a smacking on him as far transcended his wildest dreams of the weight, power, and pertinacity of the human arm.

The words Richard Bassett had shot her flying with were these:

"Too late! I've SEEN THE PARSON'S BRAT."

Richard Bassett mounted his horse and rode over to Wheeler, for he could no longer wheedle the man of law over to Highmore, and I will very briefly state why.

1st. About three years ago an old lady, one of his few clients, left him three thousand pounds, just reward of a very little law and a vast deal of gossip.

2d. The head solicitor of the place got old and wanted a partner. Wheeler bought himself in, and thenceforth took his share of a good business, and by his energy enlarged it, though he never could found one for himself.

3d. He married a wife.

4th. She was a pretty woman, and blessed with jealousy of a just and impartial nature: she was equally jealous of women, men, books, business--anything that took her husband from her.

No more sleeping out at Highmore; no more protracted potations; no more bachelor tricks for Wheeler. He still valued his old client and welcomed him; but the venue was changed, so to speak.

Richard Bassett was kept waiting in the outer office; but when he did get in he easily prevailed on Wheeler to send the next client or two to his partner, and give him a full hearing.

Then he opened his business. "Well," said he, "I've seen him at last!"

"Seen him? seen whom?"

"The boy they have set up to rob my boy of the estate. I've seen him, Wheeler, seen him close; and HE'S AS BLACK AS MY HAT."

CHAPTER XXXIV.

WHEELER, instead of being thunder-stricken, said quietly, "Oh, is he? Well?"

"Sir Charles is lighter than I am: Lady Bassett has a skin like satin, and red hair."

"Red! say auburn gilt. I never saw such lovely hair."

"Well," said Richard, impatiently, "then the boy has eyes like sloes, and a brown skin, like an Italian, and black hair almost; it will be quite."

"Well," said Wheeler, "it is not so very uncommon for a dark child to be born of fair parents, or *vice versa.* I once saw an urchin that was like neither father nor mother, but the image of his father's grandfather, that died eighty years before he was born. They used to hold him up to the portrait."

Said Bassett, "Will you admit that it is uncommon?"

"Not so uncommon as for a high-bred lady, living in the country, and adored by her husband, to trifle with her marriage vow, for that is what you are driving at."

"Then we have to decide between two improbabilities: will you grant me that, Mr. Wheeler?"

"Yes."

"Then suppose I can prove fact upon fact, and coincidence upon coincidence, all tending one way! Are you so prejudiced that nothing will convince you?"

"No. But it will take a great deal: that lady's face is full of purity, and she fought us like one who loved her husband."

"Fronti nulla fides: and as for her fighting, her infidelity was the weapon she defeated us with. Will you hear me?"

"Yes, yes; but pray stick to facts, and not conjectures."

"Then don't interrupt me with childish arguments:

"Fact 1.--Both reputed parents fair; the boy as black as the ace of spades.

"Fact 2.--A handsome young fellow was always buzzing about her ladyship, and he was a parson, and ladies are remarkably fond of parsons.

"Fact 3.--This parson was of Italian breed, dark, like the boy.

"Fact 4.--This dark young man left Huntercombe one week, and my lady left it the next, and they were both in the city of Bath at one time.

"Fact 5.--The lady went from Bath to London. The dark young man went from Bath to London."

"None of this is new to me," said Wheeler, quietly.

"No; but it is the rule, in estimating coincidences, that each fresh one multiplies the value of the others. Now the boy looking so Italian is a new coincidence, and so is what I am going to tell you--at last I have found the medical man who attended Lady Bassett in London."

"Ah!"

"Yes, sir; and I have learned *Fact 6.*--Her ladyship rented a house, but hired no servants, and engaged no nurse. She had no attendant but a lady's maid, no servant but a sort of charwoman.

"Fact 7.--She dismissed this doctor unusually soon, and gave him a very large fee.

"Fact 8.--She concealed her address from her husband."

"Oh! can you prove that?"

"Certainly. Sir Charles came up to town, and had to hunt for her, came to this very medical man, and asked for the address his wife had not given him; but lo! when he got there the bird was flown.

"Fact 9.--Following the same system of concealment, my lady levanted from London within ten days of her confinement.

"Now put all these coincidences together. Don't you see that she had a lover, and that he was about her in London and other places? Stop! *Fact 10.*--Those two were married for years, and had no child but this equivocal one; and now four years and a half have passed, during all which time they have had none, and the young parson has been abroad during that period."

Wheeler was staggered and perplexed by this artful array of coincidences.

"Now advise me," said Bassett.

"It is not so easy. Of course if Sir Charles was to die, you could claim the estate, and give them a great deal of pain and annoyance; but the burden of proof would always rest on you. My advice is not to breathe a syllable of this; but get a good detective, and push your inquiries a little further among house agents, and the women they put into houses; find that charwoman, and see if you can pick up anything more."

"Do you know such a thing as an able detective?"

"I know one that will work if I instruct him."

"Instruct him, then."

"I will."

CHAPTER XXXV.

LADY BASSETT, as her time of trial drew near, became despondent. She spoke of the future, and tried to pierce it; and in all these little loving speculations and anxieties there was no longer any mention of herself. This meant that she feared her husband was about to lose her. I put the fear in the very form it took in that gentle breast.

Possessed with this dread, so natural to her situation, she set her house in order, and left her little legacies of clothes and jewels, without the help of a lawyer; for Sir Charles, she knew, would respect her lightest wish.

To him she left her all, except these trifles, and, above all--a manuscript book. It was the history of her wedded life. Not the bare outward history; but such a record of a sensitive woman's heart as no male writer's pen can approach.

It was the nature of her face and her tongue to conceal; but here, on this paper, she laid bare her heart; here her very subtlety operated, not to hide, but to dissect herself and her motives.

But oh, what it cost her to pen this faithful record of her love, her trials, her doubts, her perplexities, her agonies, her temptations, and her crime! Often she laid down the pen, and hid her face in her hands. Often the scalding tears ran down that scarlet face. Often she writhed at her desk, and wrote on, sighing and moaning. Yet she persevered to the end. It was the grave that gave her the power. "When he reads this," she said, "I shall be in my tomb. Men make excuses for the dead. My Charles will forgive me when I am gone. He will know I loved him to desperation."

It took her many days to write; it was quite a thick quarto; so much may a woman feel in a year or two; and, need I say that, to the reader of that volume, the mystery of her conduct was all made clear as daylight; clearer far, as regards the revelation of mind and feeling, than I, dealer in broad facts, shall ever make it, for want of a woman's mental microscope and delicate brush.

And when this record was finished, she wrapped it in paper, and sealed it with many seals, and wrote on it,

"Only for my husband's eye. From her who loved him not wisely, But too well."

And she took other means that even the superscription should never be seen of any other eye but his. It was some little comfort to her, when the book was written.

She never prayed to live. But she used to pray, fervently, piteously, that her child might live, and be a comfort and joy to his father.

The person employed by Wheeler discovered the house agent, and the woman he had employed.

But these added nothing to the evidence Bassett had collected.

At last, however, this woman, under the influence of a promised reward, discovered a person who was likely to know more about the matter--viz., the woman who was in the house with Lady Bassett at the very time.

But this woman scented gold directly: so she held mysterious language; declined to say a word to the officer; but intimated that she knew a great deal, and that the matter was, in truth, well worth looking into, and she could tell some strange tales, if it was worth her while.

This information was sent to Bassett; he replied that the woman only wanted money for her intelligence, and he did not blame her; he would see her next time he went to town, and felt sure she would complete his chain of evidence. This put Richard Bassett into extravagant spirits. He danced his little boy on his knee, and said, "I'll run this little horse against the parson's brat; five to one, and no takers."

Indeed, his exultation was so loud and extravagant that it jarred on gentle Mrs. Bassett. As for Jessie, the Scotch servant, she shook her head, and said the master was fey.

In the morning he started for London, still so exuberant and excited that the Scotch woman implored her mistress not to let him go; there would be an accident on the railway, or something. But Mrs. Bassett knew her husband too well to interfere with his journeys.

Before he drove off he demanded his little boy.

"He must kiss me," said he, "for I'm going to work for him. D'ye hear that, Jane? This day makes him heir of Huntercombe and Bassett."

The nurse brought word that Master Bassett was not very well this morning.

"Let us look at him," said Bassett.

He got out of his gig, and went to the nursery. He found his little boy had a dry cough, with a little flushing.

"It is not much," said he; "but I'll send the doctor over from the town."

He did so, and himself proceeded up to London.

The doctor came, and finding the boy labored in breathing, administered a full dose of ipecacuanha. This relieved the child for the time; but about four in the afternoon he was distressed again, and began to cough with a peculiar grating sound.

Then there was a cry of dismay--"The croup!" The doctor was gone for, and a letter posted to Richard Bassett, urging him to come back directly.

The doctor tried everything, even mercury, but could not check the fatal discharge; it stiffened into a still more fatal membrane.

When Bassett returned next afternoon, in great alarm, he found the poor child thrusting its fingers into its mouth, in a vain attempt to free the deadly obstruction.

A warm bath and strong emetics were now administered, and great relief obtained. The patient even ate and drank, and asked leave to get up and play with a new toy he had. But, as often happens in this disorder, a severe relapse soon came, with a spasm of the glottis so violent and prolonged that the patient at last resigned the struggle. Then pain ceased forever; the heavenly smile came; the breath went; and nothing was left in the little white bed but a fair piece of tinted clay, that must return to the dust, and carry thither all the pride, the hopes, the boasts of the stricken father, who had schemed, and planned, and counted without Him in whose hands are the issues of life and death.

As for the child himself, his lot was a happy one, if we could but see what the world is really worth. He was always a bright child, that never cried, nor complained: his first trouble was his last; one day's pain, then bliss eternal: he never got poisoned by his father's spirit of hate, but loved and was beloved during his little lifetime; and, dying, he passed from his Noah's ark to an inheritance a thousand times richer than Huntercombe, Bassett, and all his cousin's lands.

The little grave was dug, the bell tolled, and a man bowed double with grief saw his child and his ambition laid in the dust.

Lady Bassett heard the bell tolled, and spoke but two words: "Poor woman!"

She might well say so. Mrs. Bassett was in the same condition as herself, yet this heavy blow must fall on her.

As for Richard Bassett, he sat at home, bowed down and stupid with grief.

Wheeler came one day to console him; but, at the sight of him, refrained from idle words. He sat down by him for an hour in silence. Then he got up and said, "Good-by."

"Thank you, old friend, for not insulting me," said Bassett, in a broken voice.

Wheeler took his hand, and turned away his head, and so went away, with a tear in his eye.

A fortnight after this he came again, and found Bassett in the same attitude, but not in the same leaden stupor. On the contrary, he was in a state of tremor; he had lost, under the late blow, the sanguine mind that used to carry him through everything.

The doctor was upstairs, and his wife's fate trembled in the balance.

"Stay by me," said he, "for all my nerve is gone. I'm afraid I shall lose her; for I have just begun to value her; and that is how God deals with his creatures--the merciful God, as they call him."

Wheeler thought it rather hard God Almighty should be blamed because Dick Bassett had taken eight years to find out his wife's merit; but he forbore to say so. He said kindly that he would stay.

Now while they sat in trying suspense the church-bells struck up a merry peal.

Bassett started violently and his eyes gave a strange glare. "That's the other!" said he; for he had heard about Lady Bassett by this time.

Then he turned pale. "They ring for him: then they are sure to toll for me."

This foreboding was natural enough in a man so blinded by egotism as to fancy that all creation, and the Creator himself, must take a side in Bassett *v.* Bassett.

Nevertheless, events did not justify that foreboding. The bells had scarcely done ringing for the happy event at Huntercombe, when joyful feet were heard running on the stairs; joyful voices clashed together in the passage, and in came a female servant with joyful tidings. Mrs. Bassett was safe, and the child in the world. "The loveliest little girl you ever saw!"

"A girl!" cried Richard Bassett with contemptuous amazement. Even his melancholy forebodings had not gone that length. "And what have they got at Huntercombe?"

"Oh, it is a boy, sir, there."

"Of course."

The ringers heard, and sent one of their number to ask him if they should ring.

"What for?" asked Bassett with a nasty glittering eye; and then with sudden fury he seized a large piece of wood from the basket to fling at his insulter. "I'll teach you to come and mock me."

The ringer vanished, ducking.

"Gently," said Wheeler, "gently."

Bassett chucked the wood back into the basket, and sat down gloomily, saying, "Then how dare he come and talk about ringing bells for a girl? To think that I should have all this fright, and my wife all this trouble--for a girl!"

It was no time to talk of business then; but about a fortnight afterward Wheeler said, "I took the detective off, to save you expense."

"Quite right," said Bassett, wearily.

"I gave you the woman's address; so the matter is in your hands now, I consider."

"Yes," said Bassett, wearily; "Move no further in it."

"Certainly not; and, frankly, I should be glad to see you abandon it."

"I *have* abandoned it. Why should I stir the mud now? I and mine are thrown out forever; the only question is, shall a son of Sir Charles or the parson's son inherit? I'm for the wrongful heir. Ay," he cried, starting up, and beating the air with his fists in sudden fury, "since the right Bassetts are never to have it, let the wrong Bassetts be thrown out, at all events; I'm on my back, but Sir Charles is no better off; a bastard will succeed him, thanks to that cursed woman who defeated *me.*"

This turn took Wheeler by surprise. It also gave him real pain. "Bassett," said he, "I pity you. What sort of a life has yours been for the last eight years? Yet, when there's no fuel left for war and hatred, you blow the embers. You are incurable."

"I am," said Richard. "I'll hate those two with my last breath and curse them in my last prayer."

CHAPTER XXXVI.

L ADY BASSETT'S forebodings, like most of our insights into the future, were confuted by the event.

She became the happy mother of a flaxen-haired boy. She insisted on nursing him herself; and the experienced persons who attended her raised no objection.

In connection with this she gave Sir Charles a peck, not very severe, but sudden, and remarkable as the only one on record.

He was contemplating her and her nursling with the deepest affection, and happened to say, "My own Bella, what delight it gives me to see you!"

"Yes," said she, "we will have only one mother this time, will we, my darling? and it shall be Me." Then suddenly, turning her head like a snake, "Oh, I saw the looks you gave that woman!"

This was the famous peck; administered in return for a look that he had bestowed on Mary Gosport not more than five years ago.

Sir Charles would, doubtless, have bled to death on the spot, but either he had never been aware how he looked, or time and business had obliterated the impression, for he was unaffectedly puzzled, and said, "What woman do you mean, dear?"

"No matter, darling," said Lady Bassett, who had already repented her dire severity: "all I say is that a nurse is a rival I could not endure now; and another thing, I do believe those wet-nurses give their disposition to the child: it is dreadful to think of."

"Well, if so, baby is safe. He will be the most amiable boy in England."

"He shall be more amiable than I am--scolding my husband of husbands;" and she leaned toward him, baby and all, for a kiss from his lips.

We say at school "Seniores priores"--let favor go by seniority; but where babies adorn the scene, it is "juniores priores" with that sex to which the very young are confided.

To this rule, as might be expected, Lady Bassett furnished no exception; she was absorbed in baby, and trusted Mr. Bassett a good deal to his attendant, who bore an excellent character for care and attention.

Now Mr. Bassett was strong on his pins and in his will, and his nurse-maid, after all, was young; so he used to take his walks nearly every day to Mrs. Meyrick's: she petted him enough, and spoiled him in every way, while the nurse-maid was flirting with the farm-servants out of sight.

Sir Charles Bassett was devoted to the boy, and used always to have him to his study in the morning, and to the drawing-room after dinner, when the party was small, and that happened much oftener now than heretofore; but at other hours he did not look after him, being a business man, and considering him at that age to be under his mother's care.

One day the only guest was Mr. Rolfe; he was staying in the house for three days, upon a condition suggested by himself--viz., that he might enjoy his friends' society in peace and comfort, and not be set to roll the stone of conversation up some young lady's back, and obtain monosyllables in reply, faintly lisped amid a clatter of fourteen knives and forks. As he would not leave his writing-table on any milder terms, they took him on these.

After dinner in came Mr. Bassett, erect, and a proud nurse with little Compton, just able to hold his nurse's gown and toddle.

Rolfe did not care for small children; he just glanced at the angelic, fair-haired infant, but his admiring gaze rested on the elder boy.

"Why, what is here--an Oriental prince?"

The boy ran to him directly. "Who are you?"

"Rolfe the writer. Who are you--the Gipsy King?"

"No; but I am very fond of gypsies. I'm **Mister** Bassett; and when papa dies I shall be Sir Charles Bassett."

Sir Charles laughed at this with paternal fatuity, especially as the boy's name happened to be Reginald Francis, after his grandfather.

Rolfe smiled satirically, for these little speeches from children did much to reconcile him to his lot.

"Meantime," said he, "let us feed off him; for it may be forty years before we can dance over his grave. First let us see what is the unwholesomest thing on the table."

He rose, and to the infinite delight of Mr. Bassett, and even of Master Compton, who pointed and crowed from his mother's lap, he got up on his chair, and put on a pair of spectacles to look.

"Eureka!" said he; "behold that dish by Lady Bassett; those are ***marrons glaces;*** fetch them here, and let us go in for a fit of the gout at once."

"Gout! what's that?" inquired Mr. Bassett.

"Don't ask me."

"You don't know."

"Not know! What, didn't I tell you I was Rolfe the writer? Writers know everything. That is what makes them so modest."

Mr. Bassett was now unnaturally silent for five minutes, munching chestnuts; this enabled his guests to converse; but as soon as he had cleared his plate, he cut right across the conversation, with that savage contempt for all topics but his own which characterizes gentlemen of his age, and says he to Rolfe, "You know everything? Then what's a parson's brat?"

"Well, that's the one thing I don't know," said Rolfe; "but a brat I take to be a boy who interrupts ladies and gentlemen with nonsense when they are talking sense."

"I am very much obliged to you, Mr. Rolfe," said Lady Bassett. "That remark was very much needed."

Then she called Reginald to her, and lectured him, ***sotto voce,*** to the same tune.

"You old bachelors are rather hard," said Sir Charles, not very well pleased.

"We are obliged to be; you parents are so soft. After all, it is no wonder. What a superb boy it is!--Here is nurse. I'm so sorry. Now we shall be cabined, cribbed, confined to rational conversation, and I shall not be expected to--(good-night, little flaxen angel; good-by, handsome and loquacious demon; kiss and be friends)--expected to know, all in a minute, what is a parson's brat. By-the-by, talking of parsons, what has become of Angelo?"

"He has been away a good many years. Consumption, I hear."

"He was a fine-built fellow too; was he not, Lady Bassett?"

"I don't know; but he was beautifully strong. I think I see him now carrying dear Charles in his arms all down the garden."

"Ah, you see he was raised in a university that does not do things by halves, but trains both body and mind, as they did at Athens; for the union of study and athletic sports is spoken of as a novelty, but it is only a return to antiquity."

Here letters were brought by the second post. Sir Charles glanced at his, and sent them to his study. Lady Bassett had but one. She said, *"May* I?" to both gentlemen, and then opened it.

"How strange!" said she. "It is from Mr. Angelo: just a line to say he is coming home quite cured."

She began this composedly, but blushed afterward--blushed quite red.

"May I?" said she, and tossed it delicately half-way to Rolfe. He handed it to Sir Charles.

Some remarks were then made about the coincidence, and nothing further passed worth recording at that time.

Next day Lady Bassett, with instinctive curiosity, asked Master Reginald how he came to put such a question as that to Mr. Rolfe.

"Because I wanted to know."

"But what put such words into your head? I never heard a gentleman say such words; and you must never say them again, Reginald."

"Tell me what it means, and I won't," said he.

"Oh," said Lady Bassett, "since you bargain with me, sir, I must bargain with you. Tell me first where you ever heard such words."

"When I was staying at nurse's. Ah, that was jolly."

"You like that better than being here?"

"Yes."

"I am sorry for that. Well, dear, did nurse say that? Surely not?"

"Oh, no; it was the man."

"What man?"

"Why, the man that came to the gate one morning, and talked to me, and I talked to him, and that nasty nurse ran out and caught us, and carried me in, and gave me such a hiding, and all for nothing."

"A hiding! What words the poor child picks up! But I don't understand why nurse should beat **you.**"

"For speaking to the man. She said he was a bad man, and she would kill me if ever I spoke to him again."

"Oh, it was a bad man, and said bad words--to somebody he was quarreling with?"

"No, he said them to nurse because she took me away."

"What **did** he say, Reginald?" asked Lady Bassett, becoming very grave and thoughtful all at once.

"He said, 'That's too late; I've seen the parson's brat.'"

"Oh!"

"And I've asked nurse again and again what it meant, but she won't tell me. She only says the man is a liar, and I am not to say it again; and so I never did say it again--for a long time; but last night, when Rolfe the writer said he knew everything, it struck my head--what is the matter, mamma?"

"Nothing; nothing."

"You look so white. Are you ill, mamma?" and he went to put his arms round her, which was a mighty rare thing with him.

She trembled a good deal, and did not either embrace him or repel him. She only trembled.

After some time she recovered herself enough to say, in a voice and with a manner that impressed itself at once on this sharp boy: "Reginald, your nurse was quite right. Understand this: the man was your enemy--and mine; the words he said you must not say again. It would be like taking up dirt and flinging some on your own face and some on mine."

"I won't do that," said the boy, firmly. "Are you afraid of the man that you look so white?"

"A man with a woman's tongue--who can help fearing?"

"Don't you be afraid; as soon as I'm big enough, I'll kill him."

Lady Bassett looked with surprise at the child, he uttered this resolve with such a steady resolution.

She drew him to her, and kissed him on the forehead.

"No, Reginald," said she; "we must not shed blood; it is as wicked to kill our enemies as to kill any one else. But never speak to him, never even listen to him; if he tries to speak to you, run away from him, and don't let him--he is our enemy."

That same day she went to Mrs. Meyrick, to examine her. But she found the boy had told her all there was to tell.

Mrs. Meyrick, whose affection for her was not diminished, was downright vexed. "Dear me!" said she; "I did think I had kept that from vexing of you. To think of the dear child hiding it for nigh two years, and then to blurt it out like that! Nobody heard him I hope?"

"Others heard; but--"

"Didn't heed; the Lord be praised for that."

"Mary," said Lady Bassett, solemnly, "I am not equal to another battle with Mr. Richard Bassett; and such a battle! Better tell all, and die."

"Don't think of it," said Mary. "You're safe from Richard Bassett now. Times are changed since he came spying to my gate. His own boy is gone. You have got two. He'll lie still if you do. But if you tell your tale, he must hear on't, and he'll tell his. For God's sake, my lady, keep close. It is the curse of women that they can't just hold their tongues, and see how things turn. And is this a time to spill good liquor? Look at Sir Charles! why, he is another man; he have got flesh on his bones now, and color into his cheeks, and 'twas you and I made a man of him. It is my belief you'd never have had this other little angel but for us having sense and courage to see what *must* be done. Knock down our own work, and send him wild again, and give that Richard Bassett a handle? You'll never be so mad."

Lady Bassett replied. The other answered; and so powerfully that Lady Bassett yielded, and went home sick at heart, but helpless, and in a sea of doubt.

Mr. Angelo did not call. Sir Charles asked Lady Bassett if he had called on her. She said "No."

"That is odd," said Sir Charles. "Perhaps he thinks we ought to welcome him home. Write and ask him to dinner."

"Yes, dear. Or you can write."

"Very well, I will. No, I will call."

Sir Charles called, and welcomed him home, and asked him to dinner. Angelo received him rather stiffly at first, but accepted his invitation.

He came, looking a good deal older and graver, but almost as handsome as ever; only somewhat changed in mind. He had become a zealous clergyman, and his soul appeared to be in his work. He was distant and very respectful to Lady Bassett; I might say obsequious. Seemed almost afraid of her at first.

That wore off in a few months; but he was never quite so much at his ease with her as he had been before he left some years ago.

And so did time roll on.

Every morning and every night Lady Bassett used to look wistfully at Sir Charles, and say--

"Are you happy, dear? Are you sure you are happy?"

And he used always to say, and with truth, that he was the happiest man in England, thanks to her.

Then she used to relax the wild and wistful look with which she asked the question, and give a sort of sigh, half content, half resignation.

In due course another fine boy came, and filled the royal office of baby in his turn.

But my story does not follow him.

Reginald was over ten years old, and Compton nearly six. They were as different in character as complexion--both remarkable boys.

Reginald, Sir Charles's favorite, was a wonderful boy for riding, running, talking; and had a downright genius for melody; he whistled to the admiration of the village, and latterly he practiced the fiddle in woods and under hedges, being aided and abetted therein by a gypsy boy whom he loved, and who, indeed, provided the instrument.

He rode with Sir Charles, and rather liked him; his brother he never noticed, except to tease him. Lady Bassett he admired, and almost loved her while she was in the act of playing him undeniable melodies. But he liked his nurse Meyrick better, on the whole; she flattered him more, and was more uniformly subservient.

With these two exceptions he despised the whole race of women, and affected male society only, especially of grooms, stable-boys, and gypsies; these last welcomed him to their tents, and almost prostrated themselves before him, so dazzled were they by his beauty and his color. It is believed they suspected him of having gypsy blood in his veins. They let him into their tents, and even into some of their secrets, and he promised them they should have it all their own way as soon as he was Sir Reginald; he had outgrown his original theory that he was to be Sir Charles on his father's death.

He hated in-doors; when fixed by command to a book, would beg hard to be allowed to take it into the sun; and at night would open his window and poke his black head out to wash in the moonshine, as he said.

He despised ladies and gentlemen, said they were all affected fools, and gave imitations of all his father's guests to prove it; and so keen was this child of nature's eye for affectation that very often his disapproving parents were obliged to confess the imp had seen with his fresh eye defects custom had made them overlook, or the solid good qualities that lay beneath had overbalanced.

Now all this may appear amusing and eccentric, and so on, to strangers; but after the first hundred laughs or so with which paternal indulgence dismisses the faults of childhood, Sir Charles became very grave.

The boy was his darling and his pride. He was ambitious for him. He earnestly desired to solve for him a problem which is as impossible as squaring the circle, viz., how to transmit our experience to our children. The years and the health he had wasted before he knew Bella Bruce, these he resolved his successor should not waste. He looked higher for this beautiful boy than for himself. He had fully resolved to be member for the county one day; but he did not care about it for himself; it was only to pave the way for his successor; that Sir Reginald, after a long career in the Commons, might find his way into the House of Peers, and so obtain dignity in exchange for antiquity; for, to tell the truth, the ancestors of four-fifths of the British House of Peers had been hewers of wood and drawers of water at a time when these Bassetts had already been gentlemen of distinction for centuries.

All this love and this vicarious ambition were now mortified daily. Some fathers could do wonders for a brilliant boy, and with him; they expect him, and a dull boy appears; that is a bitter pill; but this was worse. Reginald was a sharp boy; he could do anything; fasten him to a book for twenty minutes, he would learn as much as most boys in an hour; but there was no keeping him to it, unless you strapped him or nailed him, for he had the will of a mule, and the suppleness of an eel to carry out his will. And then his tastes--low as his features were refined; he was a sort of moral dung-fork; picked up all the slang of the stable and scattered it in the dining-room and drawing-room; and once or twice he stole out of his comfortable room at night, and slept in a gypsy's tent with his arm round a gypsy boy, unsullied from his cradle by soap.

At last Sir Charles could no longer reply to his wife at night as he had done for this ten years past. He was obliged to confess that there was one cloud upon his happiness. "Dear Reginald grieves me, and makes me dread the future; for if the child is father to the man, there is a bitter disappointment in store for us. He is like no other boy; he is like no human creature I ever saw. At his age, and long after, I was a fool; I was a fool till I knew you; but surely I was a gentleman. I cannot see myself again--in my first-born."

CHAPTER XXXVII.

LADY BASSETT was paralyzed for a minute or two by this speech. At last she replied by asking a question--rather a curious one. "Who nursed you, Charles?"

"What, when I was a baby? How can I tell? Yes, by-the-by, it was my mother nursed me--so I was told."

"And your mother was a Le Compton. This poor boy was nursed by a servant. Oh, she has some good qualities, and is certainly devoted to us--to this day her face brightens at sight of me--but she is essentially vulgar; and do you remember, Charles, I wished to wean him early; but I was overruled, and the poor child drew his nature from that woman for nearly eighteen months; it is a thing unheard of nowadays."

"Well, but surely it is from our parents we draw our nature."

"No; I think it is from our nurses. If Compton or Alec ever turn out like Reginald, blame nobody but their nurse, and that is Me."

Sir Charles smiled faintly at this piece of feminine logic, and asked her what he should do.

She said she was quite unable to advise. Mr. Rolfe was coming to see them soon; perhaps he might be able to suggest something.

Sir Charles said he would consult him; but he was clear on one thing--the boy must be sent from Huntercombe, and so separated from all his present acquaintances.

Mr. Rolfe came, and the distressed father opened his heart to him in strict confidence respecting Reginald.

Rolfe listened and sympathized, and knit his brow, and asked time to consider what he had heard, and also to study the boy for himself.

He angled for him next day accordingly. A little table was taken out on the lawn, and presently Mr. Rolfe issued forth in a uniform suit of dark blue flannel and a sombrero hat, and set to work writing a novel in the sun.

Reginald in due course descried this figure, and it smacked so of that Bohemia to which his own soul belonged that he was attracted thereby, but made his approaches stealthily, like a little cat.

Presently a fiddle went off behind a tree, so close that the novelist leaped out of his seat with an eldrich screech; for he had long ago forgotten all about Mr. Reginald, and, when he got heated in this kind of composition, any sudden sound seemed to his tense nerves and boiling brain about ten times as loud as it really was.

Having relieved himself with a yell, he sat down with the mien of a martyr expecting tortures; but he was most agreeably disappointed; the little monster played an English melody, and played it in tune. This done, he whistled a quick tune, and played a slow second to it in perfect harmony; this done, he whistled the second part and played the quick treble--a very simple feat, but still ingenious for a boy, and new to his hearer.

"Bravo! bravo!" cried Rolfe, with all his heart,

Mr. Reginald emerged, radiant with vanity. "You are like me, Mr. Writer," said he; "you don't like to be cooped up in-doors."

"I wish I could play the fiddle like you, my fine fellow."

"Ah, you can't do that all in a minute; see the time I have been at it."

"Ah, to be sure, I forgot your antiquity."

"And it isn't the time only; it's giving your mind to it, old chap."

"What, you don't give your mind to your books, then, as you do to your fiddle, *young gentleman?*"

"Not such a flat. Why, lookee here, governor, if you go and give your mind to a thing you don't like, it's always time wasted, because some other chap, that does like it, will beat you, and what's the use working for to be beat?"

"'For' is redundant," objected Rolfe.

"But if you stick hard to the things you like, you do 'em downright well. But old people are such fools, they always drive you the wrong way. They make the gals play music six hours a day, and you might as well set the hen bullfinches to pipe. Look at the gals as come here, how they rattle up and down the piano, and can't make it sing a morsel. Why, they ***couldn't*** rattle like that, if they'd music in their skins, d--n 'em; and they drive me to those stupid books, because I'm all for music and moonshine. Can you keep a secret?"

"As the tomb."

"Well, then, I can do plenty of things well, besides fiddling; I can set a wire with any poacher in the parish. I have caught plenty of our old man's hares in my time; and it takes a workman to set a wire as it should be. Show me a wire, and I'll tell you whether it was Hudson, or Whitbeck, or Squinting Jack, or who it was that set it. I know all their work that walks by moonlight hereabouts."

"This is criticism; a science; I prefer art; play me another tune, my bold Bohemian."

"Ah, I thought I should catch ye with my fiddle. You're not such a muff as the others, old 'un, not by a long chalk. Hang me if I won't give ye 'Ireland's music,' and I've sworn never to waste that on a fool."

He played the old Irish air so simply and tunably that Rolfe leaned back in his chair, with half closed eyes, in soft voluptuous ecstasy.

The youngster watched him with his coal-black eye.

"I like you," said he, "better than I thought I should, a precious sight."

"Highly flattered."

"Come with me, and hear my nurse sing it."

"What, and leave my novel?"

"Oh, bother your novel."

"And so I will. That will be tit for tat; it has bothered me. Lead on, Bohemian bold."

The boy took him, over hedge and ditch, the short-cut to Meyrick's farm; and caught Mrs. Meyrick, and said she must sing "Ireland's music" to Rolfe the writer.

Mrs. Meyrick apologized for her dress, and affected shyness about singing: Mr. Reginald stared at first, then let her know that, if she was going to be affected like the girls that came to the Hall, he should hate her, as he did them, and this he confirmed with a naughty word.

Thus threatened, she came to book, and sang Ireland's melody in a low, rich, sonorous voice; Reginald played a second; the harmony was so perfect and strong that certain glass candelabra on the mantel-piece rang loudly, and the drops vibrated. Then he made her sing the second, and he took the treble with his violin; and he wound up by throwing in a third part himself, a sort of countertenor, his own voice being much higher than the woman's.

The tears stood in Rolfe's eyes. "Well," said he, "you have got the soul of music, you two. I could listen to you 'From morn till noon, from noon till dewy eve.'"

As they returned to Huntercombe, this mercurial youth went off at a tangent, and Rolfe saw him no more.

He wrote in peace, and walked about between the heats.

Just before dinner-time the screams of women were heard hard by, and the writer hurried to the place in time to see Mr. Basset hanging by the shoulder from the branch of a tree, about twenty feet from the ground.

Rolfe hallooed, as he ran, to the women, to fetch blankets to catch him, and got under the tree, determined to try and catch him in his arms, if necessary; but he encouraged the boy to hold on.

"All right, governor," said the boy, in a quavering voice.

It was very near the kitchen; maids and men poured out with blankets; eight people held one, under Rolfe's direction, and down came Mr. Bassett in a semi-circle, and bounded up again off the blanket, like an India-rubber ball.

His quick mind recovered courage the moment he touched wool.

"Crikey! that's jolly," said he; "give me another toss or two."

"Oh no! no!" said a good-natured maid. "Take an' put him to bed right off, poor dear."

"Hold your tongue, ye bitch," said young hopeful; "if ye don't toss me, I'll turn ye all off, as soon as ever the old un kicks the bucket."

Thus menaced, they thought it prudent to toss him; but, at the third toss, he yelled out, "Oh! oh! oh! I'm all wet; it's blood! I'm dead!"

Then they examined, and found his arm was severely lacerated by an old nail that had been driven into the tree, and it had torn the flesh in his fall: he was covered with blood, the sight of which quenched his manly spirit, and he began to howl.

"Old linen rag, warm water, and a bottle of champagne," shouted Rolfe: the servants flew.

Rolfe dressed and bandaged the wound for him, and then he felt faint: the champagne soon set that right; and then he wanted to get drunk, alleging, as a reason, that he had not been drunk for this two months.

Sir Charles was told of the accident, and was distressed by it, and also by the cause.

"Rolfe," said he, sorrowfully, "there is a ring-dove's nest on that tree: she and hers have built there in peace and safety for a hundred years, and cooed about the place. My unhappy boy was climbing the tree to take the young, after solemnly promising me he never would: that is the bitter truth. What shall I do with the young barbarian?"

He sighed, and Lady Bassett echoed the sigh.

Said Rolfe, "The young barbarian, as you call him, has disarmed me: he plays the fiddle like a civilized angel."

"Oh, Mr. Rolfe!"

"What, you his mother, and not found that out yet? Oh yes, he has a heaven-born genius for music."

Rolfe then related the musical feats of the urchin.

Sir Charles begged to observe that this talent would go a very little way toward fitting him to succeed his father and keep up the credit of an ancient family.

"Dear Charles, Mr. Rolfe knows that; but it is like him to make the best of things, to encourage us. But what do you think of him, on the whole, Mr. Rolfe? has Sir Charles more to hope or to fear?"

"Give me another day or two to study him," said Rolfe.

That night there was a loud alarm. Mr. Bassett was running about the veranda in his night-dress.

They caught him and got him to bed, and Rolfe said it was fever; and, with the assistance of Sir Charles and a footman, laid him between two towels steeped in tepid water, then drew blankets tight over him, and, in short, packed him.

"Ah!" said he, complacently; "I say, give me a drink of moonshine, old chap."

"I'll give you a bucketful," said Rolfe; then, with the servant's help, took his little bed and put it close to the window; the moonlight streamed in on the boy's face, his great black eyes glittered in it. He was diabolically beautiful. "Kiss me, moonshine," said he; "I like to wash in you."

Next day he was, apparently, quite well, and certainly ripe for fresh mischief.

Rolfe studied him, and, the evening before he went, gave Sir Charles and Lady Bassett his opinion, but not with his usual alacrity; a weight seemed to hang on him, and, more than once, his voice trembled.

"I shall tell you," said he, "what I see--what I foresee--and then, with great diffidence, what I advise.

"I see--what naturalists call a reversion in race, a boy who resembles in color and features neither of his parents, and, indeed, bears little resemblance to any of the races that have inhabited England since history was written. He suggests rather some Oriental type."

Sir Charles turned round in his chair, with a sigh, and said, "We are to have a romance, it seems."

Lady Bassett stared with all her eyes, and began to change color.

The theorist continued, with perfect composure, "I don't undertake to account for it with any precision. How can I? Perhaps there is Moorish blood in your family, and here it has revived; you look incredulous, but there are plenty of examples, ay, and stronger than this: every child that is born resembles some progenitor; how then do you account for Julia Pastrana, a young lady who dined with me last week, and sang me 'Ah perdona,' rather feebly, in the evening? Bust and figure like any other lady, hand exquisite, arms neatly turned, but with long, silky hair from the elbow to the wrist. Face, ugh! forehead made of black leather, eyes all pupil, nose an excrescence, chin pure monkey, face all covered with hair; briefly, a type extinct ten thousand years before Adam, yet it could revive at this time of day. Compared with La Pastrana, and many much weaker examples of antiquity revived, that I have seen, your Mauritanian son is no great marvel, after all."

"This is a *little* too far-fetched," said Sir Charles, satirically; "Bella's father was a very dark man, and it is a tradition in our family that all the Bassetts were as black as ink till they married with you Rolfes, in the year 1684."

"Oho!" said Rolfe, "is it so? See how discussion brings out things."

"And then," said Lady Bassett, "Charles dear, tell Mr. Rolfe what I think."

"Ay, do," said Rolfe; "that will be a new form of circumlocution."

Sir Charles complied, with a smile. "Lady Bassett's theory is, that children derive their nature quite as much from their wet-nurses as from their parents, and she thinks the faults we deplore in Reginald are to be traced to his nurse; by-the-by, she is a dark woman too."

"Well," said Rolfe, "there's a good deal of truth in that, as far as regards the disposition. But I never heard color so accounted for; yet why not? It has been proved that the very bones of young animals can be colored pink, by feeding them on milk so colored."

"There!" said Lady Bassett.

"But no nurse could give your son a color which is not her own. I have seen the woman; she is only a dark Englishwoman. Her arms were embrowned by exposure, but her forehead was not brown. Mr. Reginald is quite another thing. The skin of his body, the white of his eye, the pupil, all look like a reversion to some Oriental type; and, mark the coincidence, he has mental peculiarities that point toward the East."

Sir Charles lost patience. "On the contrary," said he, "he talks and feels just like an English snob, and makes me miserable."

"Oh, as to that, he has picked up vulgar phrases at that farm, and in your stables; but he never picked up his musical genius in stables and farms, far less his poetry."

"What poetry?"

"What poetry? Why, did not you hear him? Was it not poetical of a wounded, fevered boy to beg to be laid by the window, and to say 'Let me drink the moonshine?' Take down your Homer, and read a thousand lines haphazard, and see whether you stumble over a thought more poetical than that. But criticism does not exist: whatever the dead said was good; whatever the living say is little; as if the dead were a race apart, and had never been the living, and the living would never be the dead."

Heaven knows where he was running to now, but Sir Charles stopped him by conceding that point. "Well you are right: poor child, it was poetical," and the father's pride predominated, for a moment, over every other sentiment.

"Yes; but where did it come from? That looks to me a typical idea; I mean an idea derived, not from his luxurious parents, dwellers in curtained mansions, but from some out-door and remote ancestor; perhaps from the Oriental tribe that first colonized Britain; they worshiped the sun and the moon, no doubt; or perhaps, after all, it only came from some wandering tribe that passed their lives between the two lights of heaven, and never set foot in a human dwelling."

"This," said Sir Charles, "is a flattering speculation, but so wild and romantic that I fear it will lead us to no practical result. I thought you undertook to advise me. What advice can you build on these cobwebs of your busy brain?"

"Excuse me, my practical friend," said Rolfe. "I opened my discourse in three heads. What I see--what I foresee--and what, with diffidence, I advise. Pray don't disturb my methods, or I am done for; never disturb an artist's form. I have told you what I see. What I foresee is this: you will have to cut off the entail with Reginald's consent, when he is of age, and make the Saxon boy Compton your successor. Cutting off entails runs in families, like everything else; your grandfather did it, and so will you. You should put by a few thousands every year, that you may be able to do this without injustice either to your Oriental or your Saxon son."

"Never!" shouted Sir Charles: then, in a broken voice, "He is my first-born, and my idol; his coming into the world rescued me out of a morbid condition: he healed my one great grief. Bar the entail, and put his younger brother in his place--never!"

Mr. Rolfe bowed his head politely, and left the subject, which, indeed, could be carried no farther without serious offense.

"And now for my advice. The question is, how to educate this strange boy. One thing is clear; it is no use trying the humdrum plan any longer; it has been tried, and failed. I should adapt his education to his nature. Education is made as stiff and unyielding as a board; but it need not be. I should abolish that spectacled tutor of yours at once, and get a tutor, young, enterprising, manly, and supple, who would obey orders; and the order should be to observe the boy's nature, and teach accordingly. Why need men teach in a chair, and boys learn in a chair? The Athenians studied not in chairs. The Peripatetics, as their name imports, hunted knowledge afoot; those who sought truth in the groves of Academus were not seated at that work. Then let the tutor walk with him, and talk with him by sunlight and moonlight, relating old history, and commenting on each new thing that is done, or word spoken, and improve every occasion. Why, I myself would give a guinea a day to walk with William White about the kindly aspects and wooded slopes of Selborne, or with Karr about his garden. Cut Latin and Greek clean out of the scheme. They are mere cancers to those who can never excel in them. Teach him not dead languages, but living facts. Have him in your justice-room for half an hour a day, and give him your own comments on what he has heard there. Let his tutor take him to all Quarter Sessions and Assizes, and stick to him like diaculum, especially out-of-doors; order him never to be admitted to the stable-yard; dismiss every biped there that lets him come. Don't let him visit his nurse so often, and never without his tutor; it was she who taught him to look forward to your decease; that is just like these common women. Such a tutor as I have described will deserve 500 pounds a year. Give it him; and dismiss him if he plays humdrum and doesn't earn it. Dismiss half a dozen, if necessary, till you get a fellow with a grain or two of genius for tuition. When the boy is seventeen, what with his Oriental precocity, and this system of education, he will know the world as well as a Saxon boy of twenty-one, and that is not saying much. Then, if his nature is still as wild, get him a large tract in Australia; cattle to breed, kangaroos to shoot, swift horses to thread the bush and gallop mighty tracts; he will not shirk business, if it avoids the repulsive form of sitting down in-doors, and offers itself in combination with riding, hunting, galloping, cracking of rifles, and of colonial whips as loud as rifles, and drinking sunshine and moonshine in that mellow clime, beneath the Southern Cross and the spangled firmament of stars unknown to us."

His own eyes sparkled like hot coals at this Bohemian picture.

Then he sighed and returned to civilization. "But," said he, "be ready with eighty thousand pounds for him, that he may enjoy his own way and join you in barring the entail. I forgot, I must say no more on that subject; I see it is as offensive--as it is inevitable. Cassandra has spoken wisely, and, I see, in vain. God bless you both--good-night."

And he rolled out of the room with a certain clumsy importance.

Sir Charles treated all this advice with a polite forbearance while he was in the room, but on his departure delivered a sage reflection.

"Strange," said he, "that a man so valuable in any great emergency should be so extravagant and eccentric in the ordinary affairs of life. I might as well drive to Bellevue House and consult the first gentleman I met there."

Lady Bassett did not reply immediately, and Sir Charles observed that her face was very red and her hands trembled.

"Why, Bella," said he, "has all that rhodomontade upset you?"

Lady Bassett looked frightened at his noticing her agitation, and said that Mr.

Rolfe always overpowered her. "He is so large, and so confident, and throws such new light on things."

"New light! Wild eccentricity always does that; but it is the light of Jack-o'-lantern. On a great question, so near my heart as this, give me the steady light of common sense, not the wayward coruscations of a fiery imagination. Bella dear, I shall send the boy to a good school, and so cut off at one blow all the low associations that have caused the mischief."

"You know what is best, dear," said Lady Bassett; "you are wiser than any of us."

In the morning she got hold of Mr. Rolfe, and asked him if he could put her in the way of getting more than three per cent for her money *without risk.*

"Only one," said. Rolfe. "London freeholds in rising situations let to substantial tenants. I can get you five per cent that way, if you are always ready to buy. The thing does not offer every day."

"I have twenty thousand pounds to dispose of so," said Lady Bassett.

"Very well," said Rolfe. "I'll look out for you, but Oldfield must examine titles and do the actual business. The best of that investment is, it is always improving; no ups and downs. Come," thought he, "Cassandra has not spoken quite in vain."

Sir Charles acted on his judgment, and in due course sent Mr. Bassett to a school at some distance, kept by a clergyman, who had the credit in that county of exercising sharp supervision and strict discipline.

Sir Charles made no secret of the boy's eccentricities. Mr. Beecher said he had one or two steady boys who assisted him in such cases.

Sir Charles thought that a very good idea; it was like putting a wild colt into the break with a steady horse.

He missed the boy sadly at first, but comforted himself with the conviction that he had parted with him for his good: that consoled him somewhat.

The younger children of Sir Charles and Lady Bassett were educated entirely by their mother, and taught as none but a loving lady can teach.

Compton, with whom we have to do, never knew the thorns with which the path of letters is apt to be strewn. A mistress of the great art of pleasing made knowledge from the first a primrose path to him. Sparkling all over with intelligence, she impregnated her boy with it. She made herself his favorite companion; she would not keep her distance. She stole and coaxed knowledge and goodness into his heart and mind with rare and loving cunning.

She taught him English and French and Latin on the Hamiltonian plan, and stored his young mind with history and biography, and read to him, and conversed with him on everything as they read it.

She taught him to speak the truth, and to be honorable and just.

She taught him to be polite, and even formal, rather than free-and-easy and rude. She taught him to be a man. He must not be what brave boys called a molly-coddle: like most womanly women, she had a veneration for man, and she gave him her own high idea of the manly character.

Natural ability, and habitual contact with a mind so attractive and so rich, gave this intelligent boy many good ideas beyond his age.

When he was six years old, Lady Bassett made him pass his word of honor that he would never go into the stable-yard; and even then he was far enough advanced to keep his word religiously.

In return for this she let him taste some sweets of liberty, and was not always after him. She was profound enough to see that without liberty a noble character cannot be formed; and she husbanded the curb.

One day he represented to her that, in the meadow next their lawn, were great stripes of yellow, which were possibly cowslips; of course they might be only but-tercups, but he hoped better things of them; he further reported that there was an iron gate between him and this paradise: he could get over it if not objectionable; but he thought it safest to ask her what she thought of the matter; was that iron gate intended to keep little boys from the cowslips, because, if so, it was a misfortune to which he must resign himself. Still, it *was* a misfortune. All this, of course, in the simple language of boyhood.

Then Lady Bassett smiled, and said, "Suppose I were to lend you a key of that iron gate?"

"Oh, mamma!"

"I have a great mind to."

"Then you will, you will."

"Does that follow?"

"Yes: whenever you say you think you'll do something kind, or you have a great mind to do it, you know you always do it; and that is one thing I do like you for, mamma--you are better than your word."

"Better than my word? Where does the child learn these things?"

"La, mamma, papa says that often."

"Oh, that accounts for it. I like the phrase very much. I wish I could think I deserved it. At any rate, I will be as good as my word for once; you shall have a key of the gate."

The boy clapped his hands with delight. The key was sent for, and, meantime, she told him one reason why she had trusted him with it was because he had been as good as his word about the stable.

The key was brought, and she held it up half playfully, and said, "There, sir, I deliver you this upon conditions: you must only use it when the weather is quite dry, because the grass in the meadow is longer, and will be wet. Do you promise?"

"Yes, mamma."

"And you must always lock the gate when you come back, and bring the key to one place--let me see--the drawer in the hall table, the one with marble on it; for you know a place for every thing is our rule. On these conditions, I hereby deliver you this magic key, with the right of egress and ingress."

"Egress and ingress?"

"Egress and ingress."

"Is that foreign for cowslips, mamma--and oxlips?"

"Ha! ha! the child's head is full of cowslips. There is the dictionary; look out Egress, and afterward look out Ingress."

When he had added these two words to his little vocabulary, his mother asked him if he would be good enough to tell her why he did not care much about all the beautiful flowers in the garden, and was so excited about cowslips, which appeared to her a flower of no great beauty, and the smell rather sickly, begging his pardon.

This question posed him dreadfully: he looked at her in a sort of comic distress, and then sat gravely down all in a heap, about a yard off, to think.

Finally he turned to her with a wry face, and said, "Why *do* I, mamma?"

She smiled deliciously. "No, no, sir," said she. "How can I get inside your little head and tell what is there? There must be a reason, I suppose; and you know you and I are never satisfied till we get at the reason of a thing. But there is no hurry, dear. I give you a week to find it out. Now, run and open the gate--stay, are there any cows in that field?"

"Sometimes, mamma; but they have no horns, you know."

"Upon your word?"

"Upon my honor. I am not fond of them with horns, myself."

"Then run away, darling. But you must come and hunt me up, and tell me how you enjoyed yourself, because that makes me happy, you know."

This is mawkish; but it will serve to show on what terms the woman and boy were.

On second thoughts, I recall that apology, and defy creation. "THE MAWK-ISH" is a branch of literature, a great and popular one, and I have neglected it savagely.

Master Compton opened the iron gate, and the world was all before him where to choose.

He chose one of those yellow stripes that had so attracted him. Horror! it was all buttercups and deil a cowslip.

Nevertheless, pursuing his researches, he found plenty of that delightful flower scattered about the meadow in thinner patches; and he gathered a double handful and dirtied his knees.

Returning, thus laden, from his first excursion, he was accosted by a fluty voice.

"Little boy!"

He looked up, and saw a girl standing on the lower bar of a little wooden gate painted white, looking over.

"Please bring me my ball," said she, pathetically.

Compton looked about; and saw a soft ball of many colors lying near.

He put down his cowslips gravely, and, brought her the ball. He gave it her with a blush, because she was a strange girl; and she blushed a little, because he did.

He returned to his cowslips.

"Little boy!" said the voice, "please bring me my ball again."

He brought it her, with undisturbed politeness. She was giggling; he laughed too, at that.

"You did it on purpose that time," said he, solemnly.

"La! you don't think I'd be so wicked," said she.

Compton shook his head doubtfully, and, considering the interview at an end turned to go, when instantly the ball knocked his hat off, and nothing of the male-factress was visible but a black eye sparkling with fun and mischief, and a bit of forehead wedged against the angle of the wall.

This being a challenge, Compton said, "Now you come out after that, and stand a shot, like a man."

The invitation to be masculine did not tempt her a bit; the only thing she put out was her hand, and that she drew in, with a laugh, the moment he threw at it.

At this juncture a voice cried, "Ruperta! what are you doing there?"

Ruperta made a rapid signal with her hand to Compton, implying that he was to run away; and she herself walked demurely toward the person who had called her.

It was three days before Compton saw her again, and then she beckoned him royally to her.

"Little boy," said she, "talk to me."

Compton looked at her a little confounded, and did not reply.

"Stand on this gate, like me, and talk," said she.

He obeyed the first part of this mandate, and stood on the lower bar of the little gate; so their two figures made a V, when they hung back, and a tenpenny nail when they came forward and met, and this motion they continued through the dialogue; and it was a pity the little wretches could not keep still, and send for my friend the English Titian: for, when their heads were in position, it was indeed a pretty picture of childish and flower-like beauty and contrast; the boy fair, blue-eyed, and with exquisite golden hair; the girl black-eyed, black-browed, and with eyelashes of incredible length and beauty, and a cheek brownish, but tinted, and so glowing with health and vigor that, pricked with a needle, it seemed ready to squirt carnation right into your eye.

She dazzled Master Compton so that he could do nothing but look at her.

"Well?" said she, smiling.

"Well," replied he, pretending her "well" was not an interrogatory, but a con-cise statement, and that he had discharged the whole duty of man by according a prompt and cheerful consent.

"You begin," said the lady.

"No, you."

"What for?"

"Because--I think--you are the cleverest."

"Good little boy! Well, then, I will. Who are you?"

"I am Compton. Who are you, please?"

"I am Ruperta."

"I never heard that name before."

"No more did I. I think they measured me for it: you live in the great house there, don't you?"

"Yes, Ruperta."

"Well, then, I live in the little house. It is not very little either. It's Highmore. I saw you in church one day; is that lady with the hair your mamma?"

"Yes, Ruperta."

"She is beautiful."

"Isn't she?"

"But mine is so good."

"Mine is very good, too, Ruperta. Wonderfully good."

"I like you, Compton--a little."

"I like you a good deal, Ruperta."

"La, do you? I wonder at that: you are like a cherub, and I am such a black thing."

"But that is why I like you. Reginald is darker than you, and oh, so beautiful!"

"Hum!--he is a very bad boy."

"No, he is not."

"Don't tell stories, child; he is. I know all about him. A wicked, vulgar, bad boy."

"He is not," cried Compton, almost sniveling; but he altered his mind, and fired up. "You are a naughty, story-telling girl, to say that."

"Bless *me!*" said Ruperta, coloring high, and tossing her head haughtily.

"I don't like you *now,* Ruperta," said Compton, with all the decent calmness of a settled conviction.

"You don't!" screamed Ruperta. "Then go about your business directly, and don't never come here again! Scolding *me!* How dare you?--oh! oh! oh!" and the little lady went off slowly, with her finger in her eye; and Master Compton looked rather rueful, as we all do when this charming sex has recourse to what may be called "liquid reasoning." I have known the most solid reasons unable to resist it.

However, "mens conscia recti," and, above all, the cowslips, enabled Compton to resist, and he troubled his head no more about her that day.

But he looked out for her the next day, and she did not come; and that rather disappointed him.

The next day was wet, and he did not go into the meadow, being on honor not to do so.

The fourth day was lovely, and he spent a long time in the meadow, in hopes: he saw her for a moment at the gate; but she speedily retired.

He was disappointed.

However, he collected a good store of cowslips, and then came home.

As he passed the door out popped Ruperta from some secret ambush, and said, "Well?"

CHAPTER XXXVIII.

"WELL," replied Compton.

"Are you better, dear?"

"I'm very well, thank you," said the boy.

"In your mind, I mean. You were cross last time, you know."

Compton remembered his mother's lessons about manly behavior, and said, in a jaunty way, "Well, I s'pose I was a little cross."

Now the other cunning little thing had come to apologize, if there was no other way to recover her admirer. But, on this confession, she said, "Oh, if you are sorry for it, I forgive you. You may come and talk."

Then Compton came and stood on the gate, and they held a long conversation; and, having quarreled last time, parted now with rather violent expressions of attachment.

After that they made friends and laid their little hearts bare to each other; and it soon appeared that Compton had learned more, but Ruperta had thought more for herself, and was sorely puzzled about many things, and of a vastly inquisitive mind. "Why," said she, "is good thing's so hard, and had things so nice and easy? It would be much better if good things were nice and bad ones nasty. That is the way I'd have it, if I could make things."

Mr. Compton shook his head and said many things were very hard to understand, and even his mamma sometimes could not make out all the things.

"Nor mine neither; I puzzle her dreadful. I can't help that; things shouldn't come and puzzle me, and then I shouldn't puzzle her. Shall I tell you my puzzles? and perhaps you can answer them because you are a boy. I can't think why it is wicked for me to dig in my little garden on a Sunday, and it isn't wicked for Jessie to cook and Sarah to make the beds. Can't think why mamma told papa not to be cross, and, when I told her not to be cross, she put me in a dark cupboard all among the dreadful mice, till I screamed so she took me out and kissed me and gave me pie. Can't think why papa called Sally 'Something' for spilling the ink over his papers, and when I called the gardener the very same for robbing my flowers, all their hands and eyes went up, and they said I was a shocking girl. Can't think why papa giggled the next moment, if I was a shocking girl: it is all puzzle--puzzle--puzzle."

One day she said, "Can you tell me where all the bad people are buried? for that puzzles me dreadful."

Compton was posed at first, but said at last he thought they were buried in the churchyard, along with the good ones.

"Oh, indeed!" said she, with an air of pity. "Pray, have you ever been in the churchyard, and read the writings on the stones?"

"No."

"Then I have. I have read every single word; and there are none but good people buried *there,* not one." She added, rather pathetically, "You should not answer me without thinking, as if things were easy, instead of so hard. Well, one comfort, there are not many wicked people hereabouts; they live in towns; so I suppose they are buried in the garden, poor things, or put in the water with a stone."

Compton had no more plausible theory ready, and declined to commit himself to Ruperta's; so that topic fell to the ground.

One day he found her perched as usual, but with her bright little face overclouded.

By this time the intelligent boy was fond enough of her to notice her face. "What's the matter, Perta?"

"Ruperta. The matter? Puzzled again! It is very serious this time."

"Tell me, Ruperta."

"No, dear."

"Please."

The young lady fixed her eyes on him, and said, with a pretty solemnity, "Let us play at catechism."

"I don't know that game."

"The governess asks questions, and the good little boy answers. That's catechism. I'm the governess."

"Then I'm the good little boy."

"Yes, dear; and so now look me full in the face."

"There--you're very pretty, Ruperta."

"Don't be giddy; I'm hideous; so behave, and answer all my questions. Oh, I'm so unhappy. Answer me, is young people, or old people, goodest?"

"You should say best, dear. Good, better, best. Why, old people, to be sure--much."

"So I thought; and that is why I am so puzzled. Then your papa and mine are much betterer--will that do?--than we are?"

"Of course they are."

"There he goes! Such a child for answering slap bang I never."

"I'm not a child. I'm older than you are, Ruperta."

"That's a story."

"Well, then, I'm as old; for Mary says we were born the same day--the same hour--the same minute."

"La! we are twins."

She paused, however, on this discovery, and soon found reason to doubt her hasty conclusion. "No such thing," said she: "they tell me the bells were ringing for you being found, and then I was found--to catechism you."

"There! then you see I *am* older than you, Ruperta."

"Yes, dear," said Ruperta, very gravely; "I'm younger in my body, but older in my head."

This matter being settled so that neither party could complain, since antiquity was evenly distributed, the catechizing recommenced.

"Do you believe in 'Let dogs delight?'"

"I don't know."

"What!" screamed Ruperta. "Oh, you wicked boy! Why, it comes next after the Bible."

"Then I do believe it," said Compton, who, to tell the truth, had been merely puzzled by the verb, and was not afflicted with any doubt that the composition referred to was a divine oracle.

"Good boy!" said Ruperta, patronizingly. "Well, then, this is what puzzles me; your papa and mine don't believe in 'Dogs delight.' They have been quarreling this twelve years and more, and mean to go on, in spite of mamma. She *is* good. Didn't you know that your papa and mine are great enemies?"

"No, Ruperta. Oh, what a pity!"

"Don't, Compton, don't: there, you have made me cry."

He set himself to console her.

She consented to be consoled.

But she said, with a sigh, "What becomes of old people being better than young ones, now? Are you and I bears and lions? Do we scratch out each other's eyes? It is all puzzle, puzzle, puzzle. I wish I was dead! Nurse says, when I'm dead I shall understand it all. But I don't know; I saw a dead cat once, and she didn't seem to know as much as before; puzzle, puzzle. Compton, do you think they are puzzled in heaven?"

"No."

"Then the sooner we both go there, the better."

"Yes, but not just now."

"Why not?"

"Because of the cowslips."

"Here's a boy! What, would you rather be among the cowslips than the angels? and think of the diamonds and pearls that heaven is paved with."

"But *you* mightn't be there."

"What! Am I a wicked girl, then--wickeder than you, that is a boy?"

"Oh no, no, no; but see how big it is up there;" they cast their eyes up, and, taking the blue vault for creation, were impressed with its immensity. "I know where to find you here, but up there you might be ever so far off me."

"La! so I might. Well, then, we had better keep quiet. I suppose we shall get wiser as we get older. But Compton, I'm so sorry your papa and mine are bears and lions. Why doesn't the clergyman scold them?"

"Nobody dare scold my papa," said Compton, proudly. Then, after reflection, "Perhaps, when we are older, we may persuade them to make friends. I think it is very stupid to quarrel; don't you?"

"As stupid as an owl."

"You and I had a quarrel once, Ruperta."

"Yes, you misbehaved."

"No, no; you were cross."

"Story! Well, never mind: we *did* quarrel. And you were miserable directly."

"Not so very," said Compton, tossing his head.

"I *was,* then," said Ruperta, with unguarded candor.

"So was I."

"Good boy! Kiss me, dear."

"There--and there--and there--and--"

"That will do. I want to talk, Compton."

"Yes, dear."

"I'm not very sure, but I rather think I'm in love with you--a little, little bit, you know."

"And I'm sure I'm in love with you, Ruperta."

"Over head an' ears?"

"Yes."

"Then I love you to distraction. Bother the gate! If it wasn't for that, I could run in the meadow with you; and marry you perhaps, and so gather cowslips together for ever and ever."

"Let us open it."

"You can't."

"Let us try."

"I have. It won't be opened."

"Let *me* try. Some gates want to be lifted up a little, and then they will open. There, I told you so."

The gate came open.

Ruperta uttered an exclamation of delight, and then drew back.

"I'm afraid, Compton," said she, "papa would be angry."

She wanted Compton to tempt her; but that young gentleman, having a strong sense of filial duty, omitted so to do.

When she saw he would not persuade her, she dispensed. "Come along," said she, "if it is only for five minutes."

She took his hand, and away they scampered. He showed her the cowslips, the violets, and all the treasures of the meadow; but it was all hurry, and skurry, and excitement; no time to look at anything above half a minute, for fear of being found out: and so, at last, back to the gate, beaming with stolen pleasure, glowing and sparkling with heat and excitement.

The cunning thing made him replace the gate, and then, after saying she must go for about an hour, marched demurely back to the house.

After one or two of these hasty trips, impunity gave her a sense of security, and, the weather getting warm, she used to sit in the meadow with her beau and weave wreaths of cowslips, and place them in her black hair, and for Comp-ton she made coronets of bluebells, and adorned his golden head.

And sometimes, for a little while, she would nestle to him, and lean her head, with all the feminine grace of a mature woman, on his shoulder.

Said she, "A boy's shoulder does very nice for a girl to put her nose on."

One day the aspiring girl asked him what was that forest.

"That is Bassett's wood."

"I will go there with you some day, when papa is out."

"I'm afraid that is too far for you," said Compton.

"Nothing is too far for me," replied the ardent girl. "Why, how far is it?"

"More than half a mile."

"Is it very big?"

"Immense."

"Belong to the queen?"

"No, to papa."

"Oh!"

And here my reader may well ask what was Lady Bassett about, or did Comp-ton, with all his excellent teaching, conceal all this from his mother and his friend.

On the contrary, he went open-mouthed to her and told her he had seen such a pretty little girl, and gave her a brief account of their conversation.

Lady Bassett was startled at first, and greatly perplexed. She told him he must on no account go to her; if he spoke to her, it must be on papa's ground. She even made him pledge his honor to that.

More than that she did not like to say. She thought it unnecessary and undesirable to transmit to another generation the unhappy feud by which she had suffered so much, and was even then suffering. Moreover, she was as much afraid of Richard Bassett as ever. If he chose to tell his girl not to speak to Compton, he might. She was resolved not to go out of her way to affront him, through his daughter. Besides, that might wound Mrs. Bassett, if it got round to her ears; and, although she had never spoken to Mrs. Bassett, yet their eyes had met in church, and always with a pacific expression. Indeed, Lady Bassett felt sure she had read in that meek woman's face a regret that they were not friends, and could not be friends, because of their husbands. Lady Bassett, then, for these reasons, would not forbid Compton to be kind to Ruperta in moderation.

Whether she would have remained as neutral had she known how far these young things were going, is quite another matter; but Compton's narratives to her were, naturally enough, very tame compared with the reality, and she never dreamed that two seven-year-olds could form an attachment so warm, as these little plagues were doing.

And, to conclude, about the time when Mr. Compton first opened the gate for his inamorata, Lady Bassett's mind was diverted, in some degree, even from her beloved boy Compton, by a new trouble, and a host of passions it excited in her own heart.

A thunder-clap fell on Sir Charles Bassett, in the form of a letter from Reginald's tutor, informing him that Reginald and another lad had been caught wiring hares in a wood at some distance and were now in custody.

Sir Charles mounted his horse and rode to the place, leaving Lady Bassett a prey to great anxiety and bitter remorse.

Sir Charles came back in two days, with the galling news that his son and heir was in prison for a month, all his exertions having only prevailed to get the case summarily dealt with.

Reginald's companion, a young gypsy, aged seventeen, had got three months, it being assumed that he was the tempter: the reverse was the case, though.

When Sir Charles told Lady Bassett all this, with a face of agony, and a broken voice, her heart almost burst: she threw every other consideration to the winds.

"Charles," she cried, "I can't bear it: I can't see your heart wrung any more, and your affections blighted. Tear that young viper out of your breast: don't go on wasting your heart's blood on a stranger; HE IS NOT YOUR SON."

CHAPTER XXXIX.

AT this monstrous declaration, from the very lips of the man's wife, there was a dead silence, Sir Charles being struck dumb, and Lady Bassett herself terrified at the sound of the words she had uttered.

After a terrible pause, Sir Charles fixed his eyes on her, with an awful look, and said, very slowly, "Will--you--have--the--goodness-- to--say that again? but first think what you are saying."

This made Lady Bassett shake in every limb; indeed the very flesh of her body quivered. Yet she persisted, but in a tone that of itself showed how fast her courage was oozing. She faltered out, almost inaudibly, "I say you must waste no more love on him--he is not your son."

Sir Charles looked at her to see if she was in her senses: it was not the first time he had suspected her of being deranged on this one subject. But no: she was pale as death, she was cringing, wincing, quivering, and her eyes roving to and fro; a picture not of frenzy, but of guilt unhardened.

He began to tremble in his turn, and was so horror-stricken and agitated that he could hardly speak. "Am I dreaming?" he gasped.

Lady Bassett saw the storm she had raised, and would have given the world to recall her words.

"Whose is he, then?" asked Sir Charles, in a voice scarcely human.

"I don't know," said Lady Bassett doggedly.

"Then how dare you say that he isn't mine?"

"Kill me, Charles," cried she, passionately; "but don't look at me so and speak to me so. Why I say he is not yours, is he like you either in face or mind?"

"And he is like--whom?"

Lady Bassett had lost all her courage by this time: she whimpered out, "Like nobody except the gypsies."

"Bella, this is a subject which will part you and me for life unless we can agree upon it--"

No reply, in words, from Lady Bassett.

"So please let us understand each other. Your son is not my son. Is that what you look me in the face and tell me?"

"Charles, I never said *that.* How could he be my son, and not be yours?"

And she raised her eyes, and looked him full in the face: nor fear nor cringing now: the woman was majestic.

Sir Charles was a little alarmed in his turn; for his wife's soft eyes flamed battle for the first time in her life.

"Now you talk sense," said he; "if he is yours, he is mine; and, as he is certainly yours, this is a very foolish conversation, which must not be renewed, otherwise--"

"I shall be insulted by my own husband?"

"I think it very probable. And, as I do not choose you to be insulted, nor to think yourself insulted, I forbid you ever to recur to this subject."

"I will obey, Charles; but let me say one word first. When I was alone in London, and hardly sensible, might not this child have been imposed upon me and you? I'm sure he was."

"By whom?"

"How can I tell? I was alone--that woman in the house had a bad face--the gypsies do these things, I've heard."

"The gypsies! And why not the fairies?" said Sir Charles, contemptuously. "Is that all you have to suggest--before we close the subject forever?"

"Yes," said Lady Bassett sorrowfully. "I see you take me for a mad-woman; but time will show. Oh that I could persuade you to detach your affections from that boy--he will break your heart else--and rest them on the children that resemble us in mind and features."

"These partialities are allowed to mothers; but a father must be just. Reginald is my first-born; he came to me from Heaven at a time when I was under a bitter trial, and from the day he was born till this day I have been a happy man. It is not often a father owes so much to a son as I do to my darling boy. He is dear to my heart in spite of his faults; and now I pity him, as well as love him, since it seems he has only one parent, poor little fellow!"

Lady Bassett opened her mouth to reply, but could not. She raised her hands in mute despair, then quietly covered her face with them, and soon the tears trickled through her white fingers.

Sir Charles looked at her, and was touched at her silent grief.

"My darling wife," said he, "I think this is the only thing you and I cannot agree upon. Why not be wise as well as loving, and avoid it."

"I will never seek it again," sobbed Lady Bassett. "But oh," she cried, with sudden wildness, "something tells me it will meet me, and follow me, and rob me of my husband. Well, when that day comes, I shall know how to die."

And with this she burst away from him, like some creature who has been stung past endurance.

Sir Charles often meditated on this strange scene: turn it how he could he came back to the same conclusion, that she must have an hallucination on this subject. He said to himself, "If Bella really believed the boy was a changeling, she would act upon her conviction, she would urge me to take some steps to recover our true child, whom the gypsies or the fairies have taken, and given us poor dear Reginald instead."

But still the conversation, and her strange looks of terror, lay dormant in his mind: both were too remarkable to be ever forgotten. Such things lie like certain seeds, awaiting only fresh accidents to spring into life.

The month rolled away, and the day came for Reginald's liberation. A dogcart was sent for him, and the heir of the Bassetts emerged from a county jail, and uttered a whoop of delight; he insisted on driving, and went home at a rattling pace.

He was in high spirits till he got in sight of Huntercombe Hall; and then it suddenly occurred to his mercurial mind that he should probably not be received with an ovation, petty larceny being a novelty in that ancient house whose representative he was.

When he did get there he found the whole family in such a state of commotion that his return was hardly noticed at all.

Master Compton's dinner hour was two P.M., and yet, at three o'clock of this day, he did not come in.

This was reported to Lady Bassett, and it gave her some little anxiety; for she suspected he might possibly be in the company of Ruperta Bassett; and, although she did not herself much object to that, she objected very much to have it talked about and made a fuss. So she went herself to the end of the lawn, and out into the meadow, that a servant might not find the young people together, if her suspicion was correct.

She went into the meadow and called "Compton! Compton!" as loud as she could, but there was no reply.

Then she came in, and began to be alarmed, and sent servants about in all directions.

But two hours elapsed, and there were no tidings. The thing looked serious.

She sent out grooms well mounted to scour the country. One of these fell in with Sir Charles, who thereupon came home and found his wife in a pitiable state. She was sitting in an armchair, trembling and crying hysterically.

She caught his hand directly, and grasped it like a vise.

"It is Richard Bassett!" she cried. "He knows how to wound and kill me. He has stolen our child."

Sir Charles hurried out, and, soon after that, Reginald arrived, and stood awestruck at her deplorable condition.

Sir Charles came back heated and anxious, kissed Reginald, told him in three words his brother was missing, and then informed Lady Bassett that he had learned something very extraordinary; Richard Bassett's little girl had also disappeared, and his people were out looking after her.

"Ah, they are together," cried Lady Bassett.

"Together? a son of mine consorting with that viper's brood!"

"What does that poor child know? Oh, find him for me, if you love that dear child's mother!'"

Sir Charles hurried out directly, but was met at the door by a servant, who blurted out, "The men have dragged the fish-ponds, Sir Charles, and they want to know if they shall drag the brook."

"Hold your tongue, idiot!" cried Sir Charles, and thrust him out; but the wiseacre had not spoken in vain. Lady Bassett moaned, and went into worse hysterics, with nobody near her but Reginald.

That worthy, never having seen a lady in hysterics, and not being hardened at all points, uttered a sympathetic howl, and flung his arms round her neck. "Oh! oh! oh! Don't cry, mamma."

Lady Bassett shuddered at his touch, but did not repel him.

"I'll find him for you," said the boy, "if you will leave off crying."

She stared in his face a moment, and then went on as before.

"Mamma," said he, getting impatient, "do listen to me. I'll find him easy enough, if you will only listen."

"You! you!" and she stared wildly at him.

"Ay, I know a sight more than the fools about here. I'm a poacher. Just you put me on to his track. I'll soon run into him, if he is above ground."

"A child like you!" cried Lady Bassett; "how can you do that?" and she began to wring her hands again.

"I'll show you," said the boy, getting very impatient, "if you will just leave off crying like a great baby, and come to any place you like where he has been to-day and left a mark--"

"Ah!" cried Lady Bassett.

"I'm a poacher," repeated Reginald, quite proudly; "you forget that."

"Come with me," cried Lady Bassett, starting up. She whipped on her bonnet, and ran with him down the lawn.

"There, Reginald," said she, panting, "I think my darling was here this afternoon; yes, yes, he must; for he had a key of the door, and it is open."

"All right," said Reginald; "come into the field."

He ran about like a dog hunting, and soon found marks among the cowslips.

"Somebody has been gathering a nosegay here to-day," said he; "now, mamma, there's only two ways put of this field--let us go straight to that gate; that is the likeliest."

Near the gate was some clay, and Reginald showed her several prints of small feet.

"Look," said he, "here's the track of two--one's a gal; how I know, here's a sole to this shoe no wider nor a knife. Come on."

In the next field he was baffled for a long time; but at last he found a place in a dead hedge where they had gone through.

"See," said he, "these twigs are fresh broken, and here's a bit of the gal's frock. Oh! won't she catch it?":

"Oh, you brave, clever boy!" cried Lady Bassett.

"Come on!" shouted the urchin.

He hunted like a beagle, and saw like a bird, with his savage, glittering eye. He was on fire with the ardor of the chase; and, not to dwell too long on what has been so often and so well written by others, in about an hour and a half he brought the anxious, palpitating, but now hopeful mother, to the neighborhood of Bassett's wood. Here he trusted to his own instinct. "They have gone into the wood," said he, "and I don't blame 'em. I found my way here long before his age. I say, don't you tell; I've snared plenty of the governor's hares in that wood."

He got to the edge of the wood and ran down the side. At last he found the marks of small feet on a low bank, and, darting over it, discovered the fainter traces on some decaying leaves inside the wood.

"There," said he; "now it is just as if you had got them in your pocket, for they'll never find their way out of this wood. Bless your heart, why *I* used to get lost in it at first."

"Lost in the wood!" cried Lady Bassett; "but he will die of fear, or be eaten by wild beasts; and it is getting so dark."

"What about that? Night or day is all one to me. What will you give me if I find him before midnight?"

"Anything I've got in the world."

"Give me a sovereign?"

"A thousand!"

"Give me a kiss?"

"A hundred!"

"Then I'll tell you what I'll do--I don't mind a little trouble, to stop your crying, mamma, because you are the right sort. I'll get the village out, and we will tread the wood with torches, an' all for them as can't see by night; I can see all one; and you shall have your kid home to supper. You see, there's a heavy dew, and he is not like me, that would rather sleep in this wood than the best bed in London city; a night in a wood would about settle his hash. So here goes. I can run a mile in six minutes and a half."

With these words, the strange boy was off like an arrow from a bow.

Lady Bassett, exhausted by anxiety and excitement, was glad to sit down; her trembling heart would not let her leave the place that she now began to hope contained her child. She sat down and waited patiently.

The sun set, the moon rose, the stars glittered; the infinite leaves stood out dark and solid, as if cut out of black marble; all was dismal silence and dread suspense to the solitary watcher.

Yet the lady of Huntercombe Hall sat on, sick at heart, but patient, beneath that solemn sky.

She shuddered a little as the cold dews gathered on her, for she was a woman nursed in luxury's lap; but she never moved.

The silence was dismal. Had that wild boy forgotten his promise, or were there no parents in the village, that their feet lagged so?

It was nearly ten o'clock, when her keen ears, strained to the utmost, discovered a faint buzzing of voices; but where she could not tell.

The sounds increased and increased, and then there was a temporary silence; and after that a faint hallooing in the wood to her right. The wood was five hundred acres, and the bulk of it lay in front and to her left.

The hallooing got louder and louder; the whole wood seemed to echo; her heart beat high; lights glimmered nearer and nearer, hares and rabbits pattered by and startled her, and pheasants thundered off their roosts with an incredible noise, owls flitted, and bats innumerable, disturbed and terrified by the glaring lights and loud resounding halloos.

Nearer, nearer came the sounds, till at last a line of men and boys, full fifty carrying torches and lanterns, came up, and lighted up the dew-spangled leaves, and made the mother's heart leap with joyful hope at succor so powerful.

Oh, she could have kissed the stout village blacksmith, whose deep sonorous lungs rang close to her. Never had any man's voice sounded to her so like a god's as this stout blacksmith's "hilloop! hilloop!" close and loud in her ear, and those at the end of the line hallooed "hillo-op; hillo-op!" like an echo; and so they passed on, through bush and brier, till their voices died away in the distance.

A boy detached himself from the line, and ran to Lady Bassett with a traveling rug. It was Reginald.

"You put on this," said he. He shook it, and, standing on tiptoe, put it over her shoulders.

"Thank you, dear," said she. "Where is papa?"

"Oh, he is in the line, and the Highmore swell and all."

"Mr. Richard Bassett?"

"Air, his kid is out on the loose, as well as ours."

"Oh, Reginald, if they should quarrel!"

"Why, our governor can lick him, can't he?"

CHAPTER XL.

O
H, don't talk so. I wouldn't for all the world they should quarrel."

"Well, we have got enough fellows to part them if they do."

"Dear Reginald, you have been so good to me, and you are so clever; speak to some of the men, and let there be no more quarreling between papa and that man."

"All right," said the boy.

"On second thoughts take me to papa; I'll be by his side, and then they cannot."

"You want to walk through the wood? that is a good joke. Why, it is like walking through a river, and the young wood slapping your eyes, for you can't see every twig by this light, and the leaves sponging your face and shoulders: and the briers would soon strip your gown into ribbons, and make your little ankles bleed. No, you are a lady; you stay where you are, and let us men work it. We shan't find him yet awhile. I must get near the governor. When we find my lord, I'll give a whistle you could hear a mile off."

"Oh, Reginald, are you sure he is in the wood?"

"I'd bet my head to a chany orange. You might as well ask me, when I track a badger to his hole, and no signs of his going out again, whether old long-claws is there. I wish I was as sure of never going back to school as I am of finding that little lot. The only thing I don't like is, the young muff's not giving us a halloo back. But, any way, I'll find 'em, *alive or dead.*"

And, with this pleasing assurance, the little imp scudded off, leaving the mother glued to the spot with terror.

For full an hour more the torches gleamed, though fainter and fainter; and so full was the wood of echoes, that the voices, though distant, seemed to halloo all round the agonized mother.

But presently there was a continuous yell, quite different from the isolated shouts, a distant but unmistakable howl of victory that made a bolt of ice shoot down her back, and then her heart to glow like fire.

It was followed by a keen whistle.

She fell on her knees and thanked God for her boy.

In the middle of this wood was a shallow excavation, an old chalk-pit, unused for many years. It was never deep, and had been half filled up with dead leaves; these, once blown into the hollow, or dropped from the trees, had accumulated.

The very middle of the line struck on this place, and Moss, the old keeper, who was near the center, had no sooner cast his eyes into it than he halted, and uttered a stentorian halloo well known to sportsmen--"SEE HO!"

A dead halt, a low murmur, and in a very few seconds the line was a circle, and all the torches that had not expired held high in a flaming ring over the prettiest little sight that wood had ever presented.

The old keeper had not given tongue on conjecture, like some youthful hound. In a little hollow of leaves, which the boy had scraped out, lay Master Compton and Miss Ruperta, on their little backs, each with an arm round the other's neck, enjoying the sweet sound sleep of infancy, which neither the horror of their situation--babes in the wood--nor the shouts of fifty people had in the smallest degree disturbed; to be sure, they had undergone great fatigue.

Young master wore a coronet of bluebells on his golden bead, young miss a wreath of cowslips on her ebon locks. The pair were flowers, cherubs, children--everything that stands for young, tender, and lovely.

The honest villagers gaped, and roared in chorus, and held high their torches, and gazed with reverential delight. Not for them was it to finger the little gentle-folks, but only to devour them with admiring eyes.

Indeed, the picture was carried home to many a humble hearth, and is spoken of to this day in Huntercombe village.

But the pale and anxious fathers were in no state to see pictures--they only saw their children Sir Charles and Richard Bassett came round with the general rush, saw, and dashed into the pit.

Strange to say, neither knew the other was there. Each seized his child, and tore it away from the contact of the other child, as if from a viper; in which natural but harsh act they saw each other for the first time, and their eyes gleamed in a moment with hate and defiance over their loving children.

Here was a picture of a different kind, and if the melancholy Jaques, or any other gentleman with a foible for thinking in a wood; had been there, methinks he had moralized very prettily on the hideousness of hate and the beauty of the sentiment it had interrupted so fiercely. But it escaped this sort of comment for about eight years. Well, all this woke the bairns; the lights dazzled them, the people scared them. Each hid a little face on the paternal shoulder.

The fathers, like wild beasts, each carrying off a lamb, withdrew, glaring at each other; but the very next moment the stronger and better sentiment prevailed, and they kissed and blessed their restored treasures, and forgot their enemies for a time.

Sir Charles's party followed him, and supped at Huntercombe, every man Jack of them.

Reginald, who had delivered a terrific cat-call, now ran off to Lady Bassett. There she was, still on her knees.

"Found! found!" he shouted.

She clasped him in her arms and wept for joy.

"My eyes!" said he, "what a one you are to cry! You come home; you'll catch your death o' cold."

"No, no; take me to my child at once."

"Can't be done; the governor has carried him off through the wood; and I ain't a going to let you travel the wood. You come with me; we'll go the short cut, and be home as soon as them."

She complied, though trembling all over.

On the way he told her where the children had been discovered, and in what attitude.

"Little darlings!" said she. "But he has frightened his poor mother, and nearly broken her heart. Oh!"

"If you cry any more, mamma--Shut up, I tell you!"

"Must I? Oh!"

"Yes, or you'll catch pepper."

Then he pulled her along, gabbling all the time. "Those two swells didn't quarrel after all, you see."

"Thank Heaven!"

"But they looked at each other like hobelixes, and pulled the kids away like pison. Ha! ha! I say, the young 'uns ain't of the same mind as the old 'uns. I say, though, our Compton is not a bad sort; I'm blowed if he hadn't taken off his tippet to put round his gal. I say, don't you think that little chap has begun rather early? Why, *I* didn't trouble my head about the gals till I was eleven years old."

Lady Bassett was too much agitated to discuss these delicate little questions just then.

She replied as irrelevantly as ever a lady did. "Oh, you good, brave, clever boy!" said she.

Then she stopped a moment to kiss him heartily. "I shall never forget this night, dear. I shall always make excuses for you. Oh, shall we never get home?"

"We shall be home as soon as they will," said Reginald. "Come on."

He gabbled to her the whole way; but the reader has probably had enough of his millclack.

Lady Bassett reached home, and had just ordered a large fire in Compton's bedroom, when Sir Charles came in, bringing the boy.

The lady ran out screaming, and went down on her knees, with her arms out, as only a mother can stretch them to her child.

There was not a word of scolding that night. He had made her suffer; but what of that? She had no egotism; she was a true mother. Her boy had been lost, and was found; and she was the happiest soul in creation.

But the fathers of these babes in the wood were both intensely mortified, and took measures to keep those little lovers apart in future. Richard Bassett locked up his gate: Sir Charles padlocked his; and they both told their wives they really must be more vigilant. The poor children, being in disgrace, did not venture to remonstrate! But they used often to think of each other, and took a liking to the British Sunday; for then they saw each other in church.

By-and-by even that consolation ceased. Ruperta was sent to school, and passed her holidays at the sea-side.

To return to Reginald, he was compelled to change his clothes that evening, but was allowed to sit up, and, when the heads of the house were a little calmer, became the hero of the night.

Sir Charles, gazing on him with parental pride, said, "Reginald, you have begun a new life to-day, and begun it well. Let us forget the past, and start fresh to-day, with the love and gratitude of both your parents."

The boy hung his head and said nothing in reply.

Lady Bassett came to his assistance. "He will; he will. Don't say a word about the past. He is a good, brave, beautiful boy, and I adore him."

"And I like you, mamma," said Reginald graciously.

From that day the boy had a champion in Lady Bassett; and Heaven knows, she had no sinecure; poor Reginald's virtues were too eccentric to balance his faults for long together. His parents could not have a child lost in a wood every day; but good taste and propriety can be offended every hour when one is so young, active, and savage as Master Reginald.

He was up at five, and doing wrong all day.

Hours in the stables, learning to talk horsey, and smell dunghilly.

Hours in the village, gossiping and romping.

In good company, an owl.

In bad, or low company, a cricket, a nightingale, a magpie.

He was seen at a neighboring fair, playing the fiddle in a booth to dancing yokels, and receiving their pence.

He was caught by Moss wiring hairs in Bassett's wood, within twenty yards of the place where he had found the babes in the wood so nobly.

Remonstrated with tenderly and solemnly, he informed Sir Charles that poaching was a thing he could not live without, and he modestly asked to have Bassett's wood given him to poach in, offering, as a consideration, to keep all other poachers out: as a greater inducement, he represented that he should not require a house, but only a coarse sheet to stretch across an old saw-pit, and a pair of blankets for winter use--one under, one over.

Sir Charles was often sad, sometimes indignant.

Lady Bassett excused each enormity with pathetic ingenuity; excused, but suffered, and indeed pined visibly, for all this time he was tormenting her as few women in her position have been tormented. Her life was a struggle of contesting emotions; she was wounded, harassed, perplexed, and so miserable, she would have welcomed death, that her husband might read that Manuscript and cease to suffer, and she escape the shame of confessing, and of living after it.

In one word, she was expiating.

Neither the excuses she made nor the misery she suffered escaped Sir Charles.

He said to her at last, "My own Bella, this unhappy boy is killing you. Dear as he is to me, you are dearer. I must send him away again."

"He saved our darling," said she, faintly, but she could say no more. He had exhausted excuse.

Sir Charles made inquiries everywhere, and at last his attention was drawn to the following advertisement in the *Times:*

UNMANAGEABLE, Backward, or other BOYS, carefully TRAINED, and EDU-CATED, by a married rector. Home comforts. Moderate terms. Address Dr. Beech-er, Fennymore, Cambridgeshire.

He wrote to this gentleman, and the correspondence was encouraging. "These scapegraces," said the artist in tuition, "are like crab-trees; abominable till you graft them, and then they bear the best fruit."

While the letters were passing, came a climax. Reckless Reginald could keep no bounds intact: his inward definition of a boundary was "a thing you should go a good way out of your way rather than not overleap."

Accordingly, he was often on Highmore farm at night, and even in Highmore garden; the boundary wall tempted him so.

One light but windy night, when everybody that could put his head under cover, and keep it there, did, reckless Reginald was out enjoying the fresh breezes; he mounted the boundary wall of Highmore like a cat, to see what amusement might offer. Thus perched, he speedily discovered a bright light in Highmore din-ing-room.

He dropped from the wall directly, and stole softly over the grass and peered in at the window.

He saw a table with a powerful lamp on it; on that table, and gleaming in that light, were several silver vessels of rare size and workmanship, and Mr. Bassett, with his coat off, and a green baize apron on, was cleaning one of these with brush and leather. He had already cleaned the others, for they glittered prodigiously.

Reginald's black eye gloated and glittered at this unexpected display of wealth in so dazzling a form.

But this was nothing to the revelation in store. When Mr. Bassett had done with that piece of plate he went to the paneled wall, and opened a door so nicely adapted to the panels, that a stranger would hardly have discovered it. Yet it was an enormous door, and, being opened, revealed a still larger closet, lined with green velvet and fitted with shelves from floor to ceiling.

Here shone, in all their glory, the old plate of two good families: that is to say, half the old plate of the Bassetts, and all the old plate of the Goodwyns, from whom came Highmore to Richard Bassett through his mother Ruperta Goodwyn, so named after her grandmother; so named after her aunt; so named after her godmother; so named after her father, Prince Rupert, cavalier, chemist, glass-blower, etc., etc.

The wall seemed ablaze with suns and moons, for many of the chased goblets, plates, and dishes were silver-gilt: none of your filmy electro-plate, but gold laid on thick, by the old mercurial process, in days when they that wrought in precious metals were honest--for want of knowing how to cheat.

Glued to the pane, gloating on this constellation of gold suns and silver moons, and trembling with Bohemian excitement, reckless Reginald heard not a stealthy step upon the grass behind him.

He had trusted to a fact in optics, forgetting the doctrine of shadows.

The Scotch servant saw from a pantry window the shadow of a cap projected on the grass, with a face, and part of a body. She stepped out, and got upon the grass.

Finding it was only a boy, she was brave as well as cunning; and, owing to the wind and his absorption, stole on him unheard, and pinned him with her strong hands by both his shoulders.

Young Hopeful uttered a screech of dismay, and administered a back kick that made Jessie limp for two days, and scream very lustily for the present.

Mr. Bassett, at this dialogue of yells, dropped a coffee-pot with a crash and a tinkle, and ran out directly, and secured young Hopeful, who thereupon began to quake and remonstrate.

"I was only taking a look," said he. "Where's the harm of that?"

"You were trespassing, sir," said Richard Bassett.

"What is the harm of that, governor? You can come over all our place, for what

I care."

"Thank you. I prefer to keep to my own place."

"Well, I don't. I say, old chap, don't hit me. 'Twas I put 'em all on the scent of your kid, you know."

"So I have heard. Well, then, this makes us quits."

"Don't it? You ain't such a bad sort, after all."

"Only mind, Mr. Bassett, if I catch you prying here again, that will be a fresh account, and I shall open it with a horsewhip."

He then gave him a little push, and the boy fled like the wind. When he was gone, Richard Bassett became rather uneasy. He had hitherto concealed, even from his own family, the great wealth his humble home contained. His secret was now public. Reginald had no end of low companions. If burglars got scent of this, it might be very awkward. At last he hit upon a defense. He got one of those hooks ending in a screw which are used for pictures, and screwed it into the inside of the cupboard door near the top. To this he fastened a long piece of catgut, and carried it through the floor. His bed was just above the cupboard door, and he attached the gut to a bell by his bedside. By this means nobody could open that cupboard without ringing in his ears.

Jessie told Tom, Tom told Maria and Harriet; Harriet and Maria told everybody; somebody told Sir Charles. He was deeply mortified.

"You young idiot!" said he, "would nothing less than this serve your turn? must you go and lower me and yourself by giving just offense to my one enemy?--the man I hate and despise, and who is always on the watch to injure or affront me. Oh, who would be a father! There, pack up your things; you will go to school next morning at eight o'clock."

Mr. Reginald packed accordingly, but that did not occupy long; so he sallied forth, and, taking for granted that it was Richard Bassett who had been so mean as to tell, he purchased some paint and brushes and a rope, and languished until midnight.

But when that magic hour came he was brisk as a bee, let himself down from his veranda, and stole to Richard Bassett's front door, and inscribed thereon, in large and glaring letters,

"JERRY SNEAK, ESQ., Tell-Tale Tit."

He then returned home much calmed and comforted, climbed up his rope and into his room, and there slept sweetly, as one who had discharged his duty to his neighbor and society in general.

In the morning, however, he was very active, hurried the grooms, and was off before the appointed time.

Sir Charles came down to breakfast, and lo! young Hopeful gone, without the awkward ceremony of leave-taking.

Sir Charles found, as usual, many delicacies on his table, and among them one rarer to him than ortolan, pin-tail, or wild turkey (in which last my soul delights); for he found a letter from Richard Bassett, Esq.

"SIR--Some nights since we caught your successor that is to be, at my dining-room window, prying into my private affairs. Having the honor of our family at heart, I was about to administer a little wholesome correction, when he reminded me he had been instrumental in tracking Miss Bassett, and thereby rescuing her: upon this I was, naturally, mollified, and sent him about his business, hoping to have seen the last of him at Highmore.

"This morning my door is covered with opprobrious epithets, and as Mr. Bassett bought paint and brushes at the shop yesterday afternoon, it is doubtless to him I am indebted for them.

"I make no comments; I simply record the facts, and put them down to your credit, and your son's.

"Your obedient servant,

"RICHARD BASSETT."

Lady Bassett did not come down to breakfast that morning; so Sir Charles digested this dish in solitude.

He was furious with Reginald; but as Richard Bassett's remonstrance was intended to insult him, he wrote back as follows:

"SIR--I am deeply grieved that a son of mine should descend to look in at your windows, or to write anything whatever upon your door; and I will take care it shall never recur.

"Yours obediently,

"CHARLES DYKE BASSETT."

This little correspondence was salutary; it fanned the coals of hatred between the cousins.

Reckless Reginald soon found he had caught a Tartar in his new master.

That gentleman punished him severely for every breach of discipline. The study was a cool dark room, with one window looking north, and that window barred. Here he locked up the erratic youth for hours at a time, upon the slightest escapade.

Reginald wrote a honeyed letter to Sir Charles, bewailing his lot, and praying to be removed.

Sir Charles replied sternly, and sent him a copy of Mr. Richard Bassett's letter. He wrote to Mr. Beecher at the same time, expressing his full approval.

Thus disciplined, the boy began to change; he became moody, sullen, silent, and even sleepy. This was the less wonderful, that he generally escaped at night to a gypsy camp, and courted a gypsy girl, who was nearly as handsome as himself, besides being older, and far more knowing.

His tongue went like a mill, and the whole tribe soon knew all about him and his parents.

One morning the servants got up supernaturally early, to wash. Mr. Reginald was detected stealing back to his roost, and reported to the master.

Mr. Beecher had him up directly, locked him into the study alone, put the other students into the drawing-room, and erected bars to his bedroom window.

A few days of this, and he pined like a bird in a cage.

A few more, and his gypsy girl came fortune-telling to the servants, and wormed out the truth.

Then she came at night under his window, and made him a signal. He told her his hard case, and told her also a resolution he had come to. She informed the tribe. The tribe consulted. A keen saw was flung up to him; in two nights he was through the bars; the third he was free, and joined his sable friends.

They struck their tents, and decamped with horses, asses, tents, and baggage, and were many miles away by daybreak, without troubling turnpikes.

The boy left not a line behind him, and Mr. Beecher half hoped he might come back; still he sent to the nearest station, and telegraphed to Huntercombe.

Sir Charles mounted a fleet horse, and rode off at once into Cambridgeshire. He set inquiries on foot, and learned that the boy had been seen consorting with a tribe of gypsies. He heard, also, that these were rather high gypsies, many of them foreigners; and that they dealt in horses, and had a farrier; and that one or two of the girls were handsome, and also singers.

Sir Charles telegraphed for detectives from London; wrote to the mayors of towns; advertised, with full description and large reward, and brought such pressure to bear upon the Egyptians, that the band begin to fear: they consulted, and took measures for their own security; none too soon, for, they being encamped on Grey's Common in Oxfordshire, Sir Charles and the rural police rode into the camp and demanded young Hopeful.

They were equal to the occasion; at first they knew nothing of the matter, and, with injured innocence, invited a full inspection.

The invitation was accepted.

Then, all of a sudden, one of the women affected to be struck with an idea. "It is the young gentleman who wanted to join us in Cambridgeshire."

Then all their throats opened at once. "Yes, gentleman, there was a lovely young gentleman wanted to come with us; but we wouldn't have him. What could we do with him?"

Sir Charles left them under surveillance, and continued his researches, telegraphing Lady Bassett twice every day.

A dark stranger came into Huntercombe village, no longer young, but still a striking figure: had once, no doubt, been superlatively handsome. Even now, his long hair was black and his eye could glitter: but his life had impregnated his noble features with hardness and meanness; his large black eye was restless, keen, and servile: an excellent figure for a painter, though; born in Spain, he was not afraid of color, had a red cap on his snaky black hair, and a striped waistcoat.

He inquired for Mr. Meyrick's farm.

He soon found his way thither, and asked for Mrs. Meyrick.

The female servant who opened the door ran her eye up and down him, and said, bruskly, "What do you want with her, my man? because she is busy."

"Oh, she will see me, miss."

Softened by the "miss," the girl laughed, and said, "What makes you think that, my man?"

"Give her this, miss," said the gypsy, "and she will come to me."

He held her out a dirty crumpled piece of paper.

Sally, whose hands were wet from the tub, whipped her hand under the corner of her checkered apron, and so took the note with a finger and thumb operating through the linen. By this means she avoided two evils--her fingers did not wet the letter, and the letter did not dirty her fingers.

She took it into the kitchen to her mistress, whose arms were deep in a wash-tub.

Mrs. Meyrick had played the fine lady at first starting, and for six months would not put her hand to anything. But those twin cajolers of the female heart, Dignity and Laziness, made her so utterly wretched, that she returned to her old habits of work, only she combined with it the sweets of domination.

Sally came in and said, "It's an old gypsy, which he have brought you this."

Mrs. Meyrick instantly wiped the soapsuds from her brown but shapely arms, and, whipping a wet hand under her apron, took the note just as Sally had. It contained these words only:

"NURSE--The old Romance will tell you all about me.

"REGINALD."

She had no sooner read it than she took her sleeves down, and whipped her shawl off a peg and put it on, and took off her apron--and all for an old gypsy. No stranger must take her for anything but a lady.

Thus embellished in a turn of the hand, she went hastily to the door.

She and the gypsy both started at sight of each other, and Mrs. Meyrick screamed.

"Why, what brings you here, old man?" said she, panting. The gypsy answered with oily sweetness, "The little gentleman sent me, my dear. Why, you look like a queen."

"Hush!" said Mrs. Meyrick.--"Come in here."

She made the old gypsy sit down, and she sat close to him.

"Speak low, daddy," said she, "and tell me all about my boy, my beautiful boy."

The old gypsy told Mrs. Meyrick the wrongs of Reginald that had driven him to this; and she fell to crying and lamenting, and inveighing against all concerned--schoolmaster, Sir Charles, Lady Bassett, and the gypsies. Them the old man defended, and assured her the young gentleman was in good hands, and would be made a little king of, all the more that Keturah had told them there was gypsy blood in him.

Mrs. Meyrick resented this loudly, and then returned to her grief.

When she had indulged that grief for a long time, she felt a natural desire to quarrel with somebody, and she actually put on her bonnet, and was going to the Hall to give Lady Bassett a bit of her mind, for she said that lady had never shown the feelings of a woman for the lamb.

But she thought better of it, and postponed the visit. "I shall be sure to say something I shall be sorry for after," said she; so she sat down again, and returned to her grief.

Nor could she ever shake it off as thoroughly as she had done any other trouble in her life.

Months after this, she said to Sally, with a burst of tears, "I never nursed but one, and I shall never nurse another; and now he is across the seas."

She kept the old gypsy at the farm; or, to speak more correctly, she made the farm his headquarters. She assigned him the only bedroom he would accept, viz., a cattle-shed, open on one side. She used often to have him into her room when she was alone; she gave him some of her husband's clothes, and made him wear a decent hat; by these means she effaced, in some degree, his nationality, and then she compelled her servants to call him "the foreign gent."

The foreign gent was very apt to disappear in fine weather, but rain soon drove him back to her fireside, and hunger to her flesh-pots.

On the very day the foreign gent came to Meyrick's farm Lady Bassett had a letter by post from Reginald.

"DEAR MAMMA--I am gone with the gypsies across the water. I am sorry to leave you. You are the right sort: but they tormented me so with their books and their dark rooms. It is very unfortunate to be a boy. When I am a man, I shall be too old to be tormented, and then I will come back.

"Your dutiful son,

"REGINALD."

Lady Bassett telegraphed Sir Charles, and he returned to Huntercombe, looking old, sad, and worn.

Lady Bassett set herself to comfort and cheer him, and this was her gentle office for many a long month.

She was the more fit for it, that her own health and spirits revived the moment Reginald left the country with his friends the gypsies; the color crept back to her cheek, her spirits revived, and she looked as handsome, and almost as young, as when she married. She tasted tranquillity. Year after year went by without any news of Reginald, and the hope grew that he would never cross her threshold again, and Compton be Sir Charles's heir without any more trouble.

CHAPTER XLI.

OUR story now makes a bold skip. Compton Bassett was fourteen years old, a youth highly cultivated in mind and trained in body, but not very tall, and rather effeminate looking, because he was so fair and his skin so white.

For all that, he was one of the bowlers in the Wolcombe Eleven, whose cricket-ground was the very meadow in which he had erst gathered cowslips with Ruperta Bassett; and he had a canoe, which he carried to adjacent streams, however narrow, and paddled it with singular skill and vigor. A neighboring miller, suffering under drought, was heard to say, "There ain't water enough to float a duck; nought can swim but the dab-chicks and Muster Bassett."

He was also a pedestrian, and got his father to take long walks with him, and leave the horses to eat their oats in peace.

In these walks young master botanized and geologized his own father, and Sir Charles gave him a little politics, history, and English poetry, in return. He had a tutor fresh from Oxford for the classics.

One day, returning with his father from a walk, they met a young lady walking toward them from the village; she was tall, and a superb brunette.

Now it was rather a rare thing to see a lady walking through that village, so both Sir Charles and his son looked keenly at her as she came toward them.

Compton turned crimson, and raised his hat to her rather awkwardly.

Sir Charles, who did not know the lady from Eve, saluted her, nevertheless, and with infinite grace; for Sir Charles, in his youth, had lived with some of the elite of French society, and those gentlemen bow to the person whom their companion bows to. Sir Charles had imported this excellent trait of politeness, and always practiced it, though not the custom in England, the more the pity.

As soon as the young lady had passed and was out of hearing, Sir Charles said to Compton, "Who is that lovely girl? Why, how the boy is blushing!"

"Oh, papa!"

"Well, what is the matter?"

"Don't you see? It is herself come back from school."

"I have no doubt it is herself, and not her sister, but who is herself?"

"Ruperta Bassett."

"Richard Bassett's daughter! impossible. That young lady looks seventeen or eighteen years of age."

"Yes, but it is Ruperta. There's nobody like her. Papa!"

"Well?"

"I suppose I may speak to her now."

"What for?"

"She is so beautiful."

"That she really is. And therefore I advise you to have nothing to say to her. You are not children now, you know. Were you to renew that intimacy, you might be tempted to fall in love with her. I don't say you would be so mad, for you are a sensible boy; but still, after that little business in the wood--"

"But suppose I did fall in love with her?"

"Then that would be a great misfortune. Don't you know that her father is my enemy? If you were to make any advances to that young lady, he would seize the opportunity to affront you, and me through you."

This silenced Compton, for he was an obedient youth.

But in the evening he got to his mother and coaxed her to take his part.

Now Lady Bassett felt the truth of all her husband had said; but she had a positive wish the young people should be on friendly terms, at all events; she wanted the family feud to die with the generation it had afflicted. She promised, therefore, to speak to Sir Charles; and so great was her influence that she actually obtained terms for Compton: he might speak to Miss Bassett, if he would realize the whole situation, and be very discreet, and not revive that absurd familiarity into which, their childhood had been betrayed.

She communicated this to him, and warned him at the same time that even this concession had been granted somewhat reluctantly, and in consideration of his invariable good conduct; it would be immediately withdrawn upon the slightest indiscretion.

"Oh, I will be discretion itself," said Compton; but the warmth with which he kissed his mother gave her some doubts. However, she was prepared to risk something. She had her own views in this matter.

When he had got this limited permission, Master Compton was not much nearer the mark; for he was not to call on the young lady, and she did not often walk in the village.

But he often thought of her, her loving, sprightly ways seven years ago, and the blaze of beauty with which she had returned.

At last, one Sunday afternoon, she came to church alone. When the congregation dispersed, he followed her, and came up with her, but his heart beat violently.

"Miss Bassett!" said he, timidly.

She stopped, and turned her eyes on him; he blushed up to the temples. She blushed too, but not quite so much.

"I am afraid you don't remember me," said the boy, sadly.

"Yes, I do, sir," said Ruperta, shyly.

"How you are grown!"

"Yes, sir."

"You are taller than I am, and more beautiful than ever."

No answer, but a blush.

"You are not angry with me for speaking to you?"

"No, sir."

"I wouldn't offend you."

"I am not offended. Only--"

"Oh, Miss Bassett, of course I know you will never be--we shall never be--like we used."

A very deep blush, and dead silence.

"You are a grown-up young lady, and I am only a boy still, somehow. But it **would** have been hard if I might not even speak to you. Would it not?"

"Yes," said the young lady, but after some hesitation, and only in a whisper.

"I wonder where you walk to. I have never seen you out but once."

No reply to this little feeler.

Then, at last, Compton was discouraged, partly by her beauty and size, partly by her taciturnity.

He was silent in return, and so, in a state of mutual constraint, they reached the gate of Highmore.

"Good-by," said Compton reluctantly.

"Good-by."

"Won't you shake hands?"

She blushed, and put out her hand halfway. He took it and shook it, and so they parted.

Compton said to his mother disconsolately, "Mamma, it is all over. I have seen her, and spoken to her; but she has gone off dreadfully."

"Why, what is the matter?"

"She is all changed. She is so stupid and dignified got to be. She has not a word to say to a fellow."

"Perhaps she is more reserved; that is natural. She is a young lady now."

"Then it is a great pity she did not stay as she was. Oh, the bright little darling! Who'd think she could ever turn into a great, stupid, dignified thing? She is as tall as you, mamma."

"Indeed! She has made use of her time. Well, dear, don't take ***too much*** notice of her, and then you will find she will not be nearly so shy."

"Too much notice! I shall never speak to her again--perhaps."

"I would not be violent, one way or the other. Why not treat her like any other acquaintance?"

Next Sunday afternoon she came to church alone.

In spite of his resolution, Mr. Compton tried her a second time. Horror! she was all monosyllables and blushes again.

Compton began to find it too up-hill. At last, when they reached Highmore gate, he lost his patience, and said, "I see how it is. I have lost my sweet playmate forever. Good-by, Ruperta; I won't trouble you any more." And he held out his hand to the young lady for a final farewell.

Ruperta whipped both her hands behind her back like a school-girl, and then, recovering her dignity, cast one swift glance of gentle reproach, then suddenly assuming vast stateliness, marched into Highmore like the mother of a family. These three changes of manner she effected all in less than two seconds.

Poor Compton went away sorely puzzled by this female kaleidoscope, but not a little alarmed and concerned at having mortally offended so much feminine dignity.

After that he did not venture to accost her for some time, but he cast a few sheep's-eyes at her in church.

Now Ruperta had told her mother all; and her mother had not forbidden her to speak to Compton, but had insisted on reserve and discretion.

She now told her mother she thought he would not speak to her any more, she had snubbed him so.

"Dear me!" said Mrs. Bassett, "why did you do that? Can you not be polite and nothing more?"

"No, mamma."

"Why not? He is very amiable. Everybody says so."

"He is. But I keep remembering what a forward girl I was, and I am afraid he has not forgotten it either, and that makes me hate the poor little fellow; no, not hate him; but keep him off. I dare say he thinks me a cross, ill-tempered thing; and I *am* very unkind to him, but I can't help it."

"Never mind," said Mrs. Bassett; "that is much better than to be too forward. Papa would never forgive that."

By-and-by there was a cricket-match in the farmer's meadow, Highcombe and Huntercombe eleven against the town of Staveleigh. All clubs liked to play at Huntercombe, because Sir Charles found the tents and the dinner, and the young farmers drank his champagne to their hearts' content.

Ruperta took her maid and went to see the match. They found it going against Huntercombe. The score as follows--

Staveleigh. First innings, a hundred and forty-eight runs.

Huntercombe eighty-eight.

Staveleigh. Second innings, sixty runs, and only one wicket down; and Johnson and Wright, two of their best men, well in, and masters of the bowling.

This being communicated to Ruperta, she became excited, and her soul in the game.

The batters went on knocking the balls about, and scored thirteen more before the young lady's eyes.

"Oh, dear!" said she, "what is that boy about? Why doesn't he bowl? They pretend he is a capital bowler."

At this time Compton was standing long-field on, only farther from the wicket than usual.

Johnson, at the wicket bowled to, being a hard but not very scientific hitter, lifted a half volley ball right over the bowler's head, a hit for four, but a skyscraper. Compton started the moment he hit, and, running with prodigious velocity, caught the ball descending, within a few yards of Ruperta; but, to get at it, he was obliged to throw himself forward into the air; he rolled upon the grass, but held the ball in sight all the while.

Mr. Johnson was out, and loud acclamations rent the sky.

Compton rose, and saw Ruperta clapping her hands close by.

She left off and blushed, directly he saw her. He blushed too, and touched his cap to her, with an air half manly, half sheepish, but did not speak to her.

This was the last ball of the over, and, as the ball was now to be delivered from the other wicket, Compton took the place of long-leg.

The third ball was overpitched to leg, and Wright, who, like most country players, hit freely to leg, turned half, and caught this ball exactly right, and sent it whizzing for five.

But the very force of the stroke was fatal to him; the ball went at first bound right into Compton's hands, who instantly flung it back, like a catapult, at Wright's wicket.

Wright, having hit for five, and being unable to see what had become of the ball, started to run, as a matter of course.

But the other batsman, seeing the ball go right into long-leg's hands like a bullet, cried, "Back!"

Wright turned, and would have got back to his wicket if the ball had required handling by the wicket-keeper; but, by a mixture of skill with luck, it came right at the wicket. Seeing which, the wicket-keeper very judiciously let it alone, and it carried off the bails just half a second before Mr. Wright grounded his bat.

"How's that, umpire?" cried the wicket-keeper.

"Out!" said the Staveleigh umpire, who judged at that end.

Up went the ball into the air, amid great excitement of the natives.

Ruperta, carried away by the general enthusiasm, nodded all sparkling to Compton, and that made his heart beat and his soul aspire. So next over he claimed his rights, and took the ball. Luck still befriended him: he bowled four wickets in twelve overs; the wicket-keeper stumped a fifth: the rest were "the tail," and disposed of for a few runs, and the total was no more than Huntercombe's first innings.

Our hero then took the bat, and made forty-seven runs before he was disposed of, five wickets down for a hundred and ten runs. The match was not won yet, nor sure to be; but the situation was reversed.

On going out, he was loudly applauded; and Ruperta naturally felt proud of her admirer.

Being now free, he came to her irresolutely with some iced champagne.

Ruperta declined, with thanks; but he looked so imploringly that she sipped a little, and said, warmly, "I hope we shall win: and, if we do, I know whom we shall have to thank."

"And so do I: you, Miss Bassett."

"Me? Why, what have *I* done in the matter?"

"You brought us luck, for one thing. You put us on our mettle. Staveleigh shall never beat *me,* with you looking on."

Ruperta blushed a little, for the boy's eyes beamed with fire.

"If I believed that," said she, "I should hire myself out at the next match, and charge twelve pairs of gloves."

"You may believe it, then; ask anybody whether our luck did not change the moment you came."

"Then I am afraid it will go now, for I am going."

"You will lose us the match if you do," said Compton.

"I can't help it: now you are out, it is rather insipid. There, you see I can pay compliments as well as you."

Then she made a graceful inclination and moved away.

Compton felt his heart ache at parting. He took a thought and ran quickly to a certain part of the field.

Ruperta and her attendant walked very slowly homeward.

Compton caught them just at their own gate. "Cousin!" said he, imploringly, and held her out a nosegay of cowslips only.

At that the memories rushed back on her, and the girl seemed literally to melt. She gave him one look full of womanly sensibility and winning tenderness, and said, softly, "Thank you, cousin."

Compton went away on wings: the ice was broken.

But the next time he met her it had frozen again apparently: to be sure she was alone; and young ladies will be bolder when they have another person of their own sex with them.

Mr. Angelo called on Sir Charles Bassett to complain of a serious grievance.

Mr. Angelo had become zealous and eloquent, but what are eloquence and zeal against sex? A handsome woman had preached for ten minutes upon a little mound outside the village, and had announced she should say a few parting words next Sunday evening at six o'clock.

Mr. Angelo complained of this to Lady Bassett.

Lady Bassett referred him to Sir Charles.

Mr. Angelo asked that magistrate to enforce the law against conventicles.

Sir Charles said he thought the Act did not apply.

"Well, but," said Angelo, "it is on your ground she is going to preach."

"I am the proprietor, but the tenant is the owner in law. He could warn *me* off his ground. I have no power."

"I fear you have no inclination," said Angelo, nettled.

"Not much, to tell the truth," replied Sir Charles coolly. "Does it matter so very much *who* sows the good seed, or whether it is flung abroad from a pulpit or a grassy knoll?"

"That is begging the question, Sir Charles. Why assume that it is good seed? it is more likely to be tares than wheat in this case."

"And is not that begging the question? Well, I will make it my business to know: and if she preaches sedition, or heresy, or bad morals, I will strain my power a little to silence her. More than that I really cannot promise you. The day is gone by for intolerance."

"Intolerance is a bad thing; but the absence of all conviction is worse, and that is what we are coming to."

"Not quite that: but the nation has tasted liberty; and now every man assumes to do what is right in his own eyes."

"That mean's what is wrong in his neighbor's."

Sir Charles thought this neat, and laughed good-humoredly: he asked the rector to dine on Sunday at half-past seven. "I shall know more about it by that time," said he.

They dined early on Sunday, at Highmore, and Ruperta took her maid for a walk in the afternoon, and came back in time to hear the female preacher.

Half the village was there already, and presently the preacher walked to her station.

To Ruperta's surprise, she was a lady, richly dressed, tall and handsome, but with features rather too commanding. She had a glove on her left hand, and a little Bible in her right hand, which was large, but white, and finely formed.

She delivered a short prayer, and opened her text:

"Walk honestly; not in strife and envying."

Just as the text was given out, Ruperta's maid pinched her, and the young lady, looking up, saw her father coming to see what was the matter. Maid was for hiding, but Ruperta made a wry face, blushed, and stood her ground. "How can he scold me, when he comes himself?" she whispered.

During the sermon, of which, short as it was, I can only afford to give the outline, in crept Compton Bassett, and got within three or four of Ruperta.

Finally Sir Charles Bassett came up, in accordance with his promise to Angelo.

The perfect preacher deals in generalities, but strikes them home with a few personalities.

Most clerical preachers deal only in generalities, and that is ineffective, especially to uncultivated minds.

Mrs. Marsh, as might be expected from her sex, went a little too much the other way.

After a few sensible words, pointing out the misery in houses, and the harm done to the soul, by a quarrelsome spirit, she lamented there was too much of it in Huntercombe: with this opening she went into personalities: reminded them of the fight between two farm servants last week, one of whom was laid up at that moment in consequence. "And," said she, "even when it does not come to fighting, it poisons your lives and offends your Redeemer."

Then she went into the causes, and she said Drunkenness and Detraction were the chief causes of strife and contention.

She dealt briefly but dramatically with Drunkenness, and then lashed Detraction, as follows:

"Every class has its vices, and Detraction is the vice of the poor. You are ever so much vainer than your betters: you are eaten up with vanity, and never give your neighbor a good word. I have been in thirty houses, and in not one of those houses has any poor man or poor woman spoken one honest word in praise of a neighbor. So do not flatter yourselves this is a Christian village, for it is not. The only excuse to be made for you, and I fear it is not one that God will accept on His judgment-day, is that your betters set you a bad example instead of a good one. The two principal people in this village are kinsfolk, yet enemies, and have been enemies for twenty years. That's a nice example for two Christian gentlemen to set to poor people, who, they may be sure, will copy their sins, if they copy nothing else.

"They go to church regularly, and believe in the Bible, and yet they defy both Church and Bible.

"Now I should like to ask those gentlemen a question. How do they mean to manage in Heaven? When the baronet comes to that happy place, where all is love, will the squire walk out? Or do they think to quarrel there, and so get turned out, both of them? I don't wonder at your smiling; but it is a serious consideration, for all that. The soul of man is immortal: and what is the soul? it is not a substantial thing, like the body; it is a bundle of thoughts and feelings: the thoughts we die with in this world, we shall wake up with them in the next. Yet here are two Christians loading their immortal souls with immortal hate. What a waste of feeling, if it must all be flung off together with the body, lest it drag the souls of both down to bottomless perdition.

"And what do they gain in this world?--irritation, ill-health, and misery. It is a fact that no man ever reached a great old age who hated his neighbor; still less a *good* old age; for, if men would look honestly into their own hearts, they would own that to hate is to be miserable.

"I believe no men commit a sin for many years without some special warnings; and to neglect these, is one sin more added to their account. Such a warning, or rather, I should say, such a pleading of Divine love, those two gentlemen have had. Do you remember, about eight years ago, two children were lost on one day, out of different houses in this village?" (A murmur from the crowd.)

"Perhaps some of you here present were instrumental, under God, in finding that pretty pair." (A louder murmur.)

"Oh, don't be afraid to answer me. Preaching is only a way of speaking; and I'm only a woman that is speaking to you for your good. Tell me--we are not in church, tied up by stait-laced rules to keep men and women from getting within arm's-length of one another's souls--tell me, who saw those two lost children?"

"I, I, I, I, I," roared several voices in reply.

"Is it true, as a good woman tells me, that the innocent darlings had each an arm round the other's neck?"

"Ay."

"And little coronets of flowers, to match their hair?" (That was the girl's doing.)

"Ay."

"And the little boy had played the man, and taken off his tippet to put round the little lady?"

"Ay!" with a burst of enthusiasm from the assembled rustics.

"I think I see them myself; and the torches lighting up the dewy leaves overhead, and that Divine picture of innocent love. Well, which was the prettiest sight, and the fittest for heaven--the hatred of the parents, or the affection of the children?

"And now mark what a weapon hatred is, in the Devil's hands. There are only two people in this parish on whom that sight was wasted; and those two being gentlemen, and men of education, would have been more affected by it than humble folk, if Hell had not been in their hearts, for Hate comes from Hell, and takes men down to the place it comes from.

"Do you, then, shun, in that one thing, the example of your betters: and I hope those children will shun it too. A father is to be treated with great veneration, but above all is our Heavenly Father and His law; and that law, what is it?--what has it been this eighteen hundred years and more? Why, Love.

"Would you be happy in this world, and fit your souls to dwell hereafter even in the meanest of the many mansions prepared above, you *must,* above all things, be charitable. You must not run your neighbor down behind his back, or God will hate you: you must not wound him to his face, or God will hate you. You must overlook a fault or two, and see a man's bright side, and then God will love you. If you won't do that much for your neighbor, why, in Heaven's name, should God overlook a multitude of sins in you?

"Nothing goes to heaven surer than Charity, and nothing is so fit to sit in heaven. St. Paul had many things to be proud of and to praise in himself--things that the world is more apt to admire than Christian charity, the sweetest, but humblest of all the Christian graces: St. Paul, I say, was a bulwark of learning, an anchor of faith, a rock of constancy, a thunder-bolt of zeal: yet see how he bestows the palm.

"'Knowledge puffeth up: but charity edifieth. Though I speak with the tongues of men and of angels, and have not charity, I am become as sounding brass, or a tinkling cymbal. And though I have the gift of prophecy, and understand all mysteries and all knowledge; and though I have all faith, so that I could remove mountains, and have not charity, I am nothing. And though I bestow all my goods to feed the poor, and though I give my body to be burned, and have not charity, it profiteth me nothing. Charity suffereth long, and is kind; charity envieth not; charity vaunteth not itself, is not puffed up, doth not behave itself unseemly, seeketh not her own, is not easily provoked, thinketh no evil; rejoiceth not in iniquity, but rejoiceth in the truth; beareth all things, believeth all things, hopeth all things, endureth all things. Charity never faileth; but prophecies--they shall fail; tongues--they shall cease; knowledge--it shall vanish away. And now abideth Faith, Hope, Charity, these three; but the greatest of these is charity.'"

The fair orator delivered these words with such fire, such feeling, such trumpet tones and heartfelt eloquence, that for the first time those immortal words sounded in these village ears true oracles of God.

Then, without pause, she went on. "So let us lift our hearts in earnest prayer to God that, in this world of thorns, and tempers, and trials, and troubles, and cares, He will give us the best cure for all--the great sweetener of this mortal life--the sure forerunner of Heaven--His most excellent gift of charity." Then, in one generous burst, she prayed for love divine, and there was many a sigh and many a tear, and at the close an "Amen!" such as, alas! we shall never, I fear, hear burst from a hundred bosoms where men repeat beautiful but stale words and call it prayer.

The preacher retired, but the people still lingered spell-bound, and then arose that buzz which shows that the words have gone home.

As for Richard Bassett, he had turned on his heel, indignant, as soon as the preacher's admonitions came his way.

Sir Charles Bassett stood his ground rather longer, being steeled by the conviction that the quarrel was none of his seeking. Moreover, he was not aware what a good friend this woman had been to him, nor what a good wife she had been to Marsh this seventeen years. His mind, therefore, made a clear leap from Rhoda Somerset, the vixen of Hyde Park and Mayfair, to this preacher, and he could not help smiling; than which a worse frame for receiving unpalatable truths can hardly be conceived. And so the elders were obdurate. But Compton and Ruperta had no armor of old age, egotism, or prejudice to turn the darts of honest eloquence. They listened, as to the voice of an angel; they gazed, as on the face of an angel; and when those silvery accents ceased, they turned toward each other and came toward each other, with the sweet enthusiasm that became their years. "Oh, Cousin Ruperta!" quavered Compton. "'Oh, Cousin Compton!" cried Ruperta, the tears trickling down her lovely cheeks.

They could not say any more for ever so long.

Ruperta spoke first. She gave a final gulp, and said, "I will go and speak to her, and thank her."

"Oh, Miss Ruperta, we shall be too late for tea," suggested the maid.

"Tea!" said Ruperta. "Our souls are before our tea! I must speak to her, or else my heart will choke me and kill me. I will go--and so will Compton."

"Oh, yes!" said Compton.

And they hurried after the preacher.

They came up with her flushed and panting; and now it was Compton's turn to be shy--the lady was so tall and stately too.

But Ruperta was not much afraid of anything in petticoats. "Oh, madam," said she, "if you please, may we speak to you?"

Mrs. Marsh turned round, and her somewhat aquiline features softened instantly at the two specimens of beauty and innocence that had run after her.

"Certainly, my young friends;" and she smiled maternally on them. She had children of her own.

"Who do you think we are? We are the two naughty children you preached about so beautifully."

"What! *you* the babes in the wood?"

"Yes, madam. It was a long, long while ago, and we are fifteen now--are we not, Cousin Compton?"

"Yes, madam."

"And we are both so unhappy at our parents' quarreling. At least I am."

"And so am I."

"And we came to thank you. Didn't we, Compton?"

"Yes, Ruperta."

"And to ask your advice. How are we to make our parents be friends? Old people will not be advised by young ones. They look down on us so; it is dreadful."

"My dear young lady," said Mrs. Marsh, "I will try and answer you: but let me sit down a minute; for, after preaching, I am apt to feel a little exhausted. Now, sit beside me, and give me each a hand, if you please.

"Well, my dears, I have been teaching you a lesson; and now you teach me one, and that is, how much easier it is to preach reconciliation and charity than it is to practice it under certain circumstances. However, my advice to you is first to pray to God for wisdom in this thing, and then to watch every opportunity. Dissuade your parents from every unkind act: don't be afraid to speak--with the word of God at your back. I know that you have no easy task before you. Sir Charles Bassett and Mr. Bassett were both among my hearers, and both turned their backs on me, and went away unsoftened; they would not give me a chance; would not hear me to an end, and I am not a wordy preacher neither."

Here an interruption occurred. Ruperta, so shy and cold with Compton, flung her arms round Mrs. Marsh's neck, with the tears in her eyes, and kissed her eagerly.

"Yes, my dear," said Mrs. Marsh, after kissing her in turn, "I *was* a little mortified. But that was very weak and foolish. I am sorry, for their own sakes, they would not stay; it was the word of God: but they saw only the unworthy instrument. Well, then, my dears, you **have** a hard task; but you must work upon your mothers, and win them to charity."

"Ah! that will be easy enough. My mother has never approved this unhappy quarrel."

"No more has mine."

"Is it so? Then you must try and get the two ladies to speak to each other. But something tells me that a way will be opened. Have patience; have faith; and do not mind a check or two; but persevere, remembering that 'blessed are the peacemakers.'"

She then rose, and they took leave of her.

"Give me a kiss, children," said she. "You have done me a world of good. My own heart often flags on the road, and you have warmed and comforted it. God bless you!"

And so they parted.

Compton and Ruperta walked homeward. Ruperta was very thoughtful, and Compton could only get monosyllables out of her. This discouraged, and at last vexed him.

"What have I done," said he, "that you will speak to anybody but me?"

"Don't be cross, child," said she; "but answer me a question. Did you put your tippet round me in that wood?"

"I suppose so."

"Oh, then you don't remember doing it, eh?"

"No; that I don't."

"Then what makes you think you did?"

"Because they say so. Because I must have been such an awful cad if I didn't. And I was always much fonder of you than you were of me. My tippet! I'd give my head sooner than any harm should come to you, Ruperta!"

Ruperta made no reply, but, being now at Highmore, she put out her hand to him, and turned her head away. He kissed her hand devotedly, and so they parted.

Compton told Lady Bassett all that happened, and Ruperta told Mrs. Bassett.

Those ladies readily promised to be on the side of peace, but they feared it could only be the work of time, and said so.

By-and-by Compton got impatient, and told Ruperta he had thought of a way to compel their fathers to be friends. "I am afraid you won't like the idea at *first,*" said he; "but the more you think of it, the more you will see it is the surest way of all."

"Well, but what is it?"

"You must let me marry you."

Ruperta stared, and began to blush crimson.

"Will you, cousin?"

"Of course not, child. The idea!"

"Oh, Ruperta," cried the boy in dismay, "surely you don't mean to marry anybody else but me!"

"Would that make you very unhappy, then?"

"You know it would, wretched for my life."

"I should not like to do that. But I disapprove of early marriages. I mean to wait till I'm nineteen; and that is three years nearly."

"It is a fearful time; but if you will promise not to marry anybody else, I suppose I shall live through it."

Ruperta, though she made light of Compton's offer, was very proud of it (it was her first). She told her mother directly.

Mrs. Bassett sighed, and said that was too blessed a thing ever to happen.

"Why not?" said Ruperta.

"How could it," said Mrs. Bassett, "with everybody against it but poor little me!"

"Compton assures me that Lady Bassett wishes it."

"Indeed! But Sir Charles and papa, Ruperta?"

"Oh, Compton must talk Sir Charles over, and I will persuade papa. I'll begin this evening, when he comes home from London."

Accordingly, as he was sitting alone in the dining-room sipping his glass of port, Ruperta slipped away from her mother's side and found him.

His face brightened at the sight of her; for he was extremely fond and proud of this girl, for whom he would not have the bells rung when she was born.

She came and hung round his neck a little, and kissed him, and said softly, "Dear papa, I have something to tell you. I have had a proposal."

Richard Bassett stared.

"What, of marriage?"

Ruperta nodded archly.

"To a child like you? Scandalous! No, for, after all, you look nineteen or twenty. And who is the highwayman that thinks to rob me of my precious girl?"

"Well, papa, whoever he is, he will have to wait three years, and so I told him. It is my cousin Compton."

"What!" cried Richard Bassett, so loudly that the girl started back dismayed. "That little monkey have the impudence to offer marriage to my daughter? Surely, Ruperta, you have offered him no encouragement?"

"N--no."

"Your mother promised me nothing but common civility should pass between you and that young gentleman."

"She promised for me, but she could not promise for him--poor little fellow!"

"Marry a son of the man who has robbed and insulted your father!"

"Oh, papa! is it so? Are you sure you did not begin?"

"If you can think that, it is useless to say more. I thought ill-fortune had done its worst; but no; blow upon blow, and wound upon wound. Don't spare me, child. Nobody else has, and why should you? Marry my enemy's son, his younger son, and break your father's heart."

At this, what could a sensitive girl of sixteen do but burst out crying, and promise, round her father's neck, never to marry any one whom he disliked.

When she had made this promise, her father fondled and petted her, and his tenderness consoled her, for she was not passionately in love with her cousin.

Yet she cried a good deal over the letter in which she communicated this to Compton.

He lay in wait for her; but she baffled him for three weeks.

After that she relaxed her vigilance, for she had no real wish to avoid him, and was curious to see whether she had cured him.

He met her; and his conduct took her by surprise. He was pale, and looked very wretched.

He said solemnly, "Were you jesting with me when you promised to marry no one but me?"

"No, Compton. But you know I could never marry you without papa's consent."

"Of course not; but, what I fear, he might wish you to marry somebody else."

"Then I should refuse. I will never break my word to you, cousin. I am not in love with you, you are too young for that--but somehow I feel I could not make you unhappy. Can't you trust my word? You might. I come of the same people as you. Why do you look so pale?--we are very unhappy."

Then the tears began to steal down her cheeks; and Compton's soon followed.

Compton consulted his mother. She told him, with a sigh, she was powerless. Sir Charles might yield to her, but she had no power to influence Mr. Bassett at present. "The time may come," said she. She could not take a very serious view of this amour, except with regard to its pacific results. So Mr. Bassett's opposition chilled her in the matter.

While things were so, something occurred that drove all these minor things out of her distracted heart.

One summer evening, as she and Sir Charles and Compton sat at dinner, a servant came in to say there was a stranger at the door, and he called himself Bassett.

"What is he like?" said Lady Bassett, turning pale.

"He looks like a foreigner, my lady. He says he is Mr. Bassett," repeated the man, with a scandalized air.

Sir Charles got up directly, and hurried to the hall door. Compton followed to the door only and looked.

Sure enough it was Reginald, full-grown, and bold, as handsome as ever, and darker than ever.

In that moment his misconduct in running away never occurred either to Sir Charles or Compton; all was eager and tremulous welcome. The hall rang with joy. They almost carried him into the dining-room.

The first thing they saw was a train of violet-colored velvet, half hidden by the table.

Compton ran forward with a cry of dismay.

It was Lady Bassett, in a dead swoon, her face as white as her neck and arms, and these as white and smooth as satin.

CHAPTER XLII.

LADY BASSETT was carried to her room, and did not reappear. She kept her own apartments, and her health declined so rapidly that Sir Charles sent for Dr. Willis. He prescribed for the body, but the disease lay in the mind. Martyr to an inward struggle, she pined visibly, and her beautiful eyes began to shine like stars, preternaturally large. She was in a frightful condition: she longed to tell the truth and end it all; but then she must lose her adored husband's respect, and perhaps his love; and she had not the courage. She saw no way out of it but to die and leave her confession; and, as she felt that the agony of her soul was killing her by degrees, she drew a somber resignation from that.

She declined to see Reginald. She could not bear the sight of him.

Compton came to her many times a day, with a face full of concern, and even terror. But she would not talk to him of herself.

He brought her all the news he heard, having no other way to cheer her.

One day he told her there were robbers about. Two farmhouses had been robbed, a thing not known in these parts for many years.

Lady Bassett shuddered, but said nothing.

But by-and-by her beloved son came to her in distress with a grief of his own.

Ruperta Bassett was now the beauty of the county, and it seems Mr. Rutland had danced with her at her first ball, and been violently smitten with her; he had called more than once at Highmore, and his attentions were directly encouraged by Mr. Bassett. Now Mr. Rutland was heir to a peerage, and also to considerable estates in the county.

Compton was sick at heart, and, being young, saw his life about to be blighted; so now he was pale and woe-begone, and told her the sad news with such deep sighs, and imploring, tearful eyes, that all the mother rose in arms. "Ah!" said she, "they say to themselves that I am down, and cannot fight for my child; but I would fight for him on the edge of the grave. Let me think all by myself, dear. Come back to me in an hour. I shall do something. Your mother is a very cunning woman--for those she loves."

Compton kissed her gown--a favorite action of his, for he worshiped her--and went away.

The invalid laid her hollow cheek upon her wasted hand, and thought with all her might. By degrees her extraordinary brain developed a twofold plan of action; and she proceeded to execute the first part, being the least difficult, though even that was not easy, and brought a vivid blush to her wasted cheek.

She wrote to Mrs. Bassett.

"MADAM--I am very ill, and life is uncertain. Something tells me you, like me, regret the unhappy feud between our houses. If this is so, it would be a consolation to me to take you by the hand and exchange a few words, as we already have a few kind looks.

"Yours respectfully,

"BELLA BASSETT."

She showed this letter to Compton, and told him he might send a servant with it to Highmore at once.

"Oh, mamma!" said he, "I never thought you would do that: how good you are! You couldn't ask Ruperta, could you? Just in a little postscript, you know."

Lady Bassett shook her head.

"That would not be wise, my dear. Let me hook that fish for you, not frighten her away."

Great was the astonishment at Highmore when a blazing footman knocked at the door and handed Jessie the letter with assumed nonchalance, then stalked away, concealing with professional art his own astonishment at what he had done.

It was no business of Jessie's to take letters into the drawing-room; she would have deposited any other letter on the hall table; but she brought this one in, and, standing at the door, exclaimed, "Here a letter fr' Huntercombe!"

Richard Bassett, Mrs. Bassett, and Ruperta, all turned upon her with one accord.

"From where?"

"Fr' Huntercombe itsel'. Et isna for you, nor for you, missy. Et's for the mester-ress."

She marched proudly up to Mrs. Bassett and laid the letter down on the table; then drew back a step or two, and, being Scotch, coolly waited to hear the contents. Richard Basset, being English, told her she need not stay.

Mrs. Bassett cast a bewildered look at her husband and daughter, then opened the letter quietly; read it quietly; and, having read it, took out her handkerchief and began to cry quietly.

Ruperta cried, "Oh, mamma!" and in a moment had one long arm round her mother's neck, while the other hand seized the letter, and she read it aloud, cheek to cheek; but, before she got to an end, her mother's tears infected her, and she must whimper too.

"Here are a couple of geese," said Richard Bassett. "Can't you write a civil reply to a civil letter without sniveling? I'll answer the letter for you."

"No!" said Mrs. Bassett.

Richard was amazed: Ruperta ditto.

The little woman had never dealt in "Noes," least of all to her husband; and besides this was such a plump "No." It came out of her mouth like a marble.

I think the sound surprised even herself a little, for she proceeded to justify it at once. "I have been a better wife than a Christian this many years. But there's a limit. And, Richard, I should never have married you if you had told me we were to be at war all our lives with our next neighbor, that everybody respects. To live in the country, and not speak to our only neighbor, that is a life I never would have left my father's house for. Not that I complain: if you have been bitter to them, you have always been good and kind to me; and I hope I have done my best to deserve it; but when a sick lady, and perhaps dying, holds out her hand to me---write her one of your cold-blooded letters! That I WON'T. Reply? my reply will be just putting on my bonnet and going to her this afternoon. It is Passion-week, too; and that's not a week to play the heathen. Poor lady! I've seen in her sweet eyes this many years that she would gladly be friends with me; and she never passed me close but she bowed to me, in church or out, even when we were at daggers drawn. She is a lady, a real lady, every inch. But it is not that altogether. No, if a sick woman called me to her bedside this week, I'd go, whether she wrote from Huntercombe Hall or the poorest house in the place; else how could I hope my Saviour would come to *my* bedside at my last hour?"

This honest burst, from a meek lady who never talked nonsense, to be sure, but seldom went into eloquence, staggered Richard Bassett, and enraptured Ruperta so, that she flung both arms round her mother's neck, and cried, "Oh, mamma! I always thought you were the best woman in England, and now I know it."

"Well, well, well," said Richard, kindly enough; then to Ruperta, "Did I ever say she was not the best woman in England? So you need not set up your throats neck and neck at me, like two geese at a fox. Unfortunately, she is the simplest woman in England, as well as the best, and she is going to visit the cunningest. That Lady Bassett will turn our mother inside out in no time. I wish you would go with her; you are a shrewd girl."

"My daughter will not go till she is asked," said Mrs. Bassett, firmly.

"In that case," said Richard, dryly, "let us hope the Lord will protect you, since it is for love of Him you go into a she-fox's den."

No reply was vouchsafed to this aspiration, the words being the words of faith, but the voice the voice of skepticism.

Mrs. Bassett put on her bonnet, and went to Huntercombe Hall.

After a very short delay she was ushered upstairs, to the room where Lady Bassett was lying on a sofa.

Lady Bassett heard her coming, and rose to receive her.

She made Mrs. Bassett a court courtesy so graceful and profound that it rather frightened the little woman. Seeing which, Lady Bassett changed her style, and came forward, extending both hands with admirable grace, and gentle amity, not overdone.

Mrs. Bassett gave her both hands, and they looked full at each other in silence, till the eyes of both ladies began to fill.

"You would have come--like this--years ago--at a word?" faltered Lady Bassett.

"Yes," gulped Mrs. Bassett.

Then there was another long pause.

"Oh, Lady Bassett, what a life! It is a wonder it has not killed us both."

"It will kill one of us."

"Not if I can help it."

"God bless you for saying so! Dear madam, sit by me, and let me hold the hand I might have had years ago, if I had had the courage."

"Why should you take the blame?" said Mrs. Bassett. "We have both been good wives: too obedient, perhaps. But to have to choose between a husband's commands and God's law, that is a terrible thing for any poor woman."

"It is, indeed."

Then there was another silence, and an awkward pause. Mrs. Bassett broke it, with some hesitation. "I hope, Lady Bassett, your present illness is not in any way--I hope you do not fear anything more from my husband?"

"Oh, Mrs. Bassett! how can I help fearing it--especially if we provoke him? Mr. Reginald Bassett has returned, and you know he once gave your husband cause for just resentment."

"Well, but he is older now, and has more sense. Even if he should, Ruperta and I must try and keep the peace."

"Ruperta! I wish I had asked you to bring her with you. But I feared to ask too much at once."

"I'll send her to you to-morrow, Lady Bassett."

"No, bring her."

"Then tell me your hour."

"Yes, and I will send somebody out of the way. I want you both to myself."

While this conversation was going on at Huntercombe, Richard Bassett, being left alone with his daughter, proceeded to work with his usual skill upon her young mind.

He reminded her of Mr. Rutland's prospects, and said he hoped to see her a countess, and the loveliest jewel of the Peerage.

He then told her Mr. Rutland was coming to stay a day or two next week, and requested her to receive him graciously.

She promised that at once.

"That," said he, "will be a much better match for you than the younger son of Sir Charles Bassett. However, my girl is too proud to go into a family where she is not welcome."

"Much too proud for that," said Ruperta.

He left her smarting under that suggestion.

While he was smoking his cigar in the garden, Mrs. Bassett came home. She was in raptures with Lady Bassett, and told her daughter all that had passed; and, in conclusion, that she had promised Lady Bassett to take her to Huntercombe to-morrow.

"Me, dear!" cried Ruperta; "why, what can she want of me?"

"All I know is, her ladyship wishes very much to see you. In my opinion, you will be *very* welcome to poor Lady Bassett."

"Is she very ill?"

Mrs. Bassett shook her head. "She is much changed. She says she should be better if we were all at peace; but I don't know."

"Oh, mamma, I wish it was to-morrow."

They went to Huntercombe next day; and, ill as she was, Lady Bassett received them charmingly. She was startled by Ruperta's beauty and womanly appearance, but too well bred to show it, or say it all in a moment. She spoke to the mother first; but presently took occasion to turn to the daughter, and to say, "May I hope, Miss Bassett, that you are on the side of peace, like your dear mother and myself?"

"I am," said Ruperta, firmly; "I always was--especially after that beautiful sermon, you know, mamma."

Says the proud mother, "You might tell Lady Bassett you think it is your mission to reunite your father and Sir Charles."

"Mamma!" said Ruperta, reproachfully. That was to stop her mouth. "If you tell all the wild things I say to you, her ladyship will think me very presumptuous."

"No, no," said Lady Bassett, "enthusiasm is not presumption. Enthusiasm is beautiful, and the brightest flower of youth."

"I am glad you think so, Lady Bassett; for people who have no enthusiasm seem very hard and mean to me."

"And so they are," said Lady Bassett warmly.

But I have no time to record the full details of the conversation. I can only present the general result. Lady Bassett thought Ruperta a beautiful and noble girl, that any house might be proud to adopt; and Ruperta was charmed by Lady Bassett's exquisite manners, and touched and interested by her pale yet still beautiful face and eyes. They made friends; but it was not till the third visit, when many kind things had passed between them, that Lady Bassett ventured on the subject she had at heart. "My dear," said she to Ruperta, "when I first saw you, I wondered at my son Compton's audacity in loving a young lady so much more advanced than himself; but now I must be frank with you; I think the poor boy's audacity was only a proper courage. He has all my sympathy, and, if he is not quite indifferent to you, let me just put in my word, and say there is not a young lady in the world I could bear for my daughter-in-law, now I have seen and talked with you, my dear."

"Thank you, Lady Bassett," said Mrs. Bassett; "and, since you have said so much, let me speak my mind. So long as your son is attached to my daughter, I could never welcome any other son-in-law. I HAVE GOT THE TIPPET."

Lady Bassett looked at Ruperta, for an explanation. Ruperta only blushed, and looked uncomfortable. She hated all allusion to the feats of her childhood.

Mrs. Bassett saw Lady Bassett's look of perplexity, and said, eagerly, "You never missed it? All the better. I thought I would keep it, for a peacemaker partly."

"My dear friend," said Lady Bassett, "you are speaking riddles to me; what tippet?"

"The tippet your son took off his own shoulders, and put it round my girl, that terrible night they were lost in the wood. Forgive me keeping it, Lady Bassett--I know I was little better than a thief; but it was only a tippet to you, and to me it was much more. Ah! Lady Bassett, I have loved your darling boy ever since; you can't wonder, you are a mother;" and, turning suddenly on Ruperta, "why do you keep saying he is only a boy? If he was man enough to do that at seven years of age, he must have a manly heart. No; I couldn't bear the sight of any other son-in-law; and when you are a mother you'll understand many things, and, for one, you'll--under--stand--why I'm so--fool--ish; seeing the sweet boy's mother ready--to cry--too--oh! oh! oh!"

Lady Bassett held out her arms to her, and the mothers had a sweet cry together in each other's arms.

Ruperta's eyes were wet at this; but she told her mother she ought not to agitate Lady Bassett, and she so ill.

"And that is true, my good, sensible girl," said Mrs. Bassett; "but it has lain in my heart these nine years, and I could not keep it to myself any longer. But you are a beauty and a spoiled child, and so I suppose you think nothing of his giving you his tippet to keep you warm."

"Don't say that, mamma," said Ruperta, reproachfully. "I spoke to dear Compton about it not long ago. He had forgotten all about it, even."

"All the more to his credit; but don't you ever forget it, my own girl."

"I never will, mamma."

By degrees the three became so unreserved that Ruperta was gently urged to declare her real sentiments.

By this time the young beauty was quite cured of her fear lest she should be an unwelcome daughter-in-law; but there was an obstacle in her own mind. She was a frank, courageous girl; but this appeal tried her hard.

She blushed, fixed her eyes steadily on the ground, and said, pretty firmly and very slowly, "I had always a great affection for my cousin Compton; and so I have now. But I am not in love with him. He is but a boy; now I--"

A glance at the large mirror, and a superb smile of beauty and conscious womanhood, completed the sentence.

"He will get older every day," said Mrs. Bassett.

"And so shall I."

"But you will not look older, and he will. You have come to your full growth. He hasn't."

"I agree with the dear girl," said Lady Bassett, adroitly. "Compton, with his fair hair, looks so young, it would be ridiculous at present. But it is possible to be engaged, and wait a proper time for marriage; what I fear is, lest you should be tempted by some other offer. To speak plainly, I hear that Mr. Rutland pays his addresses to you, and visits at Highmore."

"Yes, he has been there twice."

"He is welcome to your father; and his prospects are dazzling; and he is not a boy, for he has long mustaches."

"I am not dazzled by his mustaches, and still less by his prospects," said the fair young beauty.

"You are an extraordinary girl."

"That she is," said Mrs. Bassett. "Her father has no more power over her than I have."

"Oh, mamma! am I a disobedient girl, then?"

"No, no. Only in this one thing, I see you will go your own way."

Lady Bassett put in her word. "Well, but this one thing is the happiness or misery of her whole life. I cannot blame her for looking well before she leaps."

A grateful look from Ruperta's glorious eyes repaid the speaker.

"But," said Lady Bassett, tenderly, "it is something to have two mothers when you marry, instead of one; and you would have two, my love; I would try and live for you."

This touched Ruperta to the heart; she curled round Lady Bassett's neck, and they kissed each other like mother and daughter.

"This is too great a temptation," said Ruperta. "Yes; I *will* engage myself to Cousin Compton, if papa's consent can be obtained. Without his consent I could not marry any one."

"Nobody can obtain it, if you cannot," said Mrs. Bassett.

Ruperta shook her head. "Mark my words, mamma, it will take me years to gain it. Papa is as obstinate as a mule. To be sure, I am as obstinate as fifty."

"It shall not take years, nor yet months," said Lady Bassett. "I know *Mr. Bassett's* objection, and I will remove it, cost me what it may."

This speech surprised the other two ladies so, they made no reply.

Said Lady Bassett firmly, "Do you pledge yourself to me, if I can obtain Mr. Bassett's consent?"

"I do," said Ruperta. "But--"

"You think my power with your father must be smaller than yours. I hope to show you you are mistaken."

The ladies rose to go: Lady Bassett took leave of them thus: "Good-by, my most valued friend, and sister in sorrow; good-by, my dear daughter."

At the gate of Huntercombe, whom should they meet but Compton Bassett, looking very pale and unhappy.

He was upon honor not to speak to Ruperta; but he gazed on her with a wistful and terrified look that was very touching. She gave him a soft pitying smile in return, that drove him almost wild with hope.

That night Richard Bassett sat in his chair, gloomy.

When his wife and daughter spoke to him in their soft accents, he returned short, surly answers. Evidently a storm was brewing.

At last it burst. He had heard of Ruperta's repeated visits to Huntercombe Hall. "You are not dealing fairly with me, you two," said he. "I allowed you to go once to see a woman that says she is very ill; but I warned you she was the cunningest woman in creation, and would make a fool of you both; and now I find you are always going. This will not do. She is netting two simple birds that I have the care of. Now, listen to me; I forbid you two ever to set foot in that house again. Do you hear me?"

"We hear you, papa," said Mrs. Bassett, quietly; "we must be deaf, if we did not."

Ruperta kept her countenance with difficulty.

"It is not a request, it is a command."

Mrs. Bassett for once in her life fired up. "And a most tyrannical one," said she.

Ruperta put her hand before her mother's mouth, then turned to her father.

"There was no need to express your wish so harshly, papa. We shall obey."

Then she whispered her mother, "And Mr. Rutland shall pay for it."

Mrs. Bassett communicated this behest to Lady Bassett in a letter.

Then Lady Bassett summoned all her courage, and sent for her son Compton. "Compton," said she, "I must speak to Reginald. Can you find him?"

"Oh yes, I can find him. I am sorry to say anybody can find him at this time of day."

"Why, where is he?"

"I hardly like to tell you."

"Do you think his peculiarities have escaped me?"

"At the public-house."

"Ask him to come to me."

Compton went to the public-house, and there, to his no small disgust, found Mr. Reginald Bassett playing the fiddle, and four people, men and women, dancing to the sound, while one or two more smoked and looked on.

Compton restrained himself till the end of that dance, and then stepped up to Reginald and whispered him, "Mamma wants to see you directly."

"Tell her I'm busy."

"I shall tell her nothing of the kind. You know she is very ill, and has not seen you yet; and now she wants to. So come along at once, like a good fellow."

"Youngster," said Reginald, "it is a rule with me never to leave a young woman for an old one."

"Not for your mother?"

"No, nor my grandmother either."

"Then you were born without a heart. But you shall come, whether you like it or not--though I have to drag you there by the throat."

"Learn to spell 'able' first."

"I'll spell it on your head, if you don't come."

"Oh, that is the game, young un, is it?"

"Yes."

"Well, don't let us have a shindy on the bricks; there is a nice little paddock outside. Come out there and I'll give you a lesson."

"Thank you; I don't feel inclined to assist you in degrading our family."

"Chaps that are afraid to fight shouldn't threaten. Come now, the first knock-down blow shall settle it. If I win, you stay here and dance with us. If you win, I go to the old woman."

Compton consented, somewhat reluctantly; but to do him justice, his reluctance arose entirely from his sense of relationship, and not from any fear of his senior.

The young gentlemen took off their coats, and proceeded to spar without any further ceremony.

Reginald, whose agility was greater than his courage, danced about on the tips of his toes, and succeeded in planting a tap or two on Compton's cheek.

Compton smarted under these, and presently, in following his antagonist, who fought like a shadow, he saw Ruperta and her mother looking horror-stricken over the palings.

Infuriated with Reginald for this exposure, he rushed in at him, received a severe cut over the eye, but dealt him with his mighty Anglo-Saxon arm a full straightforward smasher on the forehead, which knocked him head over heels like a nine-pin.

That active young man picked himself up wondrous slowly; rheumatism seemed to have suddenly seized his well-oiled joints; he then addressed his antagonist, in his most ingratiating tones--"All right, sir," said he. "You are the best man. I'll go to the old lady this minute."

"I'll see you go," said Compton, sternly; "and mind I can run as well as hit: so none of your gypsy tricks with me."

Then he came sheepishly to the palings and said, "It is not my fault, Miss Bassett; he would not come to mamma without, and she wants to speak to him."

"Oh! he is hurt! he is wounded!" cried Ruperta. "Come here to me."

He came to her, and she pressed her white handkerchief tenderly on his eyebrow; it was bleeding a little.

"Well, are you coming?" said Reginald, ironically, "or do **you** like young women better than old ones?"

Compton instantly drew back a little, made two steps, laid his hand on the palings, vaulted over, and followed Reginald.

"That's your **boy,**" said Mrs. Bassett.

Ruperta made no reply, but began to gulp.

"What is the matter, darling?"

"The fighting--the blood"--said Ruperta, sobbing.

Mrs. Bassett drew her on one side, and soon soothed her.

When their gentle bosoms got over their agitation, they rather enjoyed the thing, especially Ruperta: she detested Reginald for his character, and for having insulted her father.

All of a sudden, she cried out, "He has taken my handkerchief. How dare he?" And she affected anger.

"Never mind, dear," said Mrs. Bassett, coolly, "we have got his tippet."

CHAPTER XLIII.

COULD any one have looked through the keyhole at Lady Bassett waiting for Reginald, he would have seen, by the very movements of her body, the terrible agitation of the mind. She rose--she sat down--she walked about with wild energy--she dropped on the sofa, and appeared to give it up as impossible; but ere long that deadly languor gave way to impatient restlessness again.

At last her quick ear heard a footstep in the corridor, accompanied by no rustle of petticoats, and yet the footstep was not Compton's.

Instantly she glanced with momentary terror toward the door.

There was a tap.

She sat down, and said, with a tone from which all agitation was instantly banished, "Come in."

The door opened, and the swarthy Reginald, diabolically handsome, with his black snaky curls, entered the room.

She rose from her chair, and fixed her great eyes on him, as if she would read him soul and body before she ventured to speak.

"Here I am, mamma: sorry to see you look so ill."

"Thank you, my dear," said Lady Bassett, without relaxing for a moment that searching gaze.

She said, still covering him with her eye, "Would you cure me if you could?"

To appreciate this opening, and Lady Bassett's sweet engaging manner, you must understand that this young man was, in her eyes, a sort of black snake. Her flesh crept, with fear and repugnance, at the sight of him. Yet that is how she received him, being a mother defending her favorite son.

"Of course I would," said Reginald. "Just you tell me how."

Excellent words. But the lady's calm infallible eye saw a cunning twinkle in those black twinkling orbs. Young as he was, he was on his guard, and waiting for her. Nor was this surprising: Reginald, naturally intelligent, had accumulated a large stock of low cunning in his travels and adventures with the gypsies, a smooth and cunning people. Lady Bassett's fainting upon his return, his exclusion from her room, and one or two minor circumstances, had set him thinking.

The moment she saw that look, Lady Bassett, with swift tact, glided away from the line she had intended to open, and, after merely thanking him, and saying, "I believe you, dear," though she did not believe him, she resumed, in a very impressive tone, "You see me worse than ever to-day, because my mind is in great trouble. The time is come when I must tell you a secret, which will cause you a bitter disappointment. Why I send for you is, to see whether I cannot do something for you to make you happy, in spite of that cruel disappointment."

Not a word from Reginald.

"Mr. Bassett--forgive me, if you can--for I am the most miserable woman in England--you are not the heir to this place; you are not Sir Charles Bassett's son."

"What!" shouted the young man.

Her fortitude gave way for a moment. She shook her head, in confirmation of what she had said, and hid her burning face and scalding tears in her white and wasted hands.

There was a long silence.

Reginald was asking himself if this could be true, or was it a maneuver to put her favorite Compton over his head.

Lady Bassett looked up, and saw this paltry suspicion in his face. She dried her tears directly, and went to a bureau, unlocked it, and produced the manuscript confession she had prepared for her husband.

She bade Reginald observe the superscription and the date.

When he had done so, she took her scissors and opened it for him.

"Read what I wrote to my beloved husband at a time when I expected soon to appear before my Judge."

She then sank upon the sofa, and lay there like a log; only, from time to time, during the long reading, tears trickled from her eyes.

Reginald read the whole story, and saw the facts must be true: more than that, being young, and a man, he could not entirely resist the charm of a narrative in which a lady told at full the love, the grief, the terror, the sufferings, of her heart, and the terrible temptation under which she had gone astray.

He laid it down at last, and drew a long breath.

"It's a devil of a job for *me,*" said he; "but I can't blame you. You sold that Dick Bassett, and I hate him. But what is to become of *me?*"

"What I offer you is a life in which you will be happier than you ever could be at Huntercombe. I mean to buy you vast pasture-fields in Australia, and cattle to feed. Those noble pastures will be bounded only by wild forests and hills. You will have swift horses to ride over your own domain, or to gallop hundreds of miles at a stretch, if you like. No confinement there; no fences and boundaries; all as free as air. No monotony: one week you can dig for gold, another you can ride among your flocks, another you can hunt. All this in a climate so delightful that you can lie all night in the open air, without a blanket, under a new firmament of stars, not one of which illumines the dull nights of Europe."

The bait was too tempting. "Well, you *are* the right sort," cried Reginald.

But presently he began to doubt. "But all that will cost a lot of money."

"It will, but I have a great deal of money."

Reginald thought, and said, suspiciously, "I don't know why you should do all this for me."

"Do you not? What! when I have brought you into this family, and encouraged you in such vast expectations, could I, in honor and common humanity, let you fall into poverty and neglect? No. I have many thousand pounds, all my own, and you will have them all, and perhaps waste them all; but it will take you some time, because, while you are wasting, I shall be saving more for you."

Then there was a pause, each waiting for the other.

Then Lady Bassett said, quietly, and with great apparent composure, "Of course there is a condition attached to all this."

"What is that?"

"I must receive from you a written paper, signed by yourself and by Mrs. Meyrick, acknowledging that you are not Sir Charles's son, but distinctly pledging yourself to keep the secret so long as I continue to furnish you with the means of living. You hesitate. Is it not fair?"

"Well, it looks fair; but it is an awkward thing, signing a paper of that sort."

"You doubt me, sir; you think that, because I have told one great falsehood, from good but erring motives, I may break faith with you. Do not insult me with these doubts, sir. Try and understand that there are ladies and gentlemen in the world, though you prefer gypsies. Have you forgotten that night when you laid me under so deep a debt, and I told you I never would forget it? From that day was I not always your friend? was I not always the one to make excuses for you?"

Reginald assented to that.

"Then trust me. I pledge you my honor that I am this day the best friend you ever had, or ever can have. Refuse to sign that paper, and I shall soon be in my grave, leaving behind me my confession, and other evidence, on which you will be dismissed from this house with ignominy, and without a farthing; for your best friend will be dead, and you will have killed her."

He looked at her full: he said, with a shade of compunction, "I am not a gentleman, but you are a lady. I'll trust you. I'll sign anything you like."

"That confidence becomes you," said Lady Bassett; "and now I have no objection to show you I deserve it. Here is a letter to Mr. Rolfe, by which you may learn I have already placed three thousand pounds to his account, to be laid out by him for your benefit in Australia, where he has many confidential friends; and this is a check for five hundred pounds I drew in your favor yesterday. Do me the favor to take it."

He did her that favor with sparkling eyes.

"Now here is the paper I wish you to sign; but your signature will be of little value to me without Mary Meyrick's."

"Oh, she will sign it directly: I have only to tell her."

"Are you sure? Men can be brought to take a dispassionate view of their own interest, but women are not so wise. Take it, and try her. If she refuses, bring her to me *directly.* Do you understand? Otherwise, in one fatal hour, her tongue will ruin *you,* and destroy me."

Impressed with these words, Reginald hurried to Mrs. Meyrick, and told her, in an off-hand way, she must sign that paper directly.

She looked at it and turned very white, but went on her guard directly.

"Sign such a wicked lie as that!" said she. "That I never will. You *are* his son, and Huntercombe shall be yours. She is an unnatural mother."

"Gammon!" said Reginald. "You might as well say a fox is the son of a gander. Come now; I am not going to let you cut my throat with your tongue. Sign at once, or else come to her this moment and tell her so."

"That I will," said Mary Meyrick, "and give her my mind."

This doughty resolution was a little shaken when she cast eyes upon Lady Bassett, and saw how wan and worn she looked.

She moderated her violence, and said, sullenly, "Sorry to gainsay *you,* my lady, and you so ill, but this is a paper I never can sign. It would rob him of Huntercombe. I'd sooner cut my hand off at the wrist."

"Nonsense, Mary!" said Lady Bassett, contemptuously.

She then proceeded to reason with her, but it was no use. Mary would not listen to reason, and defied her at last in a loud voice.

"Very well," said Lady Bassett. "Then since you will not do it my way, it shall be done another way. I shall put my confession in Sir Charles's hands, and insist on his dismissing him from the house, and you from your farm. It will kill me, and the money I intended for Reginald I shall leave to Compton."

"These are idle words, my lady. You daren't."

"I dare anything when once I make up my mind to die."

She rang the bell.

Mary Meyrick affected contempt.

A servant came to the door.

"Request Sir Charles to come to me immediately."

CHAPTER XLIV.

D ON'T you be a fool," said Reginald to his nurse.

"Sir Charles will send you to prison for it," said Lady Bassett.

"For what I done along with you?"

"Oh, he will not punish his wife; he will look out for some other victim."

"Sign, you d--d old fool!" cried Reginald, seizing Mary Meyrick roughly by the arm.

Strange to say, Lady Bassett interfered, with a sort of majestic horror. She held up her hand, and said, "Do not dare to lay a finger on her!"

Then Mary burst into tears, and said she would sign the paper.

While she was signing it, Sir Charles's step was heard in the corridor.

He knocked at the door just as she signed. Reginald had signed already.

Lady Bassett put the paper into the manuscript book, and the book into the bureau, and said "Come in," with an appearance of composure belied by her beating heart.

"Here is Mrs. Meyrick, my dear."

In those few seconds so perfect a liar as Mary Meyrick had quite recovered herself.

"If you please, sir," said she, "I be come to ast if you will give us a new lease, for ourn it is run out."

"You had better talk to the steward about that."

"Very well, sir," and she made her courtesy.

Reginald remained, not knowing exactly what to do.

"My dear," said Lady Bassett, "Reginald has come to bid us good-by. He is going to visit Mr. Rolfe, and take his advice, if you have no objection."

"None whatever; and I hope he will treat it with more respect than he does mine."

Reginald shrugged his shoulders, and was going out, when Lady Bassett said, "Won't you kiss me, Reginald, as you are going away?"

He came to her: she kissed him, and whispered in his ear, "Be true to me, as I will be to you."

Then he left her, and she felt like a dead thing, with exhaustion. She lay on the sofa, and Sir Charles sat beside her, and made her drink a glass of wine.

She lay very still that afternoon; but at night she slept: a load was off her mind for the present.

Next day she was so much better she came down to dinner.

What she now hoped was, that entire separation, coupled with the memory of the boy's misdeeds, would cure Sir Charles entirely of his affection for Reginald; and so that, after about twenty years more of conjugal fidelity, she might find courage to reveal to her husband the fault of her youth at a time when all its good results remained to help excuse it, and all its bad results had vanished.

Such was the plan this extraordinary woman conceived, and its success so far had a wonderful effect on her health.

But a couple of days passed, and she did not hear either from Reginald or Mr. Rolfe. That made her a little anxious.

On the third day Compton asked her, with an angry flush on his brow, whether she had not sent Reginald up to London.

"Yes, dear," said Lady Bassett.

"Well, he is not gone, then."

"Oh!"

"He is living at his nurse's. I saw him talking to an old gypsy that lives on the farm."

Lady Bassett groaned, but said nothing.

"Never mind, mamma," said Compton. "Your other children must love you all the more."

This news caused Lady Bassett both anxiety and terror. She divined bad faith and all manner of treachery, none the less terrible for being vague.

Down went her health again and her short-lived repose.

Meantime Reginald, in reality, was staying at the farm on a little business of his own.

He had concerted an expedition with the foreign gent, and was waiting for a dark and gusty night.

He had undertaken this expedition with mixed motives, spite and greed, especially the latter. He would never have undertaken it with a 500 pound check in his pocket; but some minds are so constituted they cannot forego a bad design once formed: so Mr. Reginald persisted, though one great motive existed no longer.

On this expedition it is now our lot to accompany him.

The night was favorable, and at about two o'clock Reginald and the foreign gent stood under Richard Bassett's dining-room window, with crape over their eyes, noses and mouths, and all manner of unlawful implements in their pockets.

The foreign gent prized the shutters open with a little crowbar; he then, with a glazier's diamond, soon cut out a small pane, inserted a cunning hand and opened the window.

Then Reginald gave him a leg, and he got into the room.

The agile youth followed him without assistance.

They lighted a sort of bull's-eye, and poured the concentrated light on the cupboard door, behind which lay the treasure of glorious old plate.

Then the foreign gent produced his skeleton keys, and after several ineffective trials, opened the door softly and revealed the glittering booty.

At sight of it the foreign gent could not suppress an ejaculation, but the younger one clapped his hand before his mouth hurriedly.

The foreign gent unrolled a sort of green baize apron he had round him; it was, in reality, a bag.

Into this receptacle the pair conveyed one piece of plate after another with surprising dexterity, rapidity, and noiseless-ness. When it was full, they began to fill the deep pockets of their shooting-jackets.

While thus employed, they heard a rapid footstep, and Richard Bassett opened the door. He was in his trousers and shirt, and had a pistol in his hand.

At sight of him Reginald uttered a cry of dismay; the foreign gent blew out the light.

Richard Bassett, among whose faults want of personal courage was not one, rushed forward and collared Reginald.

But the foreign gent had raised the crowbar to defend himself, and struck him a blow on the head that made him stagger back.

The foreign gent seized this opportunity, and ran at once at the window and jumped at it.

If Reginald had been first, he would have gone through like a cat, but the foreign gent, older, and obstructed by the contents of his pocket, higgled and stuck a few seconds in the window.

That brief delay was fatal; Richard Bassett leveled his pistol deliberately at him, fired, and sent a ball through his shoulder; he fell like a log upon the ground outside.

Richard then leveled another barrel at Reginald, but he howled out for quarter, and was immediately captured, and with the assistance of the brave Jessie, who now came boldly to her master's aid, his hands were tied behind him and he was made prisoner, with the stolen articles in his pocket.

When they were tying him, he whimpered, and said it was only a lark; he never meant to keep anything. He offered a hundred pounds down if they would let him off.

But there was no mercy for him.

Richard Bassett had a candle lighted, and inspected the prisoner. He lifted his crape veil, and said "Oho!"

"You see it was only a lark," said Reginald, and shook in every limb.

Richard Bassett smiled grimly, and said nothing. He gave Jessie strict orders to hold her tongue, and she and he between them took Reginald and locked him up in a small room adjoining the kitchen.

They then went to look for the other burglar.

He had emptied his pockets of all the plate, and crawled away. It is supposed he threw away the plate, either to soften Reginald's offense, or in the belief that he had received his death wound, and should not require silver vessels where he was going.

Bassett picked up the articles and brought them in, and told Jessie to light the fire and make him a cup of coffee.

He replaced all the plate, except the articles left in Reginald's pocket.

Then he went upstairs, and told his wife that burglars had broken into the house, but had taken nothing; she was to give herself no anxiety. He told her no more than this, for his dark and cruel nature had already conceived an idea he did not care to communicate to her, on account of the strong opposition he foresaw from so good a Christian: besides, of late, since her daughter came home to back her, she had spoken her mind more than once.

He kept them then in the dark, and went downstairs again to his coffee.

He sat and sipped it, and, with it, his coming vengeance.

All the defeats and mortifications he had endured from Huntercombe returned to his mind; and now, with one masterstroke he would balance them all.

Yet he felt a little compunction.

Active hostilities had ceased for many years.

Lady Bassett, at all events, had held out the hand to his wife. The blow he meditated was very cruel: would not his wife and daughter say it was barbarous? Would not his own heart, the heart of a father, reproach him afterward?

These misgivings, that would have restrained a less obstinate man, irritated Richard Bassett: he went into a rage, and said aloud, "I must do it: I will do it, come what may."

He told Jessie he valued her much: she should have a black silk gown for her courage and fidelity; but she must not be faithful by halves. She must not breathe one word to any soul in the house that the burglar was there under lock and key; if she did, he should turn her out of the house that moment.

"Hets!" said the woman, "der ye think I canna haud my whist, when the maister bids me? I'm nae great clasher at ony time, for my pairt."

At seven o'clock in the morning he sent a note to Sir Charles Bassett, to say that his house had been attacked last night by two armed burglars; he and his people had captured one, and wished to take him before a magistrate at once, since his house was not a fit place to hold him secure. He concluded Sir Charles would not refuse him the benefit of the law, however obnoxious he might be.

Sir Charles's lips curled with contempt at the man who was not ashamed to put such a doubt on paper.

However, he wrote back a civil line, to say that of course he was at Mr. Bassett's service, and would be in his justice-room at nine o'clock.

Meantime, Mr. Richard Bassett went for the constable and an assistant; but, even to them, he would not say precisely what he wanted them for.

His plan was to march an unknown burglar, with his crape on his face, into Sir Charles's study, give his evidence, and then reveal the son to the father.

Jessie managed to hold her tongue for an hour or two, and nothing occurred at Highmore or in Huntercombe to interfere with Richard Bassett's barbarous revenge.

Meantime, however, something remarkable had occurred at the distance of a mile and a quarter.

Mrs. Meyrick breakfasted habitually at eight o'clock.

Reginald did not appear.

Mrs. Meyrick went to his room, and satisfied herself he had not passed the night there.

Then she went to the foreign gent's shed.

He was not there.

Then she went out, and called loudly to them both.

No answer.

Then she went into the nearest meadow, to see if they were in sight.

The first thing she saw was the foreign gent staggering toward her.

"Drunk!" said she, and went to scold him; but, when she got nearer, she saw at once that something very serious had happened. His dark face was bloodless and awful, and he could hardly drag his limbs along; indeed they had failed him a score of times between Highmore and that place.

Just as she came up with him he sank once more to the ground, and turned up two despairing eyes toward her.

"Oh, daddy! what is it? Where's Reginald? Whatever have they done to you?"

"Brandy!" groaned the wounded man.

She flew into the house, and returned in a moment with a bottle. She put it to his lips.

He revived and told her all, in a few words.

"The young bloke and I went to crack a crib. I'm shot with a bullet. Hide me in that loose hay there; leave me the bottle, and let nobody come nigh me. The beak will be after me very soon."

Then Mrs. Meyrick, being a very strong woman, dragged him to the haystack, and covered him with loose hay.

"Now," said she, trembling, "where's my boy?"

"He's nabbed."

"Oh!"

"And he'll be lagged, unless you can beg him off."

Mary Meyrick uttered a piercing scream.

"You wretch! to tempt my boy to this. And him with five hundred pounds in his pocket, and my lady's favor. Oh, why did we not keep our word with her? She was the wisest, and our best friend. But it is all your doing; you are the devil that tempted him, you old villain!"

"Don't miscall me," said the gypsy.

"Not miscall you, when you have run away, and left them to take my boy to jail! No word is bad enough for you, you villain!"

"I'm your father--and a dying man," said the old gypsy, calmly, and folded his hands upon his breast with Oriental composure and decency.

The woman threw herself on her knees.

"Forgive me, father--tell me, where is he?"

"Highmore House."

At that simple word her eyes dilated with wild horror, she uttered a loud scream, and flew into the house.

In five minutes she was on her way to Highmore.

She reached that house, knocked hastily at the door, and said she must see Mr. Richard Bassett that moment.

"He is just gone out," said the maid.

"Where to?"

The girl knew her, and began to gossip. "Why, to Huntercombe Hall. What! haven't you heard, Mrs. Meyrick? Master caught a robber last night. Laws! you should have seen him: he have got crape all over his face; and master, and the constable, and Mr. Musters, they be all gone with him to Sir Charles, for to have him committed--the villain! Why, what ails the woman?"

For Mary Meyrick turned her back on the speaker, and rushed away in a moment.

She went through the kitchen at Huntercombe: she was so well known there, nobody objected: she flew up the stairs, and into Lady Bassett's bedroom. "Oh, my lady! my lady!"

Lady Bassett screamed, at her sudden entrance and wild appearance.

Mary Meyrick told her all in a few wild words. She wrung her hands with a great fear.

"It's no time for that," cried Mary, fiercely. "Come down this moment, and save him."

"How can I?"

"You must! You shall!" cried the other. "Don't ask me how. Don't sit wringing your hands, woman. If you are not there in five minutes to save him, I'll tell all."

"Have mercy on me!" cried Lady Bassett. "I gave him money, I sent him away. It's not my fault."

"No matter; he must be saved, or I'll ruin you. I can't stay here: I must be there, and so must you."

She rushed down the stairs, and tried to get into the justice-room, but admission was refused her.

Then she gave a sort of wild snarl, and ran round to the small room adjoining the justice-room. Through this she penetrated, and entered the justice-room, but not in time to prevent the evidence from being laid before Sir Charles.

What took place in the meantime was briefly this: The prisoner, handcuffed now instead of tied, was introduced between the constable and his assistant; the door was locked, and Sir Charles received Mr. Bassett with a ceremonious bow, seated himself, and begged Mr. Bassett to be seated.

"Thank you," said Mr. Bassett, but did not seat himself. He stood before the prisoner and gave his evidence; during which the prisoner's knees were seen to knock together with terror: he was a young man fit for folly, but not for felony.

Said Richard Bassett, "I have a cupboard containing family plate. It is valuable, and some years ago I passed a piece of catgut from the door through the ceiling to a bell at my bedside.

"Very late last night the bell sounded. I flung on my trousers, and went down with a pistol. I caught two burglars in the act of rifling the cupboard. I went to collar one; he struck me on the head with a crowbar--constable, show the crowbar--I staggered, but recovered myself, and fired at one of the burglars: he was just struggling through the window. He fell, and I thought he was dead, but he got away. I secured the other, and here he is--just as he was when I took him. Constable, search his pockets."

The constable did so, and produced therefrom several pieces of silver plate stamped with the Bassett arms.

"My servant here can confirm this," added Mr. Bassett.

"It is not necessary here," said Sir Charles. Then to the criminal, "Have you anything to say?"

"It was only a lark," quavered the poor wretch.

"I would not advise you to say that where you are going."

He then, while writing out the warrant, said, as a matter of course, "Remove his mask."

The constable lifted it, and started back with a shout of dismay and surprise: Jessie screamed.

Sir Charles looked up, and saw in the burglar he was committing for trial his first-born, the heir to his house and his lands.

The pen fell from Sir Charles's fingers, and he stared at the wan face, and wild, imploring eyes that stared at him.

He stared at the lad, and then put his hand to his heart, and that heart seemed to die within him.

There was a silence, and a horror fell on all. Even Richard Bassett quailed at what he had done.

"Ah! cruel man! cruel man!" moaned the broken father. "God judge you for this--as now I must judge my unhappy son. Mr. Bassett, it matters little to you what magistrate commits you, and I must keep my oath. I am--going--to set you an--example, by signing a warrant--"

"No, no, no!" cried a woman's voice, and Mary Meyrick rushed into the room.

Every person there thought he knew Mary Meyrick; yet she was like a stranger to them now. There was that in her heart at that awful moment which transfigured a handsome but vulgar woman into a superior being. Her cheek was pale, her black eyes large, and her mellow voice had a magic power. "You don't know what you are doing!" she cried. "Go no farther, or you will all curse the hand that harmed a hair of his head; you, most of all, Richard Bassett."

Sir Charles, in any other case, would have sent her out of the room; but, in his misery, he caught at the straw.

"Speak out, woman," he said, "and save the wretched boy, if you can. I see no way."

"There are things it is not fit to speak before all the world. Bid those men go, and I'll open your eyes that stay."

Then Richard Bassett foresaw another triumph, so he told the constable and his man they had better retire for a few minutes, "while," said he, with a sneer, "these wonderful revelations are being made."

When they were gone, Mary turned to Richard Bassett, and said "Why do you want him sent to prison?--to spite Sir Charles here, to stab his heart through his son."

Sir Charles groaned aloud.

The woman heard, and thought of many things. She flung herself on her knees, and seized his hand. "Don't you cry, my dear old master; mine is the only heart shall bleed. HE IS NOT YOUR SON."

"What!" cried Sir Charles, in a terrible voice.

"That is no news to me," said Richard. "He is more like the parson than Sir Charles Bassett."

"For shame! for shame!" cried Mary Meyrick. "Oh, it becomes you to give fathers to children when you don't know your own flesh and blood! He is YOUR SON, RICHARD BASSETT."

"My son!" roared Bassett, in utter amazement.

"Ay. I should know; FOR I AM HIS MOTHER."

This astounding statement was uttered with all the majesty of truth, and when she said "I am his mother," the voice turned tender all in a moment.

They were all paralyzed; and, absorbed in this strange revelation, did not hear a tottering footstep: a woman, pale as a corpse, and with eyes glaring large, stood among them, all in a moment, as if a ghost had risen from the earth.

It was Lady Bassett.

At sight of her, Sir Charles awoke from the confusion and amazement into which Mary had thrown him, and said, "Ah--! Bella, do you hear what she says, that he is not our son? What, then, have you agreed with your servant to deceive your husband?"

Lady Bassett gasped, and tried to speak; but before the words would come, the sight of her corpse-like face and miserable agony moved Mary Wells, and she snatched the words out of her mouth.

"What is the use of questioning *her?* She knows no more than you do. I done it all; and done it for the best. My lady's child died; I hid that from her; for I knew it would kill her, and keep you in a mad-house. I done for the best: I put my live child by her side, and she knew no better. As time went on, and the boy so dark, she suspected; but know it she couldn't till now. My lady, I am his mother, and there stands his cruel father; cruel to me, and cruel to him. But don't you dare to harm him; I've got all your letters, promising me marriage; I'll take them to your wife and daughter, and they shall know it is your own flesh and blood you are sending to prison. Oh, I am mad to threaten him! my darling, speak him fair; he is your father; he may have a bit of nature in his heart somewhere, though I could never find it."

The young man put his hands together, like an Oriental, and said, "Forgive me," then sank at Richard Bassett's knees.

Then Sir Charles, himself much shaken, took his wife's arm and led her, trembling like an aspen leaf, from the room.

Perhaps the prayers of Reginald and the tears of his mother would alone have sufficed to soften Richard Bassett, but the threat of exposure to his wife and daughter did no harm. The three soon came to terms.

Reginald to be liberated on condition of going to London by the next train, and never setting his foot in that parish again. His mother to go with him, and see him off to Australia. She solemnly pledged herself not to reveal the boy's real parentage to any other soul in the world.

This being settled, Richard Bassett called the constable in, and said the young gentleman had satisfied him that it was a practical joke, though a very dangerous one, and he withdrew the charge of felony.

The constable said he must have Sir Charles's authority for that.

A message was sent to Sir Charles. He came. The prisoner was released, and Mary Meyrick took his arm sharply, as much as to say, "Out of my hands you go no more."

Before they left the room, Sir Charles, who was now master of himself, said, with deep feeling, "My poor boy, you can never be a stranger to me. The affection of years cannot be untied in a moment. You see now how folly glides into crime, and crime into punishment. Take this to heart, and never again stray from the paths of honor. Lead an honorable life; and, if you do, write to me as if I was still your father."

They retired, but Richard Bassett lingered, and hung his head.

Sir Charles wondered what this inveterate foe could have to say now.

At last Richard said, half sullenly, yet with a touch of compunction, "Sir Charles, you have been more generous than I was. You have laid me under an obligation."

Sir Charles bowed loftily.

"You would double that obligation if you would prevail on Lady Bassett to keep that old folly of mine secret from my wife and daughter. I am truly ashamed of it; and, whatever my faults may have been, they love and respect me."

"Mr. Bassett," said Sir Charles, "my son Compton must be told that he is my heir; but no details injurious to you shall transpire: you may count on absolute secrecy from Lady Bassett and myself."

"Sir Charles," said Richard Bassett, faltering for a moment, "I am very much obliged to you, and I begin to be sorry we are enemies. Good-morning."

The agitation and terror of this scene nearly killed Lady Bassett on the spot. She lay all that day in a state of utter prostration.

Meantime Sir Charles put this and that together, but said nothing. He spoke cheerfully and philosophically to his wife--said it had been a fearful blow, terrible wrench: but it was all for the best; such a son as that would have broken his heart before long.

"Ah, but your wasted affections!" groaned Lady Bassett; and her tears streamed at the thought.

Sir Charles sighed; but said, after a while, "Is affection ever entirely wasted? My love for that young fool enlarged my heart. There was a time he did me a deal of good."

But next day, having only herself to think of now, Lady Bassett could live no longer under the load of deceit. She told Sir Charles Mary Meyrick had deceived him. "Read this," she said, "and see what your miserable wife has done, who loved you to madness and crime."

Sir Charles looked at her, and saw in her wasted form and her face that, if he did read it, he should kill her; so he played the man: he restrained himself by a mighty effort, and said, "My dear, excuse me; but on this matter I have more faith in Mary Meyrick's exactness than in yours. Besides, I know your heart, and don't care to be told of your errors in judgment, no, not even by yourself. Sorry to offend an authoress; but I decline to read your book, and, more than that, I forbid you the subject entirely for the next thirty years, at least. Let by-gones be by-gones."

That eventful morning Mr. Rutland called and proposed to Ruperta. She declined politely, but firmly.

She told Mrs. Bassett, and Mrs. Bassett told Richard in a nervous way, but his answer surprised her. He said he was very glad of it; Ruperta could do better.

Mrs. Bassett could not resist the pleasure of telling Lady Bassett. She went over on purpose, with her husband's consent.

Lady Bassett asked to see Ruperta. "By all means," said Richard Bassett, graciously.

On her return to Highmore, Ruperta asked leave to go to the Hall every day and nurse Lady Bassett. "They will let her die else," said she. Richard Bassett assented to that, too. Ruperta, for some weeks, almost lived at the Hall, and in this emergency revealed great qualities. As the malevolent small-pox, passing through the gentle cow, comes out the sovereign cow-pox, so, in this gracious nature, her father's vices turned to their kindred virtues; his obstinacy of purpose shone here a noble constancy; his audacity became candor, and his cunning wisdom. Her intelligence saw at once that Lady Bassett was pining to death, and a weak-minded nurse would be fatal: she was all smiles and brightness, and neglected no means to encourage the patient.

With this view, she promised to plight her faith to Compton the moment Lady Bassett should be restored to health; and so, with hopes and smiles, and the novelty of a daughter's love, she fought with death for Lady Bassett, and at last she won the desperate battle.

This did Richard Bassett's daughter for her father's late enemy.

The grateful husband wrote to Bassett, and now acknowledged *his* obligation.

A civil, mock-modest reply from Richard Bassett.

From this things went on step by step, till at last Compton and Ruperta, at eighteen years of age, were formally betrothed.

Thus the children's love wore out the father's hate.

That love, so troubled at the outset, left, by degrees, the region of romance, and rippled smoothly through green, flowery meadows.

Ruperta showed her lover one more phase of girlhood; she, who had been a precocious and forward child, and then a shy and silent girl, came out now a bright and witty young woman, full of vivacity, modesty, and sensibility. Time cured Compton of his one defect. Ruperta stopped growing at fifteen, but Compton went slowly on; caught her at seventeen, and at nineteen had passed her by a head. He won a scholarship at Oxford, he rowed in college races, and at last in the University race on the Thames.

Ruperta stood, in peerless beauty, dark blue from throat to feet, and saw his boat astern of his rival, saw it come up with, and creep ahead, amid the roars of the multitude. When she saw her lover, with bare corded arms, as brown as a berry, and set teeth, filling his glorious part in that manly struggle within eight yards of her, she confessed he was not a boy now.

But Lady Bassett accepted no such evidence: being pestered to let them marry at twenty years of age, she clogged her consent with one condition--they must live three years at Huntercombe as man and wife.

"No boy of twenty," said she, "can understand a young woman of that age. I must be in the house to prevent a single misunderstanding between my beloved children."

The young people, who both adored her, voted the condition reasonable. They were married, and a wing of the spacious building allotted to them.

For their sakes let us hope that their wedded life, now happily commenced, will furnish me no materials for another tale: the happiest lives are uneventful.

The foreign gent recovered his wound, but acquired rheumatism and a dislike for midnight expeditions.

Reginald galloped a year or two over seven hundred miles of colony, sowing his wild oats as he flew, but is now a prosperous squatter, very fond of sleeping in the open air. England was not big enough for the bold Bohemian. He does very well where he is.

Old Meyrick died, and left his wife a little estate in the next county. Drake asked her hand at the funeral. She married him in six months, and migrated to the estate in question; for Sir Charles refused her a lease of his farm, not choosing to have her near him.

Her new abode was in the next parish to her sister's.

La Marsh set herself to convert Mary, and often exhorted her to penitence; she bore this pretty well for some time, being overawed by old reminiscences of sisterly superiority: but at last her vanity rebelled. "Repent! and Repent!" cried she. "Why you be like a cuckoo, all in one song. One would think I had been and robbed a church. 'Tis all very well for you to repent, as led a fastish life at starting: *but I never done nothing as I'm ashamed on.*"

Richard Bassett said one day to Wheeler, "Old fellow, there is not a worse poison than Hate. It has made me old before my time. And what does it all come to? We might just as well have kept quiet; for my grandson will inherit Huntercombe and Bassett, after all--"

"Thanks to the girl you would not ring the bells for."

Sir Charles and Lady Bassett lead a peaceful life after all their troubles, and renew their youth in their children, of whom Ruperta is one, and as dear as any.

Yet there is a pensive and humble air about Lady Bassett, which shows she still expiates her fault, though she knows it will always be ignored by him for whose sake she sinned.

In summing her up, it may be as well to compare this with the unmixed self-complacency of Mrs. Drake.

You men and women, who judge this Bella Bassett, be firm, and do not let her amiable qualities or her good intentions blind you in a plain matter of right and wrong: be charitable, and ask yourselves how often in your lives you have seen yourselves, or any other human being, resist a terrible temptation.

My experience is, that we resist other people's temptations nobly, and succumb to our own.

So let me end with a line of England's gentlest satirist--

"Heaven be merciful to us all, sinners as we be."

The Codes Of Hammurabi And Moses
W. W. Davies

QTY

The discovery of the Hammurabi Code is one of the greatest achievements of archaeology, and is of paramount interest, not only to the student of the Bible, but also to all those interested in ancient history...

Religion   **ISBN:** *1-59462-338-4*   **Pages:132**
                                                     MSRP $12.95

The Theory of Moral Sentiments
Adam Smith

QTY

This work from 1749. contains original theories of conscience amd moral judgment and it is the foundation for systemof morals.

Philosophy **ISBN:** *1-59462-777-0*   **Pages:536**
                                                     MSRP $19.95

Jessica's First Prayer
Hesba Stretton

QTY

In a screened and secluded corner of one of the many railway-bridges which span the streets of London there could be seen a few years ago, from five o'clock every morning until half past eight, a tidily set-out coffee-stall, consisting of a trestle and board, upon which stood two large tin cans, with a small fire of charcoal burning under each so as to keep the coffee boiling during the early hours of the morning when the work-people were thronging into the city on their way to their daily toil...

                                                     Pages:84
Childrens   **ISBN:** *1-59462-373-2*   *MSRP $9.95*

My Life and Work
Henry Ford

QTY

Henry Ford revolutionized the world with his implementation of mass production for the Model T automobile. Gain valuable business insight into his life and work with his own auto-biography... "We have only started on our development of our country we have not as yet, with all our talk of wonderful progress, done more than scratch the surface. The progress has been wonderful enough but..."

                                                     Pages:300
Biographies/ **ISBN:** *1-59462-198-5*   *MSRP $21.95*

The Art of Cross-Examination
Francis Wellman

QTY

I presume it is the experience of every author, after his first book is published upon an important subject, to be almost overwhelmed with a wealth of ideas and illustrations which could readily have been included in his book, and which to his own mind, at least, seem to make a second edition inevitable. Such certainly was the case with me; and when the first edition had reached its sixth impression in five months, I rejoiced to learn that it seemed to my publishers that the book had met with a sufficiently favorable reception to justify a second and considerably enlarged edition. ..

Reference   **ISBN: *1-59462-647-2***

Pages:412

MSRP $19.95

On the Duty of Civil Disobedience
Henry David Thoreau

QTY

Thoreau wrote his famous essay, On the Duty of Civil Disobedience, as a protest against an unjust but popular war and the immoral but popular institution of slave-owning. He did more than write—he declined to pay his taxes, and was hauled off to gaol in consequence. Who can say how much this refusal of his hastened the end of the war and of slavery ?

Law   **ISBN: *1-59462-747-9***

Pages:48

MSRP $7.45

Dream Psychology Psychoanalysis for Beginners
Sigmund Freud

QTY

Sigmund Freud, born Sigismund Schlomo Freud (May 6, 1856 - September 23, 1939), was a Jewish-Austrian neurologist and psychiatrist who co-founded the psychoanalytic school of psychology. Freud is best known for his theories of the unconscious mind, especially involving the mechanism of repression; his redefinition of sexual desire as mobile and directed towards a wide variety of objects; and his therapeutic techniques, especially his understanding of transference in the therapeutic relationship and the presumed value of dreams as sources of insight into unconscious desires.

Psychology   **ISBN: *1-59462-905-6***

Pages:196

MSRP $15.45

The Miracle of Right Thought
Orison Swett Marden

QTY

Believe with all of your heart that you will do what you were made to do. When the mind has once formed the habit of holding cheerful, happy, prosperous pictures, it will not be easy to form the opposite habit. It does not matter how improbable or how far away this realization may see, or how dark the prospects may be, if we visualize them as best we can, as vividly as possible, hold tenaciously to them and vigorously struggle to attain them, they will gradually become actualized, realized in the life. But a desire, a longing without endeavor, a yearning abandoned or held indifferently will vanish without realization.

Pages:360

Self Help   **ISBN: *1-59462-644-8***

MSRP $25.45

www.bookjungle.com *email: sales@bookjungle.com fax: 630-214-0564 mail: Book Jungle PO Box 2226 Champaign, IL 61825*

QTY

The Rosicrucian Cosmo-Conception Mystic Christianity *by Max Heindel* ISBN: *1-59462-188-8* **$38.95**
The Rosicrucian Cosmo-conception is not dogmatic, neither does it appeal to any other authority than the reason of the student. It is: not controversial, but is: sent forth in the, hope that it may to clear... New Age/Religion Pages 646

Abandonment To Divine Providence *by Jean-Pierre de Caussade* ISBN: *1-59462-228-0* **$25.95**
"The Rev. Jean Pierre de Caussade was one of the most remarkable spiritual writers of the Society of Jesus in France in the 18th Century. His death took place at Toulouse in 1751. His works have gone through many editions and have been republished... Inspirational/Religion Pages 400

Mental Chemistry *by Charles Haanel* ISBN: *1-59462-192-6* **$23.95**
Mental Chemistry allows the change of material conditions by combining and appropriately utilizing the power of the mind. Much like applied chemistry creates something new and unique out of careful combinations of chemicals the mastery of mental chemistry... New Age Pages 354

The Letters of Robert Browning and Elizabeth Barret Barrett 1845-1846 vol II ISBN: *1-59462-193-4* **$35.95**
by Robert Browning and Elizabeth Barrett
Biographies Pages 596

Gleanings In Genesis (volume I) *by Arthur W. Pink* ISBN: *1-59462-130-6* **$27.45**
Appropriately has Genesis been termed "the seed plot of the Bible" for in it we have, in germ form, almost all of the great doctrines which are afterwards fully developed in the books of Scripture which follow... Religion/Inspirational Pages 420

The Master Key *by L. W. de Laurence* ISBN: *1-59462-001-6* **$30.95**
In no branch of human knowledge has there been a more lively increase of the spirit of research during the past few years than in the study of Psychology, Concentration and Mental Discipline. The requests for authentic lessons in Thought Control, Mental Discipline and... New Age/Business Pages 422

The Lesser Key Of Solomon Goetia *by L. W. de Laurence* ISBN: *1-59462-092-X* **$9.95**
This translation of the first book of the "Lernegton" which is now for the first time made accessible to students of Talismanic Magic was done, after careful collation and edition, from numerous Ancient Manuscripts in Hebrew, Latin, and French... New Age/Occult Pages 92

Rubaiyat Of Omar Khayyam *by Edward Fitzgerald* ISBN:*1-59462-332-5* **$13.95**
Edward Fitzgerald, whom the world has already learned, in spite of his own efforts to remain within the shadow of anonymity, to look upon as one of the rarest poets of the century, was born at Bredfield, in Suffolk, on the 31st of March, 1809. He was the third son of John Purcell... Music Pages 172

Ancient Law *by Henry Maine* ISBN: *1-59462-128-4* **$29.95**
The chief object of the following pages is to indicate some of the earliest ideas of mankind, as they are reflected in Ancient Law, and to point out the relation of those ideas to modern thought. Religiom/History Pages 452

Far-Away Stories *by William J. Locke* ISBN: *1-59462-129-2* **$19.45**
"Good wine needs no bush, but a collection of mixed vintages does. And this book is just such a collection. Some of the stories I do not want to remain buried for ever in the museum files of dead magazine-numbers an author's not unpardonable vanity..." Fiction Pages 272

Life of David Crockett *by David Crockett* ISBN: *1-59462-250-7* **$27.45**
"Colonel David Crockett was one of the most remarkable men of the times in which he lived. Born in humble life, but gifted with a strong will, an indomitable courage, and unremitting perseverance... Biographies/New Age Pages 424

Lip-Reading *by Edward Nitchie* ISBN: *1-59462-206-X* **$25.95**
Edward B. Nitchie, founder of the New York School for the Hard of Hearing, now the Nitchie School of Lip-Reading, Inc, wrote "LIP-READING Principles and Practice". The development and perfecting of this meritorious work on lip-reading was an undertaking... How-to Pages 400

A Handbook of Suggestive Therapeutics, Applied Hypnotism, Psychic Science ISBN: *1-59462-214-0* **$24.95**
by Henry Munro
Health/New Age/Health/Self-help Pages 376

A Doll's House: and Two Other Plays *by Henrik Ibsen* ISBN: *1-59462-112-8* **$19.95**
Henrik Ibsen created this classic when in revolutionary 1848 Rome. Introducing some striking concepts in playwriting for the realist genre, this play has been studied the world over. Fiction/Classics/Plays 308

The Light of Asia *by sir Edwin Arnold* ISBN: *1-59462-204-3* **$13.95**
In this poetic masterpiece, Edwin Arnold describes the life and teachings of Buddha. The man who was to become known as Buddha to the world was born as Prince Gautama of India but he rejected the worldly riches and abandoned the reigns of power when... Religion/History/Biographies Pages 170

The Complete Works of Guy de Maupassant *by Guy de Maupassant* ISBN: *1-59462-157-8* **$16.95**
"For days and days, nights and nights, I had dreamed of that first kiss which was to consecrate our engagement, and I knew not on what spot I should put my lips..." Fiction/Classics Pages 240

The Art of Cross-Examination *by Francis L. Wellman* ISBN: *1-59462-309-0* **$26.95**
Written by a renowned trial lawyer, Wellman imparts his experience and uses case studies to explain how to use psychology to extract desired information through questioning. How-to/Science/Reference Pages 408

Answered or Unanswered? *by Louisa Vaughan* ISBN: *1-59462-248-5* **$10.95**
Miracles of Faith in China
Religion Pages 112

The Edinburgh Lectures on Mental Science (1909) *by Thomas* ISBN: *1-59462-008-3* **$11.95**
This book contains the substance of a course of lectures recently given by the writer in the Queen Street Hail, Edinburgh. Its purpose is to indicate the Natural Principles governing the relation between Mental Action and Material Conditions... New Age/Psychology Pages 148

Ayesha *by H. Rider Haggard* ISBN: *1-59462-301-5* **$24.95**
Verily and indeed it is the unexpected that happens! Probably if there was one person upon the earth from whom the Editor of this, and of a certain previous history, did not expect to hear again... Classics Pages 380

Ayala's Angel *by Anthony Trollope* ISBN: *1-59462-352-X* **$29.95**
The two girls were both pretty, but Lucy who was twenty-one who supposed to be simple and comparatively unattractive, whereas Ayala was credited, as her Bombwhat romantic name might show, with poetic charm and a taste for romance. Ayala when her father died was nineteen... Fiction Pages 484

The American Commonwealth *by James Bryce* ISBN: *1-59462-286-8* **$34.45**
An interpretation of American democratic political theory. It examines political mechanics and society from the perspective of Scotsman James Bryce Politics Pages 572

Stories of the Pilgrims *by Margaret P. Pumphrey* ISBN: *1-59462-116-0* **$17.95**
This book explores pilgrims religious oppression in England as well as their escape to Holland and eventual crossing to America on the Mayflower, and their early days in New England... History Pages 268

QTY

The Fasting Cure *by Sinclair Upton*   ISBN: *1-59462-222-1*   **$13.95**
In the Cosmopolitan Magazine for May, 1910, and in the Contemporary Review (London) for April, 1910, I published an article dealing with my experiences in fasting. I have written a great many magazine articles, but never one which attracted so much attention... New Age/Self Help/Health Pages 164

Hebrew Astrology *by Sepharial*   ISBN: *1-59462-308-2*   **$13.45**
In these days of advanced thinking it is a matter of common observation that we have left many of the old landmarks behind and that we are now pressing forward to greater heights and to a wider horizon than that which represented the mind-content of our progenitors... Astrology Pages 144

Thought Vibration or The Law of Attraction in the Thought World   ISBN: *1-59462-127-6*   **$12.95**

by William Walker Atkinson   *Psychology/Religion Pages 144*

Optimism *by Helen Keller*   ISBN: *1-59462-108-X*   **$15.95**
Helen Keller was blind, deaf, and mute since 19 months old, yet famously learned how to overcome these handicaps, communicate with the world, and spread her lectures promoting optimism. An inspiring read for everyone... Biographies/Inspirational Pages 84

Sara Crewe *by Frances Burnett*   ISBN: *1-59462-360-0*   **$9.45**
In the first place, Miss Minchin lived in London. Her home was a large, dull, tall one, in a large, dull square, where all the houses were alike, and all the sparrows were alike, and where all the door-knockers made the same heavy sound... Childrens/Classic Pages 88

The Autobiography of Benjamin Franklin *by Benjamin Franklin*   ISBN: *1-59462-135-7*   **$24.95**
The Autobiography of Benjamin Franklin has probably been more extensively read than any other American historical work, and no other book of its kind has had such ups and downs of fortune. Franklin lived for many years in England, where he was agent... Biographies/History Pages 332

Name	
Email	
Telephone	
Address	
City, State ZIP	

☐ **Credit Card**   ☐ **Check / Money Order**

Credit Card Number	
Expiration Date	
Signature	

Please Mail to: Book Jungle
                                PO Box 2226
                                Champaign, IL 61825
or Fax to: 630-214-0564

ORDERING INFORMATION

web: *www.bookjungle.com*
email: *sales@bookjungle.com*
fax: *630-214-0564*
mail: *Book Jungle PO Box 2226 Champaign, IL 61825*
or PayPal *to sales@bookjungle.com*

Please contact us for bulk discounts

DIRECT-ORDER TERMS

**20% Discount if You Order
Two or More Books**
Free Domestic Shipping!
Accepted: Master Card, Visa,
Discover, American Express